Blood of the Oak

BLOOD OF THE OAK

A Novel

ELIOT PATTISON

COUNTERPOINT

Library of Congress Cataloging-in-Publication Data

Names: Pattison, Eliot.
Title: Blood of the oak : a novel / Eliot Pattison.
Description: Berkeley : Counterpoint, 2016. | "2015 | Series: Bone rattler ; 4
Identifiers: LCCN 2015035581 | ISBN 9781619026155 (hardcover)
Subjects: LCSH: Scots—United States—Fiction. |
  Murder—Investigation—Fiction. | United States—History—18th
  century—Fiction. | BISAC: FICTION / Mystery & Detective / Historical. |
  GSAFD: Historical fiction. | Mystery fiction.
Classification: LCC PS3566.A82497 B58 2016 | DDC 813/.54—dc23
LC record available at http://lccn.loc.gov/2015035581
ISBN 978-1-61902-615-5

COUNTERPOINT
2560 Ninth Street, Suite 318
Berkeley, CA 94710
www.counterpointpress.com

Book design by Domini Dragoone

Printed in the United States of America
Distributed by Publishers Group West

10 9 8 7 6 5 4 3 2 1

For Bear, who will forever own a piece of my heart.

Blood of the Oak

PREFACE

The 1760s were a time of seismic shifts on the North American continent. The mantle of the Old World that America had worn for a century and a half was becoming tattered and ill-fitting. If, as I have suggested in the prior chronicles of Duncan McCallum, the seeds of the American Revolution were planted during the French and Indian War, then this was the decade during which those seeds germinated. Great Britain, basking in the victory over France which made it the first global superpower, was blinded to the currents that were stirring the population of its most important colonies. For generations it had dumped onto American shores scores of thousands of emigrants with complaints about religious and political intolerance, people being marginalized for opposing the government, including thousands of displaced Scots, and victims of an overbearing criminal justice system. Almost by definition, these were spirited, determined people who often had little inclination to bow to British overlords.

In hindsight the rise of American independence may seem inevitable but the drama of the 1760s' stage was not about colonists conceiving a bold new form of government, it was about discovering what it meant to be American. A deep sense of freedom had already become instinctive in America, especially on the frontier, but it took the heat of new repressions to forge that instinct into a new identity.

As this novel opens, five years have passed since the defeat of the French. Duncan McCallum has established a peaceful existence in the seclusion of the western frontier, and is content to remain far removed from debates on politics and the workings of empire. Little does he know that secret plans hatched in London are about to sweep him into the tide that will launch the American nation.

Early Spring 1765

CHAPTER ONE

The forest embraced him as another of its wild creatures, sending its steadying power into each long stride. Duncan McCallum had learned the ways of forest running from his tribal friends but he had never experienced its deep joys until he had begun his own solitary treks among the farms and settlements of the frontier. There were roads, more and more of them stretching out from the Hudson, but he preferred the ancient trails of the tribes. With his pack on his shoulder and his long rifle in one hand, Duncan glided along the old Mohawk path with the carefree joy of a young stag, oblivious to the troubles of the world of men.

It was the rarest of days, when the sun, as if stretching from its winter sleep, burst through the budding leaves to ignite the wildflowers with blazes of red, blue, and yellow. His smile grew as the miles fell away. He would be in Edentown for supper, back with Sarah Ramsey and his particular friend Conawago, elder of the Nipmuc tribe, whom he had not seen for nearly a month. He would speak with Conawago about the new patches of medicinal herbs he had discovered and at sundown would walk hand in hand with Sarah, inspecting the new foals and lambs in their pastures.

He had been visiting Edentown's northernmost dependency, a farm built around a promising orchard, when he had been summoned by a message from the Iroquois. Adanahoe, mother of all the tribes, lay dying and had asked for him. Duncan had assumed the gentle old woman had sought him for his medicines but as she greeted him from her bed of furs, she had dismissed the healers from her lodge and announced there was something far more important than easing her discomfort.

"The embers burn low, Duncan," she had confessed to him, meaning the centuries-old Council fire that bound the tribes of the Iroquois confederation, "but as long as the spirits watch over us I will not fear." The frail old woman, who more than anyone embodied the heart of the Haudensaunee, the Iroquois people, had asked Duncan to carry her into the sacred lodge, the structure at the town's highest point where the masks of Iroquois ritual were kept. He had cradled her like a child in his arms, pausing at the doorway to let one of the protecting shamans cleanse them with fragrant cedar smoke before stepping inside.

He had been in the lodge once before, so he knew to brace himself for the distorted, grotesque masks that hung on the walls, each above altars that held offerings of feathers, small skulls, crystal stones, and animals fashioned of wood or cornhusk. The spirits that inhabited the masks were beloved and protected by the Iroquois, each responsible for one of the critical elements of tribal life. Insisting on being lowered to her feet, Adanahoe hobbled along the altars, leaning heavily on Duncan's arm. As they walked, Duncan recognized the maize spirit, the squash spirit, the healing spirit, the fire spirit.

Small pots of burning fat stood on each altar, their flickering flames giving movement to the gods above. Adanahoe halted at a corner where a pot burned below an empty space.

"He was here in the night when my grandson Siyenca and I replenished the lamps," the matriarch explained in a mournful tone.

"At dawn he was gone. And my grandson too." She scrubbed at a tear. "They brought Siyenca's body to me at noon that day. He was found floating in the river ten miles south of here, with this in his hand." She opened her palm to show Duncan a large bear claw sewn into a piece of black-and-white fur. "He wears a necklace of claws and bones."

Duncan realized she was no longer speaking of her dead grandson. "May I know his name?"

"The old ones have many names, some of which may never be spoken outside the secret societies. But at campfires he is called Blooddancer, or sometimes the Trickster. He lives in a long slab of curved oak painted red as blood and has twisted eyes and a snout of birch wood into which the teeth of a catamount are set. He has eyelashes made of four bear claws and bear claws below his chin like a beard." She lifted the claw in her hand. "This was one of them. And he has a rattle with four claws attached to it, which has always been kept on his altar—his ceremonial weapon."

Duncan was guarded in speaking about the lost spirit, for fear of breaking one of the tribes' complex taboos. "And when you pray to him what do you ask for?"

"It is hard to explain. His is an old warrior's spirit from days of long ago. In my father's time he accompanied our warriors on many successful raids. But it wasn't bravery you asked him for, it was the strength inside the bravery."

"Fortitude," Duncan suggested.

The old woman nodded. "Yes, but more. Like the marrow of our people. Like the heartwood of the oak. He is one of the anchors that keeps us safe and lets our tongues be heard by the spirits of the forest. He is old, and irritable, but he provides our link to the ancient ones, the link that makes us who we are." Her heavy wheezing breaths filled the silence. Outside the lodge a drum beat a slow rhythm.

"They say my grandson Siyenca stole the mask because there are Europeans who would pay silver coins for it. They would not help me with his death rites." She pointed to a brownish stain on the altar. "When I explained that this was still wet and crimson when I came here that morning, they said the god had wounded Siyenca in his theft."

The old woman's pain knew no depths. The Council embers were dying, her god was stolen, her grandson was dead, and now the younger generation of Iroquois were arguing with the venerable matriarch.

"You mean blood had dripped on the altar."

Adanahoe nodded. "It was taboo for Siyenca to be in here without one of us, but he must have seen the thieves. They hit him when he tried to stop them. He had a cut on his head. Then he followed to take back old Blooddancer and the thieves drowned him for it."

She turned and clamped her hands on Duncan's shoulders. Her voice was hoarse but urgent. "I had a dream. You and Conawago appear limping out of a fog, scarred and battered, nearly dead, as if from a great battle, but you bring Blooddancer back to us. Our people will drift apart without the old anchors. Siyenca will never have peace on the other side." Her eyes were full of moisture. "I will be gone before you return, my son, but I will linger by my body until our god is safely home."

As Duncan dipped his hand in a stream, his instincts cried out and he spun about, his gut tightening. There was nothing there. It had been like this ever since leaving Onondaga Castle, capital of the Iroquois League, two days earlier. He would find his stride, envelop himself in the harmony of the forest, but then with the abruptness of a rifle shot, an unnatural fear would seize him, and just as quickly fade. Duncan sought to calm himself by playing the game Conawago favored when doing chores, seeing how many birdsongs he could identify, then how many of their Iroquois names he could remember. The throaty melody of a wood thrush, the soft call of a waxwing. He paused. One of the songs had a human voice.

He crept stealthily along the trail, at first just curious, trying to make sense of the strangely familiar, forlorn words. But as he crested a low ridge his foreboding returned. There was danger here. He freed the thong that secured his belt knife and checked the priming in the pan of his rifle.

Near the bottom of the hollow a boy leaned against a log. He was Iroquois, but his words were French. *"Non je n'irai plus au bois,"* he sang in a tiny, frightened voice. *"Non je n'irai plus seulette."*

The words seized Duncan, loosening a flood of painful images. His father the Scottish rebel hanging on a British gibbet. His mother and sisters raped and killed by British soldiers. Even after so many years the haunting scenes still seized him like this, descending like an abrupt storm. Sometimes he would wake up shouting at their campfires and he would sit like a lost child as Conawago kept vigil with him, singing calming songs of the tribes.

It was a melody of Duncan's youth, one often sung by a French chambermaid in his Dutch boarding school, where he had heard of his family's destruction. *No, I'll not go into the woods again. No, I'll not alone be going.*

The Iroquois boy was singing a lonely French ballad. There were Mohawk clans who lived in Quebec, but it was rare to find one of their number so far south.

Duncan was two steps away when the youth spun about and, with catlike quickness, sprang at him. He saw the flash of the blade in enough time to deflect it from his chest, but not soon enough to avoid a slice across the back of his hand. With a swing of his rifle butt he knocked the boy to the ground, pinned his wrist with his foot, aimed his rifle at the boy's heart, and pulled back the hammer.

The boy's thin, soiled face filled with tears. "Go ahead," he said in English. "It is the way of you cowards. Shoot warriors from ambush. Kill the child who scares you." With his free hand the boy crossed himself then, to Duncan's horror, pulled the gun barrel to his chest so abruptly Duncan's finger almost pulled the trigger.

• "Warriors?" Duncan asked, then glanced back to the log where the boy had sat, seeing now a moccasined foot among the wild violets. He darted to the figure's side, the instincts of his medical training taking over. He checked for a pulse, felt for warmth on the man's forehead, but the dull, unseeing eyes were all that he needed to know. The shot that had killed him had ripped into the back of his neck. The moss he had fallen onto was stained crimson.

The man was an Iroquois in his prime, his broad shoulders, sinewy arms, and calloused thumb the marks of one who still used the bow. The narrow scalp lock at the crown of his shaven head held red pigments, matching the red that covered his ear. The tattooed image of a snake coiled around one arm, an intricate design of curving and jagged lines around the other. On the breast of his sleeveless brown waistcoat was a quillwork image of a leaping deer. On his cheek were four parallel slash marks from which blood still oozed.

"Murderer!" The boy was on his feet now, coiling as though for another assault.

Duncan ignored the knife in his hand. "I know this man," he said in surprise. "I sat with him once at the fire of the Great Council. His name was Red Jacob, of the Oneida people."

The boy halted. His hand was shaking.

"There are words to be said," Duncan continued in a level voice. "We should catch a snake or a bird so it can carry word to his family on the other side."

The boy seemed about to speak when a branch snapped on the slope above. His face drained of color and he crouched beside the log as if for cover. "If it comes back we will die," he declared in a fearful whisper.

"It?"

"The demon. The monster who eats men's bones, who plays with their bodies like dolls. I know about him, from the campfires. If you hear the shaking of his rattle you will know that you are dead."

Duncan scanned the slope uneasily, then pointed to a shape in the shadows. "It's just a stag. The smell of blood makes it uneasy."

"But it attracts others. The wolves are probably with the demon now, sharing the bones of Long Runner."

Duncan's head snapped up. "Long Runner?" He had not heard the name for two or three years, and had almost forgotten it.

"There were three of us." The boy spoke slowly, as if only half hearing. His eyes were locked on the face of the dead Oneida. "Long Runner was taken first and as he went down he shouted for us to run, that we had to make Edentown at all costs."

Duncan stood and reached for the boy, shaking him by the shoulders. "You mean an Englishman? A soldier?"

The Iroquois youth nodded. "But he speaks the Iroquois tongue like he was born to it. I only met him last week at Johnson Hall. They call him captain sometimes."

Duncan lifted his gun. "Where? Tell me where Long Runner is!"

The boy pointed up the trail that intersected from the north. "Near the top of the ridge."

Without another word Duncan sprinted away.

It was nearly a mile to the crest of the ridge, through a field of huge misshapen boulders that would have made for a perfect ambush. Duncan's instincts blazed with warning. The Oneida had died less than an hour earlier. His killer might still be near. He slacked his pace, an eye on the boulders he passed, pausing once to listen. The forest was constantly speaking, Conawago had taught him, if only you knew how to listen. Birds kept quiet when intruders were close. Carnivores were drawn toward the dead and dying.

The wolf's gaze was so intent on the base of the outcropping he did not notice Duncan until he had thrown a rock. The creature yelped as it struck his shoulder, and then faded into the shadows. Duncan ran to the limp form the wolf had meant to claim.

"Patrick!" he groaned. His friend the Long Runner showed no sign of life. Blood oozed from multiple wounds. A musket ball had ripped into his thigh, another had pierced his right side, and he had been struck in the head with an ax.

Patrick Woolford had been a captain of a company of frontier rangers during the war with France, nearly as famous as Major Rogers for accomplishing impossible feats. Declining frequent offers of positions in England and at headquarters units, he had gone west to fight in the recent rebellion of the western tribes. Even now, with the hostilities long over, he would disappear for weeks at a time with the Iroquois and frontiersmen who served in the small, elite ranger unit he commanded. It had been years since Duncan had seen him in uniform and despite the fact that, excepting Conawago, he had no closer friend, Woolford always found a way to change the conversation when Duncan asked how he served the king on his long treks in the forest.

With a sigh of relief, Duncan found a pulse. It was weak and irregular, but Woolford was alive. Duncan quickly straightened his long limbs and set to work. With a strip of cloth torn from Woolford's linen shirt, he tied the thigh above the wound to slow the hemorrrhaging. The ball had pierced the muscle and exited the back of the leg. He gazed forlornly at the chest wound. If a ball had gone through his ribs, there would be little Duncan could do but prolong his suffering. Slowly Duncan unbuttoned his friend's shirt then stared, disbelieving. Woolford had fastened an apparatus of oak slats around his torso, held together with knots of sinew. It was a form of Iroquois body armor once worn by the tribes in battle, before the arrival of firearms. Duncan had seen such artifacts on longhouse walls, even seen some, intricately decorated, under the sacred masks of the spirit lodge. Woolford's oaken vest had the patina of age and every one of its slats was inscribed with symbols. Europeans tended to speak down to the woodland natives, dismissing them for their lack of education and written language, but Duncan knew better. Some of the wisest, most intellectually active men he had ever known numbered among those tribesmen, and their wisdom flowed from a fount much deeper than those of European institutions. Such symbols, moreover, often told stories more eloquently than many European books.

The vest would have been useless in a closer battle with guns but the ball aimed at Woolford had come from afar, as if the captain had anticipated such an attack. Although it had smashed through the vest, he saw amidst the splinters of wood and bone the metal gleam of the bullet. The vest had kept it from reaching a vital organ.

More troublesome was the tomahawk blow Woolford had taken to the head. The strike had been a glancing one, as if the ranger captain had been struggling, but the gash was deep and had nearly taken off his ear.

Duncan lifted an eyelid. The pupil did not respond. He whispered Woolford's name as he poured water over the gash on his head. A patch of bright white, his friend's skull, gleamed through the ragged tissue. Death hovered over the ranger.

A stone rolled on the path and Duncan looked up to see the Iroquois boy staring fearfully at Woolford . Duncan pointed to a little stream twenty paces away. "He lives. Get me moss from that bank," he ordered the boy in the Iroquois tongue. "Then find some spiderwebs."

The boy seemed not to understand. Duncan tried again, more urgently. "What is your tribe, boy?" he finally asked, in English.

"'Cadian," the boy replied in a low voice, as if wary of being overheard.

Reminding himself that the boy was of the Canadian Mohawks, who sometimes spoke a different dialect, he explained in English what he needed.

Half an hour later Duncan had done what he could to staunch the bleeding and clean the wounds. The needle with silk thread and the sterile bandages he needed would have to wait until Edentown. For one short moment Woolford stirred toward consciousness. He reached up, grabbing Duncan's arm, though he showed no sign of recognizing his friend. "They're all going to die! Every last man will die!" he uttered with desperate effort, then collapsed.

A terrible chill rose along Duncan's back. "Edentown is less than eight miles away," he said to the boy. "Down the southern trail. You'll see its cleared fields and barns to the east after the trail passes a high waterfall. I want you to help tie the captain onto my back then run for the town. Take my pack, they will recognize it there. Go to the great house and tell them Captain Woolford is hurt bad. Bring four strong men and a litter."

"But Red Jacob—" the young Iroquois protested.

"We have to tend to the living, boy." Duncan saw the anguish on his thin face. "But we can set his body in repose, lay down some cedar to attract the spirits."

The boy gave a solemn nod, then pushed the flour sack looped over his shoulder to his back, and bent to help lift Woolford.

As they walked, Duncan, bent under the weight of his unconscious friend, pointed out strands of ground cedar, which the boy retrieved as Duncan explained how he should place a ring of the fragrant plant around the warrior. The youth ran ahead as they approached the log where the Oneida had died, and had begun the task when he cried out and backed away.

Red Jacob's left arm was gone. The eater of bones had returned.

CHAPTER TWO

The big Philadelphia clock in the downstairs sitting room struck four in the morning as Duncan finished the sutures on Woolford's head. He had been grateful his friend had not regained consciousness while he had plucked the splinters and ball from his broken ribs and reset the bones, but now he was getting worried. The ranger captain had not stirred since that first troubling moment in the forest. Duncan had no way of knowing how gravely his brain was injured.

"Mr. McCallum, surely you need some refreshment." He turned to see Jessica Ross, the young Scottish woman recently brought by Sarah from Pennsylvania as the manor's cook. She held out a tray with a cup of tea and a piece of buttered bread.

Duncan glanced back at his unseeing friend, then reluctantly rose and nodded his gratitude. "It's late," he observed.

"Oh nae, t'is early," Jess grinned. "A new day. There's fires to be lit and cows to be milked."

Returning her smile he quickly drained the teacup then consumed the bread on the way to the smithy. As he reached the low-roofed building he paused, extending his hands over the dull heat of the smoldering forge as he gazed uneasily at the body on the workbench.

"It's not that cold, Duncan," came a deep voice from the shadows. The big black man who sat on the stool in the corner would have been invisible but for his tan waistcoat. Crispin had come with the litter for

Woolford but had continued up the trail with the boy for the Oneida's body, and had not left it since.

"No," Duncan admitted. "I'm just soul weary, my friend. Too much blood. Will there never be an end to it?" In the dim light Duncan saw that Crispin, freed slave and now schoolmaster of the village, held one of the long hickory staffs that were waiting to be fixed by the smith to a shovel or hoe head, and he realized that the big man was not just keeping vigil, he was standing guard. Like Duncan, he was loath to spread an alarm but knew the killing meant danger could be lurking nearby. Duncan clenched his jaw and stepped to the workbench.

A pot of smoldering cedar, flanked by candles, lay near the head of the dead Oneida. The old man who sat beside Red Jacob was murmuring a tribal song for the dead, to ease the journey to the other side. Duncan found another high stool and sat opposite Conawago, the corpse between them.

He remembered the quiet Oneida from one of the elders' feasts in Onondaga. Red Jacob had sat beside him as they ate and spoken with surprising passion of his children, then of long journeys as a ranger around the inland seas and the great falls of Niagara. But when the sacred pipe had been passed around the circle, signifying the beginning of the elders' orations, Red Jacob's face had become as solemn as a monk's. The next day Duncan had seen him at the riverside carrying a young girl on his shoulder and joyfully encouraging a boy of eight or nine as he caught frogs. Their laughter had filled the forest.

"It's enough," he whispered as he gazed into the strong face of the Oneida. "I have laid out the bodies of too many good men of the tribes. When will it end?" he asked the dead man.

He had not intended for Conawago to hear, but he realized the singing had stopped. "When all the good men are gone," the old Nipmuc said in a matter-of-fact voice. Their eyes locked in a painful gaze. Conawago had given up on his decades-long search to find his people, lost to him as a boy after he had gone with the Jesuits to be educated in Europe. Duncan increasingly sensed that despite his stout heart, his friend was beginning to feel, like many other warriors of the rapidly shrinking tribes, that his one goal in life was to find a good way to die.

Conawago broke away and gestured to the corpse. "The Death Speaker has work to do. Do not let me disturb you."

Death Speaker. It was what the Iroquois sometimes called Duncan. Once he had aspired to be a doctor, had nearly completed medical school in Edinburgh before being arrested for harboring his aged uncle, an unrepentant Jacobite rebel. Unlike many of the natives, he was not afraid to touch the dead. He also had learned much of Conawago's native healing arts. But among the tribes he was known not so much for his healing as for his ability to learn from the dead, to coax the truth out of unexpected corpses.

Duncan saw that Conawago was staring at his chest and looked down to see that his hand was clutching the small quillwork pouch that hung from his neck. Duncan was a man of two clans, Conawago sometimes told him. Highland blood may course in his veins but the tribes and their totems, like that in the pouch, had a claim on his spirit.

He stood and whispered a prayer of his Catholic mother as he paced around the corpse. On the Oneida's feet were moccasins of thick elk hide soles fastened to doeskin with intricate quillwork, probably the gift of his wife or mother. The dark brown trous that covered his legs were of thick sailcloth, a fixture of British sailors borrowed by the rangers during the war with the French.

"Was he in the war then?" Duncan asked.

Conawago nodded. "One of Woolford's sergeants. He still carries the medallion," he added, referring to the little bronze discs inscribed with a tree that Woolford issued to the men, European and native alike, who served with him. If he still carried the disc then he was among the handful of elite rangers who remained on active duty, engaged on Woolford's cryptic missions.

Duncan lifted the pouch tied to Red Jacob's waist and upended it onto the bench. The ranger's disc, a flint, a length of knotted twine, a square piece of quillwork, two spotted feathers, and one cube from a pair of gaming dice. Or rather a piece of a dice, for the little bone cube had been crushed and half was missing.

Conawago paused with a worried expression over the four slash marks on the man's cheek, then indicated a tattoo on the left side of the warrior's neck. "The fish with the arrow through it," he offered, "is from the villages along Ontario, the inland sea. Probably his mother's people."

The other side of the Oneida's neck was in ruin. Duncan had once stood with his grandfather on a dock in the Hebrides as a dead sailor had been carried ashore. The man had endured storms and pirates sailing from the West Indies only to die in the harbor when a lightning bolt had severed a backstay, which had whipped down and with dreadful fortune snapped his neck. "Mark it boy," the old Scot had said, "each day our lives hang by inches."

In Red Jacob the difference had been an inch exactly. His assassin's ball had only snagged the outer inch of his neck. But in that span of flesh had been a vital artery.

"The shot came from the back," Duncan said, showing Conawago the clean entry at the rear and the eruption of tissue and dried blood that marked its exit.

"He died running down one of the old war trails," Conawago observed.

Duncan hesitated. "The Iroquois are no longer at war."

"Nonsense. One way or the other the tribes have been at war ever since the first European stepped off a boat."

The words pained Duncan. The gentle man he had befriended five years earlier would never have spoken so harshly. He unfastened the top buttons of the Oneida's waistcoat, exposing the tracks of a life well lived. Over a dozen small tattoos, each a badge of honor or mark of great achievement, ran in an arc between the dead man's shoulders. Duncan recognized several. A shooting star, a crescent moon, and an upraised hand each signified completion of a ritual ordeal, all of them excruciating to the body but cleansing of the spirit. A bear, an elk, and an eagle signified the touching—never the killing—of a massive grandfather of each species, one of the prime, proud specimens said to embody important forest gods. A canoe bearing several stick figures with an arrow over it marked the remarkable, inhumanly fast ranger expedition that had been dispatched from the New York colony to force the surrender of Fort Detroit at the end of the French war. Woolford too wore the symbol on his chest.

Conawago pulled away the cloth that covered the Oneida's left arm and looked up expectantly. Duncan had seen dismemberments before, had even participated in dissection of the dead at his medical college, but somehow the severing of Red Jacob's forearm deeply unsettled him. He had been with the body on the trail before the dismemberment. He sensed he had somehow failed the Oneida, by leaving his body to the butcher who had killed him. Mutilation of a warrior's corpse was a grave sin, an affront to the dead and the living alike. Red Jacob would arrive in the next world without his entire body, and would not be able to tell his ancestors that he had nobly lost his arm in battle. Some in the tribes would say the spirit of such a corpse could still feel the pain of such a wound, that it would even disrupt the journey to the next world.

Duncan, who normally maintained a doctor's reserve when examining the dead, had to clench his jaw, mastering his emotion as he gazed at the stump.

Conawago seemed to sense his discomfort, and started for him. "No sign of bleeding. He was already dead."

Duncan lifted the lantern closer and probed the flesh with his fingers. "It came off in three—no, four slices from a sharp, wide blade, wider than most war axes, more like a hand ax for timber."

"He had a tattoo on the arm," Conawago said, pointing to the spidery lines that started on the bicep and led toward the missing limb. "When I saw him last autumn he had no such markings."

Duncan searched his memory, picturing in his mind his first hurried glimpses of the dead man. "Curving and jagged lines that went around his arm and ended on the back of the hand," he recalled. "Not an animal, not a symmetrical design. A random adornment." He pressed a finger against the remaining lines above the elbow, then with new purpose grabbed a rag, dipped it in the bucket of water by the forge, and rubbed at the lines.

"Not a tattoo," he declared in surprise, indicating the smudge he made. "Just ink, India ink. It might have stayed for weeks if he did not scrub at it. Ink," he repeated in a confused tone.

"A charm then," Conawago offered. "A protection."

"Not from the one who eats the bones of men," Duncan whispered. He looked up, sensing a new chill in the air.

The old Nipmuc seemed to have stopped breathing. His voice cracked as he spoke. "Why would you say such a thing?"

"The boy said it. He was raving with fear, saying this was done by an ancient demon who eats the dead. He said the monster is coming for us, shaking his rattle, and that everyone who hears it will die. Some tale to keep children in their blankets at night."

Conawago's hand shot to the pouch holding his own spirit totem and he murmured a prayer in the tongue of his youth. "Children are not wise enough to be truly scared. It is the old chiefs and sachems who quake with fright when they hear of that rattle.

He rages against men and revels in remaking their bodies so they will be as hideous as he is."

"It's not unknown for tribal enemies to take a body part as a trophy," Duncan ventured.

Conawago was one of the bravest men Duncan knew, but he now watched as fear grew on the old man's countenance. He shook his head as if disagreeing with Duncan and studied the body. The old Nipmuc bent four fingers and raked the air over the slash marks on the Oneida's face, then pressed his fingers over Red Jacob's abdomen, pausing over a little lump below the Oneida's belly. Duncan loosened the remaining buttons of the waistcoat and pulled back the fabric.

Conawago groaned and jerked backward, holding his own belly as if he had been struck. Red Jacob's amputated hand was reaching out of a hole in his abdomen.

"This monster has a name," Conawago declared in a hoarse voice. "It is the Blooddancer."

CONAWAGO HAD BEEN AS DISTRAUGHT AS DUNCAN HAD EVER SEEN him, insisting that the body had to be cleansed again, with new prayers, and the old Nipmuc had hovered over Duncan as he had closed the incision in Red Jacob's belly, cupping fragrant smoke over him as he worked with needle and thread.

Duncan worried that the news he had from the Great Council would only alarm his friend more, but he knew he could no longer delay telling him. "Adanahoe used that name. The Blooddancer mask had been stolen, she told me, and the Great Council is deeply disturbed," he recounted as he tied off the suture and cut the thread. "Her grandson died in pursuit of the thieves. She said you and I were to track down the missing god. She saw it in a dream. I was going to tell you over breakfast."

Conawago's eyes flashed, then he fixed Duncan with a sober stare. "The mother of the tribes had a dream about us? And you wait to tell me?" To the tribes, dreams were important messages from the spirit world. He demanded every detail of Duncan's meeting with the old matriarch, but not before he had moved their stools to the back workbench, and lifted the bowl of smoldering cedar to set it between them.

The old Nipmuc, who had been trained by the Jesuits and visited great cathedrals in Europe, solemnly listened, nodding with an increasingly forlorn expression. He had decided, for reasons he had once explained to Duncan while sitting under a meteor shower, that the Christian God deserved great respect but he was a European god. The gods of the sacred lodge were for the natives of the woodlands. There was nothing irreconcilable, he insisted, about two sets of gods and saints serving two different peoples.

Conawago stared into the rising smoke a long time before responding to Duncan's report. "The farther that god is taken from his home the angrier he will become. He is capable of terrible things"—he gestured toward Red Jacob—"of slicing humans apart for the sport of it. Blooddancer is a very old god, a vengeful god. He is the Trickster, and when his blood rage is on him he will slash men with the claws of his rattle, then rip them apart and put them back together like horrible puzzles."

"She is dying, Conawago. But she says her spirit will linger near the sacred lodge until she knows Blooddancer has been returned."

Conawago's eyes filled with moisture, and when he rose he seemed to have become frail, stumbling as he returned to the dead man's side. The old Nipmuc bent and murmured into the scarlet ear.

"We should find some breakfast," Duncan said, but Conawago seemed not to hear. "It's been a hard night. We both need rest."

Without looking up, Conawago waved him away.

Duncan stepped out into the grey blush of early dawn, nodding to Crispin, who now sat outside the shed, his club on his lap. He dunked his head in the water trough by the barn and then lowered himself onto the stone mounting block beside it. He was not just bone weary, he felt strangely diluted, dissipated, as if his soul had been tapped and drained. He gazed into the blackened forest. A monster stalked the woods, the very demon he had promised to find. Blooddancer played with the dead the way children played with toys.

He looked back at the great house, reminding himself that he should check Woolford, and had taken a step in that direction when a voice, light as feathers, stopped him.

"Yesterday in the first light young fawns were playing with the lambs."

The voice banished all fatigue. He turned to see a dim figure perched on a fence rail, stroking the nose of one of the Percherons.

"And what was the mistress of the estate doing in the pastures at dawn?" he asked as he approached Sarah.

"Watching the northern trail. You were overdue. I was thinking of taking a horse and riding a few miles north."

He reached out and pulled her down, into his arms. They embraced for a long, silent moment. "Thank God you didn't," Duncan whispered into her ear.

"I didn't want to disturb you in the forge. Crispin said the dead man was an Oneida. Why would he be here? Why would he be killed here?" she added, as if correcting herself.

"He was one of Woolford's rangers. Ranger business," he said, knowing it was no real answer.

"I saw the quillwork on his waistcoat. That was Adanahoe's hand. She does that for those who serve the Great Council in some special capacity. I have heard she is dying, Duncan. We must go to her. When I was with the tribes she was like a grandmother to me. The wisest woman I have ever met."

"She sent for me when I was in the north, Sarah. She has other plans for me."

Sarah stiffened and pushed away. Duncan followed her gaze toward the forge, where a solitary candle showed Conawago bent over the corpse. He heard the low monotones of another death song.

Duncan led her into the barn, trying to leave the death behind. "The apple orchard at Brewster Creek shows great promise," he reported, desperate to change the subject. As he led her down the broad aisle flanked by stalls he spoke of his travels. Sarah called him her traveling superintendent, her ambassador among the far-flung farms and tiny settlements started by the families to whom she had allotted land out of her family's vast holdings. They could keep the land if they worked it for seven years, and meanwhile she offered them seed, tools, and Duncan's advice, though more often than not his contribution was with an ax or shovel in his hands. One of their first priorities had been getting orchards started wherever possible, an enterprise with which the Iroquois, renowned for their own fertile groves, had often lent a hand.

The Westcotts' milk cow had twin calves, he reported. The prize draft mare at Hay's Landing had thrown a fine colt. Sarah played the game, asking about Mrs. Langer's gout and the bear that had raided the Stoltz's smokehouse. She pointed out a blazing meteor that passed over the southern woods, and pulled him to a stop, finger to her lips, so they could listen to the gobbling of the turkeys in the trees beyond the pasture. Duncan did not miss her anxious glances back toward the smithy.

Suddenly Sarah skipped forward, pulling him toward the stile that traversed the pasture fence as if she too recognized the need to shake off their dark spell. She led him along the edge of the field, staying in the deepest shadows, and finally halted when they heard a thin but joyful bleat.

At first Duncan saw only small shadows darting among the spring grass, but as the sky quickly brightened he could distinguish the shapes of sheep and deer. A dozen lambs and half as many speckled fawns leapt about, running in bouncing strides. The ewes lay watching from the center of the pasture, the does from the edge of the forest.

Sarah rested her head on his shoulder, her auburn curls spilling over his waistcoat. "A new box of books arrived from Philadelphia," she whispered. "I have been reading the great philosophers."

"*Ohskenonton.*" Duncan pronounced the word slowly, as if just learning it. "It means deer."

A smile bloomed on her face. Sarah had been another skittish creature of the forest when he had first met her, a prisoner of the tribes only recently recovered by the British. Duncan had started his seven-year indenture to her Scot-hating father as her tutor. She had been a reluctant student who had forgotten most of her English while being raised by the tribes, and he had coaxed her by having her teach him an Iroquois word for each English word he taught her. Crispin had taken over as teacher when Duncan had followed Conawago into the wilderness, and now Sarah Ramsey had what was no doubt the largest library on the frontier, other than in the Mohawk River manse of their friend William Johnson, Superintendent of Indian Affairs.

"The one I am reading says symbols are the signposts of human lives, that we rely upon and use them without knowing so." She aimed her gaze back to the animals.

It took several breaths for Duncan to understand. "You mean the wild and the civilized can find a way to coexist."

She shot him a peeved glance. "You know better than to speak in such terms."

Duncan flushed. "I do." They both had repeatedly experienced the ways in which the tribes were more civilized than the Europeans. "Better I say the creatures of the forest and the creatures of the settlements."

"Those babes in the pasture make it look so simple," Sarah said with a sad smile. She turned to look back at the smithy, where the mutilated corpse of an Iroquois lay. She could pass for another refined English lady if need be but her spirit would always be with the Haudensaunee, the tribes of the Iroquois. "You didn't say what Adanahoe asked you to do."

Duncan watched as one of the great oxen emerged from the shadows by the barn. "A sacred mask was stolen. It has to be returned."

She seemed to sag. "So few words. You make it sound like she asked you to fetch some firewood."

"Her grandson Siyenca died trying to recover it."

Her fist pressed against her mouth as if to choke a sob. "A bright, energetic boy, the light of her life. And who was lost from the lodge?" The question came as a whisper.

"Blooddancer."

A sound of alarm caught in her throat and she turned toward the shadowed forest as if to collect herself. "There are those who say the Confederation of the Iroquois is crumbling away, that it has no role in the world anymore. They will say that having a god abandon it is proof. Is someone trying to destroy the Iroquois?"

He had no reply.

A deep sorrow seemed to settle on her countenance. "Blooddancer is the Trickster of death. You can't just track a god like some runaway animal. It needs someone who can speak with the old spirits, who knows how to listen to them. Surely she wouldn't expect you to go alone to find such a . . ." Her words trailed off as she looked back at the smithy. "Oh. Conawago."

"She had a dream, Sarah. The two of us brought the mask back." He did not speak of the rest. They would come back limping, as though from a great battle, nearly dead. "How could I say no to her?"

"Because you are not of the Haudensaunee. Because we need you here, Duncan," she said, then pushed herself into his arms again. "There will be time to speak of this later. You have to doctor Patrick. We have a burial to perform."

"They were attacked just north of Edentown. As if to stop them from arriving here. Has someone else been here? A stranger?"

Sarah faced away, looking at the waking settlement. A dog barked. A cow lowed, asking to be milked. "We have over a hundred souls now. It means a steady stream of visitors. Trading sutlers came. An Episcopal circuit rider. Teamsters with the wagons that bring supplies."

"Yesterday? The past week?"

"There was a tinker, who mended some pots. That circuit rider, who led us in hymns and moved on."

Threads of smoke began climbing out of village chimneys, laced with the scents of frying bacon and baking bread.

"An Episcopal circuit man," Duncan repeated, weighing their conversation. "A long, lonely ride over the mountains."

"The Scots, Duncan. Your countrymen have been flooding into these lands, all the way down the Susquehanna Valley. Those Anglican parsons can't abide the thought that Presbyterian churches might be built."

They watched as Crispin appeared, carrying a heavy tin bath-tub into the woodshed, followed by Jess the cook, singing a frolicking tune as she carried two buckets of steaming water. Conawago finally emerged from the smithy, pale and drawn from his lonely vigil.

"Messages have arrived from Jessica's family, Duncan, down the Susquehanna. A Scottish constable seized a horse train of trade goods going west. When they found it was mostly blades and guns for the tribes they destroyed it. Tons of weapons going to the western tribes."

He looked at Sarah, not certain why she chose to tell this now. "In violation of the rules against such trade."

"Some soldiers went to arrest those who did it and were taken prisoner by the constable," she said.

"Soldiers?"

"There's talk of sending troops from Philadelphia."

"The constable's a Scot named Smith," came a quiet voice over Duncan's shoulder. The dawning light seemed to be restoring color to Conawago's countenance. "He speaks of John Locke, who wrote of how citizens have a right to resist their government in protection of their own life and liberty. I confess I sometimes wonder if he is writing about the tribes, for they tend to their life and liberty so much better than Europeans."

Duncan looked at his friend in surprise, unaccustomed to hearing such sentiments from the old Nipmuc. "Notions from some philosopher with too much time on his hands," Duncan rejoined, now admiring the prosperous village as the sun's first rays washed over it. Jess appeared again, hauling two more buckets of water. "Scottish settlers are more practical. They knew if those smugglers had succeeded, the renegade tribes would have used the weapons to raid their settlements."

"The word that comes up the river," Sarah continued, "is that men on the council of government in Philadelphia had financed the shipment."

Duncan turned to her with new worry. "It does none of us good to credit idle rumors." Crispin appeared from the barn, carrying the sleepy Iroquois boy into the woodshed as another maid from the house entered with towels. "They were thinking of the safety of their families, not of some dead philosopher."

"And the government is likely to hang the lot of them for asserting their rights," Sarah retorted.

He studied her. The hint of defiance in her voice was something new. She was watching Jessica, who now sang an old Scottish droving song as she carried a bar of lye soap and a long-handled brush into the shed. "Jess has family there, among those Susquehanna

Scots," Sarah added, then cocked her head toward Conawago, who had lit his clay pipe and was watching the shed with unexpected, though weary, amusement.

A shrill protest exploded from the shed, in high-pitched, furious French. *"Allez vous en! Idiot! Dégage d'ici!"* Then the French shrieks were replaced with what sounded like an Iroquois war cry.

Crispin burst into the morning light, a shocked expression on his wide face and his skin several shades darker than usual. The brush flew past his head. By the time Duncan reached his side Conawago was making a low wheezing sound that he realized to his surprise was laughter.

"I never knew that a man with skin the color of walnut could blush," the old Nipmuc exclaimed, then saw the confusion on Duncan's face. "Did you not see it? Pierce the grime, Duncan," he explained with a grin, "and your wild Iroquois boy becomes an even wilder French girl!"

CHAPTER THREE

They ate breakfast at the long table in the great house kitchen, still smiling over Crispin's discovery. The big man took the ribbing good-naturedly and Duncan realized his friends were drawing out the incident because it was the one excuse to be lighthearted amid the death and fear that had descended on Edentown. To hear Conawago laugh after their long, despairing night had lifted all their spirits.

Analie, their young French visitor, fidgeted in a homespun shift and tugged resentfully at her newly revealed, neatly combed blonde hair as she explained that her family had been lost in the forced evacuation of the Acadians from Nova Scotia during the great war. As she emptied her second bowl of porridge she related how she had found herself among the tribes of Maine, then had been traded as an orphan slave until she settled with the Iroquois, where Red Jacob had shown compassion and agreed to help her on her journey south to find an uncle in Virginia.

As was the custom at kitchen meals, the house staff sat with them, and as Analie finished her porridge and began to nod off, Jess lifted her up and carried her into the little bedroom off the kitchen, cooing a Scottish lullabye. When she returned she explained how reluctant her young charge had been to yield her layers of grime. "Oh how she kicked and squirmed in the tub!" Jess exclaimed. "But I told her what I tell me own sisters. Cooperate and we'll keep the warm water coming.

Otherwise it's into the creek with ye. And oh that hair! Can you credit it? It was bootblacking they used to make her seem like some wild Indian, and it took long scrubbing till we saw the color of autumn straw coming through. Why would you ever try to hide such a bonny head, I asked her."

The Scottish burr in the woman's voice coaxed Duncan into a dull reverie. For long moments he basked in the sound of friendly voices, the welcoming smell of baking bread, and the warmth of the great stone hearth. Jess's infectious humor joined the table in laughter as she went on to describe how the day before, a too-curious turkey had gotten its head stuck inside a crock, and how she had tangled Conawago's hands in knots in an unsuccessful attempt at spooling yarn. She had arrived only weeks earlier but the young Scottish woman had clearly won many friends with her light heart and hard work.

His lack of rest the night before began to take its toll, and Duncan was drifting into sleep when he heard Jess suggest that Sarah herself should take a morning nap. She saw the surprised look on Duncan's face. "Do ye nae ken, Clan McCallum?" she asked. "Miss Ramsey was up all night, boiling your bandages and keeping vigil at the captain's bedside."

Duncan had indeed not known. He rose and gestured the weary Sarah toward the stairs. "How many men can you spare from the fields?" he asked as they reached the second floor landing. "There should be patrols."

"Nonsense. I will not alarm the village unnecessarily."

"One man dead and another near death. We have reason to be alarmed."

"Nothing to do with Edentown. The troubles of the rest of the world do not affect us."

It was a discussion they'd had every few weeks for years. Sarah was fiercely determined to make Edentown an oasis, a home for orphans and outcasts of all ages, tribal and European alike. She would ask no questions of those who came, and they were welcome to stay as long as they contributed to the community.

"The three of them were coming here. What if they were attacked to keep them from reaching Edentown?"

"Patrick simply knew he could be sure of a hot meal here, nothing more." She seemed to see the protest in his eyes, and pulled him down the hall toward her bedchamber door.

"At least let me take Crispin," he told her, "so we can search—" His words died as she pressed her fingers to his lips, then wrapped her arms around him and laid her head on his shoulder. He opened his mouth to try again but gave up and embraced her tightly.

When she pulled away, his fatigue, and his protests, were gone. With a motion that was now a habit of years, she touched the paper impaled with a knife in the lintel overhead, then closed the door behind her.

Their feelings for one another burned deeply but that paper kept their relationship chaste. Sarah Ramsey, raised by fiercely independent Iroquois women, had asked for his hand years ago, had even suggested they could just cohabit in tribal style without a ceremony, but Duncan had refused. He had been her rescuer, her teacher, her mentor, her right hand in her little reign, but above all that he was her indentured servant. She may have coerced her father Lord Ramsey, who loathed Duncan, into transferring the indenture to her but he was still a servant. There would be no honor for either of them, he had insisted, in consummating their feelings before the seven-year indenture expired. The world would say she had forced him as her bond servant, or that he had coaxed himself upon her to ease his servitude. "The world's an ass," she had fumed. He had agreed, but would not relent. That night she had furiously impaled the document above the door, and it had remained there ever since.

Woolford, now resting in a bedroom down the hall, was breathing steadily and had more color, signs that he might yet survive his terrible wounds. But Duncan knew his friend would not abide the long convalescence he needed to recover. It would be like trying to keep a bull tied down, and in his current condition the struggle could still kill him. He had suffered a severe concussion. It could be days before Woolford was able to speak with him about what had happened, and why he and Red Jacob had been racing south.

After checking each of the ranger's wounds, washing them again with vinegar and then rubbing them with witch hazel, Duncan sat and studied his friend. His eyes drifted to the ancient set of Indian armor Woolford had been wearing, now hanging on a wall peg. They had been like brothers for years but much of Woolford's life was still a mystery to him. Guilt flushed his face as he realized he was looking at his friend with the eyes of the Death Speaker. "Forgive me," he murmured as he rose and began searching for Woolford's secrets.

The small pockets of the ranger's waistcoat yielded some flints, his ranger disc, a few coins and, strangely, a broken bone cube—a half-crushed gaming dice, just as Red Jacob had carried. He looked back at the fragments of the ball he had plucked from Woolford's ribs, then dropped several in a spoon and held it over a candle.

"You need sleep almost as much as he does," came a gentle voice over his shoulder. Conawago stepped beside him, looking down at the melting lead.

"It is in pieces but clearly it was a small caliber ball," Duncan explained, "not a Brown Bess musket or one of the forest rifles." The lead softened and soon formed a bright silver pool in the bottom of the spoon. "There," he said, nodding at the melted metal.

"I don't follow."

"Lead used in balls made on the frontier is melted in dirty molds over campfires and cookstoves, making it crude and dirty. This has no impurities. It was a bullet made for a gentleman's gun, one of those expensive English fowling pieces I wager. The ball that hit Red Jacob was bigger, a heavy musket ball. Two weapons. Two men."

Conawago seemed unhappy with the announcement. "Does it matter? The killers have gone. Woolford lives. You need sleep."

"Patrick would have me understand what happened. A ranger was murdered, one of his rangers, a man he ran with for years. He would have justice, even on a trickster god."

His words clearly worried his friend. "Above all, he would have us keep Edentown safe," the old Nipmuc said, and stepped to the other side of the rope bed. As if to help Duncan, Conawago untied a pouch from Woolford's belt and opened it, tumbling musket balls and a small priming horn onto his palm. As he reached in to empty the pouch, Duncan did not miss the little twist of his fingers. The old man awkwardly looked away.

"Conawago, I am trying to find the truth. The entire truth," Duncan chided. "Not merely fragments of it."

Conawago frowned and slowly turned his hand up, revealing a slip of paper between two fingers. He remained silent as Duncan took the paper and read its single word.

"Galilee," he recited. "What does it signify?"

"I do not know, Duncan. The Promised Land."

"But you were trying to hide it."

"The war may be long over but Woolford is still the ranger who works in the shadows. People pass through here all the time now, some staying overnight. His name comes up sometimes. Some speak of him with suspicion, for they fear those who work in secret. But these are troubled times and sometimes secret work must be done. The last time Sir William wrote"—meaning William Johnson, friend of the tribes and hero of the French war—"he said to be wary, not to trust outsiders, that the landscape is shifting and we must not fall when the chasms open. The frontier has always been the breeding place for troubles. I know nothing for certain, except that we can't have those troubles brought here. Edentown needs you. Sarah needs you here. I need you here," he added with an awkward glance.

"You agree then that Edentown is in danger?"

Conawago hesitated. "No. Surely not."

Duncan studied the weathered face of his friend, as vital and inscrutable as that of any wild creature in the forest. "Would you have us ignore the request of Adanahoe on her deathbed?"

"Not us."

It took a moment for the Nipmuc's meaning to sink in. "She said it was both of us in her dream."

"I have lived with the old gods all my life, Duncan. Blooddancer will not leave a trail a European can follow. He is not your god. Do you know the ancient words to say when you finally confront him? What do you know of the half king at the southern gate, who is said to be able to summon the old gods? This god travels south for a reason."

"Because it is where the thieves take him. Adanahoe did not call me to playact in some myth. Her desperation was real. Her grandson's death was real. She sent for me, not you."

"Because I was too far away," Conawago rejoined, with surprising stiffness. "You were the best messenger. I have received the message. You must stay here. I must go."

"What if it is just some treasure hunters who stole the mask? That is a trail I can follow."

"No. It was just an unhappy coincidence that Woolford and Red Jacob were attacked. Their trail crossed with the fleeing god. The god unleashed his anger and moved on. I will go south in the morning."

Duncan saw the pain on his friend's face. He had no stomach for arguing with the old man, and he knew from long experience it was pointless to argue with him about matters of the forest spirits.

"Woolford spoke of more men dying, of men who had to be saved. Those bullets were not fired by a stolen god. Patrick cannot help them. I must try."

"The words of an army officer worried about his men. He could have been delirious, invoking some memory from the wars. In any case that is government business, not ours. What you owe our friend Woolford, Duncan, is a few weeks of constant medical care."

Their exchange weighed on Duncan as he sought his long-overdue sleep, its echo stirring him awake. His relationship with Conawago was as father and son, and Duncan knew him well enough to know he was withholding something. It was unlike the old man to keep secrets from him, except when they related to sacred trusts of the tribes. He did not know how he could bring himself to defy Conawago, and he would never violate those trusts, but it wasn't a wandering god or Iroquois myths that troubled Duncan, it was a real killer, a merciless killer, on the very trail Conawago meant to take.

At last, after four hours of fretful rest, he rose, scrubbed his face with cold water, retrieved a piece of paper from the library, and returned to the forge. The coals were cold. The smith was working outside, trimming the hooves of oxen.

The dead Oneida seemed to call to Duncan, as if the two men had unfinished business. Someone had wrapped the amputated hand in linen and laid it beside the body. He set the paper on the bench beside the stump of the arm, extracted a writing lead, and replicated the lines that had been inked above the amputation, then, with clenched jaw, unwrapped the hand, which held the end of the random, wiggling lines, and sketched them as well. He folded the paper into his shirt and then stepped to Red Jacob's pack, which had been left on the back workbench.

Leaning on his pack was a hickory bow, dark with the patina of age, probably handed down for generations. Little stick figures of men and animals were etched in the wood. The pack itself had been skillfully made of heavy buckskin and decorated with a sunburst fashioned from the colored quills of a porcupine. It was fastened with two leather thongs, the end of which had been braided together. It would have made opening the pack a tedious affair, as if Red Jacob had meant to discourage a casual inspection. As Duncan moved it, however, a bundle of jerky fell out. He turned it upright. Someone had ignored the straps and opened the pack by slicing through the leather. He reached inside and emptied the pack, finding a pewter spoon, a small, chipped clay pipe, a pouch of surprisingly fine tobacco, a flint, and a striker. He lifted the tobacco again, holding the pouch under his nose. It was not the coarse tobacco of mullein and bark used in the northern tribes, but a richly scented Oronoco leaf from Virginia.

As he returned the items to the pack he tried to recall where the pack had been when he had first found Red Jacob. In his mind's eye he saw it still draped over one shoulder. The killer had been nearby, probably watching while Duncan had leaned over the body, then had come back to remove the pack, slice it open for his search, chop off the arm, sever the hand, incise the belly, and insert the hand inside. It had been a lot of work, more than one man could quickly handle.

He heard movement behind him, then a gasp. Jess Ross was staring at the dead Oneida, with her fist over her mouth. He gazed at her for a long moment before she realized he had turned toward her. "It's the captain, sir," she stammered, lowering her eyes. "He woke and asked for you."

WOOLFORD SAT PROPPED UP IN HIS BED, MAKING A MESS AS HE tried to spoon porridge from a bowl. The hand holding the bowl shook. He seemed to have trouble finding his mouth with the spoon. Jess stepped from behind Duncan to take the bowl and was warned away with a low rumble in Woolford's throat, until he saw who was helping him and relented, allowing her to feed him several spoonfuls before nodding off again. *He woke and asked for you*, the Scottish girl had said. She had been sitting with Woolford. Her fine blonde hair was combed and tied with a ribbon.

"He's going to be all right," Jess said. It was a statement, not a question.

"He suffered grievous injury to his brain," Duncan warned. "His life hangs in balance."

"He's going to be all right," the Scottish girl insisted, then sat on the bed to wipe Woolford's face with a damp cloth. Duncan was about to stop her so he could check the bandages but then paused, surprised at the tender way she cared for his friend.

Woolford's eyes fluttered open and with obvious effort he smiled at Jess, then motioned her away and turned to Duncan. The ranger's voice was so soft and hoarse that Duncan only made out his own name when he spoke. Woolford's hand shot to his ribs and a shudder wracked his body. Duncan grabbed one of the vials he had left on the stand and opened it. Laudanum, tincture of opium, would make him forget the pain for another hour or two. But as the vial touched Woolford's lips the ranger shoved it away.

He grabbed Duncan's arm. "They have their tentacles around the bard!" he gasped. "The King knows nothing!" His eyes closed again and he seemed to drift back into unconsciousness.

Shakespeare. The only part of Woolford's brain that was working was that obsessed with his beloved Shakespeare.

The floorboard squeaked. Jess was standing in the hall, as if trying to listen. She seemed strangely frightened.

Suddenly Woolford pulled him back. His eyes cleared for a moment and his words came in an urgent whisper. "The nineteen are dead and don't know it!" he groaned, the effort clearly costing him pain. "The lie will be written and they will all die! It's up to you Duncan! Go! They can be saved in Galilee! Their only hope!" he groaned, and lost consciousness.

The floorboard squeaked again. Jess had fled.

Duncan turned back to his friend with new worry. Woolford's forehead was feverish. Whether caused by the violent blow to his head, the shattering wound to his ribs, or some mortification in his blood, he was losing his grip on reality. Such ravings about tentacles and the bard and men who were dead but alive could only mean the fever was overwhelming him. Not entirely knowing why, Duncan looked again at the paper with the lines drawn from Red Jacob's arm. The killer had left Woolford alive to catch up with Red Jacob, killing him to search his pack and then cut off his arm. If it had not been a vengeful god then it had been someone who recognized something on the arm, as if that was what he had searched for. Duncan was the only hope for nineteen men, but he was given nothing but meaningless words and meaningless drawings to help him.

At midday Sarah insisted they have what she called a household dinner, with everyone who lived and worked in the great house crowding the table in the dining room. With what Duncan knew was studied effort to distract them, she made small talk, asking Crispin to explain what his students were learning that week, and soliciting Conawago's view on where they should grow pumpkins that year. A new calf had arrived that morning. At dusk the Welsh laundress had seen a mother skunk with four tiny young ones riding on her back.

Duncan's gaze drifted toward the map on the wall, a new one of the colonies fresh from the printer in London. Duncan absently lifted a piece of a cold chicken leg and looked back at the map.

"Duncan," he heard Sarah say in a raised voice. "Crispin was asking about the iron ore mine being built at Brannock's ford."

He rose from his chair. "Still clearing the ox road," he said in a distracted voice, then stepped to the map, quickening his pace as he neared it. "The northern branch of the Susquehanna!" he exclaimed as he pulled out his sketch of the lines from the dead Oneida's upper arm. He laid his paper under the river on the map. "See how the line turns out of Lake Otsego!"

"And here where the streams join to the west of here!" came Conawago's excited voice. The Nipmuc was pointing over his shoulder to the spidery lines that joined the main river.

Duncan folded over the paper so that only its bottom portion showed, where he had sketched the lines from Red Jacob's hand. He rotated the paper to the left, then the right, sliding it over the map below the Susquehanna forks.

"There!" he cried, and pointed to two rivers that lined up in the same pattern as the sketch. "There!" he repeated, more emphatically, then his voice lowered in surprise. "Virginia. It leads to Virginia. The Rappahannock and the Potomac."

Duncan spun about to face Analie. "Nineteen men to be saved. What does that mean?"

The French girl shrank back, her eyes shifting from Duncan to Conawago. "They put me in a chair to look at a book while the captain and Red Jacob talked with Sir William. I was at Johnstown, because they said maybe I should join the school there." Duncan choose not to interrupt to remind the girl she had previously told them Red Jacob was taking her to relatives in the south. "They were comparing notes, making a tally. They didn't know I listened. Twelve men had disappeared, all rangers, some of them Oneida and Mohawk. Later I asked Red Jacob why he was studying a map and he said they were going south to bring them back. Like they weren't just lost, like they were captured in a war. Twelve," she repeated. "I remember, like the apostles."

Duncan sagged. Twelve, not nineteen. For a moment he thought it was possible Woolford had not been unhinged, that his friend had not been raving but speaking an urgent truth.

A nervous voice inserted itself into the silence. "Pennsylvania rangers started disappearing months ago, and some farmers who had been in our militia." Jess Ross fixed the French girl with an inquiring gaze, as if assessing the truth of her words.

Sarah stepped forward to put her hand on the woman's shoulder as if to quiet her. "Jess, surely you would not know that."

"Rangers stop at our farm." She cast a nervous glance in Conawago's direction. "They get letters from other rangers they served with," she said to Duncan. "There's a bond, you know, between the men who run the woods."

Duncan pushed past Sarah. "How many, Jessica? How many disappeared?"

"Seven, last I heard. If the killers are going south I must send a message."

"Twelve from the north and seven from Pennsylvania," Duncan said. "Nineteen! Nineteen men to die." He needed to believe what he had heard from his delirious friend after all. "Woolford and Red Jacob were going to Virginia to save them and they were stopped. Why? The war is over." He searched the faces of his friends for answers. Conawago lowered his head. Crispin looked at Sarah, whose face was coloring. Duncan had expected fear or sorrow on her face, not the smoldering expression she fixed him with before hurrying out of the room.

The meal was over. When the table was cleared Duncan sat and faced Conawago, who lingered at the hearth, smoking his pipe.

"What do you know?" Duncan demanded. "What is it you are not telling me?"

"I know it is not the way of Edentown. Not Sarah's way of the willow." Conawago's expression turned to one of pleading. "She struggles so when you are not here, Duncan. But sometimes I think she struggles more when you are here."

Sarah had declared that the population of Edentown and its dependencies had to let the strife and violence of the outside world pass over it, that it had to bend like the willow, keeping strong, surviving by being flexible. It was a speech he had also heard at the fire of the Great Council of the Iroquois.

"I accept that she won't take sides in the affairs of governments," Duncan argued. "But surely she understands this is different. We aren't talking about government, but of brutal murder. If we alone know and don't save those men we are complicit in their deaths."

"She asked for my vow, Duncan, when I asked if there might be a place for me at Edentown. It was very simple. Above all else, keep this place protected from the world. And I told you. When you made your own vow to Adanahoe you bound me too. It is the Iroquois we must help. Not nineteen strangers who only inhabit Woolford's ravings. There is a lost relic to find, that is all we know for certain. And one of us must stay." There was pain on his friend's weathered face but also a grim determination. What was the secret the old Nipmuc refused to share with him? Duncan turned away.

He found Sarah in the little log schoolhouse, where he had helped her learn about the ways of the Europeans after her years with the tribes. She had been wild and skittish, with an insatiable curiosity about what the books called "civilization." She sat now on the very school bench she had occupied during those first days, facing the large slate on the wall where, as then, chalk-drawn images were centered over their English words.

She did not turn when he approached. "You shall not go, Duncan," she declared in a tight voice, speaking toward the slate. "You are bonded to me."

He spoke to her back. "I shall not go. I am your servant."

His words clearly saddened her. Her hand moved to her face to push aside a lock of auburn hair but he did not miss the way she also wiped at an eye.

"I used to go among the villages with my father, my one father," she said, adding the phrase that she always reserved for the beloved old chieftain who had adopted her, killed by the aristocrat who was her biological father. "Some of the villages had already lost most of their men. In many there were more captives adopted into the clans than warriors of Iroquois blood. I asked him why we must have so much war and he said because our enemies make war and our gods wanted to keep the Iroquois free. If we are not free we are nobody," she added.

He hesitated, confused at her shift in tense, as if she were speaking now of recent events. "I'm not talking about war," he said. "I'm talking about Woolford and Red Jacob and nineteen more like them. Would you have Red Jacob die for nothing? Would you ignore justice? Would you not have me try to save more men from these murderers?"

"I would have you live, Duncan McCallum. I would have you keep the troubles of the world out of Edentown. We will not become part of this trail of death you seek to follow."

"Are you so certain it is something you can decide?"

"What I am certain of is that spring planting must be done and new fields cleared. Crispin and Conawago have laid out plans for a water wheel and a new mill. We owe it to our people."

"This is not just a random killing. Nineteen men. It has the sound of a conspiracy, of a plot. I still wake at night from nightmares of my mother and sisters being bayoneted, my father and uncles swinging from gibbets. They just wanted to be left alone too. But then a few men in the English government started plotting."

Sarah clenched her fists.

"It started out with little things," Duncan continued, speaking toward the teacher's desk that had once been his. "A few bands of drovers disappearing along mountain tracks, never to be seen again. Tavern fights between English and Scots that had always ended with only a broken bone or two suddenly ending with Scots impaled on swords. A solitary traveler wearing a kilt shot from afar. Everyone wanted not to see. No one wanted to look behind the killings. Wars had come and gone in the outside world for centuries without affecting the Highlands. By the time anyone recognized the beast that had been unleashed on the clans it was too late. Villages bigger than this became inhabited only by ghosts."

"We need you here."

"There is no one else who can do it."

"Do what? Wander off to some unknown place to face God knows what to save men you have never met? You don't know what to look for. You don't even know their names." Her voice was swollen with emotion. "Death Speaker is a playactor. You are not the Death Speaker, you are my . . ." she buried her head into her hands.

"There is yet time to save them, or Woolford would not have been running south."

Sarah took a long time to reply. "Virginia, Duncan. Does it mean nothing to you? My father has plantations there. If he caught scent of you I would never see you again." Sarah's father had more than once vowed to take his vengeance on Duncan for interfering with his plans for his daughter and his scheme for carving a private kingdom out of the New York wilderness.

"Lord Ramsey will never know to look for me. I will stay away from his lands."

"No!" He had never heard her speak so forcibly. "I forbid it!" The words came in an anguished voice and she turned away, back toward the slate. "I forbid it," she said more steadily, invoking for the first time in all the years he had known her the harsh tone of the bond master. "You are indentured to me and I forbid it. If you run, Duncan, I swear I will send bounty hunters to drag you home."

Duncan stared at her back for several silent breaths, then turned and left the building.

H E RETURNED TO THE SMITHY AND SAT AGAIN BY THE DEAD MAN, now in a shroud. He owed something to Red Jacob and he would not be able to pay it. He reached for the dead man's pouch again and held the little broken die in his hand. Something about dice gnawed at the back of his mind.

As he reentered the house a pale figure was sitting halfway down the stairway, clutching the rails with white knuckles.

"Patrick!" Duncan leapt to his friend's side. "You'll kill yourself!"

"Just a stroll . . ." Woolford offered with a weak smile, "to clear my head."

Fresh blood oozed from the bandage around his chest. "We will carry you back," Duncan said.

"Nonsense. I heard frolicking on the porch. I am quite fond of frolics."

Duncan cocked his head toward the front door, which had been left open to freshen the house. Jessica Ross ran by on the lawn, followed by Analie, laughing with abandon.

When Woolford reached for the railing Duncan pushed his hand down. "Patrick, you underestimate your injuries. You suffered a terrible concussion. It took thirty stitches to close your scalp."

"A badge of honor for an Indian fighter."

"It was an Indian then?"

Woolford shrugged. "They shot from the rocks. I dropped on my knee when the first shot hit my leg, then the shot in my ribs knocked me unconscious. They weren't interested in me. When I came to, face down, I heard them rummaging in my pack. Two men, speaking English. Just as I started to raise my head, one shouted 'I see the bastard!' and ran down the slope. The other used his ax to quiet me."

Woolford made fists, tightening his knuckles against the pain. "They meant Red Jacob, didn't they?"

"He's dead."

The ranger captain closed his eyes and for a moment Duncan thought he was sinking back into his coma. "His wife is a northern Mohawk, a Christian," Woolford said. "She insisted I be the godfather to their son. What do I tell him? His father survived untold acts of heroism in the wars only to die in an ambush on some lonely trail in his own land?"

Woolford's hands starting shaking. Duncan realized his friend could pass out at any moment. "Patrick, you spoke to me of nineteen men who were going to die."

The ranger's eyes seemed to glaze over. "Fear not until Birnam Wood comes to Dunsinane," he whispered. His mind was sinking again. "That's the bard's word. But Sir William said they die when the castle comes to the wood. What could that mean? He wouldn't confuse *Macbeth* by accident."

Duncan cocked his head. Woolford was speaking of the nineteen after all. "You came from Johnson Hall? Why would Sir William know men were going to die in the south?"

Woolford leaned his head against the wall and closed his eyes. "I don't know," he continued in a choked voice. "We sat in his library. He said he had received a devastating letter from Franklin."

"Franklin? Benjamin Franklin?"

"Then his son Francis came in. He had just arrived from London and there was a dinner to celebrate his safe return. Halfway through the meal, Sir William's hands began to shake and he excused himself. He insisted Molly help him back into the library instead of to his bed," he explained, referring to Johnson's Mohawk wife Molly Brant. "When she returned she told me this was happening every few weeks, a seizure of violent tremors that left him weak as a babe.

But this was worse. He couldn't focus, he couldn't keep his balance." Woolford opened his eyes and stared absently at the door. "When Red Jacob and I went into the library he was waiting for us, said we had to run, that very hour, that nineteen men will die if we don't get there in time."

"Twelve rangers and seven Pennsylvania men," Duncan inserted. "In a place called Galilee?"

"The rangers went missing over the past three months. Corporal Larkin, Frazier, Hughes, Robson, and the others. The best of men, with me for years. Don't know about the Pennsylvanians but that makes the nineteen. Johnson handed Red Jacob a map, said he must memorize it, that they must not find it on him."

"He inked it on his arm."

Woolford winced as he tried another nod. "Then Sir William struggled to his feet and staggered to the cabinet where he keeps his tribal treasures. 'They die when Dunsinane comes to Birnam,' he said, and threw the oaken armor at me, saying I would need it. Very old, with an ancient protective charm, goes the legend."

"It deflected the bullet and saved your life," Duncan observed. "Charmed enough. Now let me help you back to your room."

Laughter rose outside again. Woolford seemed to revive. "Not yet," he said, gesturing toward the front door. "It's a poor heart that never rejoices." He began rocking forward, as if to launch himself down the stairs. Duncan extended a reluctant hand.

On the expanse of grass outside, close-cropped by sheep, Jessica played with Analie, tossing a leather lacrosse ball pinned with trailing red ribbons. From the porch Sarah cast an uneasy glance at Duncan and then called out joyful encouragement as she filled a mug of cider for Conawago. Her laugh was shallow but sincere. She worked so hard to keep the evils of the world away. Analie at least had found a place where she would be safe.

"Long Runner!" Analie ran to hug Woolford as Duncan helped him into a chair. "A strong arm, Miss Ross," Woolford called out with surprising vigor.

"Comes from pitching Pennsylvania hay," the Scottish girl quipped as she climbed onto the porch. "A more honest labor than prancing around the woods with a rifle all day," she chided good-naturedly, and poured some cider for Woolford.

"When I recover," Woolford vowed, "I'll teach you two how to play a real game of lacrosse."

"I eagerly await the occasion," Jessica cheerfully replied.

Woolford, ever the devotee of Shakespeare, tipped his mug to her, then gestured with it toward all his friends. "Those friends thou hast, grapple them to thy soul with hoops of—"

His words were cut off by a sharp crack of a rifle from the trees, instantly followed by a second shot. Conawago jerked backward and Jess seemed to sag against the wall as Duncan darted to protect Sarah. She pushed him aside and leapt to Conawago, whose shirt sprouted a bright bloom of crimson. The Nipmuc ignored her, instead bending to lift Jess.

As he cradled the Scottish girl in his arms Duncan thought the blood on her dress was from Conawago's wound. But the agony on the old man's face was not for himself. A bullet had ripped into her heart. The joyful Jessica Ross was dead.

"Jess! Noooo!" Woolford reached a trembling hand toward the girl but the effort, and the shock, proved too much. He slumped forward, unconscious.

A tear rolled down Sarah's cheek as she looked up at Duncan. "Go, damned you," she cried. "Stop them. Stop this trail of death."

CHAPTER FOUR

A CHILL HAD RISEN, IN THE AIR AND IN DUNCAN'S HEART. HE WAS leaving his friends, his comforts, even the books that he usually carried to read at his campfires. He was chasing murder and mayhem and had to be as light and stealthy as possible. At the top of the high ridge overlooking Edentown he paused. Snowflakes tumbled among the spring violets at his feet. An owl, companion of death, hooted in the greyness ahead of him.

He should have left hours earlier, as soon as their search parties had confirmed that the shooters in the forest had fled, but Sarah would not let him set out in the night, and his friends had needed him. Conawago had been shaken deeply, not by the wound in his side but by the loss of young Jess. Despite his injury—a bullet had ripped along his rib cage and exited his back—the old Nipmuc had kept vigil beside her as she was cleaned for her burial shroud. He had proclaimed that she had to be laid to rest on the little knoll above the orchard where she could watch the birds she loved so much. Sarah had dressed the Scottish woman in one of her own best dresses and, to Duncan's great surprise, Conawago had wrapped a worn wampum bead necklace around her folded hands. The necklace, he knew, had belonged to the old Nipmuc's mother, and he had carried it for decades. Duncan could not fully fathom the bond that was apparent between Conawago and the Ross woman, but he was grateful at least that between his wound and his grief Conawago had no heart for arguing that he should join in Duncan's race to the south.

Sarah had been stricken nearly beyond words, staring numbly as Crispin and Duncan led men into the forest in search of the killers. For a second dreadful night she had kept a vigil, sitting beside Jess and only murmuring short, choked syllables when spoken to. For the first time in memory she had not been there to see him off. But beside his rifle and pack there had been one of her kerchiefs, tied around a bundle of twice-cooked cornmeal balls and the venison jerky cured in maple syrup and salt that Duncan favored in his travels.

Three hours after his last glimpse of Edentown Duncan abruptly darted into an outcropping at the side of the trail, found a perch among its heavy boulders, and cocked his rifle. The instincts of the forest warrior, instilled after years with the natives, had begun to nag him.

The slight figure in brown homespun appeared minutes later, her drawstring pouch on her shoulder. Duncan slipped down the rocks, raised a stick, and tripped Analie as she hurried by. As she fell he pounced on her, pinning her none too gently with a foot on her shoulder.

"This is no trail for a sprout!" he snapped. "You are safe in Edentown and welcomed there. Go back and help Sarah. If you still want to leave in a few weeks Conawago can take you to one of the river landings to catch a trading convoy going south."

"I go where I wish!" the French girl declared defiantly. Sometimes she seemed the innocent, vulnerable child but now she spoke like a very impatient older woman.

"Your business in the south can wait."

"You do not own me, Duncan McCallum!"

Duncan pulled away his foot and the girl sat up, brushing dried leaves from her dirty blonde pigtails. "You've seen the work of the Blooddancer, Analie. I heard you singing that day. *I will never go in the woods alone*, you sang."

The reminder of Red Jacob's death took the fire from her eyes. "You don't believe in such things as the Blooddancer."

"I believe in the power that the masks hold for the Iroquois. I believe the tribes know aspects of the world that I can only glimpse. Someone tried to finish their work on Captain Woolford and tried to kill Conawago, and Jess Ross died for it. This is no longer about a wandering spirit. There is murder on this trail." He extended a hand to help her up.

"I have no home," the girl declared in her lost waif voice.

Duncan hardened his heart. "Edentown is made up of orphans and the dispossessed. There is no place better for you. Conawago has many friends among the French in Canada. It would be easier to pick up the trail of your relatives there. Speak with him and he can send letters asking about your people."

The girl cocked her head at him and then nodded. "Letters would be good."

"Go now. Hurry and you can be back before dinner."

Analie gave an exaggerated shrug, then hoisted her flour-sack pouch onto her shoulder and nodded again, backing up a few steps. With an awkward wave, she turned and began skipping back up the trail, singing one of her songs.

Duncan shook his head in the direction of the confused girl, then tightened his pack and broke into long, loping strides. He drove himself hard, aware that if he did not meet up with one of the trading convoys on the Susquehanna he would lose precious days, and fewer convoys were plying the river. Even before the wars that had discouraged the traders, the furs that drove the trade had been harder and harder to come by. The wild was being driven out of the forests.

He stopped at dusk, knowing he risked a twisted ankle or worse if he continued in the darkness. Making a shelter of some fallen limbs and hemlock boughs braced against a low ledge, he lit a fire for tea, then opened his pack, setting aside the parcel he had promised to deliver to Jessica Ross's family, and withdrew Red Jacob's pouch. He heaped on dried branches and by the light of the fire examined the contents again, lifting the piece of quillwork for closer examination. It was not crafted with the delicate, skilled hand of Adanahoe, but was clearly done by a native hand. It held the image of a fat bird, probably a grouse. It was unusually thick, and he saw now how the back side had a double layer of doeskin, forming a pocket. From it he extracted a slip of paper, which he straightened in the flickering light.

It was a verse:

> *Childe Rowland to the dark tower came,*
> *His word was still Fi, fo, and fum*
> *I smell the blood of a British man.*

ALTHOUGH THE IDEA OF THE STALKING GIANT WAS FROM ANCIENT legend, Duncan recognized this particular version as coming from *King Lear*. He doubted that Red Jacob could read, but the Oneida had been carrying a verse of Shakespeare. Not just carrying it but concealing it. Some natives considered that powerful words, when written, created powerful charms. He read the words out loud then bent closer to the light to examine the slip of paper. On the reverse, in pencil lead, was a large numeral 5. It could signify Red Jacob's squad number. It could just be a convenient chit for a gambling debt. But he recalled how the killer had searched Red Jacob's belongings. Could this be the real secret Red Jacob had been hiding?

A vision of the awful moment at the front of Sarah's house flashed through his mind. Woolford had been at the center, seated, solidly braced against movement due to the pain each motion brought, yet the shooters had missed him. The man who had killed Red Jacob had been an expert marksman, but the two shooters at Edentown had missed their mark, killing Jess and wounding Conawago. How many were in this conspiracy of murder?

He slept fitfully, grateful for his makeshift shelter when rain began to fall after midnight. A vision of men hanging on a long English gibbet haunted his sleep. At first he thought they were the bodies of his father and clansmen who so often inhabited his dreams but then he saw they were tribesmen. A raven was perched on the gibbet, watching him as he paced along, counting the rotting dead, passing before a rank of powdered British officers who took no notice of him. Seventeen, eighteen, nineteen, then two more, on a separate scaffold.

He jerked awake, his heart hammering. The last two bodies were those of Conawago and Woolford. His hand was on his knife hilt, as if part of him sensed more immediate danger. As he listened, the pounding of his heart lessened, replaced by a nearby breathing. Something large, perhaps even a bear or a catamount, was sleeping only a few feet away. He lifted his blade and looked about in the grey twilight, then rose, took a step past the remains of his fire, and cursed.

Analie had blanketed herself with dried leaves and slept with her precious sack clutched to her breast. On a flat rock beside her, like an offering, was a small pile of spring berries. He paused for a moment, admiring how she could look so peaceful, so innocent after having been so battered by life. He had had a sister, Mary, who had burned with the same energy. She had been Analie's age when he had last seen her, destined to die on a British bayonet.

He tapped her lightly with his foot, without effect, then kicked harder. She shot up, wide-eyed and frightened. The sack fell away and in the hand underneath was a treacherous little skinning knife, which she quickly hid in the folds of her dress.

"Before dark I picked wild strawberries for our breakfast," she offered in a tentative voice, accented with an uncertain smile. "I smelled tea. I like strong tea. We could drop a peppermint leaf in it; it grows by the hemlocks."

"I wasn't going to trouble with a morning fire," he growled. "I've thirty miles to span before sunset."

Her attempt at another smile was forced, but it reminded him enough of his sister that he had to look away. She looked longingly at the smoldering ashes.

"Breakfast," he conceded in a stern voice, "but then you go back."

"*Bien sûr.* Of course," she replied, then bent to coax the embers back to life.

He watched the French girl uneasily, chastising himself for sleeping so soundly. It could have as easily been the murderers who had stalked into his camp in the night.

"Do you pray, Analie?" he asked as she handed him his mug of hot tea, with the promised peppermint. He had to grudgingly acknowledge her skills in the forest.

She cut her eyes at him. For a moment her ever-changing countenance was that of a cunning fox. "To the blessed virgin, naturally!" she replied with the fervor of a choir girl, then crossed herself as the priests would have taught her. "Father, Son, and Holy Ghost," she added, then nibbled at a piece of his jerky.

"Then swear it. Swear in the name of the Holy Mother that you have finally told me the truth and that when we extinguish this breakfast fire you will follow the trail back to Edentown."

"I swear it so, Duncan McCallum," she said solemnly, crossing herself again. "Back to Edentown. Back to Miss Sarah."

Duncan nodded and gestured for her to sit on a log by the fire. "Tell me how you came to be with the Oneidas. How old were you?"

"I had just had my sixth naming day when some old British officer, stinking of wig powder, came to say we had twenty-four hours to pack and leave. My papa and uncles got us into boats that night, for he said he would never have us become slaves of the British. Forty or fifty of us fled, along the Bay of Fundy. One boat overturned and no one swam away. One couldn't sail fast enough and was taken by a British sloop. A score of us made it to Castine on the Penobscot Bay, and my father started a new farm among the French who lived there. For just a couple years, he said it would be, then we would go south, 'cause he said some of our cousins were going to the Carolinas where they would be safe. But the British kept sending troops to search for us. One night we had to flee into the woods with only the clothes on our backs. My father and brother went one way and told my mother and me to meet them in three days at the trading post in the north. We had an Indian, an Abenaki, who helped us on the farm and my father sent him with us. He kept us safe. But when we had to swim a river, he said my mama must take off her skirts or the water would pull her under. She refused, out of modesty." Analie looked into the flames. "She never came out. She was swimming one moment and was gone the next, like a beast had swallowed her up.

"My papa and brother never came to that post. We waited five days. A trapper came and said they had been shot. I became an Abenaki for a few months, and went to their big settlement at St. Francis. Then an old Dutch fur trader offered a kettle for me."

It was a rich price, Duncan knew. "Why so much?"

Analie grinned. "My singing. They all liked my singing. But that one put a slave collar on me and made me work in the fields at his cabin. One day Red Jacob saw me. He offered three otter pelts for me. The Dutchman said I would be worth a lot more when I ripened. So Red Jacob gave him three mink pelts too. When we returned to his village by Lake Oneida he said there was no honor owning another human, and he took the collar off me."

"But you stayed with him?"

Her face grew melancholy. "He made me laugh. His wife kept me fed and warm. I was accepted as one of his children."

"Still, you left them."

She nodded as she chewed more jerky. "Red Jacob was a ranger with Long Runner. They came into our lodge one day and asked if I would like to see the great Johnson Hall and the school Sir William had there for orphans. But I didn't get to see the school because they went south."

"And you followed them. Like you followed me."

She looked into the fire. "I sang for them. I could sing for you."

"Someday. When I return to Edentown. Go sing for Conawago and the Long Runner as they heal from their wounds. They would like that." Duncan finished dropping his kit into his pack and hoisted it onto his shoulder. "I will keep an eye out," Duncan promised. "If I find any Acadians I will tell them about you, let them know you are in Edentown."

"My family name is Prideau. My mother was a Cyr."

Duncan made a show of taking out his writing lead and jotting down the names. Minutes later they parted, Analie again waving farewell as she walked back up the trail. Duncan ran out of sight then hid behind a large oak. When she appeared he tripped her again, but this time he had a switch in his hand. He put her over his knee and delivered several rapid, stinging blows. "You are going to Edentown! Did you not swear to the Holy Mother? Do you not remember what happened to Red Jacob?" he barked. "You are going to go to Sarah and apologize for making her fret over you!" He delivered one last emphatic blow. "This is the end of your games, girl, do you hear me?"

Analie did not cry out but tears were streaming down her face when she looked up and nodded.

He left her there but stopped after another quarter hour to confirm she was not following. He prayed she would reach Edentown before nightfall.

THE SUSQUEHANNA WAS A GOLDEN RIBBON UNDER THE SETTING sun as he came down out of the hills, so weary from hours of running that his hands shook. He knelt at a stream, sluicing cold water over his head, before carefully scouting the broad, sandy landing place.

Half a dozen oversized cargo canoes and two dugouts were beached at the river's edge. Ragged, weary men, including a handful of natives, were arranging the bales of cargo around a circle of smoking wood where a heavy, bearded man knelt, blowing onto the flames.

Duncan waited for the fire to illuminate the camp before venturing to the edge of the clearing. He stood behind the cover of an ancient sycamore and called out. "Hullo the camp!"

His shout sent several men scrambling for weapons. In an instant three muskets were aimed in his direction.

"One man only," he called. "A friend."

The thickset, bearded man held a heavy horse pistol at the ready, but did not aim it. "That remains to be seen."

Duncan slowly stepped into the light, leaning his rifle on a log. "I seek swift passage to Shamokin, or Harris's Landing if that be your destination. I can pay."

The big man spat tobacco juice toward Duncan's feet. "I don't run a damned ferry," he groused, a Dutch accent heavy in his voice.

Duncan calmly studied the men. Four appeared to be Iroquois, who stood together, hands on their weapons. Seven Europeans, including a huge ox of a man with black curly hair, were passing around a gourd filled with spirits. "You gentle your men with easy liquor. It makes them slow to react and slow to reach full strength in the morning. I won't touch your spirits. I have paddled the length of Lake Ontario with Mohawk friends. My rifle, and my eye, were trained by the best of the rangers."

One of the natives, a tall sinewy man wearing a tattered brown waistcoat over his naked chest, stepped closer to study him.

The bearded man rubbed his hand through his long, unkempt hair, wincing as if he had a headache.

"My name is Duncan McCallum," Duncan offered.

Instantly the tall tribesman darted forward. Duncan did not resist as he unbuttoned the top of Duncan's shirt to expose his shoulder. The muscular native, wearing the scalplock and shaved pate favored by the Mohawk, studied Duncan's tattoo of a rising sun for a long moment, then offered a quick, respectful bow of his head to Duncan and murmured several words to his tribesmen. They moved to Duncan's side, smiling, patting him on the back. The dawnchaser tattoo, symbol of an ancient and tortuous ritual, had been earned by only one European and it meant most of the Iroquois accepted him as one of their own. "You are the one who walks with the Nipmuc elder," the Mohawk declared.

"I am honored to be able to call Conawago a particular friend," Duncan replied.

"I am Tanaqua," the Mohawk explained, and clamped his forearm against Duncan's in a tribal greeting. As he did so, he revealed his own tattoo, an intricate design of snakes and birds on the inside of his arm.

"I guess we've decided," the trader said with a reluctant grin. "Hans Bricklin" he offered, and gestured Duncan to the fire, where a stew pot was suspended on an iron tripod.

He found unexpected camaraderie at the campfire. Two of the Iroquois had seen Duncan introduced at the fires of the Grand Council in Onondaga, and all knew of his frequent aid to the tribes, more than once finding them justice when colonial governments offered none. They spoke of mutual acquaintances among the tribes and the rangers. Tanaqua had served with the rangers and his face flickered with pride when Duncan mentioned the legendary deeds of Woolford's and Major Roger's men during the recent wars.

Bricklin, a veteran of thirty trading seasons, was carrying bales of pelts, casks of maple syrup, and, in the big dugout that was his personal craft, a box of specimens for Dr. Benjamin Franklin and his circle of scientist friends in Philadelphia. Duncan eased into the questions he had for the trader, sharing some of his precious tea leaves and talking about the weather and poor state of the fur trade before asking about other travelers on the river. Since leaving the headwaters of the river, Bricklin explained, no other southbound travelers had passed them other than a family of Iroquois who, when hailed, said they were en route to relatives in Shamokin, the town at the junction of the Susquehanna branches that served as southern capital of the Iroquois Confederation.

The grizzled Dutchman gave orders for the night watch then laid out a groundcloth for Duncan in front of the canvas-wrapped bales. In the warmth of the fire, reflected off the bales, Duncan's exhaustion quickly overwhelmed him.

He awoke suddenly, not in heart-pounding fear but with an unfamiliar, empty feeling. This had not been one of his nightmares of dead Highlanders. He had been in the Iroquois lodge where the sacred masks lived—they were always deemed to be as alive as any man or woman—and the hideous masks had started a death chant, a chant used in battle by those who knew they were about to die. He stared for several minutes at the brilliant carpet of stars overhead, pushing down the foreboding brought by the dream, then finally rose. It was past midnight. A solitary figure sat on a log at the water's edge. It was Tanaqua's turn as sentinel.

Neither man spoke as Duncan sat beside him. Out on the river a silver ribbon erupted and, as quickly, merged back into the water. "My Nipmuc friend insists that fish try to touch the stars on nights like this," Duncan finally observed.

Tanaqua nodded. "I am certain of it. Have you never done the same?"

Duncan smiled. "When I was a young boy I burned my hand

trying to catch a star. My father said I was a fool not to realize it was a flying ember. My grandfather said to keep trying."

Tanaqua gave an amused grunt.

"Bricklin says he hasn't seen other travelers except an Iroquois family," Duncan observed.

"This river has always been a place of shadows, full of islands, cliffs, coves, and swift currents," Tanaqua said. "A man can disappear at sunset and reappear thirty or forty miles away at dawn."

Duncan hesitated, careful about his reply. Tanaqua did not drink spirits, and carried a bow. He was one of the few, Conawago would say, who still walked the ancient paths. Talking with such men was like talking to the forest, the old Nipmuc once told him, for the threads of their souls were woven into the fabric of nature. The warriors of the old ways saw life differently, experienced the world in ways unknown to Europeans. Sitting beside the man Duncan felt very small, and saddened. They both knew his breed was disappearing from the earth. "Are you saying I should not trust Bricklin?"

The Mohawk shrugged. "We keep watch. It is what we do."

Duncan turned back and surveyed the sleeping camp, wondering whom Tanaqua was including in his reference to "we." Bricklin slept with his pistol, rolled in his blanket against his dugout. The big-boned, curly-haired man, an Irishman named Teague, slept nearby with a musket at his side. Why, Duncan wondered, did the Dutchman keep a box for Dr. Franklin guarded in his dugout?

"Tomorrow the water becomes moving land. Quicksilver land," Tanaqua observed after another long silence. "Some of the gods still favor us."

Now Duncan was certain he did not understand. "Captain Woolford was attacked and nearly killed while coming into Edentown," he ventured. "An Oneida with him named Red Jacob died in an ambush, shot in the back."

Tanaqua, like Conawago, could express volumes in single syllables. "Ahhh," he said, drawing it out, filling it with pain and sorrow. "*Sakayengwaraton* will be missed at the Council Fire." Duncan
realized it was the first time he heard Red Jacob's tribal name. It
meant *Mist that rises from the ground in autumn.* The Mohawk murmured something toward the stars, then turned to Duncan. "It is
why you are here."

"You ran with the rangers."

Tanaqua nodded. "In the French war, yes. Elders in our clan said
we had to choose one king or the other."

"Rangers are missing, some of them Oneida and Mohawk. Red
Jacob and Woolford set out to look for them."

"It is a bad death for a warrior, to be shot in the back," Tanaqua
observed. "Whoever did such a thing is less than a man."

"The killer left four slash marks on his face. His arm was
taken. His belly was sliced open and his severed hand placed
inside. Conawago said it is the sign of the Trickster. Two days
before this I was in Onondaga. Grandmother Adanahoe told me
the Trickster had been stolen from his home. Her grandson was
killed trying to recover the mask. She asked me to get Conawago
and find the Trickster. But then the killers came to Edentown.
They tried to kill Woolford but missed and killed a woman and
wounded Conawago."

The words shook Tanaqua. He abruptly rose, stepped down the
pebbly beach to the water's edge, and lowered himself to his knees.
He reached into the river, cupped water in his hands and offered it to
the moon, then held the water close to his face and murmured to it.

When the Mohawk did not move for several minutes Duncan
cautiously approached and stood beside him.

"Not stolen," Tanaqua said. "A kettle gets stolen. Captured. I only
hope he was captured. Otherwise it means he fled."

Something cold gripped Duncan's heart. The Iroquois were glimpsing the end of their world. Conawago had shared a terrible secret with him months earlier. Several of the elders of the League suspected that the life had gone out of some of the sacred masks, as if the ancient spirits were abandoning the Iroquois.

"I should have gone on a purification ritual before I left," Tanaqua whispered. "I should have summoned all the members. But there was no time. And there are only four of us left. The oldest of the guardians, my half brother, knows the words to be spoken for calling the ancient ones like the Trickster. He keeps vigil in the lodge of the bear god in the west hills, and is supposed to teach me when he returns." He looked up with a forlorn expression. "To kill like that means the old Trickster is angry. Now that he has tasted blood he will keep shaking his rattle and killing. He will dance with the bodies of the dead everywhere he goes."

Duncan struggled to understand. "You knew," he said after a moment. "You knew about the stolen mask." He heard a deep despair behind the Mohawk's voice. He spoke as if he had some responsibility to the mask. Duncan's breath caught in his throat as the strange words suddenly connected. He recalled the tattoo on Tanaqua's forearm of snakes and birds, messengers of the gods. The Mohawk belonged to one of the secret Iroquois societies whose sacred duty was to protect the masks.

"Red Jacob was killed by a musket, fired by a man," Duncan said. "Two guns were fired at Edentown. They were not held by a god."

"If the Trickster passes close to a man it can seize him to do his work. Even among Christians I have heard of possession of a soul by an angry spirit."

"The Blooddancer did not kill a young Scottish woman at Edentown."

Tanaqua seemed not to hear him. There was nothing he could do to ease the Mohawk's pain.

After several minutes Duncan stepped back to his blanket. He stood with his hands over the smoldering fire, remembering nights spent in the lodges of the Iroquois elders, witnessing rituals handed down over many generations that were meant to keep the link to their gods strong. As he knelt and pulled back his blanket, something like a ceremonial rattle sounded in his mind and he looked up, half fearful that the Blooddancer was approaching.

What happened next he remembered only as a blur of something long and sinewy. The huge rattlesnake coiled underneath his blanket lunged, aiming for the exposed flesh of his neck. The war club that knocked it aside was thrown from behind him, and Tanaqua followed it an instant later, grabbing the stunned snake by its head.

The serpent was nearly as thick as the warrior's arm, and at least six feet long. Its head seemed cocked in curiosity, not anger, as Tanaqua stared into its eyes. The rattle in its tail slowed, then stopped.

Duncan spoke over his thundering heart. "If I had known this old grandfather wanted my bed I would have gladly yielded it."

The warrior nodded. His toss of the club had had no force in it, and he had pounced on the snake as much to rescue it as to help Duncan. In the tribes there was no worse luck than that which came from killing a snake. The snake was not the only small creature that served as a messenger to the gods, but only the snake brought dreams, and dreams were the way the gods sent messages to humans. Conawago would have insisted the snake was beside him when he had dreamed of the Iroquois spirit lodge.

Duncan lifted a burning stick like a torch. "Up the trail," he explained as the snake curled around Tanaqua's arm, "I passed a field of boulders. He would find a dry bed there."

They walked in silence to the boulders, then Duncan waited as Tanaqua held the serpent's head close to his own and whispered in a comforting tone. As he bent to release it, Duncan touched his arm and extended his own hand. With a look of surprise Tanaqua let Duncan take the huge snake from his hands. Duncan steadied himself, knowing that if he slipped, the viper could end his life in an instant. He put the snake's eyes inches from his own and it strangely quieted. He whispered in Gaelic, then repeated the words in English. "The spirit of my mountain and the spirit of my forest join in you. Find us life, not death before its time." Tanaqua kept his gaze fixed on Duncan, not the snake, as he released it.

They walked silently back to the river and stood again by its edge.

"Bricklin said no travelers had passed us but that one family," Tanaqua explained. "That is true but as we approached this camp today a canoe was pushing off. A man with yellow hair wearing black clothes was in it, with another who was laughing with him as they floated away. Talked like men who wore wigs. English gentlemen. Teague was waiting here when we landed."

"The Irishman was waiting?"

"Waiting for Bricklin."

"You mean he had brought those men the canoe."

"A rendezvous of three men, two who left in the canoe. Teague greeted Bricklin like an old friend, and Bricklin told us to welcome the bull of Ireland to our company."

"You too waited for Bricklin," Duncan stated.

"I don't understand."

"You have an urgent mission to retrieve the sacred mask. In a solitary canoe you could have traveled faster. But you chose to come with Bricklin."

"I saw the body of the boy who died. Siyenca, Adanahoe's grandson. In his hand was this—" Tanaqua extracted from a pocket inside his waistcoat a flat six-inch piece of wood. In the moonlight Duncan could see the many notches cut into it. It was a tally stick used by traders to keep track of transactions or inventory. "The Trickster will never travel in a straight line. All I knew was that he was going south. He will never be where he is expected." Tanaqua looked back at Bricklin's dugout, where the Dutchman slept as if guarding the little chest destined for Dr. Franklin. "But spirits follow spirits. Spirits talk with spirits, even those in a box."

CHAPTER FIVE

Neither Duncan nor Tanaqua mentioned the snake in the morning but they stayed near each other as the canoes were loaded, and took the paddles of the same canoe as Bricklin gave the order for the convoy to push away.

The Dutchman, in his faster dugout, worked his way back and forth among the big cargo canoes as if herding them downstream, conspicuously pausing to watch Duncan as he worked the paddle in long, powerful strokes. He nodded his approval and sped forward, yelling at a pair of Welshmen to balance their canoe better.

It had been many months since Duncan had been on open water, and with a flush of excitement he touched the neck pouch with his spirit totem inside. As he did so he was drawn back to the days of his youth, sailing the waters of the Hebrides with his grandfather. The bright clear water kindled powerful memories of the old Scot laughing in the teeth of a gale, diving among seals, even once rolling out onto the back of a great basking shark just for the joy of it.

After two hours of steady progress down the river he became slowly aware of a lessening of movement, and saw that Teague, in the lead canoe, had stopped paddling. Duncan watched him in confusion, then became aware of a strange new sound, a soft liquid hissing. Suddenly the river was alive with movement, rising and churning as if it were one huge beast that had abruptly grown anxious. The surface began to boil and change to silvery tones.

There were more fish than he had ever seen in one place, packed fin to fin as they swam upstream. Jubilant whoops broke out from those at the front as the silver mass passed around them, and Bricklin yelled for the boats to make for the lee of rock ledges in the middle of the river. "Give the plankers the way," he shouted with a braying laugh, then snapped up a foot-long fish in his hat.

Shad. Duncan had never fully credited the tales he had heard of the spring runs of the fish up the Susquehanna and Delaware, with fish jammed nose to tail for as far as the eye could see. But now as he witnessed the reality, the tales did the fish no justice. Hundreds of thousands, even a million fish swam before them. They were so tightly packed it seemed he could walk on their backs across the river. He paused and turned back to Tanaqua. The night before he had stated that the river would become quicksilver land this day. The Mohawk warrior seemed not to notice him. He just stared at the fish with a serene smile, then dipped his hand into the water, not to catch them but to touch the passing fish as he murmured a prayer in the forest tongue. Not all the gods had abandoned his people.

Most of the men energetically scooped up fish in hats and with their bare hands. Bricklin, trying to paddle toward the front of his fleet, gave up and let his dugout be carried backward with the throbbing, silvery mass. The blanket in front of the Dutchman began to move and a small shape leaned out, blanket over its head, to peer out over the side, and then squealed in delight. Bricklin pulled away the blanket to expose long locks of tangled hair. The girl started singing to the fish.

"Impossible!" Duncan groaned as he recognized the French girl. "I left her thirty miles from the river!"

Tanaqua, confused, shrugged at Duncan. "The moon was out. The traders always like her. *Oiseau francaise*, the little French bird they call her. Her songs always bring good luck."

It was Duncan's turn to be confused. "You know her?"

"She sometimes sings for the elders in Onondaga. But her hair was never the color of straw."

"Surely you're mistaken. She's just—" Duncan's words faded away. He did not know what she was. A liar and an enchanter. The girl's voice was casting a spell. There was a strange harmony between her voice and the watery sibilation of the fish, still passing by like a giant silver raft. The rough, powerful men in the boat were all but paralyzed, done in by the hand of nature and the call of the little French bird.

Suddenly Teague pointed as a patch of fur approached, looking like a small weasel riding the living raft. The big Irishman leapt onto the ledge beside his canoe, ran to its far side, and scooped up the fur as it passed by. With a little jig he put it on his head. It was a cap of rich fur, probably mink, of a style worn by prosperous gentlemen. When, far too small for his head, it slipped off, he snatched it and expertly threw it to Analie. She grabbed it out of the air, waved her thanks, and pulled it onto her own head without breaking her song.

Bricklin drove them hard after the shad passed, refusing to pause for a midday meal, to make up the lost time. Yet the convoy moved in high spirits, buoyed by the French girl's singing and anticipation of roasted shad and fried roe that evening.

They beached on a broad, flat island where rings of blackened stones and lean-to poles tied to trees attested to its frequent use as a campsite. The tribesmen cut green willow sticks for spitting the shad; the Welshmen were able to split a few cedar planks to cook them on; and Teague threw mounds of rich roe, the rarest of frontier delicacies, into a pan of sizzling lard.

"You lie to me Analie," Duncan said to the girl as he sat beside her with his plate. "You lie to me every time we meet. A bad habit in one so young."

The girl seemed unconcerned about his accusation. She scooped up some fried roe with her fingers, and swallowed with a satisfied smile before replying. "My mama said do whatever I had to do, say whatever I had to say, so long as I just stayed alive. That was my vow to my mother. To stay alive. I will not surrender."

"Surrender?" he asked, puzzled at her choice of words.

"To the hornets, the vipers, the catamounts, the bears, the knives, the arrows, the bullets. Not even angry gods who kill my friends." She sang an Iroquois cradle song between bites then, the impish child again, she pulled on her new mink cap, rose, curtseyed, and picked up her mug to fill from the river. She began to kneel at the water's edge, then staggered backward and screamed.

Ducks exploded from the water. Her shrieks echoed down the river. Crows, quieting for the night, fled from their roosts with angry screeches. The girl's terrified cries echoed from across the expanse of water.

Every man in the camp ran to her side, some raising muskets, scanning the riverbanks for the cause of her alarm. Then she pointed a trembling hand. The source of her horror had drifted away and snagged on a log jutting off the island bank. One of the Welshmen reached the log first then froze and backed away, crossing himself. Another man fell to his knees as Duncan passed him, retching up his dinner.

The face of the dead man, clearly a European, had been slit open and the skin on one side peeled away. Four claws had slashed the remaining cheek. His nose was gone, an ear was gone, and one eye hung loose, out of its socket.

"Jesus bloody wept!" moaned Teague, crossing himself.

Bricklin appeared with a paddle and shoved the body free of the snag.

"We didn't . . ." Duncan began as the corpse drifted away in the current. "We should . . ." His words died away. No one, including Duncan, wanted to touch the dead man. There were many kinds of death, and this one seemed somehow tainted, as if it would curse anyone who came near.

When he turned, the frightened men, one cradling Analie, had retreated to the fire. Only Tanaqua stayed, staring with a stricken expression. They had both seen the mark of the Blooddancer. "He is hungry for flesh," the Mohawk said. "The more he eats, the more he wants."

The camp fell into a grim silence as the men readied it for the night. The fire was stacked higher instead of being allowed to smolder, and Bricklin passed around a jug of rum then called for two guards on each watch. Duncan was not alone in sleeping with his hand on his knife.

By daybreak the men were trying to convince themselves that what they had seen had been the result of a tragic accident. The man had drowned and fish had worked at his face. Others argued he had capsized in rapids, and razor-sharp rocks had raked and killed him. Duncan and Tanaqua exchanged knowing glances, but neither spoke.

Duncan had revisited the image in his mind during the night. The man had dark brown hair with no sign of grey, and with his fine woolen waistcoat and matching britches had been unusually well dressed. His shoes, with silver buckles, had been made for city streets. He was a stranger to the frontier. The anomaly had troubled Tanaqua as well. Duncan had stood watch with him at midnight, and he had found the Mohawk at the tip of their little island, staring downstream.

"We used to have great wars with the tribes in the southern lands, and our war chiefs at home said the disappearance of our men there is the sign of a new war. There is an old tale of a half king of our people lost in the south somewhere. He had great powers once. Maybe he summoned the god."

"Is that what you think—that you are going to a war?"

"War has changed for us since the Europeans arrived. Now all the tribes have lost so many they can barely make up a war party. Attacking a village is nearly impossible. But attacking your enemy's gods can be done by stealth, by a handful of men." He made a gesture toward the moon, as if gesturing for it to listen. "Why?" he asked. "Why would my god trifle with a pasty-skinned man of the city? That dead man had never even heard of the Blooddancer."

"But they met."

"The Trickster doesn't meet. He stalks. He kills the ones he needs to kill. What did he need?" Tanaqua aimed the question at the moon, then turned to Duncan. "The dead man had something tied to his hand. What was it, McCallum?"

"I didn't see. I just pray he was dead before the mutilation began."

Tanaqua shook his head. "The Trickster kills a man many times before he dies."

The company remained grim through the morning and when Bricklin ordered Analie to sing, all she offered were songs of the High Church. They moved slowly, warily—all aware they were moving in the same direction as the macabre body—with the haunting notes of the "Ave Maria" and "Tantum Ergo" echoing along their passage.

It was late morning when they passed the dead man, washed onto a rock ledge in the middle of the river. The crows that worked at him already had stripped the skinned half of his face to bone. One hand, in the water, was worked back and forth by the current so he seemed to be beckoning to them.

"We should bury the poor bastard," Bricklin said, but went no closer.

Every man but Duncan and the Iroquois looked away. As the others hurried past, Tanaqua turned their canoe into the shallow water around the rising ledge. Without a word he leapt out into knee-deep water and splashed to the dead man. For a moment he examined the man's bare forearm, then his other hand, before lifting the hand trailing in the water. There was in fact nothing in it, but a piece of twine was looped around his thumb, extending into a pocket. Duncan, having trouble keeping the canoe in place, whistled. Tanaqua emptied the pocket, then ran back and leapt into the canoe just as it drifted out of the shallows.

He studied the object he had recovered, in confusion. Tied to the string was a small enameled box. The Mohawk unwrapped the long piece of twine, which judging by the many small knots tied into it had seen heavy use, then tossed the box to Duncan.

It had been an elegant piece when it had been crafted, probably in the last century, but the enameled images of a man and woman picnicking under a tree were chipped, the silver edging nicked and worn. It bore no words, no marks of any kind other than the maker marks on the bottom. He opened it and dumped the damp snuff inside into his hand, smelling it, probing it with a finger. Finding nothing else, he dropped the contents into the river and examined the interior of the box, expecting to find a secret. But there was no hidden pocket, no false bottom, just the old, corroded tin lining.

With the horror now behind them they picked up speed and by late afternoon were coasting into the landing at Shamokin. More than five years had passed since Duncan had visited the town. Then it had been the thriving southern capital of the Iroquois League, second largest settlement in the Pennsylvania lands, a place of energetic trade and favored venue of day-long lacrosse matches.

Now it was a shadow of its former self. The big sutler's store and largest tavern both lay in ashes. The proud Moravian church Duncan had visited was in ruins, replaced by a more modest log structure with a steeple of rough-hewn planks. The boisterous crowds of traders, trappers, merchants, missionaries, and natives of a dozen tribes had thinned. There were fewer European faces and nearly all the inhabitants, both European and Indian, wore nervous, cautious expressions. As he walked up from the landing, Tanaqua and Analie at his side, he saw that most carried weapons, either in their hands or on their belts.

"The Shamokin I knew was a sanctuary," he said to the Mohawk, "with laughing children, singing Germans, and Shawnee women who chanted as they dried fish. Half the town would play lacrosse while the other half wagered on them."

"That was before the uprising," Tanaqua said. "Before the Pennsylvania governor offered a bounty on Indian scalps."

"That's but a rumor." In the rebellion of the western tribes in 1763 there had been terrible bloodshed along the Pennsylvania frontier, with scalping parties active on both sides.

"No. A Delaware came to our elders with a broadside from a bounty agent in Lancaster. Five pounds for each scalp, payable in cash by the agents."

Duncan halted. Five pounds was enough to buy a small farm. "Surely not. This is William Penn's colony, the peaceable kingdom."

"Penn is long dead. They want our land. From the moment they set foot off their boats they have wanted our land," Tanaqua added in a matter-of-fact tone, then Analie pulled him toward a stable wall where animal skins were stretched for drying.

Duncan left his companions admiring a huge bear skin and approached the little Moravian church. In the cemetery behind it were several graves marked with crude split plank crosses, all but two bearing names familiar among tribal converts. Abraham Pine. Sally River. James Holdfast. Longhand Alder, he read on the first four. The last two graves, the earth freshly mounded over them, were connected by a long snakeskin, the ends draped over each cross. The black paint of the names still seemed moist. Rachel Rohrbach and Peter Rohrbach. Two precious strips of white ermine were tied above Rachel's name, with drops of blood on them. A narrow strip of paper had been pinned to Peter's cross. Duncan found himself on one knee, strangely drawn by the graves.

The paper at Peter's grave wasn't the epitaph he expected, but a most peculiar message, composed of carefully drawn images mixed with letters. An evergreen tree, the word *go*, then a drawing of a toe, followed by a fireplace grate and the letter *r*, then the letters *hap* beside a pie and bird nest. "In the ground just this morning," came a soft voice in a German accent. Duncan rose to face a middle-aged woman of square build and bleak expression, dressed in black with a pewter cross around her neck. "Everyone said it wouldn't work, a Moravian German marrying a Delaware maid. But they were too far in love to listen. We said stay in town, but they were bent on carving a farm out of the forest, a place apart to raise their children, they said. We don't even know who did it. Could be some of those western Indians who never surrendered. Or Pennsylvania scalp hunters, black-hearted sons of Satan every one. Peter had hair as black as his darling wife's."

She paused to pick up a stone. "Such vermin would redeem his scalp too," she continued, then turned and flung the stone into the bushes.

Duncan heard a cry of pain and a man stumbled into the open.

"*Abziehen!* Be gone! I'll not have you disturbing the sleep of my babes!" the matron shouted, then punctuated her warning with a surprisingly strong German curse.

The man, attired in a fine but disheveled suit of matching tan waistcoat and britches, gazed forlornly at the woman, rubbing his shoulder. He was a few years younger than Duncan, and had the appearance of an English gentleman who had suffered unexpected setbacks. His clothes were torn, his hands deeply scratched. His long brown hair was escaping the ribbon that bound it at his nape. He hesitated, looking at Duncan with a forlorn expression before another thrown stone forced him to flee.

"What did he want, Mother?" Duncan asked.

"Brumbach. I am Mother Brumbach. To take poor Peter's things. I told him I would not trust them to a stranger. I am sending them to his family in Bethlehem. The Reverend said we should have sent the body but I said I would ne'er let them glimpse the horror. He was a fine, handsome lad and best they remember him as such."

Duncan hesitated, holding the questions that leapt to his tongue, then stooped to clear away dried leaves that had blown on the graves. He paused, considering the snakeskin, then extended the two spotted feathers from Red Jacob's pouch and inserted one into the earth at the base of each cross. In the tribal world it was snakes and birds who took news of the dead to the other side.

When he straightened she nodded her approval, and he realized that while someone else had surely brought the snakeskin and fur, she had not removed them. The Moravians understood the deep spirituality of the tribes and their own faith was strong enough not to be offended by a blending of traditions.

"I had the honor of worshipping at the great sanctuary in Bethlehem," Duncan said, speaking of the Moravians' mother church in America. "They are not unfamiliar with the horrors of the wilderness."

The big woman's face drew tight. "Not like this, *junge*. Never like this."

"You mean it wasn't just another raid on a cabin."

"I have led people to believe so, for everyone's sake."

It was time for frank talk. "My name is Duncan McCallum, from the north. Some days ago I cleaned the body of an Oneida. His arm had been severed. His hand had been planted inside his stomach. His killer was moving south. Yesterday we found another man dead in the river, his face peeled away."

A deep groan escaped Mother Brumbach's throat. Her eyes filled with moisture, and she motioned Duncan inside the little church.

They sat in a front pew, and she contemplated the flickering of the eternal light on the altar for several long breaths before speaking. "Sometimes when I bake bread I like to take a couple loaves to them. It's only three miles down along the river and I enjoy the walk along the bank. They were working hard to prepare for the baby that was due next month. Peter had built a wonderful cradle of poplar wood and was carving an angel on the headboard last time I was there. Last time I saw him alive, I mean." She sighed and wrung her hands in her lap. "I called out when I arrived yesterday afternoon but no one answered. I found them in the cowshed, the blood still wet on the ground. Rachel was tied to a post with a little linen blanket over her head. When I pulled it off I felt the breath of Satan on my back. Her beautiful hair was sliced off to the bone, her cheeks slashed, the side of her head flattened with the blow of a club. The blessed baby had died within her. God help us."

Duncan recalled that there had been two strips of delicate ermine fur on her cross. One was for Rachel, the other for the unborn infant.

A tear rolled down the woman's cheek and fell onto her folded hands. "Poor Peter was in pieces. His fingers had been cut away and jammed into holes pierced in his neck so they were like some hideous necklace."

"The Blooddancer." Duncan did not realize he had said the word aloud until he saw the woman shudder.

"An old Iroquois myth, boy. Speak not of such things in the House of our God."

"There was no sign of a struggle?"

"Only footprints in the blood. Made by shoes with heels."

"And have there been strangers in town?"

"What, apart from you and the twenty traders today, and more coming and going every day? The town may be crumbling but it is still at the intersection of many paths, on water and land."

A tall native wearing a black waistcoat over his torso but only buckskin leggings and loincloth below entered the chapel and tended to the flickering lamp. He paused when he saw Duncan, then pulled up a stool and sat before them. He studied Duncan in silence before speaking in slow, carefully measured English. "It is the hand of God, Mother, that this man comes to us today."

"This man?"

"You sit with the Death Speaker."

The woman paled and inched away from Duncan, but the Christian Indian continued. Duncan realized he had met the man once, among missionaries along the Finger Lakes. "This is McCallum, brother to Sagatchie, comrade of Chief Custaloga, and the one who guided the great Chief Skanawati along his final path."

It was Duncan's turn to shudder as the native spoke of great men he had known, all Iroquois, all dead.

"Companion to Conawago," the man continued, "and to the daughter of the shaman Tashgua."

Mother Brumbach let out a breath. "The Death Speaker," she repeated in a steadier voice, then rose and gestured Duncan into a small chamber at the rear corner that served as something of a rectory office. Against the wall was a small table, spotted with ink stains, which held dog-eared song sheets, quills, and several liturgical books. Above it were shelves bearing bundles of candles, little wooden crosses, and a battered wooden box.

Mother Brumbach set the box on the table, opened it, and lowered herself into the chamber's only chair. "The cabin had been ransacked so God alone knows what was taken. But this"—she lifted out a muslin pouch—"was stuffed under the roof in the loft. His valuables." She anticipated the question in Duncan's eyes. "It's where the Mission Society teaches us to hide our few valuables."

Inside was another cryptogram, if it could be called such, written in the style of the message at Peter Rohrbach's grave. A clever, artful hand had drawn first a rendering of a deer, a pea pod, a toe, and single syllables interspersed with a saw, a star with a tail, and what looked like several human eyes, closing with an oval from which several vertical lines extended, one with a fat cap at the top. At the bottom was a hasty postscript in plain text. *Colonel Barre has offered encouraging words from London.*

Below the odd missive was a child's Bible bearing the dead man's name in crude block letters; two feathers, one red and one white, bound together with a thin strip of fur; a quillwork bracelet with the names Peter and Rachel skillfully rendered with dyed quills. Duncan upended the pouch and a small black stone tumbled out. As he gazed at its coils and seams, he at first thought it was a stone expertly carved into the shape of a snail-like creature, then he suddenly realized he had seen such a stone before, in an Edinburgh display of natural curiosities. The luminaries had not all agreed on what to call it. A mortified beast, one had said. An alchemist stone. An Aristotle rock, some insisted, because the ancient Greek had been the first to describe them. But Duncan had settled on the term used by one of his more modern professors. A fossil.

"Was Peter a natural philosopher?" he asked.

Mother Brumbach was clearly uncomfortable with the little stone. "He always had an active mind."

"Enemies?"

"Seldom would you meet a kinder soul this side of heaven. I never heard him raise his voice. Except once," she added a moment later, "when a man from Philadelphia came through a few months ago. He had a starched collar and a ledger book. He said when the new counties were organized there would be land taxes owed and he was taking note of homesteaders. Asked to see Peter's deed. I would not have credited it if I had not been there to witness it. Our gentle Peter raised an

ax handle and declared that no far-off official had the right to tell him
where to raise his family or take his hard-won earnings when giving
nothing in return. 'But I represent the governor,' the man protested,
and Peter said he never signed on to be the governor's slave. Rachel
came out with the dog, half wolf he was, and when he showed his teeth
that fool from Philadelphia turned pale as a ghost. He must have run
all the way back to town."

He looked up to see Mother Brumbach holding a cross in her
hand now. "Should I call in all our flock to stay in town?" she asked in
a tight voice. "I am not ready to dig more graves."

"This didn't happen because he was a Moravian. Was he perhaps
a friend of rangers? Of some Iroquois?"

She shook her head. "His darling wife was a Delaware, with a
face like a spring flower." The words, soft and delicate, seemed out of
place on the tongue of the big-boned woman. She wiped a tear and
turned away.

Duncan returned the items to the pouch, holding the black stone
for a moment. It looked like a small stone nautilus. Mother Brumbach
reached out and closed his fingers around it. "Take it. The thing
unsettles me. There is something dark about it, something that has no
business in a church. An old Dutchman said there were once ancient
monsters whose breath turned every living thing to stone. One of the
Senecas said he has seen a place in the mountains, a clearing where
nothing grows, where the ground is littered with such stones. He said
his old sachem told him it was the place where gods go to die." She
looked up forlornly. "Why would my Peter have such a thing?"

HE WANDERED INTO THE THREE TAVERNS LEFT IN THE TOWN, ALL
of them unclean, decaying places that stank of stale ale and unwashed
men. There was no sign of rangers, or men who might once have been
rangers. As he stood by the corner bar cage in the third, a man called

out for a cup of dice. As the tavernkeeper reached for one of five shaped leather cups on a shelf above him, Duncan saw that five small printed rectangles had been pinned to the shelf below the cups.

The barman followed his gaze. "All the way from Philadelphia they come," he groused, "just to reach into my purse to exchange my hard-won coin for little slips of paper."

Duncan recalled seeing such rectangles fixed to the back of news journals. "I thought the stamp tax was only on gazettes and legal documents."

"And playing cards. And dice, damned their eyes. The innkeeper next door refused to pay and they burned his cards and crushed his dice with a pestle."

Duncan fingered the broken cube in his pocket as he left the tavern. Both Woolford and Red Jacob had carried broken dice, though he was certain neither was a gambling man.

He sat on a ledge overlooking the river and watched a dozen native women hanging splayed shad to dry on racks, some singing to babies on their backs. He tried to piece together the sequence of the deaths. The man on the river had died no more than two days earlier. The Moravian and his wife had died less than twenty-four hours earlier. The demon killers were still working their way south.

A shadow moved across him and Tanaqua silently lowered himself onto the rock.

"The Blooddancer was here," Duncan said, and explained what he learned of the murder of Peter Rohrbach and his Delaware wife.

"I had an old uncle who would fill the winter nights with tales of the trickster Blooddancer," Tanaqua recounted. "As a young boy I buried myself in furs against the wall of the lodge and laid awake half the night in fear. Later when we fought in the wars together I asked why he did such a thing. He said there were many things to learn along the path to being a warrior but the most important thing was fear. He said a man without fear is a danger to all those around him, that I had to learn there were indeed many things to fear in this world and the next."

The Trickster. The strange symbol messages, Duncan realized, were the work of a trickster. "The killers move downstream ahead of us," he said. "Is that what Woolford feared, that nineteen men would be torn apart by an Iroquois demon?" He answered his own question. "It can't be. He came from Johnson Hall, running south. He would not have known about the missing mask."

"Colonel Johnson sent for Red Jacob. I was with Red Jacob when he read the message. *Life or death. Come now*, it said. That was the day after the mask was stolen. Sir William knew. Messages run between Onondaga and Johnson Hall almost every day."

"Why didn't you tell me this earlier?"

"It had nothing to do with the Blooddancer. You look for missing men. I look for a missing god."

"Then why did the Blooddancer kill Red Jacob? First Red Jacob, then the man on the river. Now two Moravians here at Shamokin. The Blooddancer is going south."

Tanaqua frowned, as if Duncan had insulted the god. "The Trickster does not even know Europeans exist. He is an Iroquois god."

"He knows enough to kill them. You said before, he infects those around him with his bloodlust."

Tanaqua did not reply. After a long silence he lifted a handful of the sandy soil by the rock and sprinkled it on the ledge, then made the image of a stick man with the head of a fish on his neck. "He knew how to tame angry spirits. The half king."

"The half king was half a man?"

"All the leaders at the edge of the League's territory are called half kings. But this is his particular sign. When he traveled he would cut that shape in trees or scratch it in rocks along his path. When I was a boy my uncle took me to see some, the fish men carved on trees. We found old shrines near every one of the signs." Tanaqua somehow seemed angry with himself.

Finally he turned to Duncan. "The dead man on the river. The arm with the string. He had ripped away his shirt and scratched letters on his flesh."

"You mean the killer did."

"No. Under the fingernails of his other hand there were still pieces of his own skin and flesh."

Duncan now recalled how the Mohawk had hesitated over the body and lifted the second hand for a moment. "What did it say?" Duncan asked, then saw by the flash of embarrassment on Tanaqua's face he had asked the wrong question. "I am sorry. What were the shapes of the letters?"

The Mohawk leaned over to claw up a handful of sandy soil, dropped it between them, and spread it flat. With a twig he made the letters he had seen.

A chill crept down Duncan's spine as he read them. *Fi Fo Fum.*

He shuddered at the thought of the man's last moments, probably left for dead, an eye hanging out, the shrieking agony of the mutilations wracking his body. Yet he had ripped his shirt, tied the old family heirloom to himself to protect it, then clawed at his own flesh to send a message. The urgent message left by the Philadelphia gentleman, his last desperate words, were the same unlikely words carried by the dead Oneida.

"Watch the woman on the left," Tanaqua said. Duncan followed his gaze to a middle-aged woman who stood apart from the others. "At the end of each of her racks she lays down half a fish, for the river spirits. Only her racks." Duncan glanced at the others and saw his companion was right. The Mohawk turned to him with an expectant look and when Duncan did not react he raised his brows. "She is

Lenni Lenape. The only one I have seen today," he said, then pushed off with his hands, gracefully dropping from the low ledge onto the flat where the woman worked.

Lenni Lenape. A Delaware. By the time Duncan reached them she was in earnest conversation with Tanaqua. The woman not only knew Rachel, she was her aunt. "I promised to look after her while her mother went to the Ohio country in search of her husband, who never came back from the war." As she raised her hand with another fish, Duncan saw a fresh cut on the back of her hand, and remembered the blood at Rachel's grave. It was an old, nearly extinct, part of tribal burials, slicing one's flesh to express grief.

"Had you seen your niece this week?" Duncan asked.

The woman kept working as they spoke, and Tanaqua began lifting the gutted fish from her basket and stretching the rich layers of flesh before handing them to her for the rack. She nodded. "Three days ago I took a rabbit stew to them. Rachel was sewing a little quilt for the baby. Peter was talking to those Philadelphia men, so I sat with her and helped for an hour."

"Philadelphia men? Do you know their names?"

"No names. Friends of Peter's from Philadelphia."

"What did they talk about? Did they argue?"

"Not argue. Hushed, very serious. Something important. Like when men go on a warrior's path, though those two men were no warriors. When they left, Peter had to call out to tell them they were going in the wrong direction to reach town."

"Did they say anything to you? Have you seen them here in town?"

"Nothing to me. Not like Peter's other friend who came with him from Philadelphia. Very kind man. He could speak Iroquois like he had been born in a lodge. But they argued that time. Peter said the Bible, the captain he say Shake-a-speare," she said, adding a syllable that lent it a tribal whimsy.

Duncan looked at her with a dumbfounded expression. He knew only one captain who would speak of Shakespeare on the frontier. "Woolford. Patrick Woolford."

The woman shrugged, and swung a horsehair whisk at the gathering flies. Later there would be smoky fires lit along the rows of racks that would keep away the insects. "He made Rachel laugh. Graves in the rain. Worms in the dust. He made Peter recite it again and again. No write, no write, the captain say. A book would come. No write. But later Peter write, and he made the show for Rachel." Tears trickled down the sturdy woman's cheeks. "What do I tell her mother? There is no one to make babies in our family ever again."

Duncan had no answer to her question. As Tanaqua took the woman's hand and began speaking in low comforting tones, Duncan backed away. He climbed the path to the town, once more aiming for the church. He walked slowly, trying to piece together what he had heard. He realized he should not have been surprised that Woolford had been at Shamokin. Over the years he had learned that the process of solving the puzzles of deaths was like painting on a blank canvas, filling in a tree, a cloud, a house, a flower, a road, then eventually vague human forms who, with the final strokes, at last assumed faces. But here all he had before him was a fog. Of course Woolford might have had business in Shamokin, which had become a common shore onto which the flotsam of war and lost causes drifted. But what business could the captain have had with a reclusive Moravian and his wife? For that matter, what was Woolford's business? Conawago had spoken of secretive missions in the wilderness. But Woolford had disappeared for months the year before. Duncan had not known his whereabouts until a parcel had arrived from London, enclosing a newly published work on medicine, with a letter that spoke of family and weather, its only hint of his purpose there being references to too many trips to Whitehall and Greenwich, where high officials and military leaders met behind closed doors. Woolford had a mission, one that included nineteen men, one that was taking him to Virginia. But why would the captain have not sent Duncan to the military in Albany for help? It was as if he no longer trusted the military. Duncan still could not see through the murk on his canvas. But he knew that Woolford had trusted Peter Rohrbach with a deadly secret and, disobeying Woolford, Rohrbach had written it down.

As he passed a stable, a young European man bounded around the corner, eyes locked over his shoulder, running so fast that Duncan had no time to avoid a collision. The man stumbled over his foot and with a cry of alarm tumbled heavily to the ground.

"I beg you sir! On the soul of dear mother I meant no harm! Please!" The stranger clasped his hands together toward Duncan.

Duncan looked up to see half a dozen warriors racing down the street. He grabbed the terrified fugitive by the arm and led him back down the bank, out of sight of the pursuers, then up another path that lead to the rear of the nearest tavern, where they took refuge in the woodshed.

The man's chest was heaving. His expensive waistcoat and britches were soiled and disheveled. Strands of his long brown hair hung over his face. One arm was pressed against a parcel of rolled-up leather. Duncan realized he was the man whom Mother Brumbach had chased from the cemetery.

"I thank"—his words were truncated by deep gasps—"you, kind sir . . . those bucks had rough intentions I daresay."

"What have you done?" Duncan demanded.

The stranger pressed his hand against his chest as if to calm himself. "I don't speak their language. I should have waited for Ralston to come back from sketching his birds. He knows the Indians, went into the wilderness two years ago with his uncle."

"What have you done?" Duncan asked again.

"It's a matter of anatomy, is all."

An angry shout rose from near the river. Duncan peered through an open knothole in the flimsy plank door. The pursuers had spread out along the landing and were searching among the canoes and stacks of cargo. "Anatomy?"

"My name is Rush, Benjamin Rush. I am a student of the healing arts, apprenticed to a doctor in Philadelphia. Ralston and I were just doing a favor for Dr. Franklin and his friends. He loves his birds, and the anatomy of the aboriginals is of especial interest to me. I have measured the facial features of twenty natives in Philadelphia, though of course the Indian beggars on the waterfront there do not make the best specimens for science. I corresponded with a journal in London. They said they would publish my work if I could submit a body of evidence to support my thesis."

Duncan stared at Rush in mute disbelief. He was only a few years younger than Duncan but looked like a lost boy. He pushed him down on a splitting block. "Mr. Rush, if you have any hope of surviving your journey you'll need to do a much better job of explaining yourself."

Rush propped his arms on his knees and buried his head for a moment. "This is my first venture into the frontier. They said it was tamed. Ralston and I saw it as something of a holiday." He calmed as he spoke, and his voice became that of the educated young gentleman of America's greatest city. "I have long opined that the American natives are of a different human stock. Consider their lack of reaction to severe elements, the epicanthic fold of their eyes, their inability to perspire, the fantastical way they run for hours, the extra ridge of bone many have on their feet, their lack of facial hair. I have reason to believe the digestive tracts may have different structures than those of Europeans."

Duncan eyed the tied leather roll Rush had carried through his ordeal, now resting on the pile of logs beside the young scientist. Rush sighed but did not stop him as he unrolled it, exposing a row of silvery instruments, each in its own sewn pocket. Surgical knives, tweezers, a metal rule, a small bone saw, probes, long needles with silk thread, and a reed-thin stem of metal with a tiny mirror at its end.

"An odd arsenal for the frontier," Duncan observed.

"I am a philosopher, sir. A student of humanity. When I prove the aborigine to be of a different species, just think of the lines of inquiry I will open!"

Duncan eyed the tools uneasily. "What exactly in God's name are you doing here, Rush?"

"Gathering evidence of course. With doctors in Philadelphia paying three pounds a body, there is no end of cadavers there. But it's damnable hard to find a native specimen."

A chill ran down Duncan's back. "What were you doing when those men accosted you?"

"Nothing! I swear it! I tried to make them understand what I needed. I showed them my coin. I asked about the recently dead. They did not seem to understand. Only one spoke any English, and that poorly. So I pulled out a surgical blade to help him understand. He asked what it was and I told him, very slowly, to help him grasp the word. Then he pulls out his war ax and shouts at me."

Duncan stared in mute astonishment. "You must have an angel hovering over you to have survived so long."

"Sir?"

"You come from Philadelphia, where they pay bounties for Indian hair, you show him your coin then display your blade, naming it your scalpel." Duncan repeated the word, slowly, the way Rush must have done. "Scalp-el."

The color left Rush's face. "Dear God! I didn't . . . I never meant to suggest . . . dear God!" he repeated.

Duncan stared at the forlorn man, wondering not for the first time how learned men could be so unwise in the ways of the world.

He cracked the door and looked outside. "They'll likely get thirsty and give up the search in some tavern. Make a hiding place at the back of the woodpile and cover yourself until dark. Then find your friend and make haste for Philadelphia."

Duncan had taken several steps toward the church when he paused. Analie sat on the bank with a vigilant expression, as if keeping watch over the vessels in the convoy. She seemed relieved when he asked her for the mink cap. No one had said the words aloud but they all knew the dead man had worn it. Benjamin Rush waited for his naturalist friend from Philadelphia, who had gone upriver to sketch birds. But there had been no one upriver except a well-dressed gentleman without a face.

He turned the cap over. It was the work of a fine craftsman, who had created it by sewing pelts into a broad tube, then closing one end and doubling the open end up over itself, anchoring it with heavy stitches that created little pockets around the rim.

Duncan inserted his finger into one such opening and pulled out twigs and fish scales. Between two more stitches were several duck feathers. From the next opening he extracted a small piece of oilcloth folded around a slip of paper. On it four names had been written in a refined hand. *Peter Rohrbach, Red Jacob, Captain Woolford,* and *Patrick Henry.* It was signed with a flourish at the bottom. *Franklin.*

CHAPTER SIX

Duncan stared at the words with a chill in his heart, then finally returned the note to its hiding place, rose, and made his way back to the little church. Mother Brumbach was on her knees, transplanting violets onto the fresh graves as she sang a German hymn in a low, consoling voice. Duncan knelt and helped with the digging.

"That man you chased away today. Had you seen him in Shamokin before?" he asked.

She patted the earth around Rachel's cross as she considered her answer. "Gentlemen in fine clothes come from Philadelphia most every week. Land company men mostly. Our missionaries from Bethlehem and Nazareth. Government men sometimes. Men recruiting for the southern plantations, though they get few takers here. We used to get few such strangers but now they just come and go. I never pay much mind."

"But Peter knew some of them?"

"Peter was apprenticed to a printer in Philadelphia."

Duncan chewed on the words a moment. "So he was a journeyman?" he asked, referring to those who had recently completed their apprenticeships and traveled to find work.

Mother Brumbach shook her head. "After only three years he came north."

Duncan sensed the tightness in her voice. They both knew the term of apprenticeship was seven years. "He broke his bond?"

"He just said he was done with Philadelphia and had new work to do for his master."

"New work? Those were his words? He was clearing fields and building a cabin for a Philadelphia printer?"

The German woman winced. "He was a good boy. I wasn't going to pry." She indeed suspected that he had fled his servitude, which meant he would be a fugitive from the law. There were bounty hunters who specialized in tracking down such men.

"Had he friends who were soldiers? Rangers perhaps?"

"I doubt that. The church tells us armies cause more trouble than they solve."

It seemed impossible that the dead man would have a secret message for Patrick, but Rachel's aunt had spoken of a captain who could easily have been his friend. "What about a man named Patrick Woolford, who often travels with Iroquois?"

"I wouldn't know." Her brow furrowed. "There was a nice young man with an Oneida brave visiting once when I brought bread. He was reciting Shakespeare to Rachel. '*Oh beauty, till now I never knew thee*,'" I remember. She lowered her hands a moment and spoke toward the cross with the strips of ermine. "And then, '*Is she kind as she is fair?*' following her with his hands uplifted as if praying to her, the rogue." Moisture welled in the German woman's eyes again. "Rachel was laughing like a young *fraulein*."

"That's him. Patrick Woolford. The one who killed Peter almost killed him as well. Why was Woolford there?"

"I assumed they had met in Philadelphia. They had common friends. They had business to discuss. Peter gave the man papers. Letters, I think. They talked about committees. They talked about Parliament."

"Committees?"

Mother Brumbach shrugged, "I know, silly talk for the frontier. Not my business. The only committees I know of are for building churches and helping the needy. Or maintaining cemeteries," she added in a whisper.

Duncan looked back at the crosses, joined by the snakeskin. Conawago would say Shamokin lay at the junction between many worlds, the most important of which was that between the European and native spirit worlds. He sensed that the answers he sought might lie at that intersection. He glanced at the church. "Mother, I . . ." He did not want to give offense.

"The Death Speaker wants to see his things again." She gestured toward the church. "Take whatever you wish. Anything that brings the wrath of God down on the devils who did this."

He dipped his head to the woman and had nearly reached the door with the cross on it when she called out. "That brute of a Dutchman was looking for you. He is very angry. He said you stole something of his on the river and he wants it back."

"Bricklin? I stole nothing," Duncan replied, casting a wary glance toward the street.

"Says he has salvage rights on what's taken off the water by his convoy. Then he asked about a Rush. I said rush yourself, right away from here. He said Rush was his. I told him I know no man with such a name and to please take his overfed, unholy face away from my holy grounds."

Duncan returned to the little corner closet where she had secreted Rohrbach's valuables. He took the strange letter of symbols and letters, then lifted the Bible. A slip of paper lay inside the cover. It was another verse:

Let's talk of graves, of worms and epitaphs;
Make dust our paper, and with rainy eyes
Write sorrow on the bosom of the earth.

His confusion was like a physical pain. He stared at the foreboding words, which kindled anew his grief for the young couple in the churchyard.

It made no sense that amidst the urgent, mysterious work these men were engaged in they would take time to speak of Shakespeare, to memorize passages, first from *King Lear* and now this one, from *Richard the Second*. He examined the paper more closely. On the back, dimly inscribed, was the numeral 4. He extracted the slip Red Jacob had carried and turned it over to confirm his recollection. It held the numeral 5. He shook his head in bewilderment, then took all of Rohrbach's treasures, leaving only the dog-eared Bible.

The river was streaked with a gold and purple dusk when Duncan finally left the church, holding the letter from Rohrbach's box in his hand. He did not hear Analie approach but suddenly she was pulling his arm. She guided him into the shadows between two buildings but before she could speak he thrust the cryptic images before her. "Tell me what you see, tell me what you would call these images," he asked her, and pointed to the little drawings that substituted for words.

She cocked her head, then began pointing at images she recognized. "A deer, a tree like a pine or yew," she said, "I see a toe, an eye, a saw, a world, an oinker, then cattails," she said of the last.

"Cattails," Duncan repeated slowly, then he shook the girl by both shoulders. "Of course! You have settled accounts between us, Analie!" he declared. He thought back on the message at the graves. An evergreen, the word *go*, a drawing of a toe, a grate, an *r*, the word *ha*, a pie, and a nest. *You go to greater happiness*, it had said. "I will speak with the Moravians about you before I leave. I am sure you can stay with them. They can write letters for you." He turned and motioned her toward the church. But the girl pulled his arm again.

"Tanaqua sent me. He says Bricklin and Teague and some of those others from the convoy are asking in the taverns for you. They are carrying clubs."

They stayed in the shadows until they reached the riverbank, then Duncan sent the girl on her way and turned to the woodshed where he had left the ungainly man from Philadelphia. He was fifty paces away when he saw the gang of tribesmen who had chased Rush that afternoon, drunk now and waving war axes as they resumed their search. He quickened his pace and had nearly reached the shed when he saw Rush sitting outside, reading a book in the fading light, oblivious to the danger. Duncan grabbed him roughly. "You are about to become evening sport for some unpleasant gentlemen," he warned when Rush tried to shrug him off.

Rush did not resist as Duncan pulled him down the slope, desperately looking for a vessel. Grabbing his pack and rifle, stuffed between the cargo bales where he had left them, he shoved Rush farther down the river landing. A shout rose from the group of natives, followed a moment later by one from a tavern porch. Bricklin and his men had spotted them.

"McCallum!" came the Dutchman's angry shout.

Duncan ran to the one boat that still lay half in the water, Bricklin's own dugout, shoved Rush into it, and then jumped into the river to pull it afloat, scrambling over its side as it drifted free. The shouts increased, and as Duncan clumsily extracted the paddle lying under Rush, the boat rocked with a new weight, then sank deeper a moment later under a second, heavier weight. The big dugout shot forward and Duncan paddled frantically to leave their pursuers behind. He did not turn around until the shouting behind them subsided. Analie wore an amused smile. Tanaqua only nodded and kept paddling.

"Must I read it to you, Benjamin?" Duncan demanded of Rush as they sat by their small, struggling fire. He had lost all patience for the inept scholar who seemed so blind to the death that surrounded him. "Your own letter? Mother Brumbach suspected it was black arts. I didn't dare tell her it was just a bumbling pedant who enjoys confusing people with a rebus. You knew Peter and his wife but instead of telling Mother Brumbach you just lurked about their graves as if you had something to hide."

They had paddled for four hours, with Analie perched backward, watching for pursuers on the moonlit waters, then hid the dugout and lit a fire on the far side of an outcropping, hidden from the river.

Duncan held the letter that had been saved by the dead Rohrbach near the flames, pointing to the opening with the images of the deer, for *dear*, the pea pod for the first half of the addressee's name, and a human toe for the second half. "Dear Peter," he read, then pointed to the syllable *comm* followed by a human eye, a teacup, then an ax and the word *cept* followed by a small globe, the words *end aft*, then another toe, the equation $2+2=$ and the syllable *er*. "The committee," he deciphered, "accepts world's end after summer." He ran his finger along the other combinations of letters and images, indicating a saw, a star with a tail, a knife, and a pig, interspersed with human eyes. "Then perhaps I saw a comet and I dissected a pig." He pointed to the final image at the bottom of the letter—the cattails. "Rushes. It's your way of signing. I think you were there when Peter and his wife died. Their murders might easily have been accomplished with scalpels. There are scratches on your hands, as from a struggle."

Rush pressed a hand against his mouth as he was wracked by a dry, heaving sob. "Dear God, no! I beg you, do not suggest such an unthinkable thing! Peter and I had become particular friends. We wrote each other often. He said he and Rachel always enjoyed my rebus letters. He said they helped Rachel learn to read. I was going to surprise him. I had a gift for the new baby, a little linen blanket. They knew I was coming but not the day of my arrival. Ralston insisted he needed to go up river, so I decided to spend the day with them. When I found the cabin empty I looked in the outbuilding. But they were already . . . tied to those posts, their eyes unseeing." He hung his head. "The horror. I think I shall never sleep again. I covered dear Rachel's head with the blanket and ran. I fell in the woods and cut my hands."

"What are the committees?"

"Not for me to say. I gave a vow."

"Why would they speak of the ending of the world?"

"It's all secret. There are words used between those who know. Identifying words."

"To what end?"

Rush just stared into the fire.

"How many of these have you sent? How many rebus letters?"

"A few."

"By post?"

"Of course."

"Meaning they passed through at least a score of hands. Do you have any idea how most would view such letters? Dark business. Codes are used by spies, and worse. And if someone wanted to pierce the conspiracy, you pointed them right to Rohrbach, the recipient."

Rush seemed to grow gaunt. "Surely you misunderstand. I would never . . ." his words choked away. A chill gust bent the flames and he crossed his arms over his chest.

Duncan tossed Rush the mink cap. He put it on without thinking, then hesitated and removed it with a confused expression. "But I gave this to Ralston." He glanced up warily, and tried to be inconspicuous about checking the folds of the hat.

"We found it on the river, on the backs of the shad."

"The shad! That explains it. Ralston wanted so much to observe the fabled running of the shad as Dr. Franklin had described it to us. He would have lingered to sketch them like he sketches his birds."

Rush saw the tip of a feather and pulled it out of the little brim pocket. "See! He found his ducks. Mergansers I should think. We shall laugh about all this when he returns. He will be mortified over having lost my cap."

"Ralston is already mortified, Benjamin."

The forced smile on Rush's face disappeared but he did not otherwise react. Duncan tossed the old enameled box on the ground beside him. Rush snatched it up. "His snuffbox, from his grandfather! He'll be so pleased you found it."

"It was on his body."

Rush kept turning the cap over and over in his hands. "We have to be in Philadelphia by the end of the month," he said in a hollow voice. "There is a harpsichord recital we don't want to miss. He is to attend the College of New Jersey in the autumn."

"His face was skinned away. His nose was cut off. The work of a medical man, some might say. Just like Peter Rohrbach and his wife who were carefully sliced and mutilated. Just like Analie's friend Red Jacob whose arm was neatly amputated. If the crown were to bring a prosecution for repetitive murders, you would be the logical suspect."

Rush slowly looked up, stricken as the horror of Duncan's words finally sank in. A tremor shook his body. "Ralston!" he cried in anguish. Tanaqua, standing guard above them, looked down in warning. Rush stared at the rebus Duncan had dropped in his lap, grabbed it and threw it in the fire, then wiped at his tears.

Duncan said no more until he had shared out some venison jerky. As he reached for his pouch of corn balls, Analie stopped him and produced a flour sack with three fresh loaves in it, taken from the supplies Bricklin had been stockpiling that afternoon. He watched in confusion as she cut a loaf in quarters with her little belt knife. "How would you know to take those?" he asked the girl. "Our departure was too sudden."

"Bricklin was after you, with all those angry men," she said with one of her innocent smiles. "I told you but you didn't believe me the first time. But I knew you would eventually. Remember? We don't surrender," she reminded Duncan and tossed a piece up to Tanaqua.

They ate in silence, then Duncan stood and studied the sky. "Two hours sleep then we push on. You're staying right here, Rush, unless you explain yourself. You want words to release your vow? How about the words I speak to the magistrates when they swear a warrant for your arrest? A man with his belly incised, his hand amputated and buried in his intestines. A man from a prominent Philadelphia family with his face peeled away like the skin of a fruit. A God-fearing Moravian with his hair removed and his beautiful pregnant wife mutilated with something like a scalpel. In your cap you carried the names of two of the dead, and of a third nearly so lying now in Edentown. The trial will draw great crowds in Philadelphia, your hanging even more. You've probably been to hangings. They sell pastries and ale. People always clap when the hangman tests the trap door."

Rush buried his head in his hands.

"The message in your cap. Was it from Benjamin Franklin?"

"He was sent to London on the colony's business," Rush responded. "Since he embarked his wife Deborah has carried on certain . . . sensitive business for him. She sits in on committee meetings."

Duncan began reciting the names from the note. "Red Jacob, Patrick Woolford, Peter Rohrbach. All dead or nearly so. Were they part of the committee you speak of?"

When Rush still did not answer Duncan reached down and roughly pulled his head up. "This is the frontier. There are those who would string you up from a tree if I explained those deaths to them and showed them your treacherous instruments."

"You know I did not . . . could not."

"I will put the rope around your neck myself if it means I can save nineteen innocent men. These killers are not going to stop."

Rush looked up with red-rimmed eyes. "Not one committee. A committee in Boston, one in New York, in Newport, in Philadelphia, and Williamsburg. Maybe more. They exchange ideas and sentiments. Those you cite just help with the committees. Months ago Woolford came to Philadelphia with an older, very refined gentleman from New York who was asked by Dr. Franklin about the health of William Johnson, as if they were friends. Captain Woolford brought a native ranger who stood guard outside the door, a sturdy fellow with a red ear." Duncan and Tanaqua exchanged a grim glance. "I don't know about the end of the world, just heard them talking about it. I am just their clerk, fetching them books or meals or anything else they want."

"Who from Philadelphia? Who did Woolford meet with?"

"Dr. Franklin and his wife. The doctor I apprentice with. Jared Ralston's father, the printer who had apprenticed Ralston. There was also Mr. Dickinson the lawyer. And a man named Webb who had just arrived from the south, a tall distinguished-looking man with a scar across his left cheek. He had led rangers in a Virginia company and had a farm in the Piedmont. And there was a printer from somewhere in Maryland."

"The famous scientist. An Oneida warrior. A captain in His Majesty's army. A doctor. A lawyer. A printer. A Virginia planter. What common enterprise could they have?"

Rush glanced up with a nervous expression. "I fear they were plotting to steal something."

Duncan frowned. "My friends don't steal."

"I could not make out all of the words, but I heard talk of avoiding magistrates and hiding something. I'm sure it was with the best of intentions."

Duncan kicked a log in the fire, stirring sparks toward Rush. "It's a rough walk to Philadelphia, Benjamin, but you can probably do it in nine or ten days. Do not tarry near bear dens. Do not anger the natives. If a rattlesnake curls up beside you in the night, just stay motionless. It will move on in a few hours when the morning sun hits it."

Rush stared in despair at his cap. "They are not inclined to let a mere apprentice, even a doctor's apprentice, into their full confidence. I am not a member of the committee, McCallum, but I aspire to be. When they started talking about Ralston taking an urgent message to Shamokin station, I volunteered to escort him. Ralston had made the run before, and knew Rohrbach. We thought it would be a grand adventure, that we would have a chance to pursue our scientific studies. We agreed to share the responsibility. He would memorize a passage and I would carry two messages from Mrs. Franklin secreted in my cap. It was like a test for me, to see if I could be trusted to make the run alone next time." The words died away and Rush pounded the cap against his knee before looking up. "He was cold when he paddled away so I just tossed him my cap, forgetting what was inside. I failed the great Franklin and his wife."

"I need more, Rush. Murderers are on the loose."

"I know nothing else. They open each meeting by reading reports, sometimes just from gazettes. The last time it was just a letter from Edmund Burke to the Parliament about colonial affairs."

"Peter Rohrbach had been an apprentice," Duncan pointed out. "Why did he break his bondage?"

"He would never bring such dishonor to his name. They asked him to move to Shamokin. He was apprenticed to Ralston's father, but relased from his work, trusted by the committee for something more important." Rush looked down again. "How ever can I tell his parents of their son's death? He loved it here, loved all the birds. He was going to publish his drawings." He looked up with pleading in his eyes. "Why kill Ralston?"

"Because the killers expected a messenger from Philadelphia. He was obviously from the city but they may have let him go. Except they found a message in his fur cap."

Rush went very still. He stared into the fire again, his body wracked by a long shudder. He began rocking back and forth as Duncan stretched his blanket over Analie and lay down beside her. "I cannot go home," Rush finally said. "I will find the murderer with you or I will die trying. Peter and Rachel keep calling me in my dreams."

A bundle of feathers and fur dropped in front of Rush. He recoiled for a moment, then looked up into Tanaqua's expectant eyes. The Mohawk had jumped down and was hovering over him. Rush, in his way, had been touched by the Blooddancer. "Hold that bundle and speak to me," he told Rush. "All of it, all that you have seen in your dreams of the dead."

The crisp morning air, alive with the call of birds, gradually lifted Rush out of his despairing mood. The young man from Philadelphia had a deep curiosity about the natural world, and he pointed out nesting ducks, leaping fish, and dramatic rock formations with the enthusiasm of a schoolboy. Analie joined in, motioning first toward an eagle, then a majestic heron, before breaking out in a French ditty about a drunken goose. Her voice seemed to beguile several birds, which flew beside them and even joined in at times with ragged caws, but she gradually moved from playful songs to lonely ballads and then, in a quieter voice, to the *Ave Maria*. Duncan glanced back at the energetic girl, wise beyond her years and battered by life. It was as if she had decided to remind them of their solemn task.

At midmorning they rested on a river ledge shielded by trees and watched as two southbound canoes passed along the far bank. As they passed out of sight Duncan turned to see Tanaqua bent over the wooden box addressed to Mr. B. Franklin, which had remained behind in Bricklin's dugout. Before Duncan could protest, the Mohawk had slipped off the leather strap bound around it and removed the top. Instantly Tanaqua dropped the top as if it had scalded him, and backed away. Rush darted forward with a cry of glee and lifted the largest of the black rocks from the crumpled newspaper that cushioned it.

It was another creature rock, a fossil that reminded Duncan of one of the wood lice that scattered and curled up when decaying logs were lifted from the forest floor, only gigantic in size, as big as Duncan's palm.

"Magnificent!" Rush crowed. "As if the ancient Greeks were standing before us!"

Duncan could see that Rush's excitement was forced, but he did not want to impede his effort to push back his despair. "Greeks?" he asked.

"Was it not Aristotle himself who recorded the first thoughts on animal stones? Did he not explain how they are formed by unnatural mineral vapors?" He pointed to the fossil in Duncan's hand. "I have heard that called a trilobite."

Tanaqua stared in bewilderment at the young scientist. Analie lifted the fossils one by one, and held them in a patch of sunlight, her eyes round with wonder.

"Among my people," the Mohawk stated, "these are objects of great power, not to be trifled with. What does this Franklin want with them? Is he a witch then?"

It was the first time Duncan had seen Rush smile. "I heard him describe himself as just another student of the world, obsessed with the complexity of nature."

"When I was a boy an old Cayuga came to our village with a black bone of stone as thick as his leg, as long as his arm, and as heavy as a log. He sometimes used it as a pillow, and when he did, he had dreams of a place on the other side with beasts like moving hills."

Rush's eyes widened and he dug into his pocket for a scrap of paper. "I am convinced it is evidence of the world that existed before the Great Flood," he declared as he scribbled.

"The world where the first gods chose to live," Tanaqua said. Duncan was not sure if he was disagreeing. Tanaqua turned to Duncan. "The Great Council has many such stones—seed stones—kept under the altars of the spirit masks."

"Seed stones?" Duncan asked.

It was Analie who answered, in a deeply solemn voice. "One night old grandmother Adanahoe showed me such a stone, after we had seen a shower of shooting stars. She told me they are seeds left by the gods when they departed, for the new world that needs to rise when the last good men have died. They represent a trust, she said, from one world to the next."

Tanaqua touched the neck pouch holding his spirit totem.

Rush seemed about to laugh, then saw the sober way his companions looked at the girl. "They are rocks, girl, most peculiar rocks I admit, but still rocks," he pointed out.

"And such seeds would have to be hard as rock, wouldn't they?" the French girl replied with a tone that seemed consoling, as if she felt sorry for Rush. "Do you really think some chalk-skinned scholar from Philadelphia would know more about nature than an Iroquois?"

Rush glanced uneasily at Tanaqua and chose not to answer.

Duncan stepped to the box and repacked Franklin's fossils inside their protective papers, then closed the lid and touched Rohrbach's fossil, in his pocket. When he finished, he looked up to see the girl staring at him uneasily.

"The picture letter from Philadelphia told of the world's end," she said. "Now seed stones are being sent to Philadelphia."

Analie's words seemed to transport Rush back to his dark mood. The young man from Philadelphia had sent a message about the world's end to Peter Rohrbach, and at least Rohrbach's world had ended. When they set out again Analie did not sing but laid in the front of the dugout like a bowsprit, sometimes trailing a finger in the water, sometimes predicting, always accurately, great trees, high cliffs, or other landmarks they would encounter around the next bend. She had been that way before.

Rush, whose short, laconic paddle strokes in the middle of the dugout did little to aid their passage, eventually stirred from his silence by taking up his anatomical queries. Had Tanaqua known any Indians with six fingers on one hand? Did his little toe hide behind the adjacent toe? Did he ever know a tribesman to burn his skin in the sun? Did Tanaqua know how many teeth he had? Did he know that the little fingers of Indians did not grow as straight as those of Europeans? Had he ever, perchance on a battlefield, seen the structure of a tribesman's digestive tract or the pleural membrane that covered the lungs? Even better, had he ever counted the total joints in his skull plates? The Mohawk rebuffed him with short, curt syllables, and Duncan noticed that each time he gave his paddle an extra twist to splash Rush.

"I can assure you, Mr. Rush," Duncan finally declared, "that the temporal fossa of Tanaqua's skull joins with the parietal and occipital plates just as it does in ours. His xiphoid process extends from his sternum to the back of the ninth thoracic vertebra, and his femur rises on his meniscus just as in our knees."

In the stunned silence a rumbling sound came from Tanaqua that may have been a laugh.

"Sir?" Rush finally sputtered.

"We are of the same species, I warrant you, though the best specimens of the species I have ever seen all wore loincloths."

"But you are just a . . ." Rush, for once, was at a loss for words.

"Before I wandered the frontier, Mr. Rush, I studied at the College of Medicine in Edinburgh." Duncan chose not to mention the intervening period he spent in the king's chains.

"Edinburgh?" Rush gasped. "The Edinburgh? Why it's the best medical college in the world! I dream of matriculation there!"

Duncan guided them around a patch of white, roiling water as he spoke. "I counted friends among the professors." At least, he thought, those from the Highland clans. "I could write them if you like, offer my—"

"Harris's!" Analie interrupted.

They cut the dugout close to the western bank as the girl pointed to the wide landing on the far side where the flat-bottomed ferry conveyed travelers from the eastern settlements onto the Great Wagon Road that led south.

DRAINED BY THE EFFORTS OF THE LAST TWO DAYS, THEY MADE camp on a high flat a few hundred paces from the great river, where Tanaqua had taken only a quarter hour to catch the string of fish he was spitting for the flames. While Duncan nursed the fire, Rush had spent the time quizzing him about the famed medical college of Scotland, until Duncan impatiently instructed him to tend to the smoking kindling and pulled Analie away to gather spring greens for their pot.

Duncan watched the ungainly apprentice doctor from the adjoining hill as he struggled with the fire. Rush had no skills for the frontier, seemed almost perversely uninterested in acquiring them. He was not a man who got dirt under his fingernails. The young doctor was intelligent yet inept, sophisticated in demeanor but shockingly naive, and would quickly become a victim if they encountered the Blooddancer.

Rush had been a small link in the cryptic chain of events, an assistant to well-placed men whose dealing in codes and smuggled goods seemed to have brought the wrath of an Iroquois spirit down on them. Not for the first time Duncan puzzled over the connection between the stolen mask and the conspiracies of a Philadelphia committee.

He turned back to Analie, who for now had sloughed off the darkness of recent days, and was softly singing a ditty she made up about her search for fiddleheads and wild onions. They had pushed hard, and would push even harder the next day to reach the family of Jessica Ross. For now they had earned a few moments of relaxation.

When they returned to camp with their spring bounty, Rush had Tanaqua sitting on a log, his mouth stretched wide as Rush probed his teeth. The Mohawk rolled his eyes at Duncan and patiently complied as Rush turned his head this way and that to position the slender rod with its polished mirror disc. He seemed to regard Rush as not altogether right in the mind, and the tribes treated such people as reserved by the gods for some special destiny. It explained the Mohawk's patience with the intrusive young doctor, but Duncan's own patience was wearing thin. He would not have Tanaqua put his own life in danger out of some naive inclination to protect the awkward young interloper from Philadelphia.

Rush, energetically writing in his notebook, seemed not to notice Duncan's approach. Duncan spoke to his back. "Why is it so urgent to ship fossils to Franklin if he is away in London?"

Rush spun about in surprise, dropping his bundle of instruments on the ground. "He is a collector of intellectual curiosities. His wife carries on his work in her own fashion. Using his name assures the security of the shipment, for no one would interfere with something bound for the great Franklin."

"Bricklin is delivering a box for Franklin. But Bricklin could be collaborating with the killers."

Anguish creeped back into Rush's voice. "Surely no one would dare harm anyone in the Franklin household!"

They bent to gather up the instruments. "Your friends all died," the Mohawk said. "What if the Blooddancer passed you by for a reason?"

Rush grimaced and stared into the fire." He said after a few minutes, "I am in someplace dark. I hold a candle and keep walking forward." The night before he had been too overwrought with emotion to answer Tanaqua's question about his dreams but he had clearly not forgotten it. "I hear a chant and follow the sound. I reach a chamber with a huge fire in the center. Dr. Franklin and the other one are dancing around it."

Tanaqua leaned forward. "The other one?"

Rush's gaze dropped to the ground at his feet. "He was wearing Dr. Franklin's spectacles. It was a great bear, a giant bear, more than twice as tall as any man. Yet it seemed gentle, and wise."

Tanaqua stared in astonishment at Rush, then walked away to sit by himself. He kept quiet until after sunset, and spoke to Duncan only after Rush had fallen asleep. "I told you my half brother, Kaskay, went to the cave of the spirit bear. It is said the ghost of the ancient bear dances there when the moon is full. That is known only to those of my society," he explained, meaning his secret society dedicated to preserving the old gods. "This is a sign. Kaskay and the bear need me. In the morning I must leave for the cave." Tanaqua looked at the sleeping form of Rush. "He is a messenger," the Mohawk said in a sympathetic tone, "who never understands his messages."

THEY ROSE AT DAWN AND STIRRED THE EMBERS INTO FLAME TO make tea and fry the remaining fish. As they struck camp, Duncan, still wary of being followed, once more climbed the ridge, its vegetation now rippling in a rising wind, to survey the river and western road. For several minutes he watched the little grove by the western landing where they had left Bricklin's dugout, then turned back. As the camp came into view he froze. A hulking figure was bent in the shadow of a bush, a tomahawk in his hand, creeping toward Tanaqua, who was apparently once again listening to one of Rush's soliloquies about anatomy.

Duncan shouted a warning but his words were lost in the wind. He ran headlong down the slope, cursing himself for leaving behind his rifle. With rising horror he realized he would never make it in time. He was still fifty feet away when the intruder rose, arm outstretched. Duncan shouted again, to no avail. Then a bundle of fury launched itself onto the stranger's back.

Analie hooked one arm around the man's neck, throwing him off-balance, then grabbed his wrist and bit it as he tried to swing his ax at her. With a roar of anger he broke free of her grip only to have the ax wrenched from his hand by Tanaqua. The Mohawk slammed the side of the weapon into the man's head, catching Analie as he crumpled to the ground. Duncan, reaching them, grabbed the stranger's legs and twisted them so he lay on his back. It was Bricklin's Irish bully, Teague.

Duncan and Tanaqua bound the Irishman to a tree as Rush dumped out the pack Teague had dropped at the side of the camp. There was only a drinking gourd, a bundle of jerked meat, and a bulging flour sack. Rush looked into the sack, and instantly dropped it, staggering backward before turning to retch up his breakfast. Duncan tried to reach the sack before his Mohawk friend but Tanaqua was faster. Duncan realized he shared Duncan's own suspicion about its contents, for he stepped to a flat rock and gently emptied the contents onto it.

Analie gasped and hid behind Duncan. Rush looked up and then retched again.

There were ten matted bundles of hair. Ten human scalps. Three were of the short scalplock hair favored by Mohawk warriors, the rest were of long strands, some with red and blue beads woven into their braids. They were likely from native women, or even children.

The muscles of Tanaqua's neck flexed as he glanced back and forth from the scalps to Teague. His powerful fingers opened and squeezed shut as if imagining themselves around Teague's neck. There was death in the air, and death on the face of Tanaqua. Duncan stepped between him and the Irishman, knowing that if Tanaqua could not rein in his rage there would be no way to keep Teague alive.

The Mohawk's gaze lingered for a moment on Duncan, then he looked back down at the pouch on the log. It was not totally empty. He shook it, and one last macabre bundle fell out. It was a Mohawk scalplock, the front hairs longer and decorated with ochre. It was wrapped in a wampum belt, one of the wide ribbons of beads used by the Iroquois for messages.

Tanaqua seemed to sag. He lowered himself unsteadily onto the log, then reverently laid the scalp beside him and spread the belt between his hands, staring at it with a stricken expression.

The silence was shattering.

It was Duncan who finally moved. Clenching his jaw, he carefully lifted the other scalps one by one and returned them to the sack before breaking the silence. "You knew him."

"I told you there were only four of us left," Tanaqua said in a hollow voice. "The four guardians of the masks. Now there are only three." He glanced down at the belt, and quickly folded it, putting it into one of his waistcoat pockets. It was, Duncan knew, one of the treasures of the False Face societies. His quick glance had shown it to be adorned with the sun at one end, the moon at the other, a huge bear in the center, and several angular spirit dancers on either side. It would have been handed down from guardian to guardian for generations.

"The cave where Kaskay kept vigil is on a high ledge on the Kittatinny mountain with a high open ledge at its mouth. What you would call a sentinel place, where the gods kept watch over the southern border of the Iroquois peoples. When he left, Kaskay said they had to know we still cared. He would show them by going up there and fasting for ten days, taking nothing but water, singing the old chants all the time. Kaskay would not have taken weapons to the shrine." He fixed Duncan with an anguished gaze. "The murder of a guardian would have infuriated Blooddancer. It could be why he left us." He studied the unconscious Teague with a cold eye, his hand on his war ax.

"Leave the Irishman with me, my friend," Duncan said. "There is no honor in killing him like this."

After a long moment Tanaqua gave a reluctant nod, then murmured a low prayer as he raised the scalp of his fellow shadowkeeper to the sky. When he had returned it to the sack he rose and nodded at Duncan. "You must go to the Virginia lands. I must follow my lost god. He has shown us how angry he is by his trail of blood. I will have to go to the cave and try to explain. The Trickster might still listen, if he can sense that I speak from the lair of the spirit bear."

The Mohawk extended his forearm. His eyes were distant and forlorn. Duncan had the sense that something had broken inside the warrior, and he knew not how to heal it. Tanaqua made a gesture toward the high ridge that overlooked the river. "First I will take these memories of my brothers and sisters to a high place over the river that takes the Iroquois home, and say the words that must be said."

Duncan reluctantly clamped his own arm to Tanaqua's and nodded his farewell.

Once more the Mohawk gazed with loathing at Teague, then raised his pack and began singing one of the ritual laments of his people as he set out for the ridge.

Duncan waited until Tanaqua disappeared, then turned to see Analie at the side of the unconscious Teague.

"Analie!" he cried, and leapt to pull the girl away. Her knife was out, and dripped blood. She had been working on Teague the way Iroquois women sometimes worked on enemy warrior captives, slicing a row of bloody little X marks across his cheeks from ear to ear.

Teague's eyes fluttered open. He tasted the blood dripping across his mouth and saw the bloody knife. "Bitch!" he shouted, then spat out blood. "When I lift your hair, girl, I'll boil it in a pot of walnut juice to dye it black. No one will know the difference. You're just a little white heathen bitch anyway. Worth five pounds from the governor."

Duncan struggled mightily to restrain his own temper, and lost. The Irishman had meant to kill Tanaqua, and no doubt would make good on his threat to Analie if he had the chance. Teague had been carrying scalps as they had journeyed down the river. He kicked Teague so hard in the belly he lost consciousness again, then Duncan opened Rush's pack to remove the leather roll of instruments. He extracted the largest scalpel and with shaking hands stepped to the Irishman.

"McCallum! You can't!" Rush protested from the tree where he had retreated, but he saw the fire in Duncan's eyes and had the sense not to approach.

Duncan seized a handful of Teague's greasy black hair. The scalpel was razor-sharp and the incision, running several inches along his hairline, took but an instant.

When Rush darted forward, Duncan swung around at him, extending the bloody scalpel. The young doctor held out his hands as if in surrender.

The blood that now steadily flowed down Teague's face revived him. When he looked up at Duncan and saw the scalpel his eyes went wide with fear.

"I should take your topknot and feed it to the crows," Duncan growled. "I started the job. Whether I finish it depends on what you next say."

"Boy!" Teague yelled in desperation at Rush. "He's gone mad! White men don't do this to white men!"

Rush looked down at the ground. Analie took a step closer, raising her little skinning knife again.

"Surely Duncan," Rush tried in a trembling voice, "we can't have him thinking we would—"

"Most of them scalps I just bought, like a merchant," Teague explained. "Buy one for a few shillings and sell it for five pounds to that agent in Lancaster. There's a dry goods sutler there with a commission from the governor."

Rush advanced a step.

"Get back Rush!" Duncan shouted. His fury burned white hot. He could not remember ever feeling such hatred. For Teague, the scalps were just coins in his purse. The victims had probably been taken in ambush. "Were you at Edentown?" he demanded.

Teague's only answer was to launch a violent kick at Duncan.

Duncan hovered just out of reach. "Normally a man wouldn't bleed to death from that incision but more of that could make it so. Were you at Edentown?"

"He'll kill you McCallum. You'll be dead in a week."

Duncan stepped forcefully down on Teague's leg and leaned over him with the blade. "Did you bring the canoe for the murderers' escape? Who were the men leaving in the canoe when Bricklin was arriving?"

"Kincaid and Hobart. Hobart wears spectacles. I waited at the landing for them."

"Where are they going?"

"South. The promised land. Galilee."

"You mean Virginia."

Teague grinned despite the blood on his lips. "He said he was building up a powerful black hunger. That's what he calls it. For the black rum on black nights lying with black girls."

"Why would they leave you?"

Teague stared down at a little pool of blood on the back of his hand.

Duncan asked again. When the Irishman wouldn't answer he laid the blade along his temple. "Another couple inches, Teague, and you know what will happen? Your skin will start collapsing, sliding down your skull. What a mess. A good doctor might sew it up but it will never be the same. Your face will look like one of those lumpy deerskin balls the Iroquois use in lacrosse. Children will flee at the sight of you. Women will slam their doors and windows."

"Bricklin wants to know what you took from that dead man on the river." The Irishman nodded toward the wooden box they had carried from the river. "But mostly he needs the box back."

Duncan paused, surprised. "Mr. Franklin's fossils?"

"If you got in the way he said he didn't mind if you was hurt. You were never supposed to have survived that snake."

"Get the fossils and then what?"

"Deliver them to Mr. Franklin's house then watch who comes for them."

Duncan assumed Rush had pulled Analie away to shelter behind his tree, but she had only gone for a better weapon before charging Teauge again. She slammed a broken limb as thick as her arm into the Irishman's ribs, raising a sharp cracking noise. The Irishman groaned and sank once more into unconsciousness. "Like you said about Captain Woolford," she explained, looking up at Duncan. "A man can't move fast with broken ribs." She dropped the stick, clasped her hands together, and smiled like a choirgirl.

Duncan turned to Rush. "Why the fossils?" he demanded. "Are men dying because of fossils?" Rush stared, dumbfounded, at Teague. Duncan grabbed him and shook him by the shoulders. "Why do the killers care about them? Why does Franklin want them?"

"They are of great intellectual curiosity," Rush said. "Mr. Franklin is a great natural philosopher. For him and his committee."

Duncan stared at him in frustration. He was the messenger who never understood his messages. Duncan opened the box again, puzzling once more over the contents. Surely men weren't dying for some ancient petrifications. He noticed now a sheet of paper that had fallen to the side of the box. It was addressed not to Franklin but *To My Noble Friends*, followed by three Latin words, *Audentes fortuna juvat*, and signed, with a flourish familiar to Duncan, *Sir William. Audentes fortuna juvat.* Fortune assists the daring.

He knelt and unwrapped each from its covering of old news journal pages, laying them in a line on a piece of shale. An acorn-sized snail, the oversized louse that Rush had called a trilobite, a fern, a fish, a worm, the foot of what looked like a lizard, and a huge triangular black tooth, nearly as big as his palm. Was there a message in them? Did they constitute some sort of rebus?

He turned to retrieve the paper wrappings and paused, staring at the first page he lifted as it hung in the air. Against the morning sky he could see tiny holes. He picked up another sheet, straightening it against his leg, and held it aloft. More holes, not random but in lines. He checked other sheets quickly, confirming they all had the tiny pinpricks. Each, he quickly discovered, was squarely under a letter or number of the text. He ripped off the back of a sheet, showing no holes, and pulled out his writing lead.

G, A, L, he began recording, writing the letters over each hole. The five papers each had different letters or numbers indicated by the tiny holes. After several minutes he had five clusters of letters and numbers. *Galilee*, said the first, then *World's End, Runners missing*, and *Massnyconnri*.

"I don't understand," Rush said over his shoulder.

"Messages, Benjamin. The fossils are the perfect cover. Of course some natural philosophers in Philadelphia would be interested in them, and Sir William is a friend of several. The papers would seem to be just trash."

Duncan pointed to the last group of letters. "It puts me in mind of a native name."

Rush stared intensely at the letters then grinned and, borrowing Duncan's lead, drew lines between letter groupings. "Just abbreviations. Massachusetts, New York, Connecticut, and—"

"Rhode Island," Duncan finished. "Why would Sir William think names of colonies must be kept secret?"

"I told you. I am not trusted with the details," Rush replied in a self-pitying tone. "Apparently all I do is lure people to their deaths."

As Rush repacked the fossils, Duncan lifted Teague's water gourd and poured it over the Irishman's head. Teague woke up spitting, then grimaced and clutched his ribs.

"Where is this Galilee? Is that where Kincaid and Hobart are going?"

"South. All I know is south. Down the wagon road. They had me arrange fast horses for them at Harris's Landing."

Duncan lifted the scalpel again.

"Sotweed country," Teague hastily added. "They work out of the sotweed country."

Duncan stared at the man, trying to decide if he spoke the truth, then finally turned his back on the Irishman.

Teague seemed to take it as a sign he would not die that day. "We took three at once, me and the boys. They were sleeping, under the full moon. We each knelt by one and then howled like wolves. As they sat up their throats were thrust into our blades. Cut their own throats, ye might say."

Duncan's hand was shaking again. He dropped the scalpel on top of Rush's kit for fear of what he might do.

Teague's face became a hideous mask as he grinned through the streaks of blood. "'Course the easiest way is to just get a buck drunk. Spend a shilling on a demijohn of rum and harvest a five-pound hank of hair by the end of the night." Blood trickled into his eyes and with a wince he shook his head to clear them. "I'll kill you, McCallum. I'll find you and kill you slow, that's my vow to you."

"And I'll make a vow to you Teague," Duncan returned. "If I ever find you with another scalp, if I hear you've taken another scalp, if I ever hear you are trading in scalps or even bragging about killing natives I will find you. I will tie you down in the forest, and cut open your belly. The wolves will take a day or two to finish you."

"Leave me like this and they'll finish me here."

Duncan pulled Rush to his feet and shoved him toward Teague. "This is Dr. Rush of Philadelphia. He has taken a vow to help the injured. He will sew you up with his fine silk thread and get you to the landing." Duncan reached for his pack and rifle. The frightened young doctor did not protest. "In fact he will care for you all the way to Philadelphia, just a doctor nursing a man who suffered a terrible accident on the frontier."

Teague spat blood at Duncan. "The Indians are dying. It's our job to help them on their way. People ain't safe with them in the world."

A catlike snarl rose behind Duncan. Analie charged past him and collided with Teague. It happened so quickly Teague simply stared for a moment in confusion, then more blood streamed onto his shoulder. She extended a wrinkled bit of flesh toward him like a trophy and the Irishman spattered blood across the clearing as he shook his head and roared. The French choirgirl had sliced off his ear.

CHAPTER SEVEN

"Can there be a greater thrill than coming into a new land with the dawn at your back?" Conawago had once asked him as they had traversed the Endless Mountains to the north. "I feel like a young boy climbing his first tree!" the old man had explained. "I know the gods have not forgotten me, because they have granted me the freedom to glimpse anew their power and beauty."

Duncan had indeed felt a thrill of discovery when he had first glimpsed the fertile rolling lands of the Conococheague Valley, adorned by pockets of mists glowing silver in the sunrise. But now the thrill was being rapidly replaced with foreboding. The rich hills below the Kittatinny Ridge were not heavily populated but the few settlers they encountered were uniformly cool, even openly suspicious of the two travelers. Men working horse teams in the fields did not acknowledge their waves. Women called children into their houses as they passed. Duncan found himself checking the priming in his rifle. Analie no longer skipped ahead of him but stayed close at his side. Her songs became less frequent, and more than once he cuffed her for turning about to stick her tongue out at the unfriendly strangers.

Duncan had all but decided the Acadian refugee was not the young adolescent girl she appeared to be but a mischievous, persevering sprite in the shape of a girl. She seemed so innocent singing her hymns but then at times he would find her assessing the landscape with a predator's eyes. Or was she just another lost soul, abandoned in the wilderness? On the first night after leaving the Susquehanna she woke in the early dawn, weeping and shivering, not seeming to recognize Duncan, speaking in French, and she would not be consoled. He had wrapped his arms around her until, having stopped shivering, she regained her senses, looked up in surprise, and sprang away.

As they walked along a flat stretch of the hard-packed wagon road Analie called a cheerful greeting to a tired-looking native woman carrying a basket to men plowing a field, but she only raised a hand in warning and hurried away. In the early afternoon they reached two men laying a snake rail fence along the road. "I'm looking for the Ross farm on Pine Creek," Duncan called out. He longed to put the unfriendly valley behind him but he had made a promise to Sarah.

The younger of the two stepped toward a rifle leaning on a stump. The older man studied them, then surveyed the road behind them. "Who ye bringing?"

Duncan glanced at Analie, who huddled alongside. The strangers seemed to suspect they were guides or scouts. "Just my niece." Analie put on her angelic smile and offered a shy wave.

The two men exchanged a glance, then the older man shrugged. "A mile up. Take the north track by the ancient sycamore on the far side of the next creek. But that's no place to tarry." There was warning in his words. "Not y'er fight. And if ye turn toward Fort Loudoun we will surely know it."

Only then did Duncan see two fast saddle horses tied in the trees. He saw now they had no tools. The men were not fence builders but sentinels, standing watch and ready to run with an alarm. But run from what? They weren't watching the western mountains, the direction of the hostile natives. They were watching to the east, in the direction of Lancaster and Philadelphia.

Analie quickened her pace as she saw the massive sycamore leaning over the creek but Duncan grabbed her arm and quickly pulled her into a nearby alder thicket. A moment later a boy in a red jacket and tan britches, beating a drum in slow time, appeared over the crest of the hill beyond the tree, followed by a half company of scarlet-backed soldiers, briskly marching to the beat. Duncan led Analie deeper into the shadows. An officer, stiffly mounted on a black horse, followed the patrol, watching the landscape with a sour, impatient expression. Why, he asked himself, would the army need to patrol the remote farming valley? Surely the sentinels by the fence were not keeping watch for soldiers.

The wind died as the infantrymen moved out of sight and in the distance he heard a fife and a volley of practicing muskets. He hurried Analie out of the thicket and up the hill. Below them, half a mile south of the wagon road, lay the sprawling log palisade that must have been Fort Loudoun. He stared at it in silence for several breaths, feeling a strange unease at the sight of the soldiers. Woolford was a captain in the army but it was Duncan he had asked to save the missing men, not the military.

They hastened to the sycamore and up the stream. He would see his promise fulfilled quickly so he could leave the army and the chilly souls of the valley behind.

The farm was just as Sarah had described it from Jess's tales of her home—an apparent oasis on a low shelf on the mountain, looking out over the wide valley with pastures and fields below. A sturdy two-story stone farmhouse was flanked by a stone-and-plank barn to one side and a long open-faced shed on the other, forming a large U-shaped barnyard. On a wash line between trees hung linens, clothes of home-spun and calico, and a length of plaid. In the center of the yard was a stone-walled well with a long sweep hanging over it. Between the barn and the house a kettle hung over a low fire.

Duncan and Analie had climbed halfway up the winding dirt track that led to the farm when he halted beside a pasture with half a dozen sheep and two milk cows. He studied the buildings, then handed the girl his rifle and continued on until they were a hundred feet from the barn. With a restraining hand on Analie's shoulder he spoke toward a large maple in the pasture. "We come as friends," he loudly announced.

A man edged around the trunk. "This ain't no public house. You'll find inns in Mercersburg. Take your friendship down the road."

He felt Analie tense. She too now saw the two rifles aimed at them from the shadows.

"A word with Mr. and Mrs. Ross is all I ask."

The man muttered a low complaint then stepped into the open and gestured them forward. As they reached the barnyard another guard with a musket appeared, watching them warily. These were men of the frontier, who well knew that Indian attacks would come from the west, from the wooded slopes behind them, but these men too were only watching the east, in the direction of the soldiers.

As their escort pounded on the sturdy oak door of the house, Duncan pulled Analie closer to him, not certain of what to expect in this farm that seemed armed for battle. Over the lintel was a plank on which black paint spelled out *Wilkes and Liberty*.

The door cracked open a hand's breadth. "A man to see Ross," their escort announced.

"Does he know we tarred and feathered the last spy?" came a gruff voice.

Duncan called out a Highland greeting. *"Fearsgar math.* Is this how you treat a visitor from the Hebrides?" he continued in Gaelic.

The door swung open and an auburn-haired woman in an apron planted her feet in the entryway, studying him with hands on her hips. "McLeod, McQueen, Macaulay, McKinnon, or MacDonald?"

She whimsically fingered a sprig of laurel pinned to her blouse as she sounded off the larger clans of the islands. Her face was an older version of the dead Jessica's.

"McCallum, nigh Kyle of Lochlash, though my grandfather claimed he has laird of all the sea to Stornaway."

A smile flickered on the sturdy woman's face. "The Minch can be troublesome sailing."

"The rougher the water the louder he would sing. When on land he would play his pipes in the teeth of every gale."

Her smile broadened and she whispered instructions to someone inside. A moment later an adolescent girl with russet braids appeared, extending a tin cup of milk to Analie before guiding their guests to a bench along the front of the house. The woman picked up a sewing basket left on the bench and gestured them to sit. "We can offer refreshment, McCallum of Lochlash, then off ye go."

"Why do British citizens fear British troops?" Duncan asked.

She eyed him warily. "Lean too far over and ye'll get y'er nose bit off," she replied, then called for stew. Another girl, of perhaps seven years, with the same red hair, appeared with two bowls that she filled from the large kettle over the smoldering fire by the side of the house. They were cooking for a crowd.

The girl offered the steaming bowls with a shy, uncertain smile.

"I grew up with the Mohawks," Analie abruptly declared to the girl. "I could cut out your liver and fry it."

The girl gave a squeal of fear and ran to hide in her mother's apron. Her mother only smiled. "Could you now lass? The Mohawks teach so many useful skills. Captain Smith will be most impressed."

"Captain Smith?"

"Our constable and head of the local rangers. He was captured in one of the western wars when he was young and eventually found his way to the Mohawks. He always says leaving them was the most difficult decision of his life. And our own family be great admirers of the Mohawks as well."

Analie seemed disappointed.

"We tried to farm up north of Albany for a couple years, in the Saratoga country. I miss the Mohawk. Fine, stately men and women with hearts as big as the sky. I always felt safer when Iroquois were around. They shared their squash and maize that first year when our crop failed." The older girl brought a bucket from the well. As Duncan washed, her mother spoke a warning. "This is not your fight, Mr. McCallum," she said. "Get on with y'er journey when you finish y'er bowls."

"Is your husband here, Mrs. Ross?" he asked.

"Not so you'd know it," she replied in a tone that brooked no probing.

She decided to take Duncan's silence as acquiescence and played the hostess as they sat and enjoyed the hearty stew, asking about Duncan's home on the coastal Highlands, explaining that she had been born on Skye but left for Ulster when she was ten and America when she was sixteen. Hers was a familiar tale of the Scots-Irish, who had fled to the northern counties of Ireland in search of a better life, which they ultimately found in America. The two girls sat on the ground on either side of their mother, the youngest now making faces at Analie, who energetically returned the favor.

Duncan tried to recall the names he had heard from Sarah when she had attempted to describe Jessica's family. "You must be Clare," he said to her. "And Peggy," he added with a nod to the older girl.

The woman cocked her head. "Where do ye travel from, Mr. McCallum?"

Analie answered. "Edentown, in the north."

The announcement strangely startled the woman. She fixed her visitors with an intense stare, then backed away before turning and dashing into the house, her daughters staring after her in confusion. Duncan was on his feet the instant she disappeared, approaching the big barn with an eye on the sentinels until, as they all looked away, he slipped inside.

Light from the open windows of the loft filtered down into the big central bay, revealing more than a dozen figures gathered around a barrel on which two brawny, bare-chested men were arm wrestling. Men watched from other barrels and benches as the two men's arms bulged and swayed. Four onlookers, with legs overhanging, sat in the loft, urging the wrestlers on in excited but strangely subdued voices, as if wary of being heard outside.

"Rip his arm off, Murdo!" a young man with long blond curls called to the older man in a loud whisper.

"Glory to the McBains!" cried another.

The two antagonists were built like oxen. Their veins bulged, their throats emitted animal-like grunts, and despite the quiet calls from the crowd they stared only at each other.

Duncan inched forward, trying to make sense of the oddly subdued company of Scots. Suddenly strong hands clamped around each of his arms and yanked him off his feet. In an instant he was dragged into the center bay and shoved to the floor. Before he could rise men began kicking him. Duncan grabbed a booted foot and twisted it, bringing the man down with a surprised groan. He coiled and sprang upward, scattering several men, who reacted not with anger but laughter. Duncan turned to attack the nearest man in the circle around him, shouldering him aside, then spinning from the grip of another.

"Slippery as a snake!" the man spat.

Duncan grabbed a knee and heaved upward, upending another man who took two more down when he fell. "I will speak with Mr. Ross!" he shouted.

The men before him glanced at the older of the two wrestlers, who wore an armband of copper around his forearm in the fashion of ancient island clans. As they did so, several others near the door shot backward. Analie stepped into the light, swinging a hoe in a violent arc.

A man near Duncan cursed and raised a pistol but his arm was quickly pushed down by the man with the armband. "It's the girl, you fool!"

"I know her!" another cried. "The French lark! She travels with the runners!"

"You are Ross?" Duncan asked the big man. "Murdo Ross?"

"Ye steal in here unannounced, with narry a by y'er leave," the big man barked at Duncan, "and turn the girl a'gin us! The boys might have struck her!" He took a step forward and without warning delivered two quick hammer punches to Duncan's belly.

The blows were shattering. Duncan's vision blurred. He gasped for breath as he sagged against a post. "Jessica. She's dead," he groaned, then faded into unconsciousness.

HE WOKE IN A BED OFF A SMALL ROOM AT THE BACK OF THE HOUSE, wincing and holding his belly as he put his feet on the floor. A sober company waited at the big kitchen table. Murdo Ross, his broad shoulders now covered by a homespun shirt, sat at the end, flanked by two of the younger Scots. The woman who had fed Duncan, her face tear-streaked and looking far older now, sat at the other end, her younger daughter pressed against her shoulder. At the hearth, Analie, now wearing a boy's britches and shirt, sat playing with a cat as the older daughter patched the clothes she had worn from Edentown.

"My wife, Margaret, and I owe you an apology, McCallum," Ross said. "These are stressful times in the Conococheague. I did not ken ye had spoken of Edentown to my wife."

The woman's voice was choked. "Jessica was our oldest. The bravest. A lass of firm convictions."

Duncan gave a tentative nod, not certain why her mother would speak of Jess's convictions. "There had been a murder in the forest," he began, explaining the tragic circumstances of the girl's death. They asked many questions, wanting to know the name of the dead Oneida, and the ranger captain with him, whether Jess had seemed happy at the Edentown settlement, even seeking news of Miss Ramsey, who had sent them a delightful letter the month before, reporting that their daughter's presence at Edentown was a blessing to the entire settlement.

When he explained how she had been accidentally killed by a bullet meant for Woolford, they seemed puzzled at his words. "And Shamokin?" Murdo asked. "What news from Shamokin?" Duncan looked at them in confusion. Why would they ask about the troubles at Shamokin? The runners. Some of the men had mentioned that Analie ran with the runners. As he tried to piece together their words he remembered the parcel Sarah had given him for the dead woman's parents and retrieved it from his pack.

"She died for what she believed, and we'll always have that," Murdo Ross declared.

"But as I said, it was an accident, sir," Duncan put in, more bewildered than ever. But then Murdo untied the muslin wrapper and unfolded the contents. Duncan had thought it a piece of embroidery or perhaps a small article of clothing sewn for a sister, and now stared dumbfounded.

"That's our girl," Murdo murmured in a tight voice.

It was a flag, whose image he had seen published in gazettes. On a piece of buff-colored linen Jess had sewn a snake in thirteen yellow segments, each bearing the name of one of the colonies. The segments were all separated. Underneath were the words *Join or Die*.

"Oh aye," one of the men said. "And look what's she added, the bold lass."

Murdo turned the flag into the light so they could all see the small embroidered lines that connected Massachusetts, New York, Connecticut, and Rhode Island. He lifted it higher for his wife, now at the hearth, to see.

"Ever the fighter," she said.

Duncan stared at the flag, realizing that he had seen those same colonies linked elsewhere. *Massnyconnri*, the secret message to Dr. Franklin's house in Philadelphia had said. As he struggled to understand, the older daughter lifted the shift Analie had worn to show her mother, putting a finger through two perfectly formed holes Duncan had not noticed before.

"Was this from the same day then, child?" Mrs. Ross asked the Acadian girl. "At least an angel watched over one of you."

Analie looked up, not at the Scottish woman but at Duncan, with something like embarrassment on her face.

Duncan rose and, disbelieving, put his own finger through the holes. A bullet had gone through the loose fabric of the shift below her right arm. In his mind's eye he reconstructed the shooting. The first rifle had taken Jess Ross with a shot that hit squarely in her heart. The second shooter had hit Conawago, but Analie had indeed been in the line of fire. Duncan had been a witness. How could he have been so completely wrong about what he had seen? He had assumed the killers had ineptly tried to finish the job they had started with Woolford, but their shots had been well aimed. Jessica Ross had not died by accident, but had been the target of the shooters, who had also tried to kill young Analie.

"I believe," he said in a voice thick with confusion, "it is my turn to ask questions. Perhaps someone could start by telling me about the committee runners?" he asked, and turned toward Murdo Ross.

The big Scot glanced at his companions before speaking. "T'is a perilous job," Ross said, "and we are but a way station for them. Johnson Hall, Edentown, Shamokin, Conococheague. I warned every man, I did. Their messages aren't just urgent, they are dangerous. They have been carrying fire, and someone was going to get burnt. But most were former rangers and know not of fear. The others . . ." he shook his head sadly. "You've seen the words we've taken as our creed. Wilkes and Liberty. Hell, if I were twenty years younger I probably would have joined them on the trails instead of just being their postmaster."

Duncan's head swirled. Edentown couldn't possibly be a station. Surely Sarah, so committed to separating her settlement from the evils of the rest of the world, wouldn't allow it.

"The others," his wife put in, "were good lads of this valley, from families who had felt the yoke of the oppressors in the Highlands and just wanted to keep to themselves. But they flocked to our barnyard when Mr. Smith and Murdo started public readings of Mr. Wilkes and Mr. Locke."

"The lace-headed lairds of London," one of the Scots at the table groused, "they think they would tell us how to live in the Pennsylvania hills. But they got it wrong." The words brought a chorus of "ayes" and affirming curses from the others at the table. Duncan had a sense that he was hearing something of a eulogy for Jessica Ross.

"We are not the only ones who disagree with those lairds," Murdo added. "We embrace the king, but he knows naught what his ministers do. It's not just the hills of Pennsylvania where men think this way."

"You mean the committees," Duncan put in. "The runners bear messages from one colony to the next. Running south from Johnson Hall."

Murdo eyed him uncertainly. "Have ye tried my wife's stew? She truly does wonders with rabbit and squirrel. It's those forest herbs learned from the Mohawk."

Duncan extracted Red Jacob's broken dice and dropped it on the table. "Red Jacob, shot in the back and his arm cut off while running on an urgent mission from Johnson Hall. There was another on Captain Woolford, left for dead on the same trail. Then a young gentleman from Philadelphia serving as a messenger from Dr. Franklin and his friends. He had his face sliced off while he yet lived." Mrs. Ross herded her children out of the room, covering the ears of the nearest. Duncan continued, dropping the bound feathers from Shamokin. "A Moravian named Rohrbach and his pregnant Delaware wife." He gestured to the banner. "A beautiful Scottish girl at Edentown. How many more will die?" He turned again to Ross. "Do they carry secret messages from one colony to the next?" he repeated. "I tend to think your daughter thought so when she threaded lines connecting those colonies, as a message coded into newspapers sent from Johnson Hall to Franklin confirmed. You said she was bold, that she died for what she believed in. A wasted death if her secrets die with her."

Murdo lifted the dice. "If I had more of these I'd crush every last one myself." His eyes narrowed as he saw the confusion on Duncan's face.

"Who are these men carrying messages?" Duncan pressed.

Ross spoke in a slow, tentative voice, suspicion now in his eyes. "There are men well trained to move with stealth along the frontier," he observed.

"You mean rangers are helping. But rangers are in the army. Then why do you watch for the army?"

"Rangers are on the fringe of the army," Murdo said, as if correcting him. "Shadow soldiers. What you see here," he made a broad gesture that took in the room and the open door beyond, "is something else. Something just about the Conococheague Valley. Sometimes there must be more than words."

Suddenly Duncan remembered what Sarah had told him in Edentown. He had been so obsessed with the killings he had forgotten the rest of the news he had heard in Sarah's kitchen. "You mean like stopping trade convoys."

A low rumble rose in the throat of one of the men behind Ross, who put up a hand as if to restrain him.

"Two hundred hand axes concealed in grain sacks," Murdo explained. "Thirty muskets hidden in bundles of blankets. Two kegs of flints, twenty of gunpowder marked as flour. Not trade goods, but war goods. Men in Philadelphia gave us the law that banned all shipments of weapons to the western tribes. Other men in Philadelphia thought they could put themselves above that law, that they would make a windfall by defying that law. We told the army at Fort Loudoun and they refused to intervene, even though we said those axes and muskets would come back to kill our own people. It's an old game. A piece of silver buys a blind eye.

"But we lost too many loved ones to the raiding tribes. Of course we stopped the convoy. We separated all the commercial goods and told the bastards they were free to move on with them to Fort Pitt. Then we made a pile of the contraband. It made a right pretty inferno."

Duncan recalled that there had been a confrontation with troops, that some soldiers were still missing. "And the king's troops stood by watching."

"The king's officers were blinded to the right of it." Ross abruptly pushed back his chair and stood. "When free men have the truth of something, that is all the authority they need." He pointed to a paper pinned to the wall by the hearth. "At least the English did that one thing right."

Duncan hesitantly rose and examined the paper, a page torn from a book. To his astonishment it was a plate of the Magna Carta. He eyed his host uncertainly. "Some knights writing five hundred years ago weren't thinking of hostilities with American aborigines."

Murdo gave a slow shake of his head. "What they did at Runnymede was no different than what we do here."

Duncan returned Ross's determined stare then nodded. "She died with honor. I wished I had known her better."

Ross replied with a melancholy smile then motioned Duncan toward the door. The men from the barn were outside now, milling about in small groups, some smoking clay pipes, others washing themselves at the well. Ross called over a compact man with broad, thick shoulders and introduced him. "Ian McQueen, blacksmith from the north reaches of Skye." He jerked a thumb toward Duncan. "The lad says he is of the Hebrides, Ian." Ross still wasn't totally convinced Duncan wasn't a spy.

McQueen assumed a businesslike air, seeming to recognize that he had been given a task. "So ye ken *An T-eilean Sgitheanach?*" he asked Duncan.

"The winged isle, aye," Duncan replied in a level voice. "I spent some happy summers working on Skye."

"Have ye climbed the Cuillins then?"

"McCallums were drovers and shipbuilders since before time," Duncan said. "We would comb the Cuillins with McNichols and MacLeods each fall for the shaggy beasts. We'd camp at the head of Loch Sligachan and drive the coos for the swim across the kyle, though personally I favored the seafaring side of the family. My grandfather courted selkies on every isle of the Minch."

McQueen grinned, and with a fatherly gesture tussled Duncan's hair. "He'll do, Murdo."

Ross nodded. "Stay the night, McCallum," he suggested, then marched away toward the barn.

Duncan lowered himself against an oak as if to watch Analie and Clare play with a cat, but he kept his eye on the restless men in the yard. They were like a private army. Sarah had stated that the

Conococheague men, these very men, had captured an infantry patrol, but there was no sign of the soldiers.

McQueen brought him a tankard of cider. "Captain Smith himself be coming soon, if he feels it's safe," the Scot announced.

"Safe?" Duncan asked.

"He has a farm up the strath but some fool magistrate signed a warrant for his arrest. While the misunderstanding continues he keeps on the move so no family will be charged with harboring him."

"Misunderstanding?"

"While the general in Philadelphia still misunderstands his duty to the king," McQueen explained in an earnest tone, then dipped his own cup to Duncan before drinking.

"How long have your men been watching the wagon road?"

"These six weeks and more."

"Did two men pass through recently, one with blond hair and dressed in black?"

"We don't stop each traveler, mind, just be sure they keep moving."

Duncan tried not to be obvious as he studied the landscape for the makeshift jail that must hold the soldiers. It was probably a root cellar or a cave on the mountain behind them. At least he now understood the sentinels, and the tension among the men. The farm was a powder keg. The soldiers would be furious at being restrained, and would try to escape. Or resentful troops would come to force their release. Duncan was not sure how to characterize the strange drama that was playing out in the valley but if soldiers were killed, there would be no forgiving these proud Scots.

As he watched the yard, McBain, the big man who had been wrestling Murdo Ross, bent over two men who were slumped against the barn wall, asleep, and woke each with a light kick on the leg. They responded with deferential nods. As they hurried to the well a sentinel shouted. "He's coming down the trail!"

Duncan watched in confusion as McBain gave a shrill whistle. One of the men who had been sleeping ran to the wash line and pulled away the length of tartan hanging there. He and his companions hurried after the big man, into the barn, followed by five more men. Those remaining in the yard gathered along the front of the long shed, many with expectant smiles, making an effort at standing at attention as three riders appeared from the far side of the house. Two of the riders, young men in fringed hunters' tunics, quickly dismounted and led their mounts to the trough by the well. The third rider, a man in his forties with a strong, determined countenance, stayed erect on his tall chestnut mare, studying the company with the eye of a hawk. He rode along the ragged line of men, several of whom touched deferential knuckles to their foreheads.

Captain Smith turned to the brawny owner of the farm. "Are our guests in good health, Murdo?" he asked with an uplifted eyebrow. Murdo Ross gestured toward the barn and as if on cue the Scots who had disappeared emerged at a trot. One man stumbled as he tucked his tartan under his belt. Another tried to fix his bonnet on his head while trotting toward the line being formed at the center of the yard. Each man wore a regimental kilt and bonnet. They had become soldiers. Though none wore a sword, each had kept his dagger in his belt. The captured soldiers from Fort Loudoun had been in front of Duncan the whole time.

"Sergeant McBain?" Smith called out.

The big man who had been wrestling Ross stepped forward at the end of the line. "All accounted for, sir."

"And not suffering, I take it?"

"We did hae' to endure a screechin' that McQueen called a song last night," McBain reported in an overly earnest tone.

Duncan's jaw hung open in astonishment. The Highland farmers had captured Highland soldiers. Not just Highland soldiers, he realized as he recognized the black and green tartan of the uniforms, but members of the elite Black Watch, the toughest fighters in the king's army.

Smith dismounted and turned back expectantly to Ross, who with a sheepish expression gestured several men forward then after a chastising glance from Smith sent them back to retrieve their muskets. The show of prisoners needed a show of guards.

"Captain Smith says we must keep things in perspective," explained McQueen, standing at the end of the line. "They have their duties and we have ours. A man must stay true to his duties."

Analie settled by Duncan, erupting with low giggles as Sergeant McBain inspected the troops, Smith sternly following a step behind. The sergeant berated a man for haphazardly gartering his red and white hose, another for having his bear-fur cockade twisted under his bonnet. Duncan watched with amusement as the inspection was completed, realizing he may have seen some of the men during the earlier Champlain and Quebec campaigns in the north, then laid back and languidly closed his eyes.

"It would take a great fool to come here under false pretenses," a stern voice announced at Duncan's side. He looked up into the inquiring eyes of Captain Smith. "Or a very bad provocateur," the rebel leader continued. "I can't decide which you are. If the latter I would be saddened. We have been able to avoid the shedding of blood thus far in our little affair. You play a dangerous game, McCallum, pretending to know about the runners but not even knowing about the dice."

Duncan straightened. "Sir?"

"You've led my comrades to believe you are part of the committee network. You are not. Yet you seem to do committee work and travel with our French songbird." Smith kept his tone light but Duncan saw the cool determination in his eye. "My friends may seem amiable enough but I assure you, you will feel their wrath if you are deceiving us. There is tension here you do not see. The soldiers are shamed at being taken. Campbells from the next strath have arrived and to their surprise found McDonalds among the troops," he said, referring to one of the oldest and bloodiest of the feuds between Highland clans. "They will be at each other's throats if we don't watch close." He glanced up, toward the mountain trail, and Duncan recalled Smith was in flight from an arrest warrant.

"Why not release the soldiers?" he asked.

"Because they have half a dozen of our own in the stockade at the fort. If they would only—" He was interrupted by the wail of a hunting horn from the mountainside.

As Murdo quickly herded the soldiers back inside the barn, half a dozen men grabbed muskets and ran to covered positions.

Smith pulled a small pistol from his belt, entirely crafted of metal in the Highland style, and hurried to where the trail opened out of the forest. Two quick whistles sounded from a lookout in a tree, and moments later two men on horseback appeared, one of them leading a battered, staggering prisoner by a long leather strap tied to his neck.

Analie plucked at Duncan's sleeve, but he needed no urging. He darted toward the horses, drawing his knife as he ran. Smith shouted for him to halt, and he heard the sound of at least two muskets being cocked. With one swift motion he cut the strap and spun about to face the others, standing with his back to the captive, his knife held out in threat.

"Lower your knife, McCallum," Smith called out angrily, "and we will lower our guns. Then we can both discover why a Mohawk has been treated so."

Tanaqua's face was swollen from repeated blows and he seemed about to collapse of exhaustion, but his eyes burned bright. "The gods keep pushing us together, McCallum," he said to Duncan, grinning through his obvious pain.

Pulling one of his friend's arms over his shoulder, Duncan half carried him to the side of the house and lowered him to the ground, his back to the wall. Analie appeared with a tin mug of water, which he silently drained, then offered a grateful nod as Duncan removed the end of the captive strap from the Mohawk's neck.

"Bastard was throwing our supplies off the ledge in front of the cave we were using," one of his captors loudly reported as Smith stepped to Tanaqua's side.

"True," the Mohawk said.

Smith knelt beside him. "We have to hide stores in case the army decides to interfere with our spring planting," the captain explained. "I told the men to use what caves they might find."

"He was shooting arrows at us," one of the captors groused.

"True," Tanaqua agreed again. "In your direction."

"If this man was trying to kill you," Duncan inserted, "you'd be lying in the forest with a shaft in your heart." He studied his friend. Through Tanaqua's fatigue and pain he saw a deeper melancholy.

"You placed supplies in a cave behind a high open ledge," Duncan said to the men who had dragged Tanaqua through the forest. "A cave whose walls showed painted hands and images of forest spirits."

What was left of Smith's anger was turned on the two captors. "Is that true?"

"Aye," drawled the older of the two, a bearded man who paused to spit out tobacco juice. "Just dusty things of the savages. And some old rotting fur and bones we threw over the edge."

Duncan felt a heavy weight press down on him. "It was a shrine."

"More," came Tanaqua's voice, dry as sticks. "Since before memory our holy men have gone there to pray. A secret place."

"Hell," said the bearded man. "Some windy rock ledge surrounded by gnarled trees with a cave behind. Right pretty up there. Could see for miles and miles."

Smith's face colored. With a curt wave of his hand he dismissed the two men.

"The fur was of a giant bear," Tanaqua explained in a tight voice, "who lived there when the Great League of my people was formed. He was very old and feeble even then, and when our holy men found him they sat and spoke to him for days, until he let them feed him. It was a great sign, confirming that the spirits blessed our League. They cared for him until he died. All these years. All these centuries the guardians of our spirits have gone there, to hold his fur and bones as they pray."

Smith crossed his legs under him and sat beside Tanaqua, and to Duncan's surprise began speaking in the forest tongue. "*Jiyathondek,*" he said, "*jadadeken raskerewake. Hai! Hai!*" *Hearken*, he was saying to the spirits, *thy brother of the bear clan is here. Woe! Woe!*" They were the words of a condolence ritual.

Duncan eased away and found the bearded man who had brought in Tanaqua at the well. "Was there also the body of another Iroquois?"

The stranger winced. "We had naught to do with that. He was already dead, a week or more ago. The vultures were at work on him on the rocks below."

Tanaqua had been right. Kaskay, the guardian at the shrine, had been killed and scalped. Now the shrine had been defiled. He sent Analie with cider for Tanaqua and found himself just staring, disconsolate, into the well and the water deep below. Tanaqua had hoped to invoke the spirits, to pray for Blooddancer, but instead he had seen the body and the desecration of the sacred shrine. Duncan returned to sit beside Tanaqua and Smith, joining in the condolence.

After a quarter hour, Tanaqua slumped against the wall, deep in sleep. Duncan found himself staring at a new adornment to the Mohawk's arm, carefully drawn in ochre. It was the sign of the lost half king, the stick figure with the fish's head. Smith whispered a last few words in the Mohawk tongue and then turned to Duncan. "I believe we have an unfinished conversation, sir," he declared with challenge in his voice.

"Men who numbered among the runners have been killed or gone missing." There was defiance in Duncan's voice. "I aim to strike a balance."

A bitter smile broke Smith's stern expression. "A balance of justice? You presume much. Even if there were a magistrate who would hear your case you would need to know the true nature of the crime, I suspect, to find recompense for it."

"An Oneida friend shot in the back, with his arm severed and his hand inserted into his belly. A Philadelphia scholar with his face peeled away. A young Moravian brutally murdered with his Delaware bride. I think I know enough, Mr. Smith. Not to mention the Ross daughter who died a few feet from me, in the arms of my friend Conawago."

Smith hesitated, studying Duncan more intensely, then quieted. "Jess was a brave and joyful lass, bringing a smile to every face she met. Her loss grieves her father terribly, though Murdo will never show it." Smith gazed forlornly at Jessica's mother, whose face was drained and empty as she filled buckets at the well. "These mysteries don't just cross colonies, they cross the wide ocean. You'll ne'er get to the bottom of it. There are losses on every battlefield."

Duncan swallowed the questions that leapt to his tongue. He was more confused than ever about the battle the runners fought.

"Except he's the Death Speaker," came a small, urgent voice over Smith's shoulder.

The rebel leader turned with a weary smile, apparently thinking Analie was gibing him.

She shook her head as if in rebuke. "In the Iroquois lands that is his name. When people are killed, Mr. McCallum can still follow their trails and restore the balance on their path to the other side.

Magistrates' justice ain't worth a groat in the wilds. What matters is that the families of the dead know, and the dead know."

Smith sobered, his hard stare fixed first on the girl then on Duncan. "The Death Speaker. It has an air of the supernatural. I would be disappointed if you . . ." he chose his words carefully, "created false expectations among the tribes. Or the other families of the runners."

"I know little of the supernatural," Duncan replied, "though I do have contempt for one who hides behind it to kill innocent people. I owe the dead I left in the north. I track the truth. To wherever it is hidden."

Smith sensed the challenge in his eyes. "You want our truth?" he snapped. "Why do you think we braved the Atlantic? Why do we fight so hard to keep our homes here? T'is simple. Liberty is our truth."

"A fine word to decorate your walls," Duncan shot back. "You can exercise minds with it. Mr. Wilkes can write essays about it in his comfortable study in England. Scots have been led down the path of promised freedom again and again for centuries and have but graves and heartbreak to show for it. I would be disappointed if you created false expectations with it," he echoed sharply to Smith, then flushed, knowing the man did not deserve his anger. He was weary at grasping at phantoms. "I am more interested in what you exercise your hands with. What messages do the runners carry so urgently south? Patrick Woolford sent me to save nineteen men. It's not enough that I don't know where they are, I don't even know why they are to die."

Smith turned and settled his gaze on Analie.

Duncan's emotion flared. Then he paused. You seem to do committee work, Smith had said. Analie was backing away. The little cord that bound her precious pouch was looped around her wrist. His hand darted forward. Before she could resist he had the pouch and had upended it into the ground. A scrap of bread fell out, then one of Rush's scalpels, followed by a linen-wrapped roll.

"McCallum! No!" Smith protested, but suddenly Tanaqua's hand was clamped around his arm, pulling Smith back as Duncan untied the ribbon that bound the linen and pulled away the cloth, revealing a roll of papers bound by a red ribbon. As he untied it a dozen sheets of paper fell to the ground.

The topmost was a sheet of uncut tax stamps, printed in rows of eight. Underneath were documents. He picked one up and with a chill recognized the royal seal. They were printed, copperplate forms signed and sealed by the Minister of the Exchequer in London. *By Royal Appointment,* began each of the certificates. He lifted another, and another. They were all the same, except for the name of each appointee entered in an elegant hand and for each the name of a different colonial town or county. Each was an official appointment as a commissioner, charged with collecting the new stamp tax.

CHAPTER EIGHT

"Treason!" Duncan gasped. "That's what they'll call it! I am risking life and limb so you can steal from the king? You'll have me help thieves in some conspiracy against the crown?"

"Thieves, is it?" Smith shot back. "Ye may as well call a murderer the victim. Laying a tax on a people without giving them a voice in it, that's the thieving of it. Stopping free men from talking with one another, that's the murder of freedom, McCallum."

Duncan's mind reeled. Surely it was not possible that Woolford, a ranger captain with a king's commission, or Jessica Ross, the innocent Edentown servant, could be involved in the theft of the king's documents. He reminded himself that there were others in the strange circle of secrecy. "You would have me believe that Dr. Franklin and Sir William would conspire against the king?"

"Not the king, McCallum, but against Grenville and the other bullies in Parliament, those who twisted his arm into signing a law to punish the colonies without even a by-your-leave to those who live here. They say they must raise revenue to pay for the armies that protect us. We have no enemies but the western tribes, and it is our militias that protect against them. Where was the vaunted army when arms were passing through our own valley to help those enemies? A pox on them! It is only lace-collared prigs across the ocean who benefit from these taxes. They would steal bread from our mouths to pay for their wigs and fancy London coaches. They be the traitors, lad. We be the ones to nudge them back to right thinking. The king will agree when he sees the truth of it. Meanwhile we shall do all in our power to see the tax fails."

Analie, sitting now by Tanaqua, cast Duncan an apologetic glance. She had been the one trusted with the most secret of messages. The killers had known, and had tried to kill the girl.

"But why the committees?" Duncan asked.

As if in answer Smith nodded to the barnyard, where men were raising a pole to which Jess's flag of the segmented serpent was affixed. "It's London's nightmare. Boston looks to London for its livelihood, as do Philadelphia, Williamsburg, and Charleston. The face of each colony is turned solely to England. When Massachusetts has a problem it crosses the ocean and begs on its knees by the River Thames. Virginia sends its tobacco to Britain, Georgia its indigo. When a petition is raised in America it is always sent to London by a single colony. And alone each colony inexorably bends to London's will. The fearmongers say there be ten thousand troops here to break us. I tell them they shame the schoolmasters who taught them their numbers. Ten thousand troops perhaps. But put the colonies together and there's nigh two million of us!"

"The dice," Duncan said, finally understanding. "The tax is levied not just on documents but dice as well."

"And those who are joined with us have broken their dice," Smith explained. He nodded toward the flag, so simple in its defiance, "Dr. Franklin designed that flag years ago, saying we could never vanquish the French unless the colonies united. As with much else he was ahead of his time. But now Parliament has made it possible. Franklin calls the committees his lightning rods, with the sparks rising from the hearts of colonists up and down the coast. The cursed tax can be beaten but only if we stand together. We are choking it. Collectors in Boston and Providence have already resigned their commissions after protests in the streets. We will join across the borders of the colonies, act together for the first time. We will make it happen with the messages the runners carry."

"Until you are all murdered."

Smith hesitated, cocking his head as if trying to decide whether to take threat or invitation in Duncan's words.

McQueen called out and gestured down the road. "Scout from the valley, reporting in!" Smith took a step away before turning to Duncan. "McCallum. There were McCallums at Culloden I recollect. Your clan felt the hand of the oppressor there. Not twenty years ago and ye've forgotten already?" The captain left Duncan staring at the ground. It was not the hand of oppressors he felt; it was the hand of strangers pushing him into a fight that was not his own.

WHEN DUNCAN FINALLY STIRRED, HE CONFIRMED THAT TANAQUA still slept, then wandered behind the house and sat on a chopping block by the woodshed. He could not recall ever feeling so unsure of himself. He had made a promise to Woolford, and given a vow to a dead Oneida, but he had not known the two were entangled in the games of kings and lords. He, and Sarah with him, had worked so hard to stay out of the reach of government. His Highland clan had chosen to play in such a game and had been nearly exterminated for it.

Go home! a voice inside screamed at him. This was not the fight he had bargained for. Foreboding for Sarah and Conawago gripped his heart like a fist. Surely they could not have understood the dangers they attracted by making Edentown a station for the runners. How could Woolford have done this to them? They needed to be warned. He looked back at Tanaqua, weighing the possibility of reviving his Mohawk friend and slipping away into the forest. He had no appetite for mixing his life into the politics of strangers.

An eerie wail rose from the forest, the low, drawn out sound of a dying animal. When it rose again a minute later, he stood and tentatively followed the trail toward the sound. As he climbed a low rise onto a flat, a different sound arose, like the muffled blow of an ax.

When he spied Murdo at the trunk of a tree, he assumed the big Scot had decided for some strange reason to go cut wood.

He halted ten paces away. Ross was not cutting firewood, he was pounding a dead trunk with his fists, splintering the dry wood with blows of terrible force. His fists were bloody. His face was so soaked that little shards of the splintering wood were clinging to his cheeks. He had lost his beloved daughter but would not wear his grief in the open.

Duncan watched the stricken man for several long breaths before approaching. "Shattering your hands won't bring Jessica back," he said.

Ross turned his desolate face to Duncan, not bothering to wipe away his tears. "She was the strongest of us all." His voice cracked with emotion. "She had the wit of a poet and the grace of a swan. My little angel." He looked absently at his battered knuckles, oozing blood. "When she was a wee bairn she would have me tell her the tale of Flora McDonald night after night." The story of how Flora McDonald had risked her life to save the fugitive Prince Charlie after the disaster at Culloden had become a favorite of Highlanders. "She said she was going to be just like Flora when she grew up."

"And she did it, Murdo. Even more, for Flora did not give her life for her cause," Duncan consoled. "Now let me tend to your hands."

But Ross seemed not to hear. "She convinced her mother to let her go by saying Edentown would be safer from attack by the western savages because it was in Iroquois country, and we could always count on the Iroquois. Edentown station," he muttered with a shake of his head. "She was so proud when Captain Woolford accepted her into his network. It was only about the runners at first, but she grew sweet on him. Last time he was here he asked if I would object to him writing her. I said she would need to know the codes and he laughed and said he meant as a man might write a woman."

Duncan recalled how Jessica had so carefully tended to Woolford, remembered the light in both their eyes when they had met on the porch moments before her death. He groped for words. His friend Patrick led a lonely life, away from friends for weeks at a time and cut off from his family in England. He had never known him to express affection for a woman. "Your daughter did not suffer."

Ross gave a small, grateful nod, and scrubbed at his eyes. "There's a ledge overlooking the valley just past the house. Jess's ledge, we called it. Many were the eves she and I would go there to watch the sunset, even in winter. Sometimes she would sing. Every night since she left, even in rain and snow, I've gone there to say a prayer toward the north. She promised me she would be safe . . ." His voice died away, choked with emotion.

The big Scot did not object as Duncan pushed him onto a stump and picked splinters of wood from his bloody knuckles. "She must have known some of the runners," Duncan observed.

"Good men, every one, be they white, red, or black."

"Black?"

"Oh aye, Africans out of Virginia. Fastest of all on their feet. And perhaps the bravest." Ross saw the question in Duncan's eyes. "Because once they reach here they know they are safe. A freed black can make a life in the north, raise a family on his own land. In Virginia they can still be taken and thrown back into chains. Papers evidencing their freedom can be burnt. More than once I've heard tales of slave hunters catching up with a freed man and tossing his papers in the fire so they can put chains on him again and sell him in the southern markets. No one listens to their protests. I've even heard of men taken back in chains and their tongues cut out so they can't tell their story."

"Jess was playing with Analie that last day. I think she missed her sisters. Where do they go, Murdo? Where in Virginia?"

"We're meant not to know. If ye don't know a secret ye cannot compromise it. Down the Warrior's Path, Red Jacob said once, the trail used by the Iroquois in their raids against the southern tribes. But it's just the wagon road today. Into the Shenandoah on the road then over the Blue Ridge to Williamsburg. Letters come up from Williamsburg through a route only the Virginian runners know. The next station, that's all I know. A settlement on the eastern slope called Townsend's Store, where the stationmaster lost an arm in the western wars."

"There must be a password, or some mark to identify one runner to the next."

"Each runner has a special mark, aye. It goes on the envelope, like a postmark. A letter without the marks, without the right sequence of marks, isn't trusted. Sir William and Captain Woolford came up with using symbols and not words for the sake of the Iroquois runners."

"Carrying letters between colonies? Stealing tax commissions? Why would the Iroquois even help?"

Murdo shrugged. "Because those who fought the French together trust each other with their lives. Because they are warriors always in search of a noble cause. If they can't fight in a big war they will fight in a little war." He struggled to rise. His grief had spent all his strength. Duncan pulled him to his feet. "There's a bucket in the woodshed," the Scot explained. "I need to wash off the blood before my wife sees."

He stood in the open door of the shed and let Duncan stream water over the deep cuts and pick out more shards of wood, then clean his face with a rag from a shelf above the woodpile.

As Duncan turned to set down the rag he stopped, his hand hanging in the air. He had not noticed what the rag had covered.

The old pipes were tattered but had seen loving care. A pang rose inside, of a hunger long unsated.

"I love the creaky old things," Murdo said with a melancholy smile. "They would echo through the glen when I was a lad. But I nae got the touch my father had. She won't let me play them in the house. I keep trying. It's an itch I cannot scratch."

When Duncan spoke there was a tremor in his voice. "May I?"

"Of course, lad."

The bag had been much patched, its seams ragged, the varnish on the chanter and drones worn to raw wood in places but the pipes seemed serviceable.

A satisfied grunt rose from Ross. "I've seen that look. My father wore it whenever he wrapped his hands around that chanter. He would say the souls of eight generations of our clan were speaking when they played, that in them our blood stayed alive. Go ahead, give me a pibroch."

Duncan ran his hand along the chanter, checked the drones, and stared at the pipes for several long breaths. Playing the pipes was a deeply intimate affair for him. His grandfather had said no man could master the pipes without turning his soul inside out. He reluctantly shook his head and carefully returned them to their shelf. "Do you have axle grease?"

"In the byre, aye."

"Cover your knuckles with it. It will keep them clean. Just tell Mrs. Ross you were working on the wagon."

Murdo squeezed his arm. "You're a good lad, McCallum," he offered, and set off for the stable.

Duncan wandered to the edge of the forest and discovered a flat formation of shale that overlooked the valley, realizing it must be Jess's ledge. He sat against a boulder, staring into the sky. He could not remember ever feeling so confused. Every secret had another layer of secret beneath it. Despite the temptation to flee, he knew he couldn't retreat, couldn't walk away from nineteen souls. There had been bands of Highland fugitives after Culloden, desperate men cornered by the victorious British soldiers, who had been ordered not to waste their bullets. The Scottish rebels had been skewered by blades and left for wolves. If Duncan had been there he would have helped such survivors, some of whom might have endured but for a warm meal or a safe night's sleep. If the runners were not following the rules of the government, then neither were those who pursued them.

The rocks captured the late afternoon sun, and he drifted into a warm lethargy, feeling again the exhaustion of the past days, thinking of the spring planting underway at Edentown. Sarah would be watching the lambs and fawns. Snippets of Gaelic floated on the breeze from the barnyard. A horse nickered. A cow lowed, anxious to be milked.

THE OLD SHAGGY COW WAS AS WIDE AS A TABLE BUT YOUNG DUNCAN STILL had to grab a hank of long ginger hair to stay on her back as she angled down the heathered slope. The late summer days when they roamed the high Cuillins to gather their stock were the most joyful of the year for the clan, filled with the laughter and relief of men glimpsing the reward of their long summer's labor. He eagerly anticipated reaching the camp, and could already smell the sweet bannocks cooking and hear the high-pitched sputter of old men cleaning their pipes. The revelry would last far into the night.

"Duncan boy," called his older cousin Angus, who was extending his staff toward the little flat below, where at least two dozen Highland cattle huddled. "Lowest count does the other's chores tonight."

Duncan grinned and slipped off the cow. Angus beat him to the flat, and vaulted on top of the outermost of the long cows, standing with arms spread wide before leaping onto the next broad back, then the next. "Five, six, seven," he shouted, leaping on twelve shaggy backs before landing in the heather on the far side as the last, a young bull, bellowed his disapproval.

Duncan stood up on his mount, waiting until she reached the small herd, then launched himself onto the next cow. Three, four, five, six, seven—

"Duncan Alexander Lawson McCallum!" came the furious call. Angus had tricked him, gone first because he had spotted Duncan's mother coming up the trail. He lost his footing at the angry shout, slipped, rolled across the back of the bull, and as the animal gave a surprised snort, swung out on one of the creature's long horns to land on his feet two short steps from his mother, who stood arms akimbo, a storm brewing on her face.

"I gave consent to this adventure so ye'd learn the skills of the drover, not to invent new ways to break your bones!" she fumed, then glared at Angus, supposedly his guardian on the drive.

"He's a quick learner, Auntie m'am, sure enough," his cousin stammered. "But most of the time he's looking out over the sea, asking if every other sail might be grandfather's."

His mother pushed a strand of brunette hair from her face and frowned toward the blue waters beyond the hills. "Ye both are going to fetch a sack of neeps from the village below," she declared. Angus was crestfallen over another two-mile walk. As he shoved Duncan down the trail their mother called out once more. "And you, wee Duncan. Next summer y'er bound to me father on his ketch. That'll be the end of y'er love of water."

DUNCAN AWOKE WITH A START, HIS HAND ON HIS KNIFE. SOMEONE was watching him. He sat up and turned to face Analie, perched on a low limb twenty feet away.

"And how long have you been roosting like a bird?" he growled good-naturedly.

"Long enough to hear you speaking in that dreadful Scottish tongue, sounding like a crow with his tail in a grinder. You were smiling. I didn't know you knew how to smile." She extended a piece of paper on her open palm and with a whimsical shrug let the wind carry it toward him.

Duncan shot up and grabbed the paper just before it disappeared over the ledge. Seven names were written in crude block letters. He eyed the girl then read them out loud. "Ronald Buchanan, Albert Sinclair, Adam McIndoe, Henry Innes, Jonah Barlow, Mathias Carpenter, and Erskine Burns."

Analie swung down on the limb but did not let go. "There was a nice lady knitting on a rock below the barn," she reported as she dangled in the air. "I asked why she was there and she said she was waiting for her husband. She held up what she knitted and I saw it was a tiny blue cap." The girl dropped to the ground. "She said she didn't want Erskine Burns to hear from someone else that he was to be a father. I asked how long had he been away. She said nigh ten weeks."

He saw now the little numeral ten penciled under Burns's name, and that the others all had numbers as well. Six weeks, ten weeks, six weeks, ten weeks.

"Henry Innes was the last to go. His *mere* is *tres* cross *avec Monsieur* Ross—says the boy was too young for such treacherous work. And *Albert Sinclair*"—she gave the name a French intonation—"has half an ear missing, lost to a damned Shawnee!"

He glared at her reprovingly.

"A cursed Shawnee?" she tried, then took his hand and led him toward the barnyard.

He paused when he reached the door to the farmhouse, list in hand. The sun was setting and torches were being lit. The soldiers, out of their uniforms again, were bunched by the well, looking more like prisoners now. Several of the local Scots were passing around a crock of ale.

"One of the soldiers called out that Campbells weren't born, they just fell out of a horse's bahooky," Analie reported. "What does that mean?"

"I suspect a mademoiselle of the world such as yourself needs no translation," Duncan answered as he studied the assembly. There was a new tension in the air.

"And the man shouted back that his people used to scrape McDonalds off the bottom of their boots."

It was as Smith had feared. Duncan saw that McQueen and the sergeant were moving among the men, trying to distract them, raising tankards with them, slapping some on the back. But nerves were frayed all around and many were aching for a fight.

"Get your kit ready, girl," Duncan said. "Put my rifle and pack in the shadows at the end of the barn. Then see if you can wake Tanaqua." She nodded and he stepped inside.

Young Clare lay asleep at the hearth with two cats curled against her. Two women glanced up as they played cards at the kitchen table. The sparsely furnished sitting room was empty, but voices came from a room beyond. He paused at the door, slightly ajar, long enough to confirm who was inside then pushed it open. James Smith, Murdo Ross, and his wife looked up from a small table stacked with books and papers.

"I am searching for nineteen missing men," he announced. "Seven of them are Pennsylvania runners." He read Analie's list of names. "I didn't expect them all to be from the Conococheague."

"Not all from here but all out of this station," Smith acknowledged. "All fleet of foot and trained to the forest. All eight took an oath to serve the committees." He glanced uneasily at the Rosses. "Young Jess administered the oath, hands on the Bible."

"In the name of the king, Wilkes, and Almighty God," Margaret Ross confirmed in a whisper.

Smith nodded. "'In the name of the king, Wilkes, and Almighty God I pledge to serve the committees of liberty and keep their secrets,' Jessica had them recite, then some words about being a band of brothers that Captain Woolford gave her."

"Men of the frontier are giving oaths to serve men in distant towns they have never met?" Duncan asked. He noticed a plank leaning off the mantle, bearing words in black paint. *If Liberty is taken from men without their consent, they are enslaved*, it said, then *James Otis.*

Smith nodded solemnly. "I suggested the oath should just be to Wilkes and Liberty."

Duncan, still struggling to understand, looked down at the list of names. "This shows seven. You said eight."

"Your seven plus Atticus," Murdo put in. "I told you about the Africans. Atticus had started working a parcel of land I gave him up the valley, to earn the cash to free his wife and child. But when he heard of the missing runners he left, acting as if he knew where they were. He said a warrior does not turn his back on danger, then galloped off for Townsend's Store to speak with the one-armed stationmaster. That was ten days ago."

"At first we thought them arrested by the army," put in Margaret Ross. "But the sergeant says nae. We fear the worse now that you bring word of killings."

"Woolford said nineteen men had to be saved," Duncan said. "Twelve are from the north. The others are yours. It must mean they are still alive. But how could they all be captured together?"

"Not together," Smith corrected. "As I said, each man has a section of the route, whether trail, river, or road. Between Shamokin and the Blue Ridge we are their station. There are stages and meeting points. If you start in one direction and know the right symbols you can roll them all up in sequence. Which is what must have happened. Three men on the northern route ten weeks ago, then four men going south six weeks ago."

Duncan gave voice to a question that had long nagged him. "Why? Why along the frontier? The committees are in the cities. The cities are all on the coasts, with harbors of their own. Why not communicate by ship?"

"Woolford said it had to be," Murdo said, "because the other route was compromised." He looked uneasily at his wife. "Best check the girls, Peg," he suggested.

His wife stared at his knuckles, oozing blood again. "I best stay right here, Murdo Ross. I'd say it's time I knew as much as our own dear Jess. Someone has to fill her shoes now."

Murdo sighed heavily and looked to Smith, who scratched at his unshaven whiskers, studying Duncan for a long moment before extracting a map of the colonies from under a pile of papers. As if to confirm Duncan's words he pointed to Boston. "James Otis and Samuel Adams," he observed, then indicated Newport, New York, Philadelphia, Baltimore, and Williamsburg. Each was marked with a small red cross. "They used the sea for months with ne'er a problem," he explained. "There's merchants among the committeemen, so it seemed natural to use their boats. Small trading craft would raise no suspicions. But the letters stopped coming. Reports came in of a royal navy brig stopping boats on the lanes from Philadelphia to Boston. There were witnesses from a fishing scow sitting at the edge of a fog bank off Block Island. One of the committee boats, a fast sloop out of Boston, had been stopped by cannon fire. The crew were lashed to the mast and a keg of powder used to blow open her hull. The men screamed for mercy and the man in charge on the brig could be heard laughing. A second boat left Rhode Island and disappeared, no trace ever found, though the weather had been fair all along the coast."

"The navy? Surely that is not possible. The navy doesn't attack British vessels."

"It does when they can call them smugglers or pirates. Dr. Franklin sent news from London, at great peril to his person. A secret office has been established in the Admiralty. The Kraken Club they call it. They justify themselves by saying their goal is to avoid embarrassment to the crown by taking very private actions in America. A lesson learned from the last war with the French, who were able to secretly interfere with so many of our plans. A small investment now to avoid costly wars in the future, they tell the few ministers who hear of their efforts."

"But the king would never approve of using the navy to commit cold-blooded murder."

"Dr. Franklin and his friends are convinced the king does not know."

"Surely a group of seagoing zealots have no hand in the frontier," Duncan argued. "The killers at Edentown and Shamokin were not of the British navy, I assure you. They are wrapped up in the theft of a sacred mask from Onondaga, or at least trying to make it seem so." He saw the confusion his declaration caused, and explained the disappearance of the Blooddancer and the grim evidence it had left on the path from Edentown.

"You would have us believe that what is happening is part of some intrigue among the tribes?" Smith rejoined. "Surely you are aware that the western tribes were very bitter over the Iroquois not siding with them in their recent rebellion. With the Iroquois at their side they could have driven the colonists into the sea. I am sorry, but your friend Tanaqua has his own battle to fight. Peg has given him supplies and asked that he leave at dawn. We cannot be drawn into a fight among the tribes. We must not let it distract us, McCallum."

Tentacles. Suddenly Duncan remembered Woolford's words. *They have their tentacles around the bard.* The mythical kraken had tentacles. "Woolford discovered treachery at Johnson Hall, something about these Kraken breaking the secrets of the committees I fear. He was racing south when he was ambushed." He looked up, suddenly remembering the note from Rush's cap. "A man named Patrick Henry must be warned."

"Henry? He's a committeeman in Williamsburg. Why?"

"There was an urgent note from Philadelphia. A warning I think. It had four names on it. Red Jacob was murdered. Patrick Woolford left for dead. Peter Rohrbach, murdered. The last name was Patrick Henry. The Krakens fear him for some reason."

"How could someone in Philadelphia know that?" Ross asked.

"I don't know. There was a second message taken by those who killed Ralston, one of the messengers from Philadelphia. Perhaps that would have explained it."

Murdo and Smith exchanged a worried glance.

"The channels to the south are cut off," Ross said.

"But some messages get through," Duncan suggested. "The runners have their secret ways." He followed Smith's gaze to the papers in the center of the table, and lifted one that lay on top of an open book.

"There are secrets within secrets," Smith acknowledged. "It was the way the network was set up, so one weak link would not destroy it all. The stations are given only what we need to know for our section of the route. Even then we get instructions sometimes that leave us at a loss. The key to our puzzle usually arrives with the next runner, passed from station to station—but not this time. No one knows why."

The words of the letter Duncan examined were garbled, nothing but incoherent groupings of letters.

"Usually it is instructions from Johnson Hall, or Philadelphia, or Boston, for the stations, about the route, about new runners, about new procedures even," Smith said. "But we are blind without the key." Smith pounded the table in frustration. "We cannot continue."

Duncan leaned over the book. "The works of Shakespeare? Why would you . . ." he began, then, his mind racing, he answered his own question. "Patrick Woolford designed the code."

Smith nodded. "He had attended a special academy outside London two years ago," he explained. "For battlefield intelligence, they called it. They taught secretive practices. He called this an alphabet shift. He said the way the army taught it was to use exactly the same book, the same edition at all times and all locations. They always used the Army List since every army commander has one. But he said the method he and William Johnson devised was better. Any edition will do. He left this one for us."

"An alphabet shift. You mean each letter of the alphabet just stands for another letter."

"The simplest of codes. If the first letter of the keyword is *D* then every *D* means *A*, *E* means *B*, *F* means *C*, and so on."

"But surely you can just try twenty-six versions to decode it."

"Not that simple. After every ten letters it shifts again, based on the next letter of the keyword. We are supposed to get a verse from a play. The first letter of the next line spoken by another player in the play after that verse becomes the base. And Woolford insisted on a calendar shift as an added precaution. Each month has a new verse, to be memorized by the runners working their way south and delivered to each stationmaster. I told Woolford it was too complicated for simple frontiersmen and he scoffed. He is a zealot when it comes to the bard."

"Let's talk of graves, of worms and epitaphs," Duncan recited. "Make dust our paper, and with rainy eyes write sorrow on the bosom of the earth."

Smith's brow rose. "Sir?"

"*Richard the Second* if I am not mistaken. For month four."

Murdo looked up with new interest, then frowned. "But we have just received a May letter in the girl's pouch from Johnson Hall."

"Then it is *King Lear*. Childe Rowland to the dark tower came. His word was still Fi, fo, and fum."

With boyish excitement Murdo pulled the book closer.

A quarter hour later they sat staring at the deciphered message. *Kraken in New York and Philadelphia*, it said. *Until Woolford cuts out the rot, no one south. Stay the course until the world's end.*

A shout from outside broke the silence. As they hurried out of the house, boisterous taunts were being flung across the barnyard. The soldiers had their own jug of ale now, and were passing it among them, swilling it down as if to catch up with their captors. As Smith called out for quiet, a farmer threw a stone at Sergeant McBain. The big man spun about and with a Gaelic curse charged toward the farmers, closely followed by his soldiers. Ross ran past Duncan to separate the men but the pot had already boiled over.

Duncan hastened to the side of the house, where he found Tanaqua sipping a mug of hot tea, squatting beside his replenished pack. "There will be trouble," he said to the Mohawk. "You have unfinished business at that cave. If some trace of the half king is to be found that must be where the trail lies. Would that I could help you there but my path goes south. Let me at least tend to your injuries before I leave."

"The only injury was to my pride, to be led into the camp bound like a slave." Tanaqua nodded toward the yard. "But you should look to the French lark before her feathers are pulled."

Duncan turned to see Analie in the center of the yard, standing as if paralyzed, as a man in front of her, one of the soldiers, was knocked flat by another leaping onto his back. Half the men in the yard were swinging their fists.

Duncan took a step toward the girl, then paused, and instead darted around the house. Once in the woodshed he fumbled in the dark for what he was looking for, then, outside again, he raised the pipes and, murmuring a Gaelic prayer, began filling the bag.

By the time he was ready, nearly every man was engaged in the brawl—kicking, pummeling, or wrestling on the ground. The women were at the door to the house, swatting with brooms at anyone who grew close, some calling out with curses that would have put the men to shame.

He began with a Highland lament, playing from the shadows. The men and women closest to him hesitated, then ceased all movement as they heard the notes, raising their heads high, eyes questing toward the heavens as if some Highland god were calling down. When the men wrestling on the far side of the yard did not react, the sergeant bellowed and they paused, then helped each other up as they too heard the pipes.

Duncan rounded the house and climbed onto the nearest bench as he began the doleful sounds of "The White Cockade," a Jacobite anthem. Those still wearing bonnets snatched them off. One of the soldiers began to sing in a rich baritone. The company acted as if enchanted. Mrs. Ross started to weep and soon half the assembly, men and women alike, were wiping at their eyes. Analie hugged Duncan's leg. Murdo Ross appeared at his side, wearing a sad smile, and nodded his approval.

He played until his throat was too dry and his fingers ached, then was given ale and asked to play some more. All enmity was gone. They were all Scots and the old music stirred something deep and common in their blood, a visceral bond that could never be put into words.

Mrs. Ross stood on a bench and her rich voice reached over the crowd, hushing it. "I ne'er could brook, I ne'er could brook," she sang. "A foreign loon to own and flatter. But I will sing a ranting song, that day our king comes o'er the water."

Duncan recognized the melody as "Lady Keith's Lament" and took it up with his pipes. Not a soul stirred as she continued:

I once had sons, but now ha'e nane
I bred them toiling sorely
And I wad bear them a' again
And lose them a' fer Charlie.

REQUESTS CAME FAST, AND HE RESPONDED TO EACH ONE. "ME Bonnie Highland Laddie," called McQueen, then "Charlie Is My Darling" came the call from one of the wives. His music grew faster and men and women began to dance.

McBain, only slightly slowed with ale, climbed the edge of the well and began "The Tears of Scotland" before Duncan could catch up. He switched to the sad lament and caps came off again:

Whilst the warm blood bedews my veins
And unimpaired remembrance reigns
Resentment of my country's fate
Within my filial breast shall beat.

A fiddle began playing in the silence that followed, and the dancing recommenced. He lost all track of time. The moon had arched over the darkened valley before the last man collapsed with exhaustion.

Sometime before dawn the dead African rode in.

ANALIE'S SCREAM ROUSED DUNCAN FROM THE MOST PEACEFUL sleep he had had in weeks. For a few hours he had been a Highlander again, with the joyous company of other Highlanders. But the Blooddancer had gone to great lengths to remind them they were on a trail of death.

The shirtless African had been tied to the saddle, his back braced with a narrow plank. He had been dead several hours. His eyes stared unseeing into the rising sun above cheeks that each held four long slash marks. He was heavily scarred, from the narrow, careful zigzag line that raised lighter flesh to adorn his jawbones to the hard, ugly ridges that were witness to repeated lashings. On his chest, where the dead flesh would never scar over, strips of skin had been peeled away to form the words YOUR TAX. Blood, from the torture, and from the wooden stake that had finally been driven into his throat, had soaked his britches and the saddle he sat on.

"The blood dripped onto the saddle, meaning he died after being tied to the horse," Duncan declared. "Why would the horse come here?" he asked Murdo.

"Because she's mine. She's come home from the horror. And he is one of ours too. Atticus. I told you about him. He was a freed slave but he went back down into slave country when he heard about the missing men. About the bravest thing I ever witnessed. Left ten days ago for Townsend's Store."

They began slicing away the ropes that bound the dead man when suddenly Tanaqua's hand clasped around Duncan's and pulled it away. He took a step back as the Mohawk touched the dead man's hand, which was stuffed in his pocket. A strand of old bone beads extended out of the callused hand. Tanaqua pulled out the hand to see what the dead man, in his dying, had chosen to grip.

The Mohawk unfolded the lifeless fingers, then abruptly began murmuring a prayer in the forest tongue. In the dead man's palm, tied fast by the strand of beads, was an intricately carved figure of a man, except that his head was that of a fish with eyes of red pebbles. In his death, Atticus was clutching the sign of the lost Iroquois half king.

CHAPTER NINE

They moved southward in grim silence. Duncan had known there was no point in arguing when Tanaqua had dropped his pack beside Duncan's as they prepared to leave Ross's farm. The Mohawk had meant to bury his friend but the mythical half king had reached out through the fog of time to speak to him. When Murdo Ross appeared leading three horses, his wife had gasped and run to his side.

"No Murdo! Dear God, not you too!" Margaret Ross had cried. She had pulled on his massive arms, then pounded on his chest, sobbing as he stood motionless. "Have we not lost enough already?" she pleaded.

"'Tis the monster who killed our girl, Peg," the big Scot declared when she finally tired and fell into his arms. His wife had finally nodded through her tears, then embraced him so tightly and for so long it seemed he would lose his breath.

"I'll stop any new messengers," Smith said as he shook hands with Duncan. He handed Duncan a half-burnt tax stamp, explaining it was used like the broken dice as a sign among runners. "I wish I could do more."

Duncan had forced a smile. "You can win the battle for Conococheague," he replied, then nodded to Analie, standing with the Ross children, and mounted.

They had not even reached the bottom of the mountain before the Acadian girl had come running behind them, carrying her own pack. Without a word Tanaqua had scooped her up to ride behind him.

They had pushed the horses hard the first day, cantering past settlers' wagons, sparing the mounts by leading them up the steeper hills,
and had dropped exhausted by their campfire that night.

In the small hours, with a sliver of a moon overhead, Duncan had
awakened to see that Tanaqua had replenished the fire. The Mohawk
sat with the bead necklace in his hand, with the little fish man propped
on a rock as if to keep watch.

"It is very old, the way of this strand," the Iroquois ranger said.

"You mean the bone beads."

"The white are bone, the purple are from oyster shell. But no, not
the beads, the message." He saw the uncertainty on Duncan's face.
"Yes, the way of the message. It was used between war parties long
ago. From the days before my mother's mother. It shows numbers and
places. First is the address, the destination of the message. "He pointed
to six purple beads strung together." It means Onondaga. Where the
six tribes of the League come together, the capital of the League. This
was meant for the Great Council."

Tanaqua pointed to the designs at the bottom, consisting of, first,
four figures connected at the legs by a line of white beads, followed by
a solitary purple bead surrounded by white beads. "The north star is
to their back," Tanaqua said, pointing at the solitary bead. "Captives
from the north it means."

"It was sent by an Iroquois," Duncan said, question in his voice,
and pointed to a line of solitary white beads surrounded by purple
beneath the four captives. "More than nineteen. Four Iroquois captives, and many more. It has to mean they are all together."

"From an Iroquois," came a voice from the other side of the fire,
"who knew the message system of the runners was no longer to be
trusted." Murdo was braced up on an elbow.

Tanaqua seemed not to hear, for he still puzzled over a final
design. Suddenly his eyes went round with surprise. He looked up at

Duncan then back at the belt. Duncan made out a tree with wavy lines below it, like water, and what looked like a bear on two legs roaring at it. "I have seen this only once before," the Mohawk said. "On one of the skin chronicles about my grandfather's grandfather's time. There were shaman who could drive away evil spirits by taking bear shape."

"You mean like an exorcist."

"The black robes called them such." Tanaqua ran his fingers over the intricately worked beads. "The beads ask for great spirit warriors to come." He looked up with a forlorn expression. "But all we have is the three of us." His gaze slowly turned to the little wooden carving of the fish man, propped against a log as if to watch over them. "But how could the half king know about the missing men?" the Mohawk asked.

Duncan's only reply was his own question. "How could a dead runner know about the half king?" The flickering of the flames gave movement to the wooden figure. "Surely you understand, Tanaqua, that the half king can no longer be alive. The stories about him are from long ago, decades before any of us were born."

Tanaqua shrugged. "The stories about him say he was a great war chief who became a shaman."

"You mean a priest," Murdo said.

"Your priests," Tanaqua replied, "they go among the people to speak the words and perform holy rites for assemblies of your faithful. Not this half king. He was a great warrior once, but as he grew older he saw that his path was to be the one who stays behind. The gods who live in the land can't move. He stayed alone with them to help them as their lands were . . . were changed."

"A monk then," Murdo suggested.

"A monk," Tanaqua said tentatively. "It is said he could speak with the animals of the forest. A monk of the forest spirits." He looked at Duncan with something like pleading in his eyes. He was, Duncan

knew, still having difficulty accepting that he and Duncan were following the same path, and even greater difficulty explaining himself
to Europeans. "A man like that could defy the rules of common men.
He could summon other spirits. He could—" his voice dropped to a
whisper, "summon the Blooddancer if he needed vengeance."

They had thought Analie, lying by Murdo, had been sleeping, but
now she shuddered and snugged herself up against the big Scot, who
wrapped an arm around her.

ON THE THIRD NIGHT THEY MADE THEIR CAMP BY AN ORCHARD
high above the road. Tanaqua had begun to talk openly about Duncan's
reputation as the Death Speaker, suggesting that the spirits must have
lent him such skills. As night descended Duncan sat opposite him at
the small crackling fire and tried to explain how he had been trained
to observe things in a scientific manner.

"Scientific?" the Mohawk asked.

"The study of the world around us. Breaking down the world into
all its parts and seeing how they relate to each other. Getting to the
essence of things."

"Essence," Tanaqua repeated, and contemplated Duncan's words.
"The essence of the bow lies in the stillness of the pull," he offered as
an example.

Duncan nodded. "At Edentown I melted the bullet fragments I
took from Woolford. I could see they were pure, not like the balls shot
in frontier guns."

"So the science means reducing things to their spirit."

When Duncan did not disagree, Tanaqua insisted he explain
what the Death Speaker learned about the killers at Edentown.
Duncan told him how he knew two guns had been used, how a timber hand ax, a European tool, had been used to remove Red Jacob's
arm, and how he had deciphered the map the Oneida had inked on

his body. He expressed his frustration over his lack of knowledge about what had happened at Johnson Hall to trigger the desperate run to Virginia.

"When I was young," Tanaqua said, "my grandmother told me there were invisible demons, old spirits who used to watch over what we humans do. That's what you need, Duncan, an invisible demon." The Mohawk stretched and laid back on his blanket.

As he tried to sleep, Duncan once more sought to piece together what he knew from Woolford's report of the strange night at Johnson Hall. An owl hooted from deep among the apple trees, its persistent call seeming to mock him. *Hoo hoo hoo.* He sat up. Duncan had an invisible demon.

He found the girl lying in the grass, gazing at the stars a few feet from where Murdo kept watch. "Analie," he started, "you said when you went to Johnson Hall that you sat and read books as the others talked."

"Sir William doesn't like his books taken from his house, or even into the kitchen. So he let me sit in that big room he calls his library."

"I want to hear it all, everything you recall from that visit. When I was young I played a game called Blink and Tell. You are taken to a room, or a stable, and have to study everything until you blink, then you are taken away and have to tell all that you saw."

"I like games!" the girl exclaimed.

"Excellent. Tell me everything."

"Some Cayuga boys were playing with hoops when we arrived," she began. "After an hour or so with them Red Jacob said I would need a bath if I played any longer so I went inside. We had dinner—"

Duncan interrupted. "Everything. Who was happy, who was sad. Who expressed pleasure at the arrival of Sir William's son and who didn't." Francis Johnson was of mixed blood, Duncan recalled from their one meeting years earlier, but did not call Sir William's wife

Molly Brant his mother. The baronet had shared the lodges of many
Iroquois women. "What did Francis say when he presented the letter
of Dr. Franklin from London?"

Analie squeezed her knees close to her chest and looked up at the
moon for several heartbeats. "Is it the Death Speaker I sit with?" she
asked, then raised a hand like giving a vow. "Everything. Mr. Francis
arrived as I was going into the house after playing hoops." Woolford,
Red Jacob, and the girl had watched the jubilant greetings from Sir
William on his return after nearly two years' absence. Francis had gone
to London to build trade connections and to represent Sir William's
interest as Superintendent of Indians. A fast rider from Albany had
come the night before with the news, so a festive meal had been planned,
including the company of three visiting chieftains. "He had a white
and purple disc on his watch fob, chased in silver, which the chieftains
greatly admired. They were the ones who raised their voices first."

"You mean there was an argument?"

"Mr. Francis was talking about the pursuit of Indian affairs in
London and mentioned that Lord Amherst convinced him that no
proposal for support of the tribes should be presented to Parliament
this year." The announcement would indeed have caused an eruption
at Johnson Hall. Amherst was reviled by the tribes and Johnson himself for having abandoned the Iroquois after their long and costly support of the British in the French war. "Oh, when I went with Miss
Molly to pay that dispatch rider, who had spent the day sleeping in the
stable, he said he felt guilty taking her money. She asked why and he
said Mr. Francis and his friends had been in Albany for a week and
should have been able to send a letter by regular post, but that was no
concern of his and he would take the four shillings all the same."

Duncan had no time to puzzle out her words, for Analie quickly
continued, explaining how Mr. Francis had then quieted his father by
giving him the letter from Dr. Franklin. "Sir William was overjoyed

at first, then very distressed over whatever news it sent. But then when Francis left the library Sir William acted very curiously. He laid the letter on his desk beside another he pulled from a drawer. He held his head in his hands a long time, whispering curses, then when Mr. Francis returned he quickly hid them both in his desk. Mr. Francis poured him a glass of a new currant liqueur he had brought back from England. Sir William drank and they went in to dinner."

"And then Sir William got sick?"

Analie nodded. "He drank the liqueur and got real sick."

THE NEXT AFTERNOON DUNCAN AND TANAQUA LAY ON A LEDGE looking down at the little crossroads settlement of Townsend's Store, on the eastern slope of the Blue Ridge mountains. They had ridden hard, following descriptions runners had previously given Murdo and Duncan's sketch of the map segments that had survived on Red Jacob's hand—the southernmost section. The stationmaster should be in the inn, which they decided was the largest of the buildings, with a long open-faced stable at its rear.

The rolling hills of the Virginia Piedmont country stretched before them to the eastern horizon. Duncan saw the discomfort on the Mohawk's face, then looked back at Analie and Ross. This wasn't simply a new land to all of them, it was a new world. In New York and Pennsylvania the farms and their little villages existed in pockets of cleared land surrounded by the wilderness. They had seen from their high perches that Virginia was different. Nearly the entire landscape stretching before them showed the hand of man.

"I am going in alone," Duncan declared to his friends as they reached the trees where they had tied the horses.

"What, and let you drink all the ale?" Ross protested.

"A solitary man won't raise as much suspicion. A warrior from the north will be out of place," he observed with a nod at Tanaqua. "And if any of the runners has broken and spilled secrets, one of the first would likely be about the big bull of a Scot who runs the next station to the north." He did not miss Ross's frown. "Analie needs your protection.

"Keep the papers safe," he said to the girl. "I have what I need in case I should have to win a confidence," he added, tapping his legging. "And you," he added, with a hand on her shoulder, "should sing our friends a song. They become morose." He had grown fearful for the girl as the miles stretched southward. She was unpredictable and seemed to think that by playing the innocent she could always ward off danger. She seemed to have forgotten that those they stalked had tried to kill her, but he had not.

Analie nodded, then threw her arms around him for a tight hug.

"I'll leave my rifle and pack," he said to Tanaqua. "If things go badly, just ride for Pennsylvania."

The buildings of the settlement were not of the stone and logs used in the north but of quartersawn planks and brick. The tavern was a squat, prosperous looking two-story yellow building with a wide brick chimney. In the stable yard behind it several horses were hitched to posts, and parked to one side was a wagon that had the look of a hearse, only taller, its body just a square black box.

Duncan tied his horse in the stable, then stood in the shadows to study the quiet settlement. They had found no sign of the killers on their rushed journey from Pennsylvania but he was certain they had to be close. The little crossroads was a station for runners, and here he hoped to at least find out what lay between the two rivers on Red Jacob's map. *Galilee*, had been Teague's terse reply when he had asked where the captives were. *Galilee in the sotweed country.*

He slipped from horse to horse, looking for signs of being ridden hard, then scouted the stable, even the hayloft. If the tavern truly was a station for the secret runners, there would be mounts for them nearby, and quarters for the runners to rest.

Slipping inside the side door of the tavern he found himself in a narrow corridor that connected the kitchen and the public room, where a dozen men sat at rough-hewn tables. In the corner nearest him, a stout, square-shouldered man with a black beard worked inside the half-walled cage where refreshments were kept. He leaned out and caught Duncan's eye. "Any empty table, friend," he said, then paused and gestured him closer. "We run a tidy place here. Glad to have your custom but keep your rough business outside."

"Business?"

"I know a bountyman when I see one, this being the route the runaways prefer when they bolt. If ye got a warrant of capture to be sworn, the magistrate comes in two days."

"Bolt to where?"

The innkeeper seemed confused, and examined Duncan more closely. "The tribes sometimes," he said tentatively. "Sometimes to the French along the Mississippi, who offer freedom and land to any escaped slave who settles there. There's plenty of settlers on the frontier who will take in an extra field hand without asking questions. But if a boy shows up here there'll be a fight to claim him." It had the sound of a warning. He nodded toward the other patrons. "Work is scarce and the bounties be rich."

With an ale in hand, Duncan sat and studied the ragged assortment of men at the other tables. The talk of slaves and bounties made him uneasy. He thought again of Tanaqua, hiding on the hill above. His Mohawk friend had been on the Warrior's Path as a youth, though his foray had been only a scouting party looking in the Shenandoah Valley for signs of Catawbas, ancient enemy of the Iroquois. Tanaqua had hesitated when they had first glimpsed the Shenandoah on their journey south. "This was all forest when I came before," the Mohawk had explained in a hollow voice. "The treaties that were signed at Lancaster said the Europeans would be allowed to use our Warrior's

Path but then they turned our forest path into a road and now—" he had gestured toward the landscape that rolled over the miles. In the mountains the route had been a rutted track capable of carrying small wagons and carts, still flanked by woodlands. Before them the Warrior Path had been transformed into a broad, hard-packed road winding across the countryside, sometimes extending for long spans without a tree near it. "Our trail is no longer the way a warrior can travel," he said. "The last war parties we sent never returned. It is said they were captured and put in irons to work for the Europeans."

Duncan now felt the same disorientation. This was the land where the runners had disappeared, unfamiliar terrain in every sense. Everything—the land, the murders, the mysterious half king and runaway god—was all still puzzles. He had come for justice, and to save nineteen men, but had glimpsed more mysteries than truths since leaving Edentown. He spied a dog-eared journal, the *Virginia Gazette*, on the adjacent table and retrieved it. On the front page was printed an excerpt from a speech to the Parliament in support of the new stamp tax by one of the Prime Minister's deputies. *"Will now these Americans, Children planted by our Care, nourished by our indulgence . . . and protected by our Armies, will they grudge to contribute a mite?"* the deputy had asked Parliament.

Below it the printer had marked *The Noble Reply of Colonel Isaac Barre, MP, page 4.* Duncan turned to the page and read, then reread, the explosive answer of Barre, hero of the last war, on the floor of the Commons:

> *"Planted by our Care! No! Your oppressions planted 'em in America. They fled from your Tyranny to their uncultivated and unhospitable Country—where they exposed themselves to almost all the hardships to which Human Nature is liable . . . and Yet, actuated by Principles of true English Lyberty they met all these hardships with pleasure, compared with those they suffered in*

their own Country, from the hands of those who should have been
their Friends.

"Nourished by your indulgence? They grew by your neglect of
'em as soon as you began to care about 'em. That Care was exer-
cised in sending persons to rule over 'em in one Department and
another, who were perhaps Deputies of Deputies to some member
of this house—sent to spy at their Lyberty, men whose behavior
on many occasions has caused the Blood of those Sons of Lyberty to
recoil within them."

IT WAS AN EXTRAORDINARY SPEECH. BARRE'S WORDS NOT ONLY
resonated deeply with him, he also vaguely sensed in them a binding,
a context for much of what he had learned in his quest. *The Blood of the*
Sons of Lyberty. Is that what was being spilled on the Warrior's Path?
He looked back at the name, then realized he had seen it before. He
extracted the slip of paper where he had recorded all the names he had
seen or heard while trying to piece together the mystery before him.
Colonel Barre from London had offered encouraging words, Rush had
reported to Peter Rohrbach.

He stared at the list of names and the *Gazette*. He had started
out suspecting he was caught up in some feud between warring tribal
clans, then it had become a game played by inept intellectuals from
Philadelphia, then intrigue among smugglers. Again and again he had
been wrong. It was a struggle about politics, but one that went far
beyond the wainscoted chambers of those in public office. The conspiracies not only spanned the Atlantic, they also spanned all levels of
society, from the grand Dr. Franklin to old matrons in Iroquois lodges.
He paged through the paper, discovering that many of the stories dealt
with the stamp tax. There had been public displays in half a dozen
Virginia counties against the new tax. In the corner of the last page of
the paper where the stamp should have been affixed a small rectangle
had been cut out. In the opposite corner a different rectangle of red-
inked paper had been fastened with a dobbet of wax, the size of the

government's tax stamp but bearing a skull and crossbones framed by the words *Witness to the False Tax.*

"We don't get many bounty men with such an interest in news from afar." The innkeeper was leaning over the counter, studying Duncan.

For an instant Duncan felt a pang of alarm for Tanaqua, hiding above the village, then he recalled he was in Virginia. Bounties were paid on a different race of men here. "I am no bounty man."

"Yet from the way you nosed around my stable I'd say you were stalking something." The bartender picked up a mug from a short tub of washwater and began drying it with a towel. "Curiosity be a dangerous disease in this province."

"I am a stranger to these parts—" Duncan began. The bearded man had wedged the mug between the counter and his belly to dry it. He had only one arm.

The innkeeper saw Duncan's startled reaction and paused, then watched as Duncan dropped his burnt stamp on the table. He shot out of his bar cage, covering the stamp with his towel. "Be not so reckless!" he whispered, then pushed the stamp back onto Duncan's lap as he made a show of wiping the table, before retrieving a tankard for himself.

"Now stack some coins on the table," the innkeeper whispered as he sat beside him. When Duncan stared at him in confusion, he leaned closer. "Slave catchers buy information on runaways. You want to be seen as a slave catcher. My village is a chokepoint on the route north, leading to the main pass over the mountains. It's why a stranger would speak with me."

"Can I trust you, Mr. Townsend?" Duncan asked.

"Trust no one!" the innkeeper warned. "Life is cheap on the slave routes. Mind y'er words and mind y'er back. Do y'er business and turn back north."

Duncan stared at the man, not certain how to take his blunt reply. "A former slave mounted on a bay mare was murdered on the wagon road in Pennsylvania, near Mercersburg. He was tortured, then tied to the saddle as a warning. The skin on his chest was peeled away to form the words *Your tax*. It was done while he was still alive."

Townsend's hand gripped the towel so tightly his knuckles whitened. Duncan did not miss the glance he cast toward the men eating at a table by the hearth on the far side of the room. "Atticus!" The name came out as a low groan. "As good and brave a man as ever there was. He could have gone into the hills, back to the north and freedom. I warned him that he might be choosing death, and he just said everybody dies and he would live the way of a truly free man before he died."

"Where do they go from here? Where is the next station? Is it a place called Galilee? Between two rivers."

The one-armed innkeeper winced. "A place better imagined as the Good Book intended."

"I'm sorry?"

Townsend seemed not to hear. "My boy and Atticus were friends, used to cut wood together up on the slopes after he won his freedom. When he showed up again I gave him provisions and got him back on that Pennsylvania horse, telling him to ride north and don't come back this time. But damned if the fool didn't turn that horse's head and ride south."

Duncan shuddered. The dead man had haunted him ever since leaving the Conococheague. "You were sending him to Ross's station you mean."

Townsend offered no reply.

"With what message?"

"A letter, though he knew not what it said."

"From you? In the Shakespeare code?"

"From Williamsburg. A plain text letter. From Mr. Patrick Henry."

"There was no letter on him."

"I told you. He rode the wrong way, into the teeth of the monster. Last I saw of him."

"But he carried something else, something for the Iroquois."

"Not likely, lad. What would an African from Virginia know about the Iroquois?"

Duncan saw the glance Townsend threw again toward the men at the hearth. "Why," he asked, "would Atticus not touch here when he rode back north? He was attacked only hours from the Conococheague station."

Townsend shook his head with a mournful expression. "My boy Joshua knows him," he reminded Duncan. Strangely, he gazed with expectation at Duncan. "He will want the news."

Duncan cocked his head. "Am I to meet your boy?"

Townsend said nothing, just took a long draught from his tankard as he watched half a dozen more men walk in. He wiped his beard with his towel and stood. "We're serving out fresh turkey stew. In an hour most of my patrons will be done and gone. Borrow the *Gazette* if you wish. Take a stroll in our gardens. Come back then and we will talk."

Duncan read the *Gazette* on a bench at the side of the building, then stuffed it inside his shirt and wandered into the kitchen garden, enclosed with a low picket fence along the south side of the tavern. Its well-tended beds spoke of a gardener of not just devotion but great knowledge, for it held not only the onions, lettuce, cabbage, peas, and beans he would have expected for the kitchen but also a rich selection of herbs and savories. He bent to examine the spring growth of thyme, borage, basil, fennel, and rosemary, sometimes crushing a leaf to catch its scent. Sarah was doing spring planting at Edentown and, with Conawago's help, had been nurturing her own medicinal herb garden. He paused at the small shed along whose roof beams drying herbs hung, and admired, on an interior shelf, the glass jars and decanters where someone was making infusions. Beyond the shed he found more beds of only medicinal herbs, some of which he had seen not since leaving Europe. Lovage, santolina, yarrow, lemon balm, nightshade, and hyssop.

"There's my pretty lass." The throaty words came from the other side of the high forsythia hedge at the end of the gardens. "Did ye miss me then?"

Duncan burst through the bushes and onto the path that led to the pastures. Not thirty feet away, Murdo and Analie were feeding handfuls of spring grass to two chestnut mares, as Tanaqua, sitting under a nearby chestnut tree, watched in amusement.

"What don't you understand about keeping out of sight?" Duncan demanded. "This is not a safe place to—"

"And did we not stay hidden?" Murdo interrupted. "Until my horse throws up his head and whinnies. And wasn't he just answered quick as a bee. I know this girl's voice. Would have been rude not to come down, seeing how they're mine, Duncan, used by the runners. She was foaled in the Conococheague." The big Scot lifted the mare's muzzle and kissed her. "My Jess's favorite. I've half a mind to give her head and let her run home."

Analie giggled as the compact mare she was feeding buried her muzzle against her neck. Murdo stroked her mane. "If ye ever need a mount, lass," he said to the French girl, "she's the one for ye. Fast as the wind and the best nose for direction I've ever did see. Joan of Arc, my Jess named her." He pointed to the small irregular white patch on her nose and Duncan saw that it bore a vague resemblance to a fleur-de-lis. Murdo checked himself, and Duncan saw how memory of his lost daughter momentarily twisted his features. "A sweet French lady for you, Analie," he said in a voice thick with emotion. "Dear little Joanie."

"Things inside are—" Duncan searched for a word, "unsettled. We found the station true enough. But the stationmaster is nervous. You need to stay out of sight until I come back out."

As Duncan returned to the tavern, Townsend motioned to the same table by the bar cage. Sitting there now was a man of stern countenance, a few years older than Duncan, whose thin face and spectacles gave him the air of a scholar. Townsend brought three tankards of spiced ale and pulled up a third chair. He surveyed the tavern, cleared out now but for two men sitting by the low fire in the hearth.

As Duncan took a long draught, the stranger pulled out a broken die and very deliberately laid it before him, raising an expectant eyebrow. From a waistcoat pocket, Duncan produced the burnt stamp given him by Smith. "Excellent," the man declared in a refined voice, the product, Duncan suspected, of one of the English colleges. "Your bona fides are established. Long life to Mr. Wilkes."

"Runners have gone missing," Duncan declared. "We think they are somewhere south of here."

The man leaned forward. "Distressing news. You have come to the right place. Tell me all."

Duncan felt a weight lifting off his shoulders as he confided the details of the murders and apparent abductions. The man produced a writing lead, making hurried notes, listening with a worried expression. Here at last was a man of Virginia, who would know what lay to the south. Townsend brought a second round of drinks, pushing a tankard toward Duncan, then shuddered as Duncan described the last of the murders, that of the freed African, Atticus.

"We must find this place Galilee," he said. "Between two rivers."

The stranger nodded with a thoughtful expression. "I can help with that," he offered. "But above all we must maintain the flow of correspondence. We cannot let our enemies disrupt our noble efforts. Do you have a letter for me then? There are gentleman in Williamsburg eagerly awaiting news."

Duncan hesitated. Why would the man speak so openly of matters entrusted only to code by the committees? "Are you a committeeman then?" he asked.

"Consider me the committee for northern Virginia, sir. I will have your letter." The man searched his pockets, setting a snuffbox and a folded letter on the table, then produced a scrap of paper and writing lead, which he pushed toward Duncan. "First your mark, prithee."

A cloud seemed to be forming in Duncan's head. His fatigue was overpowering him. "You have to show me . . ." he began.

The stranger grinned as Duncan reached out and opened the letter. Inside, drawn in a crude hand was a large square, with what may have been trees on two sides, wavy lines of water on another, and trees combined with water on the fourth. At the bottom was a row of what looked like little buildings. In one corner was a stain that could have been blood. Inside the square were runner marks. A stick deer. An eye, a rising sun, a crescent moon, a square with a cross in the center. A tomahawk. A fish. A little windmill. A flying bird.

His head began to spin, and he shook it to clear it. Townsend, his face clouded, was looking into his clasped hands, as if praying. The stranger watched Duncan in amusement. "I'll have the committeeman names, sir," he instructed.

Duncan felt as if he were speaking through a haze. "Wilkes and liberty," he replied.

The scholar sighed. "Oh dear. And I thought we were going to be such good friends." He turned to the innkeeper, whose face seemed to be losing its color. "Where do you keep the brandy, Townsend? Not the cow piss you sell to tinkers and traders." As he spoke a man leaned inside the entrance. "Two in the stable, sir," he reported. The bespectacled man beside Duncan made a peremptory gesture and the men at the hearth sprang up and followed the third man outside. When Townsend did not move, the smug scholar rose and stepped into the bar cage and reached for an onion-shaped bottle on a top shelf.

Duncan grabbed the letter and began moving toward the hearth. His feet were strangely heavy. His eyes seemed unable to focus. He swayed and caught himself on a table, then staggered toward the fire. An angry shout rose behind him and as the scholar ran toward him, Duncan fell to his knees and threw the paper into the flames. As he collapsed onto the hearthstone a shrill voice called out from upstairs. "Hobart! Tell that damned one-armed fool I want my tea!"

CHAPTER TEN

Duncan floated in his hammock on his grandfather's ketch, rocking with the waves, listening in the night to the groan of stays and lines, smelling the sour stench of bilge water. He gazed up at a solitary star, then decided he was too tired to rise so rolled over to sleep some more. And found his hand on a man's head.

He jerked upright, suddenly alert, his heart thumping. He was not in a boat, but in a box. The star was a nail hole in a top corner that dimly illuminated four black walls. The sounds he heard were of horse harnesses, the fetor that of unwashed men and urine. He recalled the black wagon he had seen behind the tavern. It had reminded him of a hearse and now to his horror he realized it had indeed been designed for human cargo. Townsend's Store was where escaped slaves were collected and sent back to their torment in the fields.

He made out the dim shapes of at least two others in the box, lying as if lifeless. A thunderclap of pain burst in his head with each effort at movement, and his shoulders and legs began throbbing. He had been beaten while unconscious. He pressed his hands against his head until the pain subsided, then reached out again, quickly identifying his companions in the slave wagon. Murdo Ross and Tanaqua acted as if they were in comas but seemed to be breathing steadily.

His belt knife and penknife were gone, but nothing else in his pockets and belt pouches seemed to have been touched by his captors.

With his fingers he probed for wounds on his friends and found none, then lightly touched the torn skin on his forehead, remembering how he had fallen onto the hearthstone. He fingered the stubble on his chin and looked up at the bright light seeping through the little hole. He had been unconscious for hours, through the night and into the middle of the next day. An acrid, metallic taste lay on his tongue, and he remembered the spiced ale and the fertile beds of herbs beside the inn. In the medicinal herb beds had been nightshade, the source of belladonna, the most powerful of sedatives. A heavy dose would kill a bull. A carefully administered dose could render a man comatose for many hours, even a day or more. The turncoat Townsend at least had been fastidious in his doses. He braced himself in a corner, cradling his head on his knees, and drifted into sleep again.

When he woke the light from the nail hole had faded into a smudge of grey. He stretched his legs.

"Are ye fit, McCallum?" Murdo asked.

"Fit enough."

"That bastard innkeeper brought out a loaf and a pitcher of ale for us in the stables. I thought you must have explained who we were and it was his way of extending hospitality to allies. We were fair parched and drank deep of his damn brew. Next thing I know we're in this stinking black box."

"Tanaqua?" Duncan called into the shadows.

"Our warrior friend still sleeps. Where are we bound?"

"Deeper into Virginia. Toward the river lands. I saw him, Murdo, spoke with him, though I knew not whom he was until they had already drugged me. Hobart, the man who who helped the killers from Edentown."

"The bastard Townsend played us for fools."

"Aye," Duncan said, but then recalled how the innkeeper had warned him, had even implored him to flee. "The girl?"

"Last I knew, sleeping in the loft of that stable with our gear. Alone and unaware of the danger."

The words brought a long silence. Duncan had decided that Ross had drifted into sleep when the Scot's voice reached out to him. "I was only fifteen when me and my four brothers left Ulster to return to the Highlands to fight for Prince Charlie. Killed my first Englishman at the battle of Prestonpans. At Culloden they ordered me to hold the horses and off they ran yelling the Stuart's name. But instead of fighting like men the English bastards filled the air with grapeshot from their cannons. My clan was at the front, cut down in the first discharge of the guns. So I wound up in the dungeon at Sterling Castle. Dark like this, with just the rags on my back against the cold. Rats picked at my toes when I tried to sleep. I learned to curl up my legs close and wait for 'em. Just reach out and hope you grabbed the tail so ye could dash 'em against the stone. The guards would piss in the porridge that was our only food so those rats kept me alive for months. They hanged every man until I was the last, and ready to die, but on the gallows the laird of the castle said I was but a bairn, that he grew weary of killing. They cast me out with a loaf of bread and some new trous to cover my nakedness. I went right back to Culloden to search for the bones of my brothers." The big man shifted, leaning his back against the wall beside Duncan. "I remember seeing brown McCallum plaid there, sticking out of the mud."

Neither spoke for a long time.

"Most survived the battle," Duncan finally whispered. "I was in Holland, sent to school where I would be safe and learn the modern ways, my father said. I didn't know anything until the schoolmaster pulled me out of class one day and handed me a journal from Edinburgh. He said I was excused to chapel. I didn't understand. I went outside and sat by the canal to read the paper. When I saw my father and brothers on the list of the hanged I stepped to the edge of the canal. I was going to leap in but the schoolmaster had followed me, and pulled me back inside, to the chapel. He said my duty now was to finish the education my father had wanted for me, to honor them by having a full and long life."

Silence descended once more. Duncan slept again. When he woke Tanaqua was whispering a low chant in his native tongue. Duncan recognized enough words to know it was one of the old prayers, the invocations to the old spirits that were being lost to the tribes as elders died. Fewer and fewer of their offspring showed an interest in learning the ancient words.

The road they traveled was smooth, worn from heavy use. Duncan heard cows mooing, horses whinny, and curses from the driver, impatient with the slow progress of his team. His stomach ached from hunger, his tongue raged from thirst. He leaned into a corner, bracing himself again in a despairing, fitful slumber.

Suddenly they stopped and the small hatch-like door flew open. It was the middle of the night. The man at the door tossed in half a loaf of bread, so hard it struck the floor like a stone, then a clay demijohn. Duncan and Tanaqua rushed to the opening, then fell back. Two men standing ten feet away aimed muskets at them. The man at the door gave a gloating grin and slammed it. A heavy locking bar thudded into place.

The bread shattered when Ross tried to break it, and they had to probe the soiled straw for the pieces. "The muskets," Murdo said as he chewed. "They had bayonets. Curious."

Duncan tried to visualize again what he had seen in the brief glimpse outside. Ross was right.

"Military," Tanaqua observed. "Only soldiers have bayonets."

Duncan explained to the Mohawk what he had learned from Smith about the navy secretly opposing the committees of correspondence.

"Marines would have bayonets," Ross said, "but there can't be marines in the middle of Virginia." Duncan heard him uncork the big jar then take a long swallow.

"Even the water tastes like piss," the big Scot grumbled.

Duncan extended his hand in the shadows, took the jug, and wet his fingers to sample the contents.

"It's drugged," he declared. "Probably the same belladonna they used on us at the inn."

"If they wanted us dead," Tanaqua observed, "we would never have made it out of that village alive. A man can die of thirst," he added, "but not from sleep." As the Mohawk took the jug from Duncan to drink, Murdo slumped against the wall, already drifting away. Tanaqua took a long swallow. "Rest now," he suggested, "for we are moving to where the Blooddancer wants us to be." He handed the jug to Duncan.

Nightmares gripped him in his stupor. Men tied to the masts of a sinking ship screamed for mercy. Sarah and Conawago stood at a fresh grave beside that of Jessica Ross, the stone marked *Patrick Woolford*. The dead and tortured Atticus kept riding toward him on his blood-stained horse, raising his hands to beckon Duncan. He woke with a start, his heart racing, his brow covered with sweat. Sarah's father had vowed such a tormented death for Duncan, though Atticus's fate would seem merciful compared to what Lord Ramsey would do to Duncan if they were ever to meet again. The aristocrat was in some far land, probably Jamaica or even England, but Duncan loathed him for the way his unnatural fear had wormed its way into his soul. When he drifted back to sleep the nightmares came again.

"Not the rope!" Duncan shouted as cold water on his face woke him. He had been having another nightmare of Scotland, this time of men in chains, including himself, being herded toward a gallows.

He spat the water from his mouth and wiped his eyes. He was in a pit, or rather a large square yard dug into the earth so that the level of the ground was chest high, with a fence of rough planks above. Three posts were sunk in the ground in the center of the yard, each with an iron ring near the top. A man was tied to one. Duncan wiped more muddy water from his eyes then leapt up as he saw it was Tanaqua. He managed two steps toward his friend before his feet were jerked out from under him. His ankles were bound by manacles, which were themselves chained to the nearest of the posts.

Behind him someone exploded into a wheezing laugh. He turned to see a thickset man with eyes like bright pebbles whose thin black hair was combed over a balding head. With one hand the man held his wide belly, with the other a leather-clad club as long as his arm, mounted with a stained pewter ball at the end. "What a sight!" he proclaimed in a surprisingly high-pitched voice. "You northern boys think you can just come down and have your way. But you are mine now, and your days of sassing and nosing into unwelcome places are over."

Four men emerged from the barn that formed one side of the enclosure, each carrying an appendage of Murdo Ross, who was obviously still groggy. With the speed of those habituated to their work they closed manacles around his ankles, hammering in the pins that clamped them tight, then pulled his arms out of his shirt, bound his wrists, tied a rope to the knot between his hands, and looped it through the iron ring of the center post. With a great heave two of them hauled him upright like a side of beef. His shirt fell away, exposing the chalky flesh of his broad back.

"I had the good fortune," the stout man loudly declared as he paced along the line of posts, "of being raised by an uncle who was a trainer of horses." He paused at a brazier and pushed an iron deeper into its hot coal fire. "Some overseers just release fresh stock to the fields without their ever having felt the kiss of the cat. But my uncle taught me that you always teach respect first." He reversed the club in his hand and untied a strap, releasing the cover to reveal long ribbons of leather. It was a flogging whip, fashioned after the cat-o'-nine-tails used on naval ships. Tanaqua instantly understood, and braced himself against his post as the tails snapped at his back.

"You red boys are just the damnedest thing," the man declared in his high-pitched voice as he struck Tanaqua a second time. "Ye never know when to go down. What you don't understand is I don't care if you stand or fall. I value the turd of my hound more than I value your life," he declared in a matter-of-fact tone, punctuated by another wheezing laugh, then slashed the leathers down onto the Mohawk's back again. The long welts were opening, oozing blood. The lashes glittered in the sunlight, and to his horror Duncan saw that rivets had been fastened into the tips, acting like little blades each time they struck.

With surprising, snakelike speed the man turned and cracked the lashes against Ross's back, leaving little threads of blood that quickly widened as the whip struck again and again. Murdo stirred with a moan and with a mighty strain of his muscles tried to pull out of his bindings.

"Good!" the stout man screeched as two of the men hauled Duncan to his post. "The more ye struggle the quicker ye learn." He spun again and tapped the pewter ball against Duncan's shoulder. "My name is Gabriel. Like the angel. Angel Gabriel of Galilee. Superintendent of overseers. We have only a few rules. Never disobey me. Never disrespect me. Breakfast at the dawn bell, promptly into the fields a quarter hour later, never stopping except when the bell signals a meal. No cursing in front of me or any visitor from the manor house," he said, gesturing to a large two-story brick and clapboard structure at the end of the long fields, nearly half a mile away. With an impatient gesture he summoned a man from the barn who led another man by a thick strap fastened around his neck. The man's clothes were little more than rags. He did not seem to be resisting but Duncan could tell by the tension on the strap that the prisoner was not letting the man at the other end set the pace. He was tall and walked erect despite his obvious exhaustion. His black hair was matted with filth, and Duncan wondered why the hair at his crown was longer, then suddenly realized it had once been a scalp lock. The man was an Iroquois, and his flash of recognition when he saw Tanaqua was so fleeting neither Gabriel nor his escort noticed. Duncan saw now that men were attentively watching from the upper windows of the barn, some of which seemed to have sheets of cloth on them like curtains. The building had been converted into quarters for the overseers.

"Try to escape or resist us," Gabriel continued, "and we brand an arm with an *S* for slave. Try again and we brand the other arm. Then the two cheeks. Try a fifth time and we will snip your stones." He made a cutting motion with his two fingers. "No longer a man!" he crowed. "If you survive that and are fool enough to try one last time, we will sell you to the sugar plantations in the Indies. Meaning we get paid by some fool for the right to bury you in the rot of some tropical hellhole."

The silent Iroquois's forearms bore the ugly scars of the branding iron, though the mark of the branding iron on both was blurred, meaning he must have struggled when it had been applied. The handlers seemed to have learned their lesson, for now three of them pinned him to the wall with pitchforks pressed into his abdomen and chest. One of the men handed Gabriel the red-hot iron.

"Hyanka!" Tanaqua shouted. Duncan realized he had heard the captive's name.

Duncan could smell the burning flesh as the iron was pressed against the Iroquois's cheek. Hyanka did not flinch, only kept his eyes fixed on a distant cloud.

Tanaqua turned away to hide his emotion. Gabriel mistook it for a sign of fear. "Good. Lesson understood." He tossed his whip to one of the overseers and pointed to Duncan. "A dozen, to get better acquainted."

Duncan tried to twist as the whip cracked but his bindings held him tight. The first five strikes seemed endurable, but then the whip ends dug into the flesh that had already been opened. He tried to think of Sarah, of Conawago, to banish the pit from his mind. But suddenly he knew only the shrieking pain of the lash.

THEY WERE SLAVES. AS THEY WERE SHOVED ONTO A DUSTY ROAD along the fields, Gabriel explained that the manacles would stay on for the first few days, then would be removed if they observed the rules. The superintendent mounted a big grey horse and rode behind them, laughing as the brutes who escorted them slapped rods of split cane on their raw backs to keep them at a half trot. They reached a long shed with narrow slits, a handsbreadth wide, for windows. The only entry was through a barred door in the center of the back wall, facing the fields, inside a yard defined by thick logs laid on the ground in a U against the building. In the center of the yard was a large oak tree. Along the back row of logs were two blood-stained punishment posts.

The superintendent hummed an old hymn as he dismounted and led them into their quarters. He was clearly enjoying himself.

Straw pallets covered in filthy sackcloth were strewn across the double-tiered platform along each wall. Sacks of personal belongings hung on pegs along the walls. The breeze that blew through the slitted windows stirred hanging sheets of tattered muslin that revealed, behind them, a bench with holes running along the far wall. "All the conveniences," Gabriel snickered as he pointed to the latrine.

On the walls, names and marks had been inscribed in charcoal, in many different hands. Betsy, Margaret, Rebecca, he read and also saw crude drawings of children, dogs, and horses. On one section the names of seven men had been recorded in block letters. He recognized the names of the missing Pennsylvania men. The last name, McIndoe, had a line through it. By the door were slash marks in groups of five. Twenty groups and three single lines. One hundred and three days.

"The field overseers carry clubs and whips," the superintendent explained with an amused expression. "But they also have lovely tin horns. One blast of the horn and my pharaohs fly down on the wind. Most have clubs and swords. Those riders are my elite guard. They are much less merciful than me," he declared with another of his hideous laughs. He continued as he led them back outside. "Some enjoy their own particular instruments. One has a net and trident. I saw him pierce a man at forty yards with that forked spear. Lord, what a mess. What the dogs didn't finish we gave to the pigs," he chuckled, then quickly sobered. "Leave this stable or work crew without permission, and you become fair game."

Duncan, his manacles clinking as he walked, paused at the top of the steps and stared at the landscape. The breeze carried the scent of brackish water. Across the wide, flat bottomland, just beyond the compound of the manor house, the masts of two small ships could be seen. The land before them was nothing but clear fields intersected with packed earth tracks, drainage ditches, and low hedgerows. Along the edge of the vast fields were long buildings not unlike their own sleeping shed, with the same slit openings for windows, and he realized they had all been built as drying sheds for tobacco. In the fields, teams of mules and horses pulled harrows. Where the teams had done their work, crews were shaping the soil in mounded rows. Farther down the rows, separate crews of Africans—men, women, and a few children—bent over the long rows planting seedlings.

"The best Oronoco on the river," Gabriel declared, then pointed to a cluster of three long sheds on the opposite side of the fields. "Our

Africans live there in the original sotweed sheds. If one of them catches an escapee, or tells of suspicious conduct by any of you, they get a pipe and a pouch of leaf. Some of those blackamoors do love a good pipe."

Murdo stumbled in his chains as he descended the stair. Gabriel swung his cat through the air as if he might deserve more punishment.

As Duncan stepped in front of his friend he felt blood trickling down his own back. "Why?" he demanded of the superintendent. "Why would you treat us so?"

"Treason tends to sour the milk of human kindness."

"There is no treason but that determined by a court of law," Duncan shot back.

Gabriel's mouth curled up in another sneer and he pointed to the groups of workers in the fields. "We got African slaves," he declared, then he indicated a smaller group working with the teams near the manor house. "We got a few indentured slaves. And then we got you. The slaves of the manure stables, our Judas slaves." He nodded over Duncan's shoulder.

A burly man, nearly as big as Murdo Ross and thicker in the shoulders, stood grinning at the three new slaves. His head was shaven. On his neck was a tattoo of a skull. Beside him was a younger man, barely out of his teens, watching them with an impatient expression. "Trent and young Winters are your field bosses," Gabriel explained, and nodded at the big man. "You don't want to get Trent angry. How do they say it—" he rubbed his chin. "Ah, yes! He'll grind your bones to make his bread. And don't even think about running," he reminded them, and pointed toward the big two-story barn at the base of the wooden hills, where they had been flogged.

"River on the north, the death swamp to the east, and the overseers living on the south side. We got twenty more, some almost as mean as Trent." With another wheezing laugh Gabriel turned back toward his horse, where an escort of two riders waited.

Trent raised what looked like a quarterstaff, capped with a heavy wooden knob, except that the opposite end had been split into a dozen foot-long slats, the splintered ends of which were designed to deliver stinging blows. He pointed his weapon toward a track that led into the long fields, then led them forward, the impassive Winters following a few steps behind.

They made a grim, silent procession, their passage accompanied by the metallic rattle of their chains. Crows flew over their heads, drawn by the scent of blood. Seagulls worked at the freshly turned soil. Duncan studied the masts of the ships. One had a stern mast rigged for a triangular schooner sail for sailing close into the wind, allowing greater maneuverability. The other was a square-masted brig, made for deep-water sailing, which meant they must not be far down a tributary of the Chesapeake. Red Jacob's map had pointed them toward the Potomac and the Rappahannock.

"Jesus, Mary, and Joseph," Murdo muttered.

"Silence fore and aft!" Trent growled.

Duncan followed Murdo's gaze toward a line of men, all on their knees, all eyes fixed on the ground before them. They did not look up as the newcomers were led down the silent row.

The men were wasting away. It was the only medical term that might describe them. Those with their shirts off showed ribs and long scars or more recent lash scabs on their shoulders. Their faces were gaunt, drained of strength. Some, apparently more recent arrivals, did not look as skeletal but wore the same blank, hopeless expression as the others. Hyanka, the fresh brand on his cheek, knelt at the end. Near him was a man with half an ear missing. Albert Sinclair of the Conococheague, Analie had reported, had half an ear taken by the Shawnee. Duncan kept count as he walked by them. Twenty-five. Another six had been captured with the nineteen from the north.

Trent motioned them to kneel at the end of the line, then went back to supervise a party of African women and boys who had arrived with a mule cart to distribute lunch.

"Six of the Pennsylvania men," Murdo whispered. "Burns, Sinclair, Buchanan, Innes, Carpenter, and Barlow. Don't see McIndoe."

"Hyanka and two more Iroquois rangers," Tanaqua said. "And one more of the forest," he added studying an older native who worked apart from the others.

"So this is what you call a rescue, McCallum?" Murdo chided, wincing as he walked.

"We know where they are now."

"And we be the only ones in chains."

They quieted as an adolescent boy approached, laying a slice of bread on each man's extended palm. Behind him came the slow-moving cart, with a large black kettle, from which a woman ladled a thin fish stew onto each slice. The men ate in silence, then the same woman and boy repeated their progression, this time offering a ladle of water from a cask on the cart. The boy's wide eyes locked on Duncan's, and Duncan saw a deep curiosity on his mahogany face. The woman, not looking up, gently slapped his shoulder and pushed him on.

After the meager meal they were marched to a stack of hoes and stubby, pointed sticks. Their job was to heap the freshly harrowed earth into mounded rows, into which evenly spaced holes were made by plunging one of the sticks into the soil. Behind, far down the massive field, African slaves were planting seedlings. Their little band, watched over like dangerous criminals, apparently had the lowest, meanest job on the plantation.

Trent hovered over them like a hungry predator. Anyone he caught speaking paid for it with a sharp rap from the knob at the end of his club. A man with thick red hair paused for a moment to look at Ross with a mournful expression, and quickly doubled over as

Trent slammed his staff into his belly. The men were afraid to show any acknowledgment of the newcomers. They labored without a break until nearly dusk, shadowed by the overseers.

"Here they come," Trent crowed in the late afternoon. "The mighty pharaohs." Duncan dared to look up, seeing four men on black horses trotting along the perimeter road, accompanied by a pack of hounds. The two men in the front wore dark cloths over their heads, bound by straps around their foreheads, giving them the look of ancient Egyptians. One of the riders in the rear held a long forked spear, resting in a boot affixed to his saddle. Trent lifted the horn that hung from his belt and pretended to blow on it. Gabriel and his pharaohs reigned over Galilee.

Duncan worked in numbed agony, the manacles chafing his ankles, his hands blistering around the rough handle of his hoe, the scabs on his back constantly breaking with his movement, then stinging from his sweat. Finally a bell rang from the manor house and the overseers herded the staggering, exhausted men back to their quarters, depositing them in the yard bounded by the logs. Several prisoners collapsed in the shade of the tree, while the others stood in line for a drink from a barrel set in a corner by the slave stable.

Whenever he could, Duncan stole glances at the overseers. The young overseer Winters sat on a log with a quarterstaff on his lap, watching the old native, a man with a gentle expression whose leathery, wrinkled face spoke of great age. Trent paced along the log perimeter, tapping his club in his palm with an expectant, hungry expression.

Tanaqua sat among the natives. Although the Iroquois now seemed excited to see him, none rose to greet him, as if still wary of betraying any acquaintance. Ross seemed confused over the same reaction among the Conococheague men, who reacted stiffly, frequently glancing at the overseers. Too many wore empty expressions, as if the misery had simply broken them.

No one spoke to Duncan as he stood in line, first for a drink of the tepid water, then for the wooden bowl of porridge and hard bread that served as their evening meal. He ate alone, and watched with interest as the young overseer, whose gaze had turned to the manor house, finally rose and walked among the men, then silently sat beside the old native. The man's long hair, streaked with grey, was tied at the back with a braided leather strap. Along one jaw were tattoos of fish and flying cranes that came alive as he chewed. He had wisdom in his eyes, and much sorrow. Duncan found himself drawn to the incongruous pair, and after taking another drink settled down a few feet away from them.

The old man noticed Duncan wince as the shifting manacles pinched his flesh. "Inside by the water butt there's a tub of axle grease," he said in a dry, gravelly voice, nodding at Duncan's feet where the irons were rubbing his skin raw. "I always find it eases the chafing." His voice was soft. His face was like old wood. Duncan nodded his thanks. "I have lived among the Iroquois," he ventured, "but I do not know the southern tribes."

The old man's smile seemed to express gratitude. "The rivers were once home to many tribes," he said. "There is a Nanticoke who works with the blacksmith, and some Conoys supply fish to the kitchen." With a look of great pride he tapped his own chest. "I am Jahoska of the Susquehannock."

Duncan, surprised, nodded his head deferentially. "I have heard tales of the mighty Susquehannocks. They were lords of the great river," he said, referring to the massive waterway that bore their name. Though they had been defeated and nearly exterminated in the prior century, he knew from tales around Iroquois hearths that the tribes had fielded the fiercest warriors the Iroquois had ever met. The tales all spoke of how the greatest of them fashioned helmets of bear skulls, with the lower fangs extending below their own jaws. When

Conawago had first related such a tale Duncan had remarked that it seemed they fought like the beserkers of Viking legend.

"Lords of the great Susquehanna and all the lands it touched. Now we have but a little slice of the Rappahannock," the elder added, then shrugged. "To everything there is a season." He spoke the words of Ecclesiastes with a meaningful glance at the young overseer beside him, who looked away as if somehow shamed.

The company began moving, stepping into the long stable as Trent hovered by the door, cursing at those who stumbled on the short step into the doorway. "The sun is down, old man," Winters growled to Jahoska, lifting his club. "Do I have to lift your skin to get you inside?" His words were harsh but his tone was of soft chiding, and the Susquehannock just smiled, stretched, and rose for the door.

The Judas slaves warily filed into the stable, most collapsing onto the long sleeping platforms as the young overseer counted heads, the surly Trent lingering impatiently at the entry. A moment after the door was shut Duncan heard the thud of a heavy bar locking it for the night.

The sound transformed the company. Instantly the Iroquois were on their feet, surrounding Tanaqua and firing excited questions at him in their native tongue. The Conococheague men gathered around Murdo Ross, some pummeling his shoulders and others embracing him in greeting with welcoming words in Gaelic. Ross quickly introduced Duncan to those around him—Burns, Buchanan, Innes, Carpenter, Barlow, and Sinclair, all names from Analie's list. Six names. One was missing. The remaining men, gathered at the far end of the building, stayed away. Duncan warily approached them.

They offered none of the warmth the Iroquois and Pennsylvania men were showing, just returned his look of cool appraisal. "My name is Duncan McCallum. I come from Edentown," he offered. "Edentown station." They gave no reply, only stared with unwelcoming expressions.

He saw now they stood in two groups, the smaller of which, only five men, all wore tattered green bands around their sleeves. He recited the first of the names of the missing rangers. "Corporal Larkin." A gaunt man with a salt-and-pepper beard looked up in surprise. "Robson, Hughes, Frazier," he continued. "I came to help. You are in grave danger."

Larkin offered a bitter grin. "Ye mean 'cause we might become slaves?"

"I mean because you might become dead."

The man gave a sour frown, as if Duncan's presence offended him. "Up the hill at the end of the fields is the slave graveyard. We already died, lad, when they threw us in that damned black wagon. This be our hell. Ain't we laid poor McIndoe to his rest there this past month?" McIndoe. It was the seventh name on the list of Pennsylvania runners. "Death is the relief from our hell." Larkin saw the uneasy way Duncan eyed the men with the green bands. "Virginia rangers," he explained, with a gesture toward a compact, tight-faced man wearing one of the bands who was approaching. "Sergeant Morris, he's the—"

Morris interrupted, fixing Duncan with a hard stare. "How comes a stranger by the names of the company?"

Duncan did not understand the suspicion in the man's voice. "I came down the runner's path. The remaining runners are being murdered. You're marked for death. Word will come and everyone here will die."

"Damn y'er eyes!" Before Duncan could react, Morris moved with lightning speed, shouldering Larkin aside and slamming his fist into Duncan's belly. "We know the bastards' tricks! If they can't beat it out of us they try to scare it out of us!" As Duncan staggered, two others seized his arms to hold him for his assailant. The furious sergeant had landed a third blow before Duncan was able to summon his strength, bracing against the men who held him and landing a kick on Morris's belly that sent him reeling backward.

"Woolford!" Duncan shouted as he violently twisted, throwing the men who held him off-balance enough so that he could kick one in the knee, sending him to the floor, then throwing the second man onto him. "Woolford sent me!"

"Death to spies!" a man standing on the sleeping platform shouted and leapt, locking his hands around Duncan's throat as he landed.

CHAPTER ELEVEN

Fists pounded his ribs and spine. Duncan struggled to pull away from the grasp of his captors but the blows kept coming, and he slowly sank, bending over in a futile effort to protect himself. Then one of the Virginians groaned and staggered backward. One assailant after another was jerked away and Duncan found himself lying in a ring formed by Tanaqua and his Iroquois companions. As the Virginians retreated, the youngest of the natives knelt and studied Duncan, then called for a candle and pulled down the shoulder of Duncan's torn shirt. He held the flame close and murmured a syllable of wonder as he saw the tattoo.

The Iroquois, including the battered Hyanka, bent over him, staring in surprise at the sign of the dawnchaser. The young native motioned to his chest. "Ononyot of the Oneida," he said in introduction, then pulled Duncan to his feet and helped him onto the sleeping platform. His back screamed where the lash marks had reopened and were bleeding again. His arms and shoulders throbbed where fists had pounded him. With painful effort he extracted the little metal disc inscribed with a tree and held it out for the rangers to see. "I ran the woods with Woolford in the war. I was with Johnson when Montreal fell."

A grunt of surprise came from the shadows and a man in his thirties with a dark powder scar on his cheek pushed forward. "And with Murray when the Highland troops gathered for mutiny!" he exclaimed, stepping closer to grab Duncan's hand, shaking it hard. "By Christ, it *is* you! I'll ne'er forget that night you swam the St. Lawrence. You be the one who cut the cables on the gunships that were aimed at us." He turned to his companions. "Hughes," he said to a brown-haired man with a bent nose, "McCallum saved us that night!" He gestured to Larkin. "Corporal, you know that damned scheming General Amherst would have fed us all to the crows if McCallum had not been there." He kept pumping Duncan's arm as he spoke, then introduced himself as Ian Frazier before stepping between Duncan and his assailants.

His companions did not seem convinced. Frazier leaned closer to the man who had first attacked Duncan, who glared at Frazier. "If Woolford says this man will help, Sergeant Morris, then I'd listen to him."

"Help?" Morris snarled. "He's the one wearing chains. Look at him, he can barely stand up."

With painful effort Duncan rose off the platform. "Why would you expect a spy?" he asked Frazier.

Morris pushed Frazier aside. "Because someone broke the system," the sergeant snapped. "Someone stole our secrets or we wouldn't be here. Because there's more they want to know and don't they try to beat it out of one of us most every day in that damned smokehouse of theirs. Goddamned spider will keep changing its web 'til it catches fresh meat, eh? Just when they realize the runners stand together and won't be broke, you show up."

"But you've already been captured," Duncan pressed. "What more do they need to know?" As the words left his tongue he recognized the trap he had laid for himself. Pushing to understand the secret would be exactly what a spy would do.

Frazier opened his mouth but said nothing, cut off by an angry glare from Morris, but then turned his back to Morris and bent over Duncan. "One of us gets dragged away most mornings," he explained in a low voice, "left in the root cellar by the great house, until they shove him into the smokehouse for interrogation."

"Asking about what?"

Morris grabbed Frazier's arm and roughly pulled him away.

Murdo Ross stepped to Duncan's side, followed by his Pennsylvania men. "If you don't know McCallum ye do know me," he declared to the northern runners. "Who among you hasn't taken my hospitality at the Conococheague station? Someone has infiltrated the committees. Someone is using the committees, someone urgently trying to stop communication among the colonies."

Duncan picked up the explanation. "Woolford said your lives will be forfeit."

Each of the northern rangers had been trained to stalk and kill. Except for Frazier, they still stared at him as if he were their prey. Duncan saw the old Susquehannock, Jahoska, in the shadows, listening intently.

"We're ain't frail children to quake at some stranger's words," Morris growled. "There would have to be trials, and judges."

"Last month near Edentown," Duncan continued, fixing the sergeant with a level gaze, "Captain Woolford and an Oneida ranger named Red Jacob were ambushed. Red Jacob died of a bullet in his back." Ononyot, standing near Tanaqua, whispered something and touched the spirit pouch hanging from his neck. Hyanka pounded his fist against the sleeping platform and called out something in his native tongue toward the heavens. "Woolford was wounded too severely to continue, to even explain himself to me. The next day a young Scottish woman, the daughter of Murdo Ross there"—he nodded toward the big Scot—"was killed by a shot from the forest."

"Jess!" Frazier gasped. "Not the bonnie Jessica Ross!"

Duncan answered with a solemn nod. "They tried to a kill a young French girl."

Larkin pressed forward. "Analie?" he asked. "Not our sweet Analie too!"

"Analie was traveling with Woolford and Red Jacob. They shot at her and missed. Then she followed me despite my objections. She and I continued, just behind the killers. We found a man from Philadelphia dead on the Susquehanna, son of a committeeman. Peter Rohrbach and his Delaware wife at the Shamokin station were murdered at their homestead. Then a freed slave on the road north of here. A path of killings leading here. None of them had trials. Which of you had a trial before being imprisoned here?"

"Where's the French girl?" Larkin pressed.

"We were drugged at Townsend's Store." As Duncan spoke the words the man turned toward the group who huddled further down the aisle. "We told her to flee north if anything happened."

"Drugged at Townsend's Store," Larkin repeated more loudly, staring accusingly at the young man at the front of the Virginians, a blond youth in his late teens.

"He's a good man," the youth protested.

I have a boy, the innkeeper had pled, as if asking for forgiveness. "Joshua Townsend?" Duncan asked.

The youth nodded, then stepped closer to Duncan as if for protection. His face bore fading bruises. "I thought I could be a runner. But they took me before I could carry my first message. They gave me one of my father's doses and threw me in that black coach."

"Who took you?"

"I had never seen them. But I spotted them last week patrolling the perimeter road. Some of those bullies Gabriel calls his pharaohs."

"Our misery started with spies," Morris said with growing impatience. "They ain't succeeding with interrogations so it's about time they tried something else. The killer himself would know everything you just told us."

Duncan tried to ignore the accusation, though he saw the suspicion on the faces that surrounded him. "There is a secret group in London," he explained. "The Kraken Club. They support Grenville in keeping America under London's thumb." Murdo Ross took up the explanation, acquainting the prisoners with how messengers had been intercepted and killed at sea by a naval ship, and how the Krakens were now following the network inland.

"You're daft," Larkin rejoined, and gestured to the men around him. "Boys, anyone notice a frigate cruising down the Wagon Road?"

"But we see the navy here every day," put in a slight, nervous man in his twenties who stood with the Virginia rangers.

It took a moment for Duncan to understand. "Some masts extending above the riverbank doesn't mean the navy. Surely there are merchant ships that call."

Sergeant Morris stepped in front of the young ranger. "Devon, git on with ye. Ye know nothing of such things."

But Devon would not be silenced. He shifted a step as if to avoid Morris's reach. "They stepped up patrols on the Chesapeake," he declared.

"How would you know?" Murdo asked.

"I grew up on the water. I'm the last of the water runners." Devon paused and glanced uneasily at Morris, as if he had said too much.

"Blue coats," came a gravelly voice. They turned to see that old Jahoska was close, and had been listening. "Blue," he said, running his hands along his torso. "But red here," he said, placing his hands, crossed diagonally, on his shoulders.

"Red lapels," Duncan said. "Marines. The Kraken Club started in the Admiralty. Where are the marines?" he asked the old native.

"On the ships standing guard," Jahoska replied. "And in their sleeping place. Sometimes mixing with the overseers. When they walk around the manor grounds they dress like schoolmasters."

"You mean they sleep off the ships?"

"Some do. In the big wheelhouse. Water for bread." As he spoke old Jaho extended a finger in the air and laughed, moving it as if drawing invisible figures. He seemed not to notice them anymore, and the company nervously parted to give him wide passage as he wandered down the aisle.

"Feathers for brains," Larkin muttered.

"What did he mean, the wheelhouse?" Duncan asked. No one was paying attention to the aged Susquehannock, except for Tanaqua, who watched intently as he settled onto the floor at the far end of the building, in the darkest shadows, where blankets had been fastened against the wall to form a small tentlike structure. The aged Indian blew into a bowl and coaxed a wisp of smoke from it. Duncan caught the faint scent of cedar and tobacco. He was invoking his spirits.

"Old Jaho's been here since long before any of us arrived," Larkin explained. "Crazy old bird. Sits for hours at night spouting that mumbo jumbo. Said once he had been here for all of time. Says that going into his little tent is taboo, that it would bring a curse on any European who tries." The northern ranger shrugged. "But when in his right senses he can explain the environs right well, even tells stories of days long past that have the ring of truth."

Duncan withdrew his writing lead and pointed to a blank space on the wall. "Show me what you know of Galilee."

Corporal Larkin drew quickly, after the fashion of one accustomed to making battle maps. He inscribed the curving bank of the river on the wall, showing a small bay formed by a long point of land and the bend of the river where the docks and manor house lay. "Sunday mornings they take us to the bay to wash away the stench," he explained. Around the point, over the ridge beyond the manor house, he drew a tributary stream with a cluster of buildings beside it.

"A mill," Duncan suggested. "He said water for bread. He meant where grain is crushed into flour." He glanced back at Jahoska. Tanaqua had taken a candle to him, and now both Tanaqua and Ononyot were seated beside him on the floor. In the brighter light Duncan saw leather braids pinned to the wall above the little blanket tent, holding feathers, bones, and bundles of fur.

"None of us have seen it, but aye," Larkin offered, "that was the sound of it. Most plantations have their own mill."

"A mill where His Majesty's marines sleep and conduct business," Duncan said. "Men with bayonets were guarding the wagon that brought us here. Is it marines who interrogate you?"

"No uniforms, but they wear sash belts sometimes," the Conocochéague man named Burns stated. "And take them off to strike us with them." Duncan remembered Analie's report. Erskine Burns's wife waited at the end of the lane to tell him he was going to be a father.

"They're just overseers, you fool!" Sergeant Morris insisted. "If they meant real harm we would know it. It's the way the overseers have of keeping us in line. The Navy has no business with the likes of us, they just need a rest station for the patrols. Like I keep saying, they need us until the crop comes in then it will be fare-thee-well and good riddance. Just keep y'er noses down, lads, and stay away from fearmongers," he said, then stepped in front of the runners, and glared at Duncan.

Duncan returned his stare for several breaths, then reached down to untie one of the buckskin leggings he still wore around his shins. The runners watched uncertainly as with his teeth he ripped apart the seam and extracted the paper hidden inside.

Frazier's eyes went wide as he saw it, then he took it from Duncan and stretched the paper for all to see.

"Mary Blessed Mother!" Larkin exclaimed. The prisoners who had already stretched out on the platform sat up. "A sheet of London's stamps, lads! One that McCallum got away from the goddamned lace caps!"

His words brought excitement to the weary faces.

"That many fewer tax payments for those bastards in Parliament!" Burns boasted.

"For the bastard the king," Morris spat.

Burns straightened, closing his fists. If Murdo Ross hadn't placed a restraining hand on his shoulder, Duncan suspected the man would have struck the Virginia sergeant. "The king is my country," Burns said instead. "Do not ask me to hate my king. Our grievances are with Parliament."

Frazier, still holding the sheet of stamps, gave an impatient grimace, as if he had heard such words before. "That would be the king who massacred the Jacobites and laid waste the Highlands."

"We're not all Scots here," Morris protested. "And ye weren't gathered up because y'er Scot."

"Exactly," Duncan said, taking the stamps from Frazier. "You are bound by something other than blood. Do you not see the bold stroke across the sheet?" He read the words inscribed across the stamps given to him in Conococheague. "Death to the tax! And signed by an Irish baronet! Sir William Johnson risked his freedom by signing that paper, then letting it be carried by strangers into the south."

His words did not have the effect he had hoped for. Some men were still frightened. Others shrugged in disinterest. "Don't know that northern prince," one of the Virginia rangers said as he spat tobacco juice onto the floor.

"Easy enough for Sir William lying in his comfortable castle in the north," Larkin said. "I don't see him being caned while working the sotweed from dawn to dusk." He looked down at the floor. "I told my wife and son I had to go, because I owed Captain Woolford. Told them I'd been gone for three weeks. That was four months ago. No one to do the planting."

As the men dispersed, taking up pallets along the long platforms, the blond youth lingered. Duncan suspected the bruise on his face had not been made by overseers. "You said a freed slave died," Joshua Townsend said.

Duncan recalled his conversation with the boy's father, and the older Townsend's grief over the news of Atticus's death. "I'm sorry. Your father said Atticus was your friend."

Young Townsend clenched his jaw, fighting a wave of emotion. "It wasn't his fight. He had won his fight and could have made a new life up in Pennsylvania. The fool slipped onto the fields last week and worked alongside the other Africans until I was in earshot. I could not believe it when he called out. I begged him to flee. He said he had come to see our faces, to make sure we still lived. I didn't understand."

"He was going to bring help from Pennsylvania."

"He said I mustn't think bad of my father, who was a good man being used by bad men."

"How long have you been here?" Duncan asked.

"Three months."

Duncan offered a grim nod. "They took you so they could force your father to help them."

Joshua returned his nod, then looked back toward the end of the stable. Old Jaho still sat before his little tent of blankets. He was reaching out to cup the fragrant smoke and rub it over his limbs.

"Atticus told me once that as a boy he had been the fastest runner in his village, that he had often been sent to deliver important messages to warrior chiefs on the field of battle. He said being a runner between chiefs in America meant his life had completed a circle of destiny." Joshua looked back at Duncan. "Did he suffer?"

Duncan tried to push back the image of Atticus's mutilated body. "He died a warrior's death" was all he said.

In the morning every inch of Duncan's body ached. He stumbled in his chains, collapsing onto one of the long logs in the yard as porridge was served out in the filthy wooden bowls used the night before. When he stumbled on the way to the work site Tanaqua and Ononyot were instantly at his side, lifting him by the shoulders. As they worked the field, the Iroquois prisoners stayed close to him, putting added effort into their hoes to make up for his weakness. Half the rangers and several of the Pennsylvania men still watched him with suspicion. At lunch some of Ross's friends spoke with him of Scotland, and after learning that the McCallum clan had been shipbuilders and island drovers, they warmed to him, offering tales of sailing among whales in the Hebrides and of shaggy cows tangling in washlines. With a nostalgic sigh Murdo explained how as a boy he had watched a great hairy bull plant himself on a pebble beach in a gale, and when he had appeared the next morning with his horns and body draped with kelp, his aunt had fled with a terrible shriek, insisting he was a waterhorse come to eat them.

More than once Duncan leaned on his hoe, trying to connect the strange company, and the events that had brought them to their misery. Their shared suffering seemed to have done little to unite them. The Virginian runners, who had fought in the last Indian war together, stayed to themselves, working and even sleeping near each other, as did the Pennsylvania men. Only the northern rangers and Iroquois mixed, because the Iroquois had run the woods as rangers themselves.

Nearly half the men, their backs scarred with lashes and several bearing brands on their forearms, joined the ranks of submissive slaves who mumbled "yessir" and dutifully bent when an overseer yelled, "sotweed," apparently the universal command for slaves to focus on the crop. Some, including all the natives, seemed unaffected by their servitude. Duncan did not miss the way each of the Indians in his own way paid homage to the spirits, frequently touching the totem pouches that hung around their necks, sometimes leaving little cairns of stones along the rows they worked, pausing to whisper toward the ospreys that sometimes drifted overhead. When an eagle flew low, Ononyot shouted to the creature in his native tongue, earning a blow from Trent's knob. The Oneida had been close enough for Duncan to hear. "Tell them on the other side," the young warrior had called out to the majestic bird then, ignoring Trent's second blow, "we are not ready to cross over!"

Most of the others, rangers and Scots, were angry and resentful, though when their epithets were heard by the overseers they paid with slaps of the split canes or Trent's knob against tender scars.

When they reached the end of a row old Jaho conferred briefly with Winters, then slipped away to the perimeter road to strip bark from willow branches at the edge of the swamp. Trent chastized Winters, even tapped the younger overseer on the shoulder with his staff, but, as if the Susquehannock were invisible, both overseers ignored Jaho when he returned and extended the bark for Duncan to chew. The old native opened his other hand, exposing a handful of a pasty solution that looked like swamp water mixed with a root that had been chewed. He ran his fingers over the bruises on Duncan's shoulder, which were now assuming blue-green arc shapes, then covered them with the paste.

The tribal remedies pushed down his pain, and as he grew more alert he began studying the fields and the manor house. The smaller of the ships was gone. There was a steady stream of workers, both African and European, to and from the small outbuildings scattered around the manor. A wagon pulled up and loaded new casks from what must have been a cooperage. The hammer of a forge rang out and he could see an ox in front of a low shed with a chimney, patiently standing as it was fitted with new hoof plates.

As the sun reached its zenith, men around him began watching the perimeter road, and soon a cart appeared with the kettles and kegs of the field lunches. The Africans were fed first, and as the mule cart finally progressed toward them, Winters left to meet it on the track. The young overseer, away from his duties, seemed more relaxed, even appearing to jest with the boy who led the mule, the same youth with the inquisitive eyes who had fed Duncan the day before.

By midafternoon he was feeling stronger, and even joined in an old Iroquois work chant used by the natives when tending maize fields. The Africans, never closer than a stone's throw away, also sang, more loudly, and their rhythmic songs, echoing of unknown lands, filled the emptiness of the long afternoon. On the doors of the sheds where they slept he saw strange symbols. They may have been invocations of gods, or perhaps, more likely, hex warnings against strangers entering the buildings. He found himself watching the Africans closely when his work permitted. Most, but not all, of the men were very tall and heavily muscled, and when their workpaths grew closer Duncan saw that many wore patterns of scars on their faces and necks that reminded him of the adornment often used by the woodland tribes. One of them, a heavily muscled man towering inches above Duncan's own six feet, paused to return Duncan's stare. He pressed his hand to his heart, then opened his palm outward in what Duncan took to be a greeting. When Duncan returned the gesture the big man grinned for an instant before feeling the sting of his overseer's cane.

Duncan sat with the natives as they ate their meager supper. Old Jaho acknowledged that he had worked on the plantation since its first days, and at Duncan's prodding he explained how it had started long ago as only a few cleared acres along the river, served by boats that came up from the bay once a month. With a faraway look he spoke of how before those times there had been a village of his people, a southern haven from the ravages of war and disease they had suffered in the prior century, a place made safe by the great maze of swampland that bordered it to the south where they could hide when European tempers flared. Although he did sometimes seem to drift away as if suffering some infirmity of the mind, when Jaho was cogent, the twinkle in his eye and the gentleness of his demeanor reminded Duncan so much of Conawago that a new ache rose in his heart. He looked toward the north. Conawago had begun speaking openly of the approaching day when, after decades of fruitlessly searching for his family from Nova Scotia to the Mississippi, he would finally greet them in the next life. In the past few months every time Duncan had parted company with the Nipmuc, more like family to him than anyone else alive, he had found himself praying he would see the old man on his return. He had always assumed when they were finally separated it would be by the old man's death but now, battered and enslaved, Duncan realized it could just as easily be by his own.

As the sun touched the horizon, young Winters, assisted by an older African wearing a leather apron, used a hammer and metal rod to at last pop the pins that bound their manacles, then motioned Duncan and his friends to the entry, where Trent sullenly counted off the company as they stepped back inside. Candle stubs were lit, and one of the tribesmen produced a pouch of black and white pebbles and crouched by a circle that had been inscribed on the floor, launching one of the Iroquois gambling games. Soon most of the natives and Pennsylvania Scots were watching or playing, using buttons, beads, and seedpods for their wagers.

Duncan rubbed grease around his chafed ankles then applied it to the strange arc-like bruises on his shoulders.

"He came back for you," came a low voice. Duncan looked up to see Devon, the young Virginian, staring at Duncan's bruises.

"I don't catch your meaning," Duncan said.

"The lieutenant. He has a special club with a saddle brass fixed at the end, with a little anchor set in it. We always know when he has used it at the smokehouse interrogations because it leaves the mark of the anchor. When he returns from his travels he always grabs a bottle of rum and takes one of the African girls to the mill but when he arrived with your wagon he went straight to retrieve his club."

Duncan twisted his head and saw now that the curving marks on his shoulder did indeed resemble an anchor.

"He hates all of us but he has a special hatred for you," Devon observed. "You must take care around him. What did you do to him?"

"You mean Hobart is a lieutenant?"

Devon nodded. "The men at the mill call him Mr. Hobart, though once I heard him called lieutenant, and the man earned a kick for it. Hobart was one of those in the smokehouse asking questions, but then disappeared weeks ago. Wanted to put needles under our fingernails but the doctor wouldn't let him."

"Doctor?"

"From the ship we think. Sometimes he is in the smokehouse, watching, but only when the brig is in. The *Ardent* she's called. He makes sure nothing is done to us that would impede our ability to work. It's why Morris says they are only looking for free labor. In the smokehouse they mostly use clubs wrapped with rags unless a brand has been earned but Hobart shows up for special cases. And my God, you were a special case yesterday. What did you do to raise such a rage?"

Duncan shuddered to hear how matter-of-factly Devon spoke of torture, then he paused and twisted toward Murdo as he remembered. "The letter! Hobart had left a letter on the table at the inn, gloating over it like it is a trophy. Something he had brought from the north. I was already drugged but I was able to throw it into the fire before I passed out. He was furious. It must be why they beat me after I lost consciousness. Beat me before they threw me into the wagon and after I arrived here."

"Did ye read anything of it?" Murdo asked. "See an address?"

"It bore no address. No words of any kind. A big square that was bounded by a river, forest, and a swamp."

"A map of Galilee you mean."

Duncan hesitated. "I didn't realize it then, but yes, it was a drawing of the tobacco fields here. Inside the square were runner marks, over a score. A stick-figure deer, a square divided into fourths," he began, "a beaver, an apple, a candle, a pine tree, a bell, a dog I think. Along the bottom were buildings. A house with two chimneys, a barn, what may have been a native lodge, and a church or schoolhouse."

Murdo scratched at the stubble on his face. "All the station marks are buildings. Johnson Hall has the two chimneys, the barn is mine, the lodge is Shamokin, and the schoolhouse is Edentown." Murdo surveyed the Judas slaves, several of whom had approached to listen, and indicated Burns. "The beaver," he explained, then pointed to half a dozen others in quick succession. "Pine tree, apple, bear, bell, candle, dog."

"There was blood on the letter, a few drops on the edge," Duncan recalled.

The words brought a grimace to Murdo's face. "Atticus couldn't write," the big Scot declared.

The realization stabbed Duncan like a blade. "When he left your farm you said he acted like he knew where the missing runners were."

"He was the only runner who had served in both Virginia and the north," Devon put in, and saw the confused looks on his companion's face. "Don't you see? He knew all the marks, or more than anyone else."

"Jesus wept!" Murdo muttered. "Atticus came here alone to confirm which runners had been enslaved, and made a list, in the only way he knew how."

"For the Krakens such a list would be a key, to unlock the system. Atticus gave them an unexpected treasure."

"And you destroyed it," Tanaqua observed.

"If they had made an extra copy they would not have beaten me so. No one else must have such a key."

"No one but Major Webb," Devon inserted.

They looked up in surprise at the young Virginian.

"Major?" Ross asked.

"Major of the militia in the Indian wars. He runs the last station before Williamsburg, in Louisa County. The letters go to him and he sees them to Williamsburg, where he sits in the House of Burgesses. He's the only stationmaster who sees all the marks that authenticate letters from the north. When the water route fell apart I went to see him."

Duncan chewed on the words for a few heartbeats. He had heard the name Webb before. Benjamin Rush had reported that a Virginian named Webb had attended a committee meeting in Philadelphia. "You knew the water route?"

"It took too many losses so the northerners laid out the land route. I was the only one who crossed over from water to the land routes. But the Major had me run up the Chesapeake one more time to tell Philadelphia all the messages over water had to stop. That was three months ago. Urgent, he called it, to go straight to the Franklin house."

"As if," Ross said, "the trouble had started in Virginia."

Devon agreed. "All the first Judas slaves were Virginians."

Duncan leaned toward Devon. "You were captured three months ago?"

"In Philadelphia. When I delivered my letter to the Franklin house the noble matron expressed concern that I could have been followed. She kept peeking out the window and finally sent a servant out the back to circle the block. He reported a big man with black curly hair watching from an alley. She showed me into a chamber that had been converted into a laboratory with wires and glass rods and rows of jars with metal slats sticking out of them. The electrical studio, she called it."

"You speak of Mrs. Franklin?" Duncan asked.

Devon nodded. "Deborah, she prefers to be called. An ample and jovial lady but not one to be crossed. She had me touch a silver wire that came out of a jar and I swear it sent lightning through my body, and put my hair standing on end. She laughed and had me help her rig a wire across the sill of an open window, powered by six such jars. Then she locked all the other doors and windows.

"He came in the middle of the night and yelped like a frightened goat when he touched that wire. When we saw him running away we figured he was done, and I went out to sleep in the stable. But before dawn he was back. He hit me on the head, knocking me out. The bastard kept a bag over my head until I was thrown into a boat on the Chesapeake. A big Irishman."

"Teague!" Tanaqua spat.

The name seemed to frighten Devon. "A devil incarnate. Wouldn't give me any food for all the days it took to bring me here, only water to drink."

Teague had lied, Duncan realized. He had known exactly where Galilee was.

"So the danger started in Virginia," Duncan said, "but no one in the north got the warning until that night at Johnson Hall. Red Jacob and Woolford weren't summoned urgently to Johnson Hall but they were dispatched urgently once they arrived. It all happened that night, Murdo, the night Francis Johnson arrived from London." Duncan recalled Analie's description of the events at Sir William's home. "His son had acted as though he had just rushed to the Hudson to return but in fact he had lingered with others at Albany for a week. Then he arrived at Johnson Hall, alone. I think it was that very night the Blooddancer mask was stolen in Onondaga."

"The others," Tanaqua said. "The ones who parted company with Francis Johnson in Albany went to Onondaga."

"But Sir William's alarm didn't arise from speaking with Francis," Duncan said, "it came from reading a letter from Benjamin Franklin. And then Johnson said the men of Galilee will die when the lie is written. But not until then." He turned back to Devon. "The Chesapeake station. Where is it?"

But Devon seemed not to hear. "It's all true," the young Virginian said in a hollow voice. "They killed Atticus and they will kill us."

Duncan asked the question again.

"Leave the boy alone, damn ye!" Sergeant Morris growled. "Ain't ye caused him enough grief?"

Devon's wan face took on a remote look. "It's planting time back in Culpepper. Not much tobacco there, mostly maize and wheat. I love the smell of the fields in the spring. I told Sally Mullin I'd take her to the midsummer fair." He sobered and his hand went to his neck. "I never really understood," he said, looking up at Duncan. "When the noose tightens, will I die from choking or from my neck breaking?" he asked.

CHAPTER TWELVE

Frightened cries woke Duncan before the dawn bell. Men were rolling out of their pallets, gathering at the far end of the sleeping platform. As Duncan sat up from his pallet, two men darted to the necessary bench and vomited down the holes. He pushed his way through the crowd, then wished he hadn't. Devon would not take his Sally to the fair. His lifeless eyes gazed up at the roof.

"Christ!" Sergeant Morris muttered. "I didn't know he was so frail. The cursed overseers are responsible for this. Worked him too damned hard." Duncan tried to push past the sergeant but Morris shouldered him aside. "I'm his sergeant, damned ye," he snapped, then called for Virginia rangers to rip open the pallet for a shroud.

"McCallum will have a look," Murdo Ross insisted.

Morris glared at the big Scot and seemed about to swing at Duncan when Tanaqua seized his arm. The Virginia sergeant backed away.

Duncan touched Devon's neck. It was not yet cold. He had been dead no more than two or three hours. There were bruises around his nostrils. His unseeing eyes were stained red from burst vessels. The young ranger's hands were in tight fists, the knuckles drained white. The company grew quiet as they watched Duncan lean over the dead man's head. Dried blood clung to the corners of Devon's mouth. He pulled back a lip. Two of his incisors were broken.

"He was—" Duncan began, but Tanaqua cut Duncan off, pulling him away.

"He was what?" Trent stood in the aisle, most of the other prisoners now behind him. Winters stood at the entry. "Lookee here, Mr. Winters," Trent called to him, gesturing him forward. "The new Scot is playing with a dead man."

"He is a doctor," Ross said.

"Is he now? Must be a damned good one if he is going to help this sorry fool." Trent gestured to Duncan. "Go ahead, McCallum, practice your skills on the corpse. Isn't that what the doctors like most, a patient who can't complain?" He gave a throaty laugh.

Duncan lifted the dead arms, already stiffening with rigor, then pushed on the chest. When air did not rush out of the lungs as expected he opened Devon's jaw and extended two fingers down his throat. They emerged holding a strip of cloth. He had to pull it hard, for it had been rammed in with force, and finally turned to Trent with a dirty strip of sack cloth nearly as long as his forearm. "Torn from the curtain," he said, then saw a stubby piece of wood that had rolled against the wall and pointed at it. "Pounded down his throat with that planting stick. His eyes have blood in them. He struggled mightily for air. The killer held his nostrils closed until he stopped breathing."

Trent seemed barely able to control his rage. "Blow the horn for the superintendent!" he shouted to Winters.

A quarter hour later, their breakfast in the kettle untouched, the company stood in a line by the yard's whipping posts as the superintendent paced before them.

"Five lashes for every man!" Gabriel boomed. "That's how you apologize to me for destroying the property of the plantation! You shall pay for your sin!"

Up and down the line, men cursed.

"Silence fore and aft!" Trent barked, then whirled his stick through the air so hard the split ends whistled.

Gabriel's temper seemed to boil over as he passed along the line of Judas slaves. "Ten lashes then, damned you all!" he screeched. "None for the first man who steps forward to tell me who the murderer was."

Not a man moved.

Gabriel made a strange hissing sound that propelled drops of saliva from his mouth. The braying of hounds broke the silence as he moved along the line. Four men on horseback rode along the end of the fields, escorted by the dogs. Gabriel stopped in front of Tanaqua. "Take off your shirt," he ordered. The Mohawk glared at him but complied. "You damned bucks love killing Virginians. None of the others ever lifted a hand against them. But you arrive and now I have a dead one."

"It was not him," Duncan said again. "He slept beside me and never rose."

"That's right," Murdo confirmed. "He would have had to climb over me. Never moved." Burns and Larkin murmured agreement.

Gabriel's icy smile disappeared. His jaw clenched. His face turned a deep purple. "Strip them all!" he screamed, then grabbed Trent's stick, waved its treacherous knob in front of Duncan, and abruptly slammed it into Tanaqua's ribs. "You want to sass me boy? Your companions will pay for it." He looked up as two of the wagons used for transporting seedlings to the fields approached, and ordered them to drive to the edge of the yard. "Ten lashes to every man! Fifteen for McCallum!"

The Judas slaves wordlessly followed the superintendent's orders, dropping their clothes in a row around the side of the building then standing back in line for punishment. A horse-drawn cart coming up the perimeter road from the manor house halted a hundred yards away until the naked men retreated back to the yard. Black-clad pharaohs arrived, lifting coiled whips from their saddles.

Four men at a time were tied to the wheels of the wagons and the lashes began raising bloody welts. The pharaohs were efficient at their task, quickly untying men from wheels as the cat finished with them, and as quickly binding new victims. Gabriel saved Duncan for last, and began by pressing the pewter pommel of his whip against the scabs of his prior flogging, until Duncan felt blood running from them. The superintendent had Trent count the strokes, aiming them not just at Duncan's back but also his buttocks and naked legs. Trent stopped looking at Duncan after the fifth, just calling out the numbers each time he heard the leather bite into Duncan's flesh. As Duncan was untied and dropped to his knees, gasping, blood streaming down his back, the superintendent leaned over him. "Y'er the damned troublemaker from Townsend's. God damned ye for y'er interference!" He hissed, and kicked Duncan's raw, bleeding back, sending him sprawling on the ground.

"Into the fields with the lot of ye!" Gabriel shouted. His voice had gone hoarse. "Ye'll git y'er clothes back tonight!"

"Oh nae," came a loud but steady voice. "I do'na think so." Murdo Ross had found his britches. "I will nae offend the African ladies." He tightened his belt as he spoke.

Gabriel pulled a heavy horse pistol from his belt. The veins on his bald pate were throbbing. "I'll spill y'er brains, I swear it!"

Murdo stepped closer to Gabriel. "Good. I'm tired of looking at y'er ugly face."

No one breathed. Gabriel aimed the weapon at Ross's head. The faint tone of a bosun's whistle could be heard from the river.

A low rattling sound rose from Gabriel's throat and the skin of his jaw drew tight as a drum. Duncan struggled to his feet, then sprang forward, thrust his foot around Murdo's ankle, and with a mighty shove knocked him to the ground. He hit the Scot hard, in his mouth. "You'll not wage my fights for me, damned you Ross!" he shouted. He slapped the unresisting Scot, hard enough to draw blood.

Gabriel gave one of his icy laughs, then tucked the pistol back into his belt. "Now who has the ugly face?" he quipped, and glanced back at the manor house, where figures could be seen in the yard, watching them. "No midday meal. Put your damned clothes back on before you frighten the dogs." He glared at Duncan. "What do I care if you kill each other? Put enough rats in a cage and they'll always wind up eating each other." He marched away, his rough companions a step behind.

"I'm sorry, Murdo," Duncan murmured to the big Scot.

"So ye do ken, lad, that this is only Galilee, not ancient Sparta? I donna' fancy this naked wrestling of y'ers."

The men beside them grinned and helped them to their feet.

"But it's like you said, Duncan," Murdo stated. "He was never going to pull that trigger. They're saving us for something."

"Don't bet your life on my word!" Duncan said, flinching as Tanaqua ladled water over his raw back.

Murdo grinned as he wiped blood from his jaw. "I think I just did."

Before the ravenous company was allowed to touch the kettle of fish stew waiting for them at the end of the day, the overseers lined them up to view the shrouded body of Devon, propped now in a sitting position against one of the logs. His head had been left uncovered, and his unseeing eyes seemed fixed on the kettle. No one moved toward the stew. Trent, standing near the kettle, cut a piece from a tobacco plug and popped it in his mouth with a grin.

Finally Murdo Ross stepped to the dead man. "Sorry you're dead, lad, may God forget all your sins and pull you up to his blessed embrace. Now I'm bloody well famished," he added, then crossed himself, and shut the dead eyes before turning to dip his bowl in the kettle. His actions broke the paralysis of the others but seemed to set a rule for the meal. Each man paused in front of the hideous corpse, dipped his head, and muttered a few words before taking supper.

As the sun was setting, old Jaho instructed those with the worst lash wounds to drape themselves over a log while he applied grease to their backs. He distracted the men with tales of great bravery in tribal wars, speaking of the natives who faced down the first Englishmen with bows and spears against English guns. One Susquehannock warrior had earned the name Eight Breath Wolf, Jaho recounted with pride, after he learned that he had time to rush and kill an adversary during the eight breaths it took the Englishmen to reload. Ononyot and Hyanka offered tales from the fires of their youth, about how the Susquehannocks would attack three or four times their number, of the terror caused by the wild men wearing bear skulls over their heads or shoulders who leapt out of the shadows and with three strokes of their war axes left as many dead. The company listened with solemn attention as, his eyes round with the telling, Ononyot spoke of the greatest warrior of all, the Susquehannock who not only wore a bear skull helmet but had two bear heads tattooed on his shoulders that came to life in battle, snapping at any enemy who tried to flank him.

Old Jaho chuckled. "Stories for children in their beds. My mother used to tell me of a tree that walked and let good children ride on its limbs."

"Not this one," Tanaqua said. He spoke in the tongue of the Haudensaunee now, and the other Iroquois listened with rapt attention. Duncan had seen the deference they paid to Tanaqua, and realized they had recognized him as a leader of the secret societies, a famed spirit warrior. "He was real. My grandfather knew him. Our people were so impressed that when the Susquehannocks were finally broken they made him the chief of the south, the half king of the border lands."

Jahoska smiled again. "I looked for that tree for years but never found it. But my children heard about it, just in case."

As the men began climbing onto their pallets Murdo bent over Duncan. "Did they take them, lad?"

Duncan looked up in question.

"Your papers. Gabriel had an air of playacting today. I don't think it was out of perverseness that he made us strip off our clothes."

"But he made everyone strip."

"Strip and leave their clothes behind, around the corner of the building. Why leave them where we couldn't keep them in sight? Because they wanted to search them without us knowing. That cart came up and stopped behind the stable while the pharaohs worked their whips. I reckon it held a maid from the house."

"You make no sense."

"If I'm not mistaken, she had needle and thread. Check your leggings."

Duncan did as he was told, taking the leggings to one of the slits where the last light of day filtered in. He studied the seams then looked up in surprise. "They've been opened and resewn, by a hand more skilled than mine."

"The stamps and the commission?"

"I hid them last night."

"Gabriel just needs an excuse. If he finds those papers, and discovers y'er are not a runner he may just hang ye as a thief and be done with ye."

Duncan gazed out at the purple sky, weighing Ross's words. "Someone told them about the stamps," he whispered.

"Oh, aye. A bird that sings to Gabriel. Probably the same creature who killed poor Devon."

There was just enough light left outside for Duncan to make out the corpse propped in the yard. "Why kill him?" he asked.

"You asked hard questions last night. He spoke freely, but you saw how he was wary of being overheard. He had to be silenced."

"But surely . . ." Duncan's heart seemed to shrivel. "You mean he died because I asked him questions." He looked out at Devon's body.

The Virginian would be alive but for him. "Do me a favor," he said to Ross. "Go down to the end of the building. Distract the men there while I retrieve the papers."

Ross frowned. "Aye," he reluctantly agreed.

Moments later, as Ross broke out in a loud Gaelic ballad, Duncan slipped behind the latrine curtain, stood on the bench, and retrieved the papers from where he had jammed them between a beam and a roof shingle. He walked purposefully toward the gathering around Murdo and held out the first of his treasures, the *Virginia Gazette* with Colonel Barre's speech. He recounted how he had obtained it, making sure to acknowledge that Townsend had given it to him, earning a grateful nod from the man's son, then read the speech in a slow, loud voice. Eyes that had lost their fire showed a spark, and several men gathered around the speech.

Larkin urged him to read the last passage again. "About our blood," the old ranger prompted. "—has caused the Blood of those Sons of Lyberty to recoil with them," Duncan recited.

"Amen, amen," Larkin said, and the men repeated his words in a chorus.

Duncan pinned the speech with a splinter into the wall and withdrew the tax commission.

"Mathias Lee, Caroline County," he read, "is hereby appointed revenue commissioner for His Majesty's government." He extended it into the flame of a candle.

"McCallum! No!" Frazier called out, knocking Duncan's hand from the flame.

"I never meant to be captured with this," Duncan explained. "Just having these could still be enough to stretch our necks." He looked up into the grim faces. No one protested.

Burns gave a mischievous grin and called out. "Sinclair, still have that stash of Oronoco in your sock?"

The Pennsylvania Scot grinned and darted to the pouch over his pallet as Burns methodically folded and refolded the commission. He ripped the paper along the fold, then sprinkled Sinclair's tobacco along one of the halves and rolled it into a tight cylinder. "The king's cheroot!" he declared, then bent and lit the roll, handed it to Duncan, and began rolling the second one.

Soon the scent of the fragrant tobacco filled the stable as the men, eyes gleaming, passed the cheroots around.

"Shhh!" Murdo called out with a glint in his eyes, and moved to a window slit. "What's that? Do ye not hear it?" He leaned toward the window, playfully cupping his ear before turning to his companions. "It's Prime Minister Grenville, lads. He says he has been waiting for his taxes, says we owe him for each puff!" The big Scot blew smoke out the slit. "Here's what the liberty boys said to that, sir!" he shouted, and made an obscene gesture toward the night.

The little speech, perhaps aided by the tobacco, revived the company, and men pounded fists on the platform to register assent when Murdo proposed that they leave the stub of the cheroot to shove into Devon's shroud. After Duncan drew on the second cheroot and passed it on he produced the sheet of tax stamps, then laid it flat on the platform. The men watched silently as he folded the sheet then started tearing off the stamps one by one.

When he finished, Duncan had stamps for each of the men in his hand. "These are liberty stamps. Don't take one unless you believe we will find our liberty. One we save for Devon," he added, dropping a stamp into his pocket.

As he walked along the men, each took a stamp from his palm with a solemn nod. He felt like a priest giving communion.

THE NEXT MORNING THE DENSE FOG THAT OFTEN COVERED THE swamp at night had overtaken the fields. As they stepped groggily along the gruel line Winters moved among them, tapping men with his stick. Old Jaho, Murdo Ross, Frazier of the northern rangers, Burns of the Conococheague, and finally Duncan.

"Work party to plant poor Devon," he announced.

In the night someone had secretly been at work on the dead man. A sack had been tied around his head, and a garland made of oak leaves wrapped around vines had been draped around his neck. The Virginians were clearly put off by the interference with the body, but Tanaqua and the other tribesman gazed at the garland with sober expressions, as if it secretly spoke to them. Tanaqua saw the inquiry on Duncan's face and Duncan was about to step to his friend when Trent shoved him toward the corpse, pointing to the lengths of rope and four shovels that had been dropped by the whipping post. Moments later two new overseers appeared to take over the Judas company for the morning.

Their procession through the fog had an otherworldly quality to it. The stable and every other building quickly faded from view. From the direction of the river came the sound of one of the low-pitched horns blown by sailors making way in fog. Ahead of them an owl hooted. Through the murk over the field came a disembodied, mournful African chant. The slaves from the other side of the field somehow knew about the dead man.

Jahoska, carrying a shovel on each shoulder, led the way, sometimes getting far enough ahead that wisps of the ground-hugging mist obscured his lower body, so that he appeared to be some antlered beast floating along in front of them. Winters, walking alongside the men carrying the corpse, seemed oddly contemplative, and not at all disturbed by the Susquehannock's wandering. "The overseers in the fields are given pistols on days like this," he declared. "They worry about runaways. No crews go into the fields until the bosses can see the distance of a pistol shot in every direction."

Not for the first time Duncan wondered about Winters, who often seemed uncomfortable with his duties. Even Trent was different somehow from the other overseers, for the glint in his eyes was often that of a deep-seated anger at something rather than the casual cruelty displayed by the others. Now, accompanying the burial detail, he had lost his usual surliness. "Mend y'er lines, ye lubbers," he mildly chastised when Burns stumbled and lost his grip on the carrying rope, letting the corpse touch the ground. "Level y'er ballast, damn ye," he added, though it came out as more of a dutiful reprimand.

Through the mist came a new sound. Old Jaho, almost invisible now, was speaking. Duncan knew none of the Susquehannock words, but he recognized the tone. It was a burial chant, a request for a gate to open into the next world. The words grew louder as they began to climb, and Duncan realized they must be nearing the burial plot on the side of the hill. Small white crosses materialized out of the gloom, then suddenly the air stirred and they found themselves in a pool of sunlight, surrounded by graves. A changed world opened before them. The fields were still covered in the ground fog, a grey quilt that obscured all but the highest roofs, the tallest trees, and the masts of three ships on the river.

Jahoska's chant faded away and he pointed to a patch of open ground. Winters distributed the tools and outlined the grave with his heel in the soft earth. They had dug nearly two feet into the moist soil when Duncan realized the old Susquehannock was nowhere to be seen. Trent, sitting on a boulder, was strangely reserved, just frowning at Winters, who gazed toward the top of the hill. As Trent stood and handed around a water gourd, Murdo shoved the stub of the commission-paper cheroot into Devon's shroud. The Scot had paused in front of Sergeant Morris as they had left the stable yard, extending his palm. Morris had mumbled an apology, saying he had forgotten, and dropped the remains of the cheroot into Murdo's hand.

When they had nearly finished digging, Duncan wandered toward Trent, whose gaze, not for the first time that day, had drifted toward the river. He recognized the look of a stranded sailor. "The first I make to be a brig," Duncan offered, "and the second, with the tall mast rigged fore and aft with the pennant at top, has the look of a fast cutter. But the third, the short one, I can make no sense of."

"Just one of those squat snows that ply up and down the bay. Come fall when the crop is dried and loaded into hogsheads the snows and luggers will be swarming the river." Trent caught himself and cast a peeved frown at Duncan, as if Duncan had tricked him somehow.

"I crewed my grandfather's ketch as a boy," Duncan said, "in and out of the western isles of Scotland. If we were anchored he would dive off and swim right under the keel each morning. The first time it happened I thought he had drowned for certain. I was leaning over the rail, desperately calling his name, when the old fool put his wet hand on my neck. Scared the hell out of me. He had climbed up the other side and was standing behind me the whole time I was calling him."

For the briefest of instants there was a glint in Trent's eye, then his face hardened. "That hole ain't digging itself," he barked, and with his quarterstaff pushed Duncan back toward their task.

By the time they lowered Devon into his grave, the fog had burned entirely away, exposing the wide fields below. Old Jaho had reappeared, carrying a bundle of willow bark, and patiently listened while Winters berated him halfheartedly as slovenly and irresponsible, telling the old man he had forgotten he was a slave. But when Jaho set a twig of oak on the head of the shrouded corpse the young overseer nodded.

"*Agnus Dei*," Winters declared. Before Duncan could grasp that he was speaking Latin, he continued, "*qui tollis peccata mundi, miserere nobis.*" *Lamb of God*, he had said, *who takest away the sins of the world, have mercy on us.*

In the silence Jahoska whispered, "Appointeth the moon."

Duncan saw Winters nod.

"He appointeth the moon for seasons," the young overseer went on, "the sun knoweth his going down. Thou makest darkness, and it is night, wherein all the beasts of the forests do creep forth. The young lions roar after their prey and seek their meat from God. The sun ariseth, they gather themselves together, and lay them down in dens." When he had finished Winters saw that all but Jaho stared at him. "It is a Psalm," he said as if apologizing. "One hundred seven."

Duncan saw a tiny, inscrutable smile on Jahoska's face. It may indeed have come from the Christian Bible, but it could have just as easily come from an elder at a tribal hearth.

"My father was a pastor," Winters added.

"There should be memories offered," Murdo suggested. "Ain't a proper funeral without mention of his life." No one spoke.

"I never heard him curse," Frazier volunteered.

"A good man with a hoe," Burns offered.

Duncan dropped a handful of dirt into the grave. "I marked his carefree nature. He was one of the few who kept hope in his eyes, as if he didn't believe"—Duncan glanced at the overseers—"his predicament would last."

Winters cleared his throat and spoke toward the grave. "Gates. His full name was Devon Gates, from a family of famous sharpshooters in the Shenandoah country. Corporal Gates was the youngest member of the Virginia rangers in the late Indian war. When his father was elected to the House of Burgesses, Devon would often travel with him to Williamsburg."

"You knew his family?" Duncan interrupted.

Winters shook his head. "But we were of an age. He was one of the first white slaves brought to the stable. In the early weeks we would talk at the water barrel sometimes, until Mr. Gabriel put an end to it.

Slaves are beasts of burden, he said, and it was demeaning for a man to speak with his mule. He said if I needed intercourse with a slave so badly then he would give me one of the African girls they bring to the overseers' barn on Saturday nights.

"He saw me speaking with Devon in the field last week. Don't treat with dead men, he said, and laughed that high-pitched laugh of his. The hyena, the Africans call Gabriel, whatever that means."

"Someone should send word to his parents," Murdo suggested.

"His mother died birthing a sister two years ago. His father may be in flight himself now."

"Flight?"

"The Resolves. His father helped Mr. Henry work on the Resolves."

Duncan struggled to understand. "You mean a law from the Burgesses?"

"Something about who has the right to tax free Virginians, stating that London had no right to tax us, only the assembly duly elected by Virginians. There was talk of an arrest warrant against Mr. Henry. At a dinner in his palace the night the Resolves were passed, the governor said Henry and every man who joined him in the vote should be shipped in chains back to London to apologize to the king."

"Enough palaver about London and governors!" Trent growled. "We ain't taking ease in some tavern. And ye don't want Gabriel to hear about more of y'er chatter with mules, do ye?"

"The boy stood with the oak," Old Jaho said suddenly, then lifted a shovel and began covering the body.

"Yes, well," Winters muttered, then straightened and collected himself. "Put your backs into it!" he ordered in the voice of the overseer.

When they had finished their melancholy work, Trent led them back to the company in time to share a lunch of beans mashed with lard. Winters took Jaho back to the stable, where he left the willow bark he had collected.

Three hours later Murdo gave a low whistle and nodded toward the stable. A new prisoner was being deposited there, supported by two men at his shoulders under the angry direction of Gabriel. The man appeared more dead than alive, but as they reached the door, he struggled, knocking off his powdered wig, and earning a knob on the skull from Gabriel. He was thrown inside and the door barred.

At the end of the day the door to the Judas slaves' stable was still barred and Trent stood guard. Duncan ate his meager supper quickly then approached the door. Trent glanced at the setting sun and offered no challenge as Duncan lifted the bar and entered.

The man lying on the platform jerked awake at Duncan's touch, pulling away and thrusting an arm over his face. He was perhaps forty years of age, and though his clothes were torn and soiled, they were obviously those of a gentleman. The blood on the back of his shirt showed that he had received his welcoming lashes.

"Your tormenters are gone," Duncan said. "I would tend your wounds." As he spoke he became aware of movement behind him, and saw Jaho filling a mug from a crock beside his makeshift altar.

"The willow bark," Duncan guessed as the Susquenhannock extended the mug to the new prisoner.

The old man nodded. "I would have preferred to dry it and grind it, but this will do."

Duncan took the heavily chipped mug and held it up to the man's lips. "All of it, to ease the pain."

The stranger sipped and winced at the bitterness before downing the contents of the mug. "There's been some ghastly mixup!" he blurted out. "You must take me back to the manor house. These are slave quarters. By God, I will have strong words with that damned overseer!" He paused, considering Duncan and Jaho. "You work for him?"

"We are chattels of the estate," Duncan replied. "If you were to rank the population of this plantation, there would be the unseen owner, then the aristocrats of the manor and the superintendent, after that there is the house staff, the field overseers, the Africans, the horses, the pigs, and finally those of us who inhabit this stable. Although Superintendent Gabriel might suggest the dung piles rank higher as well."

The man's anger waned, replaced by confusion. "But you sir— look at you. You are—" he searched for a word.

"Scottish," Duncan suggested.

"Yes, well. Scottish," he said with a nod, then cast an uncertain glance at Jaho. He took in his surroundings, and tried to rise, triggering a clang of metal. The color drained from his face as he discovered the manacles on his ankles, and for a moment Duncan saw despair in his eyes. Then he took a deep breath, rose from the platform, and began to brush his clothes. "These must be quarters for the Africans."

"The Africans are treated better. They are allowed their own gardens, and many live with their families. The only men we have ever seen in manacles are those of this building." Duncan put a hand on the man's shoulder. "You were not mistakingly sent here."

"I will summon a magistrate! They do not know who I am!"

"Our confinement is secret. You will not be permitted to send a message. I doubt anyone knows you are here."

"I was taken in the night," the stranger explained. "I heard a noise in my stable, went out to investigate, and was hit on the head. Secret? What can you mean, sir?"

"Secret punishment for the secret committees of correspondence. They call us the Judas slaves. Most of us were runners for the committees."

Duncan's words struck the man like a physical blow. He sank back down onto the platform. "Dear God . . ." he gasped. "They wouldn't dare . . ." He sagged and Duncan took his arm and lowered him onto the platform. He buried his head in his hands. "Not now, surely not now of all times!"

"There is food outside," Duncan said. "If you don't eat before dusk there will be nothing until tomorrow. Eat, then we will clean your wounds."

The stranger did not respond. They left him still holding his head, stricken, muttering "no, no, no" to himself.

Minutes later the new slave stepped outside. He seemed drained, so weak he clutched at the door frame. Sturgis, one of the Virginians, ran to him, helping him to a seat on the nearest log before bringing him a slab of bread and a piece of dried fish.

Duncan gave him a few minutes to eat before approaching.

"It's Major Webb, sir!" the Virginia runner explained to Duncan.

He studied the weary man. Atticus had been the only one to know all the runner marks, except Webb, Devon had declared in front of the company the night he died. It could be no coincidence that Webb was now a prisoner.

"Not anymore, Private," the gentleman said with a sigh, then looked up and extended his hand to Duncan. "Just Elijah Webb, farmer and owner of a dry goods store in Louisa County now. I have been remiss in my manners, Mr.—"

"McCallum. Duncan McCallum."

"The major was our senior officer in the militia," Sturgis explained. "When we came back after whomping the Shawnee above the Shendandoah, didn't Colonel Washington say he prayed he could find ten more just like you?"

"The war's over, son."

"Then why are good soldiers in a prison camp, sir? Perhaps a new war is beginning."

Sturgis's words seemed to shake Webb. The intense, worried stare he aimed at his former ranger was broken by Sergeant Morris, who, finally recognizing the officer, gave a sharp whistle. Moments later six men stood in a line before Morris, including young

Townsend, who saluted Webb with a knuckle to his forehead. They were a ragged, battered company but each was clearly heartened to see their former officer.

Webb struggled to his feet, declining help from Duncan, and shuffled along the line, ignoring the rattle of his chains, greeting each man by name. "Braford, is that young boy of yours up on two feet yet?"

"Prancing like a young buck, sir."

"Sturgis, still have that fast thoroughbred?"

"Swift as a Chesapeake eagle."

"Preston, did you ever find that lost hound?"

It was the first time Duncan had seen the tall, scarred man smile. "Just went into the woods to have young ones. Came back with eight whelps on her heels."

Webb studied the file of weary men, who were struggling to remain erect like good soldiers. "All of you were runners?"

Braford nodded vigorously. "Liberty and Wilkes, sir."

"How long have you been here? What is your sentence?"

Braford swallowed hard. "Death by hanging, says Mr. McCallum. Let him have a look at your wounds, sir. He's a medical gentleman—."

Webb stared at Duncan in disbelief. "Death? Ridiculous. Why would you put such a horrid notion in their heads?"

"The men behind this rolled up all the runners," Duncan explained. "Several of them are already dead, murdered and mutilated, the rest imprisoned here." Webb shuddered, and held his belly again. "Please sit, sir. We should wash your wounds while we still have light." Webb complied, and Duncan explained his journey from Edentown as he and Jaho tended the torn flesh on the major's back.

"But who would do such a thing?"

"The ones you warned Philadelphia about," Duncan replied. "What caused you to send the warning?"

"A letter from London reported that several supporters of Mr. Wilkes disappeared mysteriously. One of the lost men reached a merchant ship owned by a friend that was docked in Jamaica, his back riddled with pitiful scars and burning with fever. Said he had been knocked on the head in London and awakened in chains on the high seas, then taken to a slave plantation in Jamaica. He seemed raving mad, but used his last breath to say Wilkes had to warn his American correspondents about the Kraken Club."

"The Krakens use the runner marks for deception," Duncan observed. "Devon said you knew them all."

Webb paused and twisted to look about the company. "Was Devon captured then? Let me speak to the boy. I never meant to cause him trouble."

"He was murdered, sir. The very night he spoke your name."

The Virginia officer shook his head slowly from side to side, as if he might deny Duncan's words. "The knaves! The king will not abide such treachery!"

"If the king is told treason is afoot he will abide very much indeed."

"Treason! We simply engage in political discourse. Have they not heard of the Magna Carta? The liberty of Englishmen is protected!"

As Trent began herding them inside for the night Hughes extracted a piece of hickory from his pocket and tossed it to Webb. "They will question you about the runner marks and commissioners. They will not be polite," he added.

They left the major staring at the deep bite marks on the wood.

As the men settled onto their pallets, Duncan helped Webb find a place to sleep. "This is a nightmare," the major said. "Surely I will wake up in my featherbed in Louisa County and recall that I drank too much claret last night."

Duncan grabbed his arm as he swayed again. "You have a bruised rib, cuts on your face, lash marks on your back, and a broken tooth.

What more evidence do you need? You are a slave with the rest of us. We are dying day by day and you may be the best chance we have to leave this place alive."

"Best chance?"

"You know who is in that manor house. You know the roads, by both water and land, and the way of the tobacco trade."

They spoke no more until the door was locked behind them.

"We are on the Rappahannock, perhaps fifteen miles of deep channel from the Chesapeake." Webb shrugged. "How does that help you? The navy is on maneuvers on the bay. You can't throw an oyster shell without hitting a government ship. The river offers no escape."

It was not the news Duncan wanted to hear. "Who is in the manor house?"

"It was built by the Dawson family. The elder Dawson was a kind Christian who ran his farm to help the needy and his nephew continued his good works." Webb shrugged. "I have heard nothing of the family these two years and more."

"The tobacco. Who sells the tobacco? We need to understand who controls this place."

Webb paused, considering the question. "I suspect one of the companies seeking to take over the Oronoco market. The Rappahannock Company, I'd wager."

"And who controls the company?"

Webb shrugged. "Their proprietors hide behind lawyers and clerks. There's several such companies, given charters by the king. Shares change hands in London and Williamsburg."

"The Krakens must control it," Duncan suggested. "They must. This is their lair, where secret killers are dispatched to serve their masters and secret prisoners are punished."

"It's an old tale," came a raspy voice behind them. Larkin had been listening. "An old seafarer spoke of the krakens when I served on coasters as a boy. Great beasts that would rise up from the darkness and rip apart men and ships with their tentacles. I said surely then we must sail closer to shore to avoid them and he said it didn't matter, that a kraken moved like a ghost. It could creep right up a river and snatch one of us. And so it did," the former sailor insisted. "Poor Devon said he that he alone survived the water route. The beast took offense. It stalked him and squeezed the life out of the poor lad."

CHAPTER THIRTEEN

The days became a blur of pain and toil. The crack of a cane and the bray of "sotweed!" grew as constant as the drone of flies. At night men collapsed onto the sleeping racks but in the small hours Duncan often heard them talking in their sleep to loved ones they might never see again. Friends whispered to each other of simple things, like picking apples with a son or kittens delivered on a hearth on a snowy night. Duncan, lying on his pallet in the dark, found himself spending more and more time thinking of Edentown, and the contentment he had known in the years since the war.

Sarah and Duncan were joined by a young Oneida girl, who skipped between them, holding their hands, as they approached the grove of maple trees. A spring sugar camp was always a joyous time for the tribes, but this camp was cause for special celebration. The Edentown settlement, newly enlarged under Sarah's guidance, was busy with arrival of new craftsmen, new lambs, even two new Percheron foals in its pasture. The first year of the schoolhouse, which counted several tribal children among its students, would soon be celebrated with a picnic. Sarah had been moved beyond words when Adanahoe and four other Iroquois elders from Onondaga had arrived to share the bounty of their sugar orchards.

They stopped at a huge maple and Duncan helped the girl lift the birch-bark bucket from its tap, which she cradled in both arms to take back to the boiling kettles.

"We've done it, haven't we?" Sarah said.

Duncan wasn't certain of her meaning until he saw the contented way she watched the girl entering the joyful camp of natives and Europeans. We've made our oasis in the forest—she meant the sanctuary she had dreamed of. "You've done it," he replied.

She took his hand. "I could never have done it without you, Duncan. You were my strength. You made me believe it was possible." She squeezed his hand and seemed about to embrace him when Conawago, with an Iroquois toddler on his shoulder, called out for Duncan to come join an impromptu lacrosse game.

They did not find each other until long after sunset, when the kettle of venison and squash stewed in sap was empty, and everyone was exhausted from singing many rounds of harvest songs of the Iroquois, the Scots, and the Germans. Sarah had her sleeping blanket draped around her neck and from behind her she produced Duncan's blanket. He had led her to a bed of moss at the edge of the camp and they were lying down when several of the Iroquois children ran up and laughingly wedged themselves between Sarah and Duncan. Sarah cast Duncan a disappointed smile, then began telling the children the English and Iroquois names for the constellations overhead. As the children quieted she reached out to hold his hand, but the children had stretched them far apart. Only their fingertips could connect, and they fell asleep like that, fingertip to fingertip.

ON SUNDAY THEY WERE ESCORTED TO THE RIVER, WHERE THEY joined the other slaves in the weekly bathing and clothes washing. The sinister pharaohs watched over them from the shore, aided by two guards in separate dinghies anchored along the mouth of the little cove where the slaves were allowed to bathe.

Some of the Africans had children who splashed naked in the water and threw balls of mud at one another. At first Duncan, stripped to his britches, stayed with Webb and several of the Judas slaves who just sat in shallow water to let the river soothe their ravaged backs. Soon he ventured into the deeper water, pretending to wash his own clothes but keeping his eye on the wharf. The cutter was moored along the long dock, guarded by a marine in a scarlet tunic. In the deeper water at the end of the wharf was a broad-beamed trading snow unloading the big hogshead barrels that would be used later in the season to ship the tobacco crop to market.

Set behind the wharf was the manor house, a structure of brick and white clapboard that was not at all elegant, but certainly spacious. It had obviously been built around a farmhouse now serving as the rear wing, probably where kitchens and servant quarters were located. A low white-pillared portico extended a hundred feet from the entrance toward the wharf, flanked by flowering lilacs. A blonde woman in a blue dress was cutting the flowers, handing them to an African woman with a basket on her arm.

"The fool's asleep," Murdo whispered at his side. "Too much ale on Saturday night I wager."

Duncan followed his gaze toward the farthest dinghy, where indeed the solitary guard sat stiffly with a musket between his knees, his head braced on one hand. He studied his weary companions. Escape would be impossible if they had no will to do so. Broken men would never be able to summon the speed and courage needed for flight from the well-armed enforcers of Galilee, and the spirit they had briefly shown had flagged since the night they had burned the tax commission. Hope was steadily fading from their eyes. "How many do you think can swim?" he asked.

Murdo made a show of bending and running water over his head as he replied. "All of us from the western isles, which would be eight. Half the tribesmen and rangers perhaps, no more. But eight or ten be too weak to carry themselves. And there's not a chance for anyone in manacles."

From the moment Duncan had seen the expanse of water, much wider and deeper than he had expected, his mind had been racing. His hand had gone to the spirit pouch that always hung from his neck. The totem inside, given to him by Conawago five years earlier when scores of lives had depended on his swimming impossible waters, called him to the deeper channel. He could easily escape right there, reaching the far bank underwater, surfacing only every two or even three minutes. But he could not leave his companions. "Then it's the swamp," he said. "We will flee into the swamp where their horses and dogs will be useless."

"May the blessed Mary preserve us," Murdo said with a grim nod. "And pray the serpents and quicksand and leeches ignore us in favor of the damned pharaohs."

But Duncan knew they would never find an escape if they could not even find hope. "They need to see that it's real, that we make progress," Duncan observed as he surveyed the half-starved men. "Murdo, if that man in the boat wakens make a distraction. Shove someone. Fight over a piece of clothing. Anything to keep his eyes on you."

"Christ, Duncan, don't be foolish. The river is swift underneath. It will take ye to the bottom and we'll ne'er see ye again."

"As a bairn I lived in the water so much my friends called me the McCallum seal," Duncan replied. He touched the spirit pouch that hung from his neck, then began working his way toward the handful of men who were bathing in chest-deep water. A minute later he was among them, then slightly beyond them, dipping his head in the water, even fully immersing twice with motions of washing his long, streaming hair. The third time he did not surface.

Farther from the bank and the churning of the slaves, the water cleared. Minnows swam among long strands of weed. A hulking catfish nearly as long as Duncan himself lolled on the bottom, watching him with black pebble eyes. He surfaced silently in the shadow of the dinghy. The sentry's broad back was toward him, and the low snoring told him Murdo had been right. He could not dare put his hand on the boat for fear of rocking it, but he was able to wrap his ankles around the trailing anchor line and push up gently enough for his arm to clear the gunwale. He explored the items on the rear bench with his fingers and chose three, securing them into his britches before relaxing his grip on the line and letting himself sink into the dark water.

The Galilee rules gave them only half a day's rest on the Sabbath but they were able to linger in the stable yard as they waited for their midday meal. Duncan motioned Tanaqua and Murdo inside the stable and led them to the shadows of the necessary bench, where he revealed his bounty. A fishing knife with a long slender blade. A coil of thin rope, and a pouch which yielded a fork and spoon. "Good metal," he said of the utensils. "With enough work on a stone, their handles can become blades."

"Y'er a bloody magician!" the big Scot exclaimed.

"Just a swimmer." Duncan watched as Tanaqua tested the strength of the rope and looked up in query. "If we are going through the swamp the men will be tied together."

Tanaqua considered his words, then nodded. "Because of the quicksand."

"Tell only the men you trust from home," Duncan warned his friends. "Devon's killer is still among us."

As Tanaqua kept watch, Duncan climbed onto Murdo's back and hid their treasures in the rafters. By the time the company was led out to the fields, the Pennsylvania Scots and Iroquois had a new light in their eyes.

After an hour of readying the last row for planting, Duncan felt the gaze of old Jaho, who stood in the field as if waiting for him.

Trent, like Winters, had begun giving the Susquehannock more latitude, and walked by the old man without a word. When Duncan reached him Jaho extended his hand, enclosed around an object. Duncan hesitantly offered his open palm, thinking the old man wished to give him something, but Jaho instead extended his other hand to enclose Duncan's in a tight grip. "Ononyot says you are the Death Speaker," the Susquehannock said, "that you are touched by the spirits, and do their work."

"I respect the spirits," Duncan said in a tentative tone, "and try to understand what they desire."

Jaho nodded. "Have you ever considered, McCallum, what bears dream about in their winter sleep?"

Duncan found himself grinning at the extraordinary question. The old man seemed to live in more than one world, and Duncan had no way of knowing which the old man was in now.

"The old spirits, the ancient ones, are like sleeping bears," the Susquehannock, still gripping Duncan's hand, explained. "They only wake now and again but they have dreams and those they touch may walk with them in those dreams. Actual dreams, my mother called them. Messages between worlds. Sometimes messages between ages."

Duncan had no reply, and Jahoska seemed to expect none. His leathery face wrinkled with a smile, then he released Duncan's hand and opened his own closed hand. Duncan's heart skipped a beat. On the old man's palm was a fossil, the kind the scientists called a trilobite.

"A seed stone lies at the intersection," Jahoska said. "The Death Speaker will need to see that."

Duncan slowly reached into his own pocket and produced the fossil he had brought from Shamokin. When Jaho saw it a cry of joy escaped his throat. For some reason he seemed greatly relieved. "Intersection of what?" Duncan asked.

Jaho cocked his head as if surprised at the question, then his leathery face curled again in a grin. "The crossroads of old miracles and new miracles."

"Sotweed!" snapped Trent.

Jaho backed away, closing the fossil in his fist again and raising it toward the sky. When Duncan turned to his work, the big African slave who had greeted him before was standing alone in the field, thirty paces away, staring at him.

THE NEXT DAY TOKENS CAME UP FROM THE EARTH. TANAQUA, AT the head of the line that worked the seedling row, bent to tie his moccasin, then deftly palmed something from the soil. An hour later, as they were begrudged their morning ladle of water, the Mohawk opened his hand to give Duncan a fleeting glimpse. It was a small metal rod. Duncan did not recognize it until Webb walked by several minutes later dragging his chains, which had been left on for more than a week, as if the overseers especially feared him. It was a manacle pin, one of the little rods that when pounded down by a hammer locked the clamps around the ankles, or when pushed against another locking pin could release it.

An hour later they came upon an oak leaf pinned by a squarish, oblong rock with a channel cut into it, a hammerhead used by the old tribes. As Duncan grabbed the stone, he realized the items were not random. They had been left for the Judas slaves. Minutes later Ononyot showed him a packet of leather scraps he had found, with a needle and thread tucked into the vine that bound it.

Three men, including Major Webb, wore manacles. As soon as their door was barred for the night, Duncan and Tanaqua braced Webb's foot and went to work on his chains, using the little rod, with sharp blows of the stone hammer, to pop out the pins that bound the chains to his ankles. The manacles of the other two men quickly followed.

"Back on in the morning," Duncan said as they finished the last one. "The overseers must not suspect."

"But the pigeon will know," Ross whispered.

"The difference now since Devon's death is that everyone knows he exists. Everyone is watching for him and he must expect it. He is not as likely to sing and if he does all will be watching for it."

"I've been asking whether anyone comes back from the interrogations without injuries," Ross reported.

"It would seem the best opportunity for the spy to meet with his handlers," Duncan acknowledged. "And?"

"No one seems spared the beatings. But a man could fake a limp or even take a bruise to avoid suspicion."

"It's not one of the Iroquois," Duncan whispered. "I'd stake my life on that."

"As I would on my Conococheague men," Murdo added.

"Which leaves the northern rangers and the Virginians," Duncan concluded, "and it won't be those who are turning to skin and bones. You can bet the spy is given extra food when he goes to the smokehouse."

He studied the men, most of whom gathered around Jaho as he began applying grease to the chafed ankles. Duncan noticed that Buchanan, one of Ross's Scots, had tucked his forearm inside his tattered waistcoat. He approached and touched his arm. Buchanan's haggard face tightened in a grimace of pain, then he froze as Tanaqua clamped a hand around his shoulder. "McCallum is a healer," the big Mohawk declared.

"He was taken to the smokehouse just this morning," Ross explained to Duncan.

Duncan pushed up the man's sleeve, which was soiled with blood and dirt. His forearm was swollen in a massive green bruise. The skin along the underside was stretched in a large, unnatural lump.

"God's breath, Buchanan!" Murdo gasped. "What have they done to ye?"

"It was in the smokehouse," the young Scot explained. "They were more angry than before. They kept asking for names of the commissioners on stolen certificates, and hit me harder and harder when I gave them no answers."

"It's broken," Murdo observed.

"Oh aye," Buchanan agreed, "sounded like a stick of wood snapping." When Duncan bent to examine the arm Buchanan pulled it away.

"I studied medicine in Edinburgh."

Buchanan remained skeptical.

"He is a healer in our lodges," Tanaqua inserted.

Buchanan frowned, but slowly extended the arm. Among men of the frontier a university-trained physician was a suspect outsider, but a healer of the longhouses was always respected. In truth Duncan had seen native healers perform miracles with compounds of herbs that would baffle Edinburgh scholars. Old Jaho brought Buchanan a cup of his willow brew, then Tanaqua and Murdo pinned the Scot to the platform as Duncan performed the quick but painful resetting.

"We need a splint, two or three plain slats, and strips to tie them tight," Duncan declared to no one in particular. The words brought a flurry of activity behind him. He turned to see one of the rangers point up to a splintering rafter and then lean over. In a blur of motion one of the Iroquois rangers took a running jump, pushing off the man's back and landing on the rafter. Moments later he had peeled away several thick strips of wood, which were quickly smoothed on one of the stones that some used as headrests.

Duncan finished tying the splints around Buchanan's arm with strips torn from pallets and looked up. Every man in the stable was watching him, many wearing grins. Something had shifted. The company had acted as one. Duncan nodded at Murdo and Tanaqua, and they retrieved the items he had stolen from the dinghy.

Eyes widened as he held them out for all to see. This was resistance.

Webb lifted the knife, nodding his approval, and murmured a command. The rangers from both Virginia and New York lined up. Webb paced the line then handed the knife to Hughes. "I want this as sharp as a razor by dawn," he said. Hughes pressed a knuckle to his forehead in acknowledgment.

"From now on," Webb continued as he handed out the spoon and fork with instructions to sharpen the handles, "every man is paired with another. Together in work, when eating, always together outside or we will know why not. Sergeant Morris, sound off the men in pairs." They would not make it easy for the infiltrator.

The major walked back along the line, tapping several men on the shoulder. "Sick call," he ordered. The men obediently formed a line by Duncan and Jaho, who grinned at Webb then went to work. The major had apparently seen symptoms that Duncan had not, and soon he was examining boils, deep splinters, aching teeth, and a disjointed thumb. Compresses were heated in one of the mugs over massed candles, the thumb was reset, and long draughts of the Susquehannock's brew were dispensed. Scottish songs erupted in low tunes, and to considerable amusement Old Jaho and the Iroquois tried to learn the Jacobite songs, making many of the throat-rattling Gaelic syllables sound like bird calls. They went to sleep to the scraping of Hughes's knife on a stone.

As the charcoal marks on the wall slowly grew in number, so too did their little arsenal. The shaft of a broken hoe was worked by Tanaqua into a club, then, with the insertion of a sharpened stone, turned into a formidable war ax before being hidden in the rafters. One of the Virginian youths recounted how he had often brought down squirrels with a sling. More scraps of leather that could be worked into slings appeared one morning by one of the yard logs, a little pile of round pebbles another morning, and to their great pleasure, eight plump onions on still another. They were quickly hidden until, after the door was barred, Webb used the knife to quarter them then distributed pieces to each man.

Duncan slept lightly that night, then not long past midnight he rose and squatted by a platform where he could watch Jaho's blanket tent, where the old man was bent over his smoldering pot. It was nearly an hour before the Susquehannock crawled into the tent. Duncan waited a few minutes then crept to the tent, apologized to the spirits, and ventured inside.

It was empty. The spirits protected not just Jaho himself, but also his escape hatch. The old tobacco sheds had been built with planks that could be swung out on top pivot pins for ventilation in the drying season but those on the slave quarters were supposed to have been nailed shut. The plank at the back of the makeshift tent, however, was loose, held in place by the peg that now lay on the floor. He pushed against the board and dropped to the ground outside.

Once outside he hurried to the cover of the nearest tree, by the road that separated the fields from the vast swamp that bordered the plantation's eastern side. He thought the old man would have headed toward the hills and began stealing from tree to tree in that direction, but after a few steps he halted, then followed a low murmuring sound toward the bank that sloped down to the swamp.

The old Susquehannock was not alone as he sat in the moonlight. A deer was at his side, nibbling grass from his hand as he whispered to it. Nearby a tall, graceful shape bent at the edge of the water. A night heron.

"If you walk slowly they will not shy away. I told them you were coming," Jaho declared.

As Duncan sat beside him the heron took a step backward, then twisted its neck to give a raspy call before returning to its hunt.

They sat in silence, contemplating the starlit sky, as Duncan and Conawago had so often done.

"People of this world are scared of swamps," Jahoska said. "They stay away from them, frightened of their creatures, or kill them with wagons of stone and dirt."

Of this world. The Susquehannock once again spoke as if he were familiar with more than one world.

"But a swamp is the wilds between land and the water," the old native continued. "It is the breeder of life, the dark place that makes the light place possible."

"You could run to freedom," Duncan observed. "Instead you go out in the night and leave presents for the company."

"Freedom? Here is where you learn about freedom, McCallum. The only real chains you wear are those you put on yourself."

The deep *onk a lunk* cry of a bittern rose out of the reeds.

"Why stay in this prison?"

"Here is where you learn about freedom," Jaho repeated.

Something rippled the water between two islands of reeds. Jahoska made a gesture toward the water's edge. "She leaves a basket for him sometimes. One of the kitchen maids whose tribe lived by a big river across the ocean."

Duncan eased himself down the bank and discovered a wicker basket partially submerged in the water. It was half filled with clams, on top of which was a short knife with a thick blade. The disturbance in the water grew closer as Duncan put the blade to one of the clams.

"For your brother," Jaho urged and somehow, with a tremor of his heart, Duncan understood. "Just crack it open," his companion said, then erupted in a hoarse laugh.

On the bank, an arm's length away, an otter had materialized. Water dripped from its sleek fur as it twisted its head, gazing first at the old man, who murmured comforting words in his ancient tongue, then at Duncan.

Ever so slowly Duncan extended the clam. The otter took a step closer and shifted to brace himself upright on his hind legs and tail, then took the clam with his front paws. With a soft sound like a purr it pushed open the loosened shell and consumed the sweet meat. When Duncan offered another it froze, then warily approached. Duncan sat like a statue as it pressed its nose against the totem pouch hanging over Duncan's neck. It looked up with blazing eyes then with a single leap landed in Jaho's lap, excitedly pushing its nose into his neck as the old man laughed. "I know, I know," the Susquehannock chuckled, stroking the animal's back. "It has taken a long time."

Duncan felt a sudden and inexplicable joy. Something important had just happened, something he could not describe, something he could not ask about. He forgot about chains and the misery of the slaves, for in that moment Jaho had let him glimpse the other world he lived in. The otter played with the old man as if he were one of his own kind, curling around his body and emerging under his arms before leaping to Duncan and repeating the action. Duncan found himself joining in the laughter then, as the otter hovered like an excited pup, he opened the remaining clams, laying them in a row on the grass. The otter joyfully pounced on each one. When he had eaten them all he nudged his nose into Duncan's neck then backed away into the water and slipped under the surface, performing a dolphin-like jump before disappearing.

In the silence that followed, Duncan heard a new sound, a heavy breathing behind him. He slowly turned then shrank back as he saw a large animal sitting on its haunches. It took him a moment to recognize that the great square head was that of a dog. The animal's dark curly coat glistened with water. It seemed to be guarding Jahoska.

"Chuga used to be at the big house," Jaho explained, "but he decided he liked it in the swamp better."

Duncan extended a hand for the dog to sniff before leaning over to stroke its back. "In the swamp," he said after a moment, "there must be islands."

"Many islands."

"And perhaps there are paths that connect the islands, that would take a man through?"

"Paths found by my people, yes. Dangerous paths. One false step and you can be in bottomless mud, the killing sands. But a man could get through if he knows the way."

"And twenty-some men?"

Jaho was quiet for several breaths as he weighed the words. "If I helped you escape I could never come back."

"You would be welcome among my people."

The old Susquehannock did not reply, just rubbed the big dog behind the ears with a contemplative gaze.

"The moon will set soon," he finally said. "We should go now."

Duncan dutifully followed Jaho along the bank until they reached a drainage ditch that cut across the fields towards the ridge on the north side of the plantation. Chuga stayed at Jahoska's side, matching his steady trot with long powerful strides, as watchful as a warrior. When they passed the sheds for the Africans, Duncan heard the sound of a lonely chant.

The mill and its outbuildings sat along a stream that emptied into the river, just as Larkin had drawn on the wall. Dinghies from the larger ships were tied to the small dock. The big water wheel was not turning. A soldier sat by a flaming brazier at the door of the mill, his musket leaning against the wall. Lights flickered in the windows of the long structure built into the back of the mill, confirming that it was used for sleeping quarters.

"How long have they been here?" Duncan asked.

Jaho ran his hand along Chuga's back. "Nearly six moons. The miller disappeared and they moved in. Half a dozen of them usually, more when the bigger ships come in."

"What do they do?" Duncan spied a second guard, sitting on a keg by the dock.

"They do what soldiers do. They make war."

The improbable words tore at Duncan's gut. They were the truth no one would speak. The Judas slaves were victims of a war, a silent, anonymous war. Now at last their foes would have faces.

THE NEXT MORNING HE WAS SHOVED OUT OF LINE AS THEY HEADED to the fields. Two of the pharaohs, rough men with dull, cruel eyes, dropped a loop over his head and led him onto the perimeter road toward the manor compound. They answered each of his questions with a jerk of the neck strap, which they did not remove until they had shoved him into the smokehouse and thrust his shoulders through two loops tied to the center beam.

He was left hanging between two hams, steadied only by the balls of his feet on a low milk stool. Each movement brought spasms of pain to his shoulders. No runner had died in the smokehouse interrogations, Larkin had said. But Duncan was not a runner.

The two men were laughing as they entered. The bespectacled man Duncan now knew to be Lieutenant Hobart accepted a pinch of snuff from a little silver box offered by the taller of the two, a man of thin, refined features and icy eyes wearing a wig that was askew enough to reveal his blond hair. A shorter, darker man with the boxed braid of a seaman hanging over his neck followed them inside, shutting the door and dropping a leather bag on a barrel head.

"At last we meet our would-be nemesis," the taller man said. It was, as Duncan expected, the peremptory voice he had heard calling down the stairs at Townsend's inn.

"Lieutenant Kincaid I take it," Duncan stated. "Did Townsend ever bring your tea?"

"Excellent. A civilized conversation! What a relief. So many of your companions want to start with crude suggestions. So refreshing to have an educated man with whom to transact business." Kincaid paused to press snuff up his nostril, held out a palm, as if to ask Duncan's indulgence, then released a formidable sneeze. He shook his head, smiling. "Much better. And you, Mr. McCallum. Are you perhaps an officer of some kind yourself?"

The question took Duncan by surprise. Then he recalled they had tried to kill Woolford, captain of rangers. "If I told you I was would you cut me down or cut my throat?"

His interrogators seemed amused. "Just another complication on the landscape," Kincaid replied. "A good field officer always gets the lay of the land." Kincaid bent so close Duncan could smell the tobacco and brandy on his breath. "Who the hell are you?"

"Just a tracker from the north. Asked to find some murderers. A tall blond man aided by an Irish giant named Teague. And the man who waited for them on the Susquehanna after they killed a young Scottish woman and an Oneida."

"Asked by whom?"

"The army," Duncan tried.

He did not miss the confused glance that passed between them. Kincaid shrugged, and picked up a slat of wood. He faced Hobart for a moment as if to converse, then with snakelike speed slapped the wood against Duncan's cheek.

Pinpoints of light exploded in Duncan's eyes.

"You could be valuable to us, McCallum. Or you could be just another doomed Judas slave."

The sting of the first blow had not subsided before Kincaid struck him again. "What other commissions do you have? What commissioners do you know of?"

"James," Hobart whispered. "We have no instructions."

"What," Kincaid demanded, "are the names on the stolen commissions? Who are the revenue agents you have hidden from us?"

Duncan pushed down his pain to study the man. He had expected them to press for details of the runner network. Why would the marine lieutenant want to know about names on commissions?

When Duncan did not reply, Kincaid frowned, stepped back, and bent to the ear of the smaller man, who left the building. "Damned Welshman, forever forgetting things," Kincaid said to Duncan in a conversational tone.

Hobart loomed closer now. A new tool had materialized in his hand. Duncan recalled that the narrow blade was called a stiletto, a treacherous Italian instrument. Hobart languidly dragged the blade along Duncan's exposed arm, scraping away hair, then very carefully inserted the cold steel into Duncan's nostril. "When," he asked in a casual tone, "is the world's end?" As he twisted the blade Duncan desperately bent his head back. Hobart laughed and withdrew the stiletto. Blood dripped onto Duncan's lip. "Or should we just speak of your end?"

"It was you!" Duncan spat back. "You were with Francis Johnson in Albany!" Hobart hesitated. Kincaid kicked away the stool.

Duncan's shoulders erupted in agony as they took the full weight of his body. He stretched, desperately trying to reach the brick floor with his toes. "And you went from there to Onondaga," he gasped.

Kincaid answered with a punch to his belly, setting Duncan swinging backward, then punched him again when his body swung closer to him. "William Johnson's son is . . ." his words came in gasps as they took turns punching him, "is a spy for the Krakens."

Kincaid paused, letting Duncan swing back without a punch, then gave one of his frigid grins. "William Johnson will be killed by trunnel nails and teapots," he declared. "So why should I care, you interfering weasel!" He hit Duncan on the return.

The swinging became faster, and the punches kept pace. Duncan closed his eyes, clenching his jaw, until suddenly he realized they had stopped. He opened his eyes to see that the Welshman had returned, and was standing on the stool beside Duncan. "They never told you, did they?" Duncan said.

"Told us?" Hobart asked.

"About the curse. That mask you stole. It is very old, like the things left by the Druids in England. You know about Druid relics. They terrify people. I recall a story about a man who stole some from a museum. Within months he and his family were all dead. Where is it?" Neither Duncan nor Tanaqua had given voice to the fear he knew they shared, that the mask had been destroyed.

Kincaid cocked his head a moment, then shrugged. "Five thousand acres of Ohio bottomland if you will sing our song. When will they come to the world's end?"

"I tend to prefer mountains," Duncan replied.

Kincaid seemed pleased. Hobart gave a nod.

The pain seared through Duncan's body like a bolt of lightning.

The Welshman was fastidious about his job, steadying Duncan's forearm in one hand as he pressed the red-hot iron into Duncan's flesh with the other. The smell of singed hair and seared flesh filled the little chamber. Kincaid offered Hobart more snuff and they watched in amusement as the short man pressed the iron deeper into his arm.

When he finished, the Welshman carefully poured water over the raw S-shaped brand burnt into Duncan's forearm, then with a businesslike air tucked the iron under his arm, stowed the stool in the shadows, and left the building.

Hobart reached up with his blade and sliced through the cord binding Duncan, who collapsed onto the bricks.

"*S* for slave," Kincaid crowed. "*S* for spy. *S* for stamps."

"*S*," added Hobart, "for the simpleton who gives up his life for fools with quills."

"The committees write for freedom," Duncan said with a cracking voice.

"Wilkes and corpses," Hobart cracked as they turned to the door, laughing with Kincaid.

Duncan lay on the floor, his body wracked with dry heaves but then growing much stiller as he stared at the knotted cord tied to his shoulder, lying in front of him on the bricks.

He had a dreamlike sensation of being carried in a barrow and heaved onto a sleeping platform, then finally jerked awake as a cold cloth was draped over his forehead. He opened his eyes to see Tanaqua and Webb.

"Winters let us forego lunch," Webb explained. "We thank you for the opportunity since it looked like some slop refused by the pigs." The major propped him up as Tanaqua handed Duncan a mug of the willow brew. As Duncan downed it he deftly reached to Tanaqua's belt, lifting away the twine he had taken from the dead man on the river. As he stretched the knotted twine between his hands both men went very still. Webb glanced at the door as if to make sure it was closed.

"Red Jacob had one of these," Duncan said to the Mohawk. "Just a string, I thought, the kind a forest traveler might keep for any number of tasks. But then the dead man on the Susquehanna had one. I thought he had used his last strength to preserve his enameled box but the box was just a way to anchor the string, wasn't it? That's why you took it, not for the box but for the string. It was a message from Philadelphia."

Tanaqua did not disagree.

"Duncan," Webb began, "it's better that you don't—"

"Don't know what I am going to die for?" he snapped. "They kept asking about the world's end. I thought it was a macabre joke, a reminder that we are meant to die. But it's a place, isn't it? When at the world's end, they want to know. They wanted me to name commissioners and reveal the time at the world's end."

"It's the secret they covet most of all," Webb confessed. "No more than a handful know. They await word in Williamsburg."

"It's in Lancaster," Tanaqua said. "Captain Woolford and I ate a venison pie there once."

"An inn? The World's End is an inn?"

"It was a very good pie," the Mohawk added.

Webb sat beside Duncan and Tanaqua slipped away to a window, keeping watch.

"There's going to be a congress, Duncan," Webb explained. "The men on the committees are going to meet, gathering members of colonial governments, before the end of the year. They will seek resolutions to bind the colonies against the stamp tax. If it happens the Krakens know it means London is losing control of the colonies. They are furiously trying to stop it. Even postal carriers are being stopped and searched by government agents. Without correspondence the congress will never happen."

"But surely they can't prevent a public gathering of prominent men."

Webb nodded agreement. "So long as the planning is done in secret. At a meeting among the leaders of the committees."

"At an inn called World's End," Duncan concluded. "But they learned of the inn weeks ago," he added after a moment. "I saw a rebus letter that used symbols for it, written to Peter Rohrbach by a young doctor in Philadelphia."

"Rush?" Webb asked. "Benjamin Rush?"

As Duncan nodded Webb sighed. "Rush is well-intentioned but is so naive. He was sworn to secrecy but he knew Rohrbach already had the secret. But the date is still well guarded, kept in the hands of the Iroquois, using their system. Sir William and Captain Woolford insisted on it. They had gone to Johnson Hall to receive the date and carry it down through the network."

My God, Duncan thought, so simple, so open, and, in the hands of the illiterate natives who were so casually dismissed by the British, so ingenious.

Tanaqua stepped closer. "It is a way we have used for more years than can be counted," the Mohawk said. "A date is the simplest of things, especially if we use the English calendar, which most English think we don't understand. My father, he could send a whole story of a battle on a string of sinew, telling of who had won, how many prisoners were taken, how many dead of which tribes."

Webb took up the explanation. "New York, Rhode Island, Connecticut, and Massachusetts have sent confirmation of the date. Their confirmation comes in the form of one of the strings, accepting the date."

Duncan recalled the strange jumble of letters encoded with Franklin's fossils. *Massnyconnri.* He studied the string, then counted nine double knots and seventeen single ones. "Ralston had been bringing Pennsylvania's confirmation. September seventeenth" he whispered, then looked up at his companions. "They would kill to know it."

"They *have* killed to know it," Tanaqua corrected.

CHAPTER FOURTEEN

In the dark heart of the night Duncan slipped out of Jaho's blanketed hatch and darted to the bank of the swamp. A figure was receding out on the water, and in the light of a half moon he could dimly see the slightly muddy water where the man had passed, the track of the narrow path of firmer ground that twisted its way through the beds of quicksand.

For more than half an hour Duncan followed the old man down the narrow, treacherous path, fighting his fear when clouds briefly obscured the moon and he lost the trail. One false step and he could be pulled into the killing mud, and if he lost sight of his ghostly guide he knew he would be hopelessly trapped. In the silence, mosquitoes bit at his ears and bubbles gurgled as they burst, reeking of decay. He quickly pressed on as the moon emerged, past islets of willow and sedge, through water that was at times up to his thighs, until suddenly the moon disappeared again. He stumbled, lost his footing, and dropped into a thick ooze.

Duncan pushed with his hands, his feet, his knees, but could find no purchase in the sucking mud. He was drawn down, his shoulders going under, as he frantically tried to keep his head above water, fighting the mud that wanted to swallow him. The water touched his chin, his lips, then the foul mix was in his mouth. Sputtering, choking, he made a final desperate twist that caused him to slip further, sending his head under. As he lost consciousness the teeth of the mud bit into his arm.

Duncan awoke slowly, watching as through a fog, as a monk prayed at an altar by a crackling fire. Gradually he recognized the shapes of crumbling lodges and overgrown fire rings, even what looked like old fish-drying racks. He sat up, spitting the grit from his mouth, and saw that he was on an island of tall pines and cypress. His arm ached and his clothes were lined with damp mud. Rising unsteadily, he staggered for a moment, then a furry creature pushed against his leg to keep him upright. Duncan looked down into Chuga's black eyes, which stared at him with an oddly worried expression. As he approached the fire the murmuring of the man at the altar turned into wheezing laughter.

"Three times Chuga has pulled me from the deathsands," Jahoska declared. "He has always been an energetic retriever, glad for the practice. Now get your shirt off so we can pull away the leeches. Stand in the smoke to keep the blood bugs away."

As Jaho stretched his shirt between two sticks by the fire, Duncan saw now that the altar was the bottom of an inverted, rotting dugout set against the fallen trunk of a great cypress. Arrayed on and below the altar were small skulls, old stone mortars, chipped pots with intricate but faded designs of birds and fish.

As the old Susquehannock plucked the leeches from Duncan's torso, he saw now that the old man had not been praying, but simply singing as he worked on a heavy clamshell with a small blade. He was making an intricate image of two small children flanked by a man and a woman. Beside him on the altar were more than a dozen other such shells, each inscribed with a scene of tribal life. On one, men were dragging a massive fish out of the water; on another, what may have been a hummingbird hovered over a man and woman. A

European ship was surrounded by canoes on a shell, while on one more a crude fortress was fired on by cannons.

When Jaho finished, Duncan stepped closer to the chronicles, until halfway down the row he saw the small black stone Jaho had shown him in the field. He lifted the fossil and looked up. "It was always on the altar in our Council House when I was a boy," the Susquehannock explained. "It was believed to hold great power. Our war chiefs carried it into battle."

The old man took the fossil and held it toward the moon. "My mother said such seed stones were proof that though time always takes life, the messages of life endure through time." He bent to a squarish block of stone below the altar and slid back the top. The stone inside had been carved out to create a container. Inside was an object wrapped in what looked like eel skin. Jaho carefully unwrapped the flat rock it covered. "This too was always on our altar, from years long ago. My mother said it too was a kind of seed stone."

Duncan took the rock as Jaho extended it, not understanding. It was no fossil, of no particular geologic interest, the patterns on it seemingly random works of nature, but when he held it closer to the flames the lines took on an order. He dropped to his knees, his hands trembling. He had seen such signs as a boy, carved into the boulders of the Hebrides.

"They're called runes," he finally said. "How did you . . . where would . . ." He looked up to see Jaho's wrinkled face lifted in a smile again.

"People can reach across time," the old man replied. "The messages can tell you who you are."

"These were from mighty warriors who rode the sea," Duncan said, "dozens of lifetimes ago."

The Susquehannock dropped crosslegged in front of the fire, listening with the eagerness of a young boy, as Duncan told him of the ancient northern adventurers who left rune stones on the shores they visited. By the time he finished Jaho was rocking back and forth, his eyes out of focus. Over the past weeks Duncan had seen the ravages of advanced age on the old man, and now he realized Jaho's mind had gone somewhere else. He stared at Jaho a long time, trying to understand why he was sharing so many secrets with him. At last he returned the rune stone to its container and paced along the altar, studying the other clamshell chronicles and finding a bowl of loose wampum beads waiting to be strung, similar to those in the strand Atticus had carried in his death. Here before him were the lost treasures of a lost tribe.

At last Chuga nudged the old man and he snapped out of his trance. "You're right," Jaho said to the dog as he rose. The moonlight fades. He turned to Duncan and put a hand on his shoulder. "Sometimes you have to die a little to know how to live," he said, and gestured him back into the swamp.

The fork and spoon retrieved by Duncan were being transformed into weapons through long hours of scraping. The frame of the window slit by the door became pockmarked, for the sling throwers practiced by aiming for the narrow slit from the opposite side of the building. Stones flew, rocks scraped, and six more lines had been marked by the door before trouble hit again. One of the African work crews had worked its way close to their company, planting the last of the sotweed, when an adolescent boy tripped and dropped one of the baskets, spilling and crushing several seedlings as he fell. It was the boy with the bright, inquiring eyes who often delivered their lunches. To his misfortune, Gabriel was riding by on one of his inspections. The superintendent screeched his displeasure then sprang from his horse and bounded toward the boy, reversing his whip to use its heavy metal ball.

Suddenly Murdo Ross was bent over the boy, back toward Gabriel, who did not check the swing of his stick. His fury enflamed by the Scot's interference, he pounded it into his back, then through the shredded cloth into his skin. "You brainless ox!" the superintendent screamed. "Do not—" the ball struck again, "get between me—" it struck once more, "and my sotweed monkeys!"

But Murdo would not move. The big African whom Duncan had often seen watching them work now advanced, clenching his fists. The huge man, dark as walnut, gestured for the boy to flee, and the young slave ran into the arms of a weeping woman. The tall slave hesitated, clearly fighting the compulsion to intervene. The lines of decorative scars on his face moved up and down as he clenched his jaw. He looked toward Duncan, who shook his head in warning, then frowned and retreated to the woman's side.

Gabriel gave full vent to his wrath, slamming the metal ball down with sickening force, again and again, until at last the sturdy Scot broke, collapsing onto all fours then onto his belly. Gabriel had found a release for the wrath he felt toward Duncan and his friends. The superintendent only stopped when the blood began dripping down the shaft onto his fingers. "No one touches him!" he screamed. "No one! If anyone tries I'll feed them to my dogs! Not now! Not the rest of the day! Not tonight. Let him crawl in his filth back to his quarters!"

Tanaqua, sensing Duncan's own impulse, clamped his hand around Duncan's arm. Murdo's companions, rage in their eyes, seemed about to charge the superintendent, but then Webb appeared, pushing them back, pointing to the pharaoh riders who were now watching from the edge of the field with their dogs, waiting for the command to unleash their fury. Gabriel mounted his horse and rode off with one of his grotesque laughs.

Duncan stood motionless, gazing at his friend in despair, until Tanaqua finally pulled him back to the work crew. For over an hour

Ross did not move. The blood oozed out of his back, staining the soil. Crows landed beside him, and Duncan was about to charge at them when several well-aimed stones scattered them. The big African man with the scarred face was throwing them, as if standing guard from a distance, and when he hit one, stunning it, the others flew away. When Ross finally moved, it was only to lean up on his elbows before collapsing into unconsciousness again.

Duncan knew his spine could be broken. His brain could be bleeding under a crushed skull. Lesser wounds had killed men. Black thoughts seized Duncan. Jessica Ross appeared in his mind's eye. He had failed her again.

Another crow landed and another stone was flung from a different direction. To Duncan's surprise he saw Trent, tossing a second stone in his palm as if waiting for another bird. Winters grabbed Trent's drinking gourd from his belt and emptied it on Ross's back before taking his own water gourd from his belt and dropping it beside the Scot's outstretched hand.

"*Ai ya yi yo wayaka.*" An African woman started singing, a rhythmic chant in a strange tongue that was soon taken up by all the women in the crews working nearby. One of them, nervously watching Winters, inched forward and knelt, putting her hand on Murdo's head while raising her other hand in a beseeching gesture toward the sky, murmuring low, emphatic words. She pulled off her necklace, bearing a pendant of what looked like twisted roots and feathers, and tied it to Ross's arm. The big black man with the ring of scars around his head slowly advanced. Trent raised a restraining hand but the man did not halt until the woman rose and grabbed his arm, pointing toward the boy, who stood watching, crying now. Duncan realized he must be looking at the boy's parents. The man shook the woman off then stared toward the manor house, where Gabriel had disappeared. He began his own chant, aimed at the manor compound, more angry and much louder than that of the women, then with a finger drew symbols in the air. The Judas slaves could not understand his words but they all recognized a curse.

By the time the bell sounded for the end of the day Murdo had risen up once, to drain the gourd, then collapsed again. When they reached the yard not a man moved to the supper kettle but instead all watched as the big Scot began crawling toward the stable in slow, agonizing stages, seldom going more than fifty feet before collapsing, each time leaving a trail of blood. Winters and Trent herded the company toward the kettle, but as they ate they silently watched Murdo's slow, excruciating progress through the dying light. The rangers watched Webb, waiting for an order to rush out onto the field, but the major, with a forlorn glance toward Duncan, gestured them inside. It was dark as the last men reached the entry. Trent was pushing the door shut when he gasped and abruptly retreated. Winters, holding the bar, dropped it and stumbled backward.

A huge shadow was moving toward them. A moment later the tall African materialized out of the darkness with Murdo in his arms. Tanaqua and Ononyot pushed past the overseers and draped Murdo's arms over their shoulders as the African lowered him. The big man spoke several incomprehensible words in a rich, deep voice, then pointed to Murdo. "War-i-oor," he said, stretching out the word. "Warrior," he tried again. He thumped his own chest. "Like Ursa," he said in introduction, then looked back at Murdo.

"My son . . ." the African began, then seemed unable to find any more English. He pressed his hand over his heart, lifted it and placed it over Murdo's own heart, then spoke words in his native tongue that had the sound of a prayer. Duncan silently returned Ursa's nod as he backed away into the night.

Murdo pushed himself away from Tanaqua and, holding onto the wall, staggered into the slave shed. He collapsed onto a platform and closed his eyes as Duncan examined him. When he opened them a few minutes later he lifted his head toward the despairing companions who surrounded him. "I've been beaten, damn ye," he growled, "but I'm not beat." The big Scot paused and looked with a wrinkled brow at the bundle of feathers, now stained with his blood, that had been wrapped around his arm by the African woman.

Duncan had to touch him to get his attention, then asked him to move his feet and grip each of Duncan's hands. "He's built too much like an ox for any serious damage," Sinclair quipped. Murdo gave an affirming grunt and, as Jaho began washing his wounds, he fell asleep, his fingers on the feather totem. Amazingly, despite his terrible flailing by the metal ball, he had no broken bones. Duncan sprinkled the last of his healing herbs onto the open gashes.

"He needs better food to heal properly," Duncan declared, looking at Webb but speaking loudly enough for all to hear. "There's dandelion greens and pokeweed shoots in the field. Gather some for him tomorrow." He surveyed the gaunt faces. They had no hope of escape if they could not build their strength. "And any other you find eat yourselves."

THAT NIGHT HE AGAIN FOLLOWED JAHO OUTSIDE, REACHING HIM as Chuga emerged from the reeds to greet the old man. "No, Duncan," the Susquehannock warned when he realized Duncan did not intend to stay with him. "You will be caught. You don't know the hills the way I do. I know every outcropping, every blind spot. This is my land."

Duncan grabbed some mud from the swamp and began rubbing it over his face. "But I'm not going onto the land," he declared, rubbing Chuga's head, and then stole away along the bank toward the river.

A sliver of moon reflected on the still water of the Rappahannock. A deer at the edge of the river looked up then returned to drinking. Duncan stripped to his britches in the shadow of a cedar tree then silently eased into the water. He reached the two-masted snow after surfacing for air only three times, then hauled himself up the anchor line, clapped onto the rail, and watched the deck. The cutter and the brig that had recently arrived would have marine guards posted but a trade ship anchored in a quiet river was unlikely to follow such discipline.

There was no sign of life on deck other than a dim lantern at the stern. He moved like a shadow, the way Mohawks and rangers moved through enemy camps to rescue captives. Below the deck his nose quickly led him to the galley. Heaped beside the cold stove were baskets of produce. He filled an empty flour sack with carrots, onions, and potatoes, then dropped in three knives. He was about to throw more utensils into a second sack but thought better and filled it instead with more food. He fastened both the sacks with twine, then tied them together and draped them around his neck.

Back in the water, he carried the food to his pile of clothes on shore then returned to the river. With silent, stealthy strokes he approached the naval vessels, circling the cutter then the brig, pausing often to study their construction and rigging. The cutter had sailed away Sunday afternoon and returned four days later, and Frazier had said that was its usual schedule, as if it were routinely carrying messages back and forth to a place two days away. It made no sense for the ships to spend so much time at Galilee. He might expect an occasional call of a naval ship attached to the Chesapeake squadron but these ships were like fixtures at the remote tobacco plantation.

He pushed himself out into the current, luxuriating in the cool water and the freedom it offered, letting himself float with the slow movement of the river, then swam upriver and drifted past the manor house. He studied the manor house compound and the wharf from afar. The only room showing light was what appeared to be the dining room. Figures moved by its windows, one lifting an arm as if in a toast. The breeze carried faint sounds of laughter.

Half an hour later he was back at the stable, dropping the bag of food and knives in the shadows before sprinting along the long drainage ditch across the fields, painfully aware of the consequences if he were caught by the night patrols. He lay in the ditch, watching as two men on horseback passed the African sheds, but did not rise for several more minutes. A whippoorwill called from the hills. Frogs sang in the swamp. When he heard the crickets renew their chorus he stole to the nearest of the sheds.

Inside, someone was chanting again. He began dropping the food into one of the window slits. After the first three onions, a strong hand reached out to take the food, then when he was finished, Duncan extended his own hand. The slave inside squeezed his hand tightly and spoke a few words in an unfamiliar tongue. They sounded not so much like an expression of gratitude but as a quiet vow.

THE NEXT AFTERNOON DUNCAN WAS PULLED OUT OF THE WORK line by Winters. "Go with Trent back to the stable. Wash up," he ordered. "You're going to the compound."

Duncan received the news with a chill, and found himself clutching the still-painful burn on his arm. He had told himself he would not be sent to interrogation again so soon. With a stab of fear he realized he may have been seen the night before. Murdo and Tanaqua stared at him with worried expressions. Larkin handed him one of the little slats of hickory, riddled with teeth marks.

Trent gauged him with a disapproving eye when Duncan finished washing his hands and face at the water barrel, then motioned with his baton toward the perimeter road. Duncan tried to push away his fear by putting a label on each of the buildings as they approached the compound. The smithy, the carpenter's shop, the cooperage, the laundry shed where aproned women now toiled at a soapy kettle, the root cellar, then with a chill he found himself staring at the squat brick building with the wide chimney. Why, he asked himself, would he need to be cleaned to go back into the smokehouse?

His relief at being led past the smokehouse was momentary, for he spied the servants waiting with impatient expressions on the back portico. As he climbed the steps, a young African woman filling buckets at a pump paused and watched him with sad eyes.

Trent led him past the servants through the kitchen door.

A rotund woman wearing a bright yellow apron pounced on them. "Not a step further!" she ordered, raising a rolling pin.

Trent backed away. "It's him," he muttered.

The woman's eyes went round. "This?" she scoffed as she paced around Duncan, inspecting him.

"From the stable," Trent reminded her. "The Judas slaves."

The woman stroked her chin, rubbing flour into her cocoa-colored skin. "Titus!" she called.

A remarkably graceful man in black waistcoat, white linen shirt, and britches over white stockings appeared from a side door. He was long-boned and thin, with greying hair and a row of small, subtle decorative scars that ran from one ear into his collar. He was as tall as the big slave who had helped Murdo, but with much lighter bone structure and a narrow, refined face. Duncan was beginning to realize that Africans, like the American natives, had many different tribes.

Titus bowed his head to Duncan and led him back out onto the rear portico. With a few quick commands he launched the lingering servants into a frenzy of activity. The woman at the pump brought a bucket of water. A teenage girl dressed as a housemaid removed Duncan's filthy waistcoat with a disapproving grimace and slammed it against the wall several times before roughly brushing it. He was shoved down onto an upturned keg, his head was jerked back, and with painful tugs another began using a comb to untangle his hair.

The girl from the pump arrived and giggled as she pulled off his shoes and tattered leggings. He watched, confused and no less apprehensive, unable to shake the feeling that he was still bound for punishment, just one more refined than he had expected.

"Blessed Jehovah!" the plump cook exclaimed as his filthy shirt was peeled away. The Africans all paused, their levity gone, as they silently stared at the scars and scabs on Duncan's back. She called for a clean cloth and began dabbing cold water on them, then paused as she saw the livid brand on his arm. "Poor boy," she muttered, and stroked his arm with a motherly touch. "Poor, poor boy."

A quarter hour later he was for all appearances a new man. Fresh stockings, shoes, and a shirt had been fetched for him. The pink, nearly raw flesh of his brand had been rubbed with witch hazel and powdered over before the clean shirt was pulled over his shoulders. His waistcoat had been cleaned, sprinkled with lavender water, and a tear in its fabric hastily patched. His hair was straightened for the first time in weeks and a blue ribbon bound it at the back.

"Better," the woman in charge declared in a tone that made it clear she did not entirely approve. "Pity no time to shave you," she said, then with a finger on his shoulder pushed him deeper into the great house.

Duncan followed her down a wood-paneled hallway lined with paintings onto an ornate staircase and up to the second floor. In a bedroom overlooking the river, a man lay with a compress on his head. On the bedpost hung the jacket of a British naval officer.

"It's the malaria," came a soft tight voice from the shadows behind him. Duncan turned. The cook was gone. Rising from a daybed, rubbing sleep from her eyes, was a woman in a simple green dress. A few years older than Duncan, with high cheekbones and hazel eyes, she had a quiet elegance about her despite her obvious fatigue.

"Came back with it from a Jamaica posting, he says." She pushed back her curly brunette hair to see Duncan better. "Jamie . . . I mean Mr. Winters mentioned he had a Scottish doctor among his charges. Can it be true?"

"Edinburgh, aye," Duncan replied uncertainly, and bent over the man. He had a raging fever.

"Peruvian bark," Duncan said instantly. "He needs the bark."

"We used it all, Dr.—"

"McCallum."

"The brig. The surgeon on the brig would have some, Mrs.—"

"Alice Dawson. And Mr. Lloyd *is* the surgeon of the *Ardent*."

Duncan looked up in surprise then contemplated his patient. "He must have a medicine chest. Where is it?"

"On board."

"Some diaphoretin then. Antimony perhaps, or at least James's Powder."

"You speak beyond me, sir. We bled him yesterday. This is as bad as I have ever seen him. He passed the night shivering uncontrollably. He is unable to keep food down. Titus says we could find leeches in the swamp."

Duncan paused a moment, considering the dangers, and opportunities, before him. "He is a frequent visitor then?"

"Starting last autumn the *Ardent* started calling every few weeks, a stopping point in the bay patrol."

Duncan kept examining Lloyd as he spoke. "She's been here several days," he observed, keeping his tone casual. Their chances of escape would be far greater if the brig and her men were gone.

"Three or four months ago she started flying a pennant of Virginia and tends toward more extended stays now." Mrs. Dawson hesitated, studying Duncan a moment. "The navy is using the old mill that lies around the point in the river as something of a headquarters for provincial business. We have a wharf that accommodates ocean ships."

"And a smokehouse where fresh meat is hung," he stated. She turned her head down, and began fidgeting with a corner of the doctor's comforter.

"Do you have strong spirits?"

"Some brandy."

"We must rub it into his limbs. It will draw out the heat."

She stepped to the door, spoke a few words to someone waiting in the hallway, and moments later the housemaid who had cleaned Duncan's waistcoat appeared with a decanter.

"Nancy and I can do this, Mr. McCallum," Mrs. Dawson said as she lowered herself into the chair beside Lloyd's bed. "Polly will take you to the brig to retrieve such medicines as you find there." She nodded toward the doorway, where the plump woman from the kitchen, her apron removed now, waited with a basket in her hand. He glanced back at his hostess. Polly must have been instructed to make ready for the ship even before Mrs. Dawson had met Duncan.

Feeling as if he were caught up in some strange theater performance, Duncan followed the cook slowly, studying the house. The hallway on the opposite side of the stairway was blocked off by a row of chairs, and seemed to have a stale, unlived-in atmosphere. Portraits lined the stairway, of elegant women in silk dresses, a stern but prosperous-looking man holding a tobacco leaf in one hand and a long-stemmed clay pipe in the other, and a young boy with his arm resting on the back of a large russet-haired retriever with a brace of ducks at its paws.

In a frame at the bottom of the stairway, in a place of prominence, was a peculiar document, which caused him to pause. It was a land charter. To his astonishment he saw it was the charter for the Virginia colony, which seemed so unlikely he leaned in for a closer examination.

"If they ever lost the real one, old Mr. Dawson would say, the governor could come and just cut this out of the frame."

He turned to see Polly grinning at him, then he studied the framing. It was not an actual parchment under glass, but rather a very clever reproduction on a canvas, a seemingly perfect reproduction, right down to the royal seal. "The artist must have worked in the king's court," he suggested. Polly just laughed, and gestured him out the front door.

The *Ardent* was moored at the deepwater plantation wharf, with a guard at the top of the gangway. Polly explained their business, then produced a fresh pie from her basket, which quickly warmed the face of the stern young officer on the deck. He removed his bicorn hat to them and gestured him down a hatch, ordering a mate to guide them to the sick bay. Duncan asked the mate about the light blue band he and the rest of the men wore on their sleeves.

"In the service of the colony. Seconded to the Virginia navy, which I never knew existed until they brought out these armbands."

"Eighteen guns," Duncan observed—he had quickly surveyed the single fighting deck before descending into the shadows—"but you don't have nearly the men to work them."

"Aye," came the mate's weary response. "Over half the crew is seconded to the cutter and the yacht and most of the marines have been split between here and"—he paused and eyed Duncan more deliberately—"elsewhere."

"Yacht?"

"It's what the Commodore calls the ketch when he is aboard. Like the king's royal yacht."

"Now leave the good doctor be," Polly scolded the man as they reached the physician's station, and when the mate retreated she took up a position in front of the cramped chamber as if to assure Duncan's privacy. Opening the wooden chest that served as the brig's dispensary, he stared in amazement. It was filled with drugs, bandages, bleeding cups, lancets, even a bone saw neatly inserted into tiny brackets under the lid. He dropped a vial of laudanum, the tincture of opium, into each of his waistcoat pockets then began filling two sacks. Into the first he dropped another vial of laudanum and little jars of the diaphoretic James's Powder, and set it aside. Into the second he dropped more laudanum, wrapping each vial in a linen bandage to protect it, a small tub of unguent, and two sharp scalpels, also carefully wrapped. He stepped behind the curtain that provided privacy for the little alcove where surgery was performed, quickly removed his waistcoat and shirt, then fitted the drawstring of the second sack over his shoulder and dressed again.

As they reached the gangway to the dock, the mate put a knuckle to his forehead and dipped his head. "Give Mr. Lloyd our best, sir. Tell him we look forward to his showing us a step or two at the great ball."

Duncan paused. "The great ball?"

"When the Commodore arrives. That's what they call him, thought he ain't got no commission, just a right pretty uniform, and letters from London he takes out whenever anyone questions him. Special orders from the Lord High Admiral and the governor, they say."

"There's to be a ball?" he asked Polly as they walked back along the lilac-lined path.

"A right grand affair."

"Sometime soon?"

"Ten days or so. Word came from the Commodore that it couldn't take place until the magistrate's affairs are settled in Williamsburg."

Duncan considered the words with new foreboding. "What affairs would those be?"

"Lord, Mr. Duncan," Polly laughed. "Surely I wouldn't know. I just cook the meals and make sure the Commodore's chambers are washed down with vinegar. His rooms always have to be just so," the cook said, her voice getting tighter. "Lemon water in basins at each corner. Logs stacked just so in the hearth. He has his own peculiar ways, and may the Lord have mercy on ye if ye don't respect them."

Back in his patient's room Mrs. Dawson sat holding a cold compress to the officer's head. Duncan examined Lloyd once more, then carefully arranged the medicines he had brought on the nightstand and explained their dosages. "Without the bark, his fever will just have to run its course. The laudanum will help him sleep through most of it. Twenty drops in a cup of tea every four hours should do."

Mrs. Dawson nodded gratefully. She sank back into her chair and closed her eyes, about to drift off herself. Duncan stepped to the window. The bright, comfortable chamber was something of an oasis, removed not only from the torment of the slaves living half a mile away but from the world outside. He found the woman's devotion to the sick man strangely comforting. He had been living in a world of murder, torture, and deceit so long he had grown unaccustomed to simple human kindness.

A breeze stirred the curtains, bringing with it the sweet scent of the lilacs. "I wish these days could go on forever," Alice Dawson said behind him. "In another few weeks we will be getting the hot fetid air off the bay. But today I can smell the lilacs and the bergamot in the kitchen garden. There were wrens nesting in an old shoe on a beam at the back of the cooperage. Polly showed me the tiny eggs. Little seeds of song, she calls them."

The words sparked an unexpected memory of spring in a different world. To his surprise, Duncan began speaking of visiting eider nests with his grandfather, telling of how they would whisper to the brooding birds to make them comfortable, then take a handful of down from each nest for their winter comforters. She gave a weak laugh and told him of how one of her great joys as a girl was to be taken out on the river by a maiden aunt to watch an island rookery of night herons.

When Nancy entered to check Lloyd's bedding, Mrs. Dawson whispered to the maid, then turned back to explain with sparkling eyes how a bluebird sang from the window sill the day before. They exchanged more stories, Duncan of waking to a family of young turkeys sitting around his campfire one morning in the Catskills, and she of the amazing mating flights of the woodcocks that inhabited the river islands.

Duncan realized Nancy had returned, and was now extending a tray with a plate of cold chicken, cornbread, and a mound of butter beside a glass of milk. Ravenous as he was, he stared at the food for several long breaths before shaking his head. "I cannot."

Mrs. Dawson took the tray from the woman and set it on the table at the end of the bed. "Because you are not hungry?"

"Because I am always hungry. Because I have more than twenty companions who will only eat thin gruel and dried fish today."

"Your devotion to them is commendable, sir. But I can do nothing for the others." She looked down into her hands as she spoke, and there was a new tightness in her voice. It was the first acknowledgment she had given of the slaves of Galilee. She took a deep breath and looked up. "Would you deny me the opportunity to show compassion for one just because I am prevented to do it for all?" She looked back at the unconscious man on the bed. "We must at least have one healthy physician, sir."

"Duncan. Just Duncan." He studied the woman, surprised at the familiarity that had grown so quickly between them. She seemed so strong yet strangely fragile. He had not meant to hurt her. "I would not betray my manners by eating alone."

She smiled and pulled two chairs to the table, then sat and bit into a slice of cornbread.

"Speaking as a physician, madam, you look exhausted to the point of collapse," he said after swallowing several bites. "I prescribe sleep. Surely your husband or one of your staff could sit with Dr. Lloyd."

A melancholy smile lifted her face. "My husband was an inquisitive man, always seeking out modern techniques for farm management.

So he traveled. London. Philadelphia. Charleston. He was invited to inspect sugar plantations in Jamaica. Nearly two years ago."

Duncan lowered his fork. "Surely you made inquiries."

"Six months after he left here, a portly man dressed like a Tudor prince arrived with a paper that said the plantation was now his, surrendered by my husband to settle gaming debts." She stared out the window now. "A codicil stated that I was to be provided for, for as long as I lived. Of course I made inquiries. I had never known my husband to gamble, and he would have never risked the title of this plantation he loved so much. One man said my husband had died of the fever in Kingston. Another said he never made it to Jamaica. Lost at sea."

"If his ship sank there would have been an inquest, with proofs required."

"Only him. Lost overboard in a storm."

"But these are matters for a court."

"The Commodore is a confidant of the governor, even a member of Parliament. His papers are always crowded with seals and stamps."

Duncan lowered his glass. "Are you saying that the man the brig awaits is the man who stole your plantation?"

She glanced back at the door, as if fearful of being overheard. "He is the owner. He provides for all of us."

"Off the backs of slaves."

She did not meet his eyes as she broke off a corner of the cornbread. "We always had field hands, but it was different then. In fair weather we would have meals with them on the lawn every Sunday. My husband would send doctors and pastors to minister to them. We never allowed a lash to be used."

"Did you have Indian slaves? Scottish slaves?"

"Never a native. Not slaves at all, just indentured servants who were given land at the end of their service." She looked down into her folded hands and spoke in a voice that grew smaller with each word. "I have nowhere else to go. He brings me lovely dresses and throws balls attended by every plantation owner on the river. He likes his sashes and medallions. Sometimes he calls himself Lord of the Chesapeake, a silly notion but no one would ever dare dispute him." She grew silent for several breaths, then shrugged. "He wears me on his arm like another ornament."

Duncan stared at the woman. The elegant Mrs. Dawson was herself a slave.

She had no more words. She did indeed seem about to collapse, as though the confession had used up the last of her strength.

He prepared a draft of the laudanum, which he left by the bed, then touched her shoulder in farewell. She did not look up.

Duncan was alone as he reached the downstairs hallway, and paused again at the extraordinary painting of the document he had noticed before venturing into the largest chamber at the front of the house. Flanking an ornate marble fireplace were shelves of books. Over the fireplace was a large portrait of King George. Over a vase of lilac blossoms on a side table was a painting of a bare-breasted Indian woman on her knees, extending a handful of tobacco to a richly dressed European. Two more paintings adorned an adjoining wall, one of a native in a pose of earnest Christian prayer, the second of a fierce warrior with two eagle feathers extending from the back of his head, one upright and the other jutting at an angle. The warrior was accurately adorned with tattoos and quillwork, dressed in loincloth and leggings. Behind him was a murky forest where the dim shapes of a wolf and a bear could be seen.

He walked along the edge of the room, marveling at how such opulence could exist so close to the squalor of the slave quarters. He brushed a bundle of peacock feathers extending from a crystal jar, then looked up and froze. His knees grew so weak he had to hold onto a chair for support.

On the wall before him was a life-sized portrait of the plump, lavishly dressed man who could only be the Commodore, the Lord of the Chesapeake. But Duncan knew him by another name. It was Lord Ramsey, Sarah's ruthless and reviled father, who had vowed repeatedly to take Duncan's life.

CHAPTER FIFTEEN

R amsey!" Webb spat the name like a curse. Duncan had just described what he had discovered in the manor house. "I know the bloated prig."

Duncan felt bile rising up his throat. Seeing the portrait had been a waking nightmare. "He fashions himself as a commodore, and wears a fanciful uniform."

Webb's eyes flared. "He owns tobacco plantations in Virginia, indigo plantations in Georgia, and sugar plantations in the West Indies. Cajoled his friend the governor into granting him a commission in the Virginia navy, which at the time had maybe four dinghies and a scow in its fleet. He promised he would get ships seconded from His Majesty's navy." The militia officer looked back at the masts extending over the riverbank. "Is that the *Ardent*? That's his brig, by God!"

"The brig that sank the committees' boats, I warrant," Duncan said. "Meaning he is one of the Krakens. Franklin reported it all started at the Admiralty."

Alarm built on Webb's countenance as the words sank in. "The marines. The maritime runners blown out of the water. The pieces fit together."

"You've had dealings with Ramsey?"

"I have sat in the House of Burgesses listening as he lectured us about our obligation to support the merchants and lenders in London and Glasgow, on whose backs all prosperity rests. He was insisting that the Burgesses should guarantee all debt incurred by the planters. I dismissed him as another arrogant, ill-informed member of the brocade-and-lace set. But later I began to glimpse how powerful he is behind the scenes. He works in the shadows. It is said he gained his plantations by acquiring the annual mortgages many owners use to pay plantation expenses before the crops come in, then bringing actions in court for immediate payment when no ready cash was to be had. I know for a fact that he bought the debt of several members of the Burgesses and allows them to remain in their homes at his pleasure, meaning they must do favors for him in the government. It is said he has loaned money to the governor himself. My God," Webb said as he contemplated his own words. "It must be how he got the commission, and started his little Virginia navy."

"He stole this plantation, probably killed the rightful owner, and parades the widow on his arm."

"God in heaven! Not dear Alice Dawson? They used to call her the angel of the Rappahannock for the good works she did for the poor."

"He is likely the leader of the Kraken Club in America."

Webb's anger seemed to give way to fear. "Then our enemy is Satan himself," he whispered.

"He will arrive in a week or two. He is waiting to settle some business with a magistrate."

"Business? Ramsey never does business. He does extortion, and never to serve anyone but himself. But what would a magistrate have that Ramsey might desire?"

William Johnson's warning came back to Duncan. *The lie will arrive and they will die.* "His signature on twenty-four death warrants."

DUNCAN WAS SLEEPING HEAVILY, BONE TIRED FROM ANOTHER DAY tending the rapidly growing tobacco plants, when a hand clamped over his mouth. In the dim light of the solitary candle left by the necessary chamber, Duncan nodded at old Jaho. The Susquehannock was holding Duncan's sack of medicines. He led Duncan to his blanket tent and out into the shadows.

The moon had not risen yet, and Jaho appeared untroubled by the threat of guards. He strode purposefully across the perimeter road and knelt. Chuga appeared, pushing its head against the old man's chest as Jaho whispered to it. The dog backed away toward the water, and Jaho motioned Duncan toward the fields.

They trotted in the deep shadow of the low ditch that divided sections of the wide field. Jaho knocked on the side of the first building they reached and after a moment the board moved outward and a broad hand reached out to help them inside.

Half a dozen candles were lit along the platforms used by the Africans, and Duncan looked up at more than three dozen wary faces. Ursa, the big slave who had saved Murdo from his misery after Gabriel's beating, spoke to the others in his native tongue, and several came forward to greet Duncan, led by the man's wife and son. Duncan introduced himself and Ursa gave his hand a vigorous shake, then pulled his son forward. "Kuwali speak good," the man said of his son.

The boy gave an awkward smile. "Mrs. Dawson taught me with her children," he explained in a surprisingly refined voice. "I worked in the manor house until I dropped the Commodore's decanter one night. We have sickness. In the house they say you are a healer."

The Africans had divided their sleeping platforms with sacking and even walls of woven reeds so that the building reminded Duncan of an Iroquois longhouse, with compartments set aside for each family. Kuwali and Ursa, clearly the leader among his people, led Duncan along the quarters, first presenting him to an old woman with deeply wrinkled skin, whose eyes blazed like embers. Without thinking Duncan knelt before her. No one moved for a long moment, then she reached out and lifted his hand, running her dry fingers over his palm. She smiled, and as if it were a signal, Ursa pulled him up and pointed to the first of the compartments, where a woman lay cradling a hand with a dislocated thumb. He realized he had been called for his medical skills, and set to work.

He set the thumb in place, then gave four adults with loosening teeth and yellowing eyes instructions to eat a handful of fresh greens—dandelions, wild onions, young poke, though never the larger leaves, which could poison—each day. To be certain they understood, Duncan promised to give Kuwali samples of each when he brought lunch the next day. He set a broken fibula, binding it with the staves of a cask, and with some embarrassment, to Ursa's quiet laughter, put his hand over the womb of a nearly full-term pregnant woman and opined that the baby seemed healthy. With old Jaho assisting, he dispensed small amounts of his precious medicine, then bound tight a sprained ankle. The Africans, though clearly familiar with Jahoska, were shy with Duncan at first but, with Ursa's encouragement, they soon warmed to him.

He managed to explain that his people were the Scottish, pointing to himself. "Scoootissh," Ursa repeated in his rich bass voice, then made a gesture that included most of his audience. "Ibo!" Ursa cried out enthusiastically, then pointed to a man who was much lighter in complexion. "Fulani!" he explained, and gestured to the row of diamond-shaped scars that adorned his own jaw. "Ibo," he said again, then to the tattoos of fish on the other man's neck. "Fulani," he repeated, then asked the name of Duncan's clan. "Mc . . . Callum," he repeated several times, making a clucking sound where the *c*'s intersected.

"Titus in the big house is Mr. Jaho's old friend," Kuwali added, pride evident in his voice. "He is Ashanti."

His eyes gleaming, Ursa led Duncan to a section of the wall covered with a sacking drape and pulled it aside. On the horizontal beam before him was a line of unexpected objects, at the center of which were several human images assembled from carved bone, centered around a woman of slightly larger size. Their arms and legs were just crude suggestions of those appendages, but the heads and torsos had been expertly worked. To the left was a fierce-looking man with jagged teeth, whose wild eyes and mane-like hair suggested a great cat. On the other side was a figure with a pointed face, elongated eyes, and scales of a serpent. In the center, standing on an inverted teacup missing its handle, was a woman with plump, exaggerated breasts and a wide, serene smile. Her body had been stained brown with what looked like walnut juice. Flanking the images were items Duncan took to be offerings—dead beetles, long feathers that appeared to have come from cranes, a turtle shell, several skulls of small mammals, and flower blossoms. At either end of the little altar sat sailing ships expertly carved of bone. Hanging above the woman at the center was a disc the size of his hand, made of red and yellow feathers. He took it to be the sun.

Duncan lowered his head respectfully toward the bone figures, then Ursa pointed to the little quillwork pouch that hung from his neck and thumped his hand against his own heart as if to approve. Jaho grinned, and motioned expectantly to Duncan's medicine pouch. Duncan opened the sack and extracted one of the little blue mercury pills he had taken from the *Ardent*, brilliant as a gem, dropped it in an empty vial, and placed it beside the other offerings.

The onlookers murmured their enthusiastic approval. Ursa spoke to his son, who translated for Duncan. "Sometimes our people go to the rolling house to work. Sometimes my mother and I go there with food."

"Rolling house? You mean the mill?"

The boy nodded solemnly. "Lila is the maid there. She knows their secrets."

Duncan searched Ursa's anxious face. "I don't understand," he confessed.

"It's not their god," Kuwali translated. "It makes their god worried. It's why they keep it locked away like another slave. One of those men in scarlet jackets painted a cross on the door." Kuwali spoke for himself now, taking over the explanation. "They send us in there to bring them packets of tobacco and such." He looked to Ursa who nodded, then the boy motioned to a folded paper behind the goddess. His mother approached the altar, murmured something to the little bone woman, and lifted the paper away for Duncan. "I learned to draw from Mrs. Dawson," Kuawli added.

Duncan opened the paper and felt his heart leap into his throat. He had only seen the long spirit mask once before, but he instantly recognized the twisted red face and beard of bear claws. The British marines had imprisoned the Blooddancer.

TANAQUA WAS KEEPING A SOLITARY VIGIL OVER JAHO'S SMOLDERING cedar chips when they returned, leaning into the fragrant smoke as if praying. "In the mill," Duncan whispered as he handed him Kuwali's drawing. The Mohawk's countenance lit with a fierce intensity. He looked up at the sleeping platforms and gave the soft cry of a nighthawk. Ononyot instantly shot up, followed a moment later by Hyanka and the other Iroquois.

As they huddled around Tanaqua, Jaho handed Duncan his medicine bag. "Kuwali," the Susquehannock said, and nodded to the bag. Duncan opened it and extracted a news journal. Kuwali, who had frequent contact with the house servants, had inserted a copy of the *Maryland Gazette*, only three weeks old. "Annapolis," the dateline said.

"Riots!" Duncan did not realize he had given voice to his reaction to the lead article until he saw Webb, then Murdo, approaching, rubbing their eyes. "There's been riots over the tax!" he exclaimed as they reached him. "In Boston, Newport, even Annapolis."

Webb grabbed a candle. Ross lit another. Suddenly half a dozen men were around them. As Duncan read, more and more men rose, until soon nearly the entire company was listening. The tax commissioner in Boston had been hung in effigy, he read. Commissioners in New York and New Hampshire had resigned under public pressure. There had been a mock trial in Connecticut of a symbolic Stampman.

Ross took up the narrative when Duncan paused for a drink. "He was charged with conspiracy to kill and destroy his own mother, America!" Murdo crowed, to guffaws all around. He turned to the next story, reporting on an exchange in Parliament between William Pitt and Grenville. "'When were the colonies emancipated to choose what laws apply to them,' Grenville had asked. 'When,' said Pitt, 'were they made slaves?'"

Even the Iroquois were listening now, as Ross read the final report, about how colonists were signing pledges not to buy anything from Britain until the tax was removed. At gatherings in town squares throughout the colonies, women were sewing hundreds of dresses and britches out of homespun in lieu of wearing British fashions.

The men gleefully passed around the paper, pausing over passages and reading them aloud again. Duncan did not even notice that Frazier had backed away until Larkin hooted. "There's a bonny lad!" he said, and pointed to the wall.

On a blank space near the door, Frazier had used a piece of charcoal to inscribe the words. "I swer not to by English guds." With a flourish the young ranger signed his name, eagerly followed by Larkin. A line of grinning men added their names. The Iroquois queued at the end of the line, and when their turn came, inscribed their runner marks on the wall.

THREE HOURS AFTER SUNSET THEY WAITED AGAIN BY THE AFRICANS' shed, watching from the shadows as a night patrol trotted past. Duncan's gut tightened as he saw the dogs with the riders. "If the wind shifts they will get our scent when we cross back over to the stable," he said to Tanaqua, at his side.

"Then we will go around," the Mohawk replied, pointing toward the river. He meant they would risk venturing closer to the manor compound to get back to their quarters. His eyes blazed with a warrior's determination, had burned so since seeing Kuwali's drawing the night before.

Jaho had insisted on bringing Ursa and Kuwali with them, just as Tanaqua insisted on bringing Ononyot. Ursa led the way up the ridge behind the sheds, moving with the stealth of a warrior himself. As they began to climb, a new figure joined them. Chuga trotted silently to Jahoska's side, who murmured a greeting in his river tongue. The dog hesitated as the others moved up the trail, then turned and stepped deliberately along the bottom of the hill. Duncan and Jaho hesitated only a moment, then followed the dog, who halted at a pile of heavy timber with a long saw laid across it.

"A new outbuilding they say," Kuwali explained as he and his father caught up with them. "Some of our men have been shaving timbers and making the joints." Ursa gestured them back to the trail.

Duncan lingered, Chuga watching him as in his mind he tried to match the mortised joints chiseled in the heavy posts. There was a stairway, two long posts cut to make a high frame in the center, and no roof. Something icy seemed to grip his spine and he backed away, then ran to join his friends.

Minutes later they were looking down at the mill compound.

"One," Tanaqua whispered as he pointed to the guard on the dock.

"Two," Ononyot added, indicating a shadowed figure at the head of the riverside track to the manor.

Ursa made a clicking sound with his tongue and pointed to the latrine as another soldier emerged, buttoning his britches. In a low whisper Kuwali explained that the mask was in the center of the five storerooms built into the rear of the mill building, two of which were used as quarters for the officers and a third as an office. The Blooddancer had been leaning against the wall, on bags of grain. Tanaqua nodded, then he and Ononyot each scooped up a handful of soil and rubbed it over their exposed skin before melting into the darkness.

In the stories shared in the stable Duncan had learned that Ononyot was famed for infiltrating enemy camps, never taking a weapon other than his belt knife. It meant that he, like Tanaqua, engaged in the ancient form of tribal warfare, which did not aim for the death of enemies but for the release of captives, taking of prisoners, or other acts meant to shame the enemy and bring honor to their tribe.

A moment after the Iroquois disappeared Ursa also faded into the shadows. Duncan saw the proud smile on Kuwali's face. "My father was a war prince in our tribe, known for leading raids deep inside our enemy's territory. Once he brought back the headdress of their king, taken from his side as he slept." Not for the first time Duncan was moved by how similar the African tribes and the woodland tribes were.

"He has told me," the boy continued, "of how our warriors often fought enemies of much greater strength, pounding their shields like thunder to break the enemy's will before charging." The boy leaned forward as if trying to glimpse his father stealing among the shadows.

"That northern god is angry." Duncan looked up to see Jaho bent over Kuwali now, whispering. "He does not like being a prisoner," the old man explained in a solemn voice. "No one is feeding him. The living god must be fed like a living human. When that Blooddancer gets angry he plays with bodies like toys. Do you understand me, son?"

The African boy replied with a worried nod.

"Those in the manor house must be warned."

Ursa's son nodded once more, and Duncan cocked his head in confusion at the old Susquehannock.

The old man gave Duncan one of his serene smiles. "Is there a river where you live?"

"I'm sorry?"

"I would have to bring Chuga."

As understanding slowly sank in, Duncan returned his smile. "Chuga could swim in cool, fresh water all day long."

"In the swamp men could die from one false step."

"I have a rope. We will get more, to tie men together."

"In a few days then," Jaho said, "when the moon is at the quarter. Not too dark, not too light."

"We should get men to the island of your ancestors, then move them out a few at a time. The Virginia men will help from there."

No one spoke again until Tanaqua materialized out of the shadows. "He is there, Duncan! Just as this brave warrior told us," he added, starting a smile out of Kuwali as he offered the boy a quick bow of his head before turning to drop a metal ball in Duncan's hand. "In one of the sleeping quarters there is an English fowling gun." Duncan held the small-caliber ball up in the dim light. It was, he suspected, from the same gun that had shot Woolford.

Ononyot appeared, carrying trophies of his own foray. In one hand he held a hammer and a coil of rope. With a proud smile he opened his other hand, in which lay a little gold braid, sliced from an officer's epaulet, which he presented to Kuwali, and a small square of silk, which he handed to Duncan. "On the entry door," the Oneida explained. It was small flag, bearing the image of a castle with a gauntleted fist over it. Duncan folded the flag into his pocket.

Ursa appeared, carrying two loaves of bread, one of which he gave to Duncan before breaking off a piece of the other for his son.

"I could bring the ancient one back," Ononyot offered. "We can hide him in the woods."

Tanaqua's eyes gleamed at the prospect. He had come so far, and suffered so much, to find the lost god.

"Not yet," came a soft voice. "He is not finished with those men."

The two Mohawks stared at Jahoska and hesitantly nodded.

"You call him Blooddancer," the Susquehannock said, "but in my father's lodge he was always just the old Trickster." Jaho gave one of his wheezing laughs. "They think they captured him but they will find that it is they who have been captured."

THE NEXT DAY THE TRICKSTER STRUCK IN THE MANOR HOUSE. Duncan had been called to check on Dr. Lloyd and was descending the stairs with Alice Dawson when screams erupted from the kitchen. Servants began running out the front door. When they reached the kitchen Titus and Polly were on the back porch, futilely trying to calm the kitchen staff.

Duncan followed their terrified gazes toward the heavy work table by the hearth where a pig was being prepared for roasting. Apples and onions had spilled onto the floor. As Alice tried to calm the servants Duncan approached the table. The pig was being readied for a huge roasting pan. A knife lay by its belly where someone had started dressing it. The dead pig's black eyes seemed to stare at Duncan. One of the frightened servants at the window yelled for Duncan to run. Then the pig arched its back and rolled toward Duncan.

The maids screamed, and Duncan shot backward. He halted halfway across the chamber, realizing that expectant eyes watched from the doorway. "Duncan, please . . ." Alice Dawson said, though whether in warning or encouragement he was not sure.

The pig was writhing now, as if trying to rise on its truncated limbs. Duncan took a deep breath and advanced on the table, clamping the pig down with one hand and grabbing the knife with the other. The writhing started again as he cut, until a gluttonous lump with two eyes appeared, followed by a long serpentine body that slid out onto the table.

Duncan grabbed the creature behind the head. It was a river eel. His discovery did little to quiet the onlookers. A maid squealed in fear as the creature squirmed in his grip, another spat what sounded like an African curse.

"It's true!" Polly cried.

Titus appeared, extending a bucket of water, and Duncan dropped the eel into it. Alone of the house staff the tall Ashanti was undisturbed.

Polly took a few cautious steps into the kitchen.

"What's true?" Duncan asked her.

"That red god, he's terrible angry," the cook declared. "He don't like his people enslaved. They're the blood of the forest."

THE NEXT MORNING A SMALL BUGGY MADE A SLOW CIRCUIT OF THE fields as they worked. Titus drove the single-horse rig, while Alice Dawson, holding a parasol, studied the slaves. She directed Titus to stop repeatedly, and was so obvious about staring at them that Trent snapped out for the stablemen to avert their eyes from the mistress of the manor.

That afternoon Duncan was summoned back to the house. At first, fighting a terrible foreboding ever since seeing Ramsey's portrait, he ignored Trent's calls to him, and even turned his back on him, but finally the overseer impatiently tapped his baton on Duncan's shoulder.

They did not speak while Duncan washed at the water barrel, but as they walked up the perimeter road Duncan kept pace beside Trent instead of dutifully following. Duncan watched a group of

Africans digging holes in the knoll at the base of the fields, then noticed how the overseer's gaze kept returning to the masts visible above the riverbank.

"Were you a bay sailor then," he asked Trent, "or did you get out on blue water?"

Trent paused, and for a moment Duncan saw a faraway look in the overseer's eyes. "The Florida islands up to the Delaware Bay, all those waters were my home, lad. Farther north to Georges Bank when we had letters of marque to take French ships in the last war."

"A privateer then."

"That was the pretty word for it. Pound a ship and take her cargo and you were a hero back then. But do the same thing without the letters of marque and suddenly you're an outlaw."

Duncan puzzled out his words. "You were caught raiding British vessels and you didn't swing for it?"

"They're rare short of bay pilots. The navy made me sign a paper swearing off the wild life and agreeing to pilot His Majesty's ships."

"But here you are."

"The Commodore liked the way I handled myself. Seconded for his navy, he calls it. Said if I proved myself he would double my pay."

"Prove yourself by tormenting prisoners?"

"By taking his orders without question."

They walked on. "I miss the water," Duncan observed. "For years I was never away from it. My grandfather would sail into the teeth of a gale, howling with laughter. At first I was terrified. But later I learned to feel the joy of it."

The words brought a strange silence. "Sometimes when the wind is right," Trent finally said, "you can smell the salt from here."

Titus waited with a clean shirt in his little room off the kitchen. Duncan stood unresisting as the butler helped him change into it, then spun about at a gasp from a darkened doorway, which he had taken to be a closet. He leapt into the shadows and pulled back the woman who had flattened herself against the corridor wall.

Alice twisted out of his grasp and, pale and trembling, lowered herself onto a stool. "I am so ashamed," she said, looking at the floor. "It's only that Nancy said every man in the Judas stable received regular beatings. I didn't credit it. But look at you. A doctor, and your back lies in ruin."

"After the first ten or fifteen strokes the tips of the leathers dig into the flesh. Gabriel has little rivets set in his whip that claw away the tissue. You would be amazed at the gutters they can dig into a man's flesh."

She stared at the brand on his arm then looked up with anguish in her eyes. "I insisted on being shown your stable. You live worse even than the Africans. What have you done, Mr. McCallum, to deserve such torment?"

"Carry broken dice and ask the wrong questions," he shot back, then regretted his glibness. "The men in the stable resist the stamp tax. And deliver messages for those who do so in Boston and Philadelphia and Williamsburg."

His words seemed to genuinely confuse her. "Who does *not* speak ill of that dismal tax?" She shook her head. "The officers from the mill say you are all traitors and deserters who practiced vile crimes and would commit more if allowed to escape."

"One of those demons stands before you." She glanced up uneasily then quickly looked away. "The Commodore," Duncan continued, "is a man who trades in lies like other men trade in Oronoco leaf." Duncan pushed his arm into the sleeve held by Titus, then saw how she stared at him now, with a new, and intense, curiosity. "We are men who chafe against the yoke, and help those with more power discuss the nature of government."

She stood and straightened her dress. "I don't understand. Discuss? You make it sound as though our duties to government are negotiable. The government is the government. You may as well argue against breathing or the color of the sky."

"Is the Commodore the government then?" His question seemed to strangely wound her. She turned and he spoke to her back as he finished buttoning his shirt. "Is this truly the government that ambushes and mutilates men in the forest, who detains us and treats us so, who threatens imminent death without so much as a trial?"

She stiffened, and silently led him to the stairs.

Dr. Lloyd was much recovered, or at least in a more comfortable stage of the terrible malarial cycle. The naval surgeon, draped with a blanket, was asleep in a rocking chair by the open window. He revived as Duncan lifted his wrist for a pulse.

"I am grateful for your efforts, sir," the officer said. "I am loathe to prescribe the tincture to my sailors for fear of habituation but laudanum was the right measure for my extremity. I had a blessed rest and when I awoke the fever had passed. I should return to my ship but Mrs. Dawson makes me too comfortable. I am indebted, McCallum."

Duncan hesitated and glanced at Alice. "McLaren. My name is McLaren. An easy mistake." The woman cocked her head at him but said nothing.

Lloyd sighed. "My wits are yet dulled, sir. McLaren. Of course. You have the air of a man from the north. I myself had the honor of cruising up the St. Lawrence at the end of the late hostilities with France."

"I was there at the fall of Montreal," Duncan replied and, as Alice excused herself, the two men embarked on a quarter hour's conversation about the northern campaign that had won the war for Britain.

"I trust you will be supplied with Peruvian bark soon," Duncan said at last.

"Three days, maybe four" Lloyd offered. "The Commodore will bring fresh supplies." The genteel doctor paused as he saw the cloud on Duncan's features. "I beg your pardon. I said something to offend you. Most unintended."

Duncan stood and backed away, making a half bow. The manor house was beginning to feel like more of a prison than the stable. "I must go. I am pleased to have played a small part in your recovery, though I daresay that Mrs. Dawson deserves most of the credit."

"I was hoping to have you dine with me on board the *Ardent*. Roasted duck. I might be able to discover a passable claret in the hold."

Duncan offered a grateful nod. "I am honored, sir." He glanced up at Alice, who had appeared in the doorway. "But my time is otherwise committed," he stated, and, making a bow, left the room.

She followed him down the stairs. "What is it, Duncan? Have we offended you somehow?"

They had reached Titus's room before he replied. "You give no offense," he said. She turned her back to him as he stripped off the linen shirt. "My business here is done."

"Then tell me why you prefer the slave quarters to my home."

"Because I am a slave of the Judas stable, Mrs. Dawson."

He was prepared for her anger, her rejection, but not for the pain in her deep eyes. "Walk with me at least," she said, motioning him outside. "I am late for a daily appointment. And you well know my name is Alice."

Trent rose from a chair on the back porch as they stepped outside, but she waved him away. "The prisoner is in my care, Mr. Trent," she declared in a tone that brooked no protest, then led Duncan around the house onto the track that followed the river bank. She soon turned onto a steeper walkway that had once been carefully laid with brick, though its weeds and heaves showed it had fallen into disuse.

They paused at an overgrown terrace where Alice picked a handful of blossoms. "My husband was so proud of this garden. He had plans to expand it, and had written to a horticulturalist for boxwood to create a maze for the children to enjoy. Galilee was a happy place, Mr.—Duncan, though you would not credit it now." She led him back onto the path as she spoke. "He was a devout Christian, and when he was left this estate by his great-uncle he continued with his uncle's plan for a work farm, where debtors came for wholesome labor while they worked off their debt. On Sundays we would have an open-air church service on that little knoll in the field. Sometimes traveling troupes would stop and perform entertainments. My husband kept open accounts for all to see and gave out shares of the harvest. I still get letters from debtors who were able to renew their lives because of their time here. It heartens me, to at least know there are others with happy memories of this place." She gazed at a little clearing at the top of the hill then paused as if to collect herself, and sank her face into the blossoms before marching forward.

It was a small graveyard, with fragrant peonies and flowering shrubs enclosing three sides, sheltering half a dozen graves.

As she arranged her flowers at two gravestones Duncan examined the others. Henry Dawson, born in 1694, died 1756, must have been the great-uncle who had founded the estate. Buried beside him were his wife and infant son, dead the same day in 1741. Two other stones, without birth years, were for Magali and Tsonai, with the smaller English names Jemma Kitchen and Quiet Sam underneath. It was extraordinary to have house servants buried with the manor family. The next stone simply said Elijah Dawson, with no dates. The stones where she arranged flowers were for Elizabeth and Jeremiah Dawson, ages four and seven, dead the same month. Duncan plucked two peony blooms and laid them by the stones.

"My babies," Alice Dawson said. "They waved goodbye to their father with me at the dock. He never knew they died. They never knew he died."

"But you said his body was never recovered."

"He's dead. I have felt it all these many months." She wiped the dampness from her eyes, then rose to pull weeds from her husband's marker. "And it's God's blessing that he never saw what Galilee has become." She gazed down at the compound, where Trent could be seen still sitting on the porch, then grabbed his forearm and pulled him through the bushes to the crest of the hill, and pointed down the other side at the mill.

"There are two lieutenants of marines there, Mr. Hobart and Mr. Kincaid. They were quartered in the manor house but I ejected them after they took too many liberties with the housemaids. The girl Lila, their housekeeper, visits us most mornings. Sometimes I go down there to bring the soldiers fresh bread. We make conversation. The officers insist their work is secret but speaking with a widow bringing food can do no harm, surely, nor can letting her help clean their office."

Duncan heard the invitation in her voice and stepped closer.

"Their secrets involve records and documents and testimony obtained by coercion. They go back and forth from the *Ardent* to the mill, arranging maps and letters. Some of the letters are from London. They boast about how Lord Grenville has taken particular notice of them."

"Maps of what?"

"New York colony. Pennsylvania. I remember thinking how odd, that they would need such maps in Virginia. They placed marks on the maps, along what looks like roads or trails. Strange symbols are arranged along the routes, like something the Indians would use. A deer. A bird. A tree. And I saw big crosses marked at five places. Johnson Hall, somewhere called Edentown, then Shamokin, Conococheague, and Townsend's Store. They have lists of names pinned to the wall. Some with checkmarks beside them, and four with little Xs beside them."

She reached up a sleeve and produced several papers. "Here. Take them. I only had a moment alone in the room they use as an office. I grabbed these from a table two days ago, though I don't really know why. It's just that they are evil men, and I am sick of Galilee being used for evil." She shrugged. "The papers make no sense to me. The lieutenants deal with mounds of correspondence. The Commodore writes to Lord Amherst in London. Hobart and Kincaid are always receiving letters and other papers, and paying coin to those who bring them in. Not postmen, more like bounty hunters and sneak thieves."

Duncan put the papers inside his shirt and studied her. "Four names with X marks," he repeated. "Patrick Woolford, Red Jacob, Peter Rohrbach, and Patrick Henry."

"How could you possibly know?" she asked.

"My God, Alice, it was you! You sent the warning."

"I didn't know the significance, but those Xs filled me with foreboding. Hobart and Kincaid spoke so hatefully about Dr. Franklin, so I wrote a message to his house in Philadelphia and concealed it in a letter to a friend in Philadelphia, asking her to deliver it."

"It was a list of men marked for death. Two of them are dead already. The other names you saw on the wall are probably the Judas slaves."

Alice closed her eyes a moment, and when she opened them he saw moisture in them. "It has to do with the pig coming to life in my kitchen, doesn't it?"

Duncan looked out over the river. "It has to do with a dying Mohawk grandmother and the stamp tax. It has to do with a lost god and committees of correspondence."

"I don't understand."

"Neither do I," Duncan admitted. "But if you wish I will tell what I know. Though I caution that it may sound like a legend out of a children's storybook."

"My children and I were always quite fond of old legends." She motioned him to a flat ledge overlooking the little harbor in front of the manor house.

He spoke without interruption, of the dying Adanahoe, the theft of Blooddancer the Trickster, of the disappearance of runners and murders on the trail south, of the committees and the Kraken Club, even the little rebellion in the Conococheague Valley. At first she listened while gazing intently at Duncan, but when he described the death of the freed slave Atticus her eyes brimmed with moisture again and she stared into her folded hands with an anguished expression.

"Atticus was a house slave here," she said, "a favorite of my husband's. We let him buy his freedom and he was still working here to buy that of his wife and child. Gabriel hated him for that, and for always talking with Jaho and the other Indian slaves. Six months ago Gabriel sold his wife and child, and refused to say where they had gone. He banished Atticus from Galilee."

"Are Hobart and Kincaid here now?" he asked after a moment.

"They left on the dawn tide, taking that little cutter. God help me, but I always pray they will drown in the bay." She shrugged. "They always return in a few days."

They walked on.

"He has a dog, old Jaho," Duncan said. Increasingly he had a strange sense that the mysteries of Jahoska were as important as the mysteries that kept the runners at Galilee.

"I'm sorry?"

"Jahoska has a great water dog that stays in the swamp close to the shed where we sleep."

Her gaze grew distant, and a small smile flickered on her face. "Jaho was always here, helping, teaching the young ones. He knew so much about growing things, about young plants and animals and humans. Some called him the forest wizard. The dogs were always with him, like kin. That painting of the dog by the stairway is of my husband as a boy. The retriever in it was Chuga. Always Chuga. When one died the biggest male of the next litter was always Chuga. My husband said Jaho's people had started the name, long before we were born, as if it were always the same dog, just in a different body. We relied on Jaho so much in the early days but he always refused to be paid. When Gabriel and the soldiers came Chuga disappeared. I thought Gabriel had killed him. Jaho refused to take their orders and was banished to the slave quarters. He was close to Atticus. Sometimes there were reports that Atticus had been spotted, speaking with Jaho. Gabriel kept calling on those dreadful pharaohs of his to capture him."

When they returned to the track along the river, Duncan extracted the square of silk Ononyot had taken from the mill. She grimaced as he unfolded it. "His flag," she said, "that's what the Commodore calls it, the insignia of his military empire." Alice caught his eye. "Titus saw you discover the portrait of the Commodore. He said you were like to faint from the shock of it."

"It was Ramsey's indenture that took me from a Scottish prison to America."

"Dear God! You are bound to that monster?"

"His daughter forced him to hand over the bond and his northern estate to her. I live with her at Edentown."

Alice noticed his choice of words. "Live with her?" She paused and turned her face toward Duncan's. "You didn't say *serve* her."

"I am bound to her. My body and my heart." He looked across the wide river. "If Ramsey finds me he will destroy me. He has vowed more than once to kill me."

"It is why you denied your name in front of Dr. Lloyd," she observed, then her face darkened. "You must go, Duncan!" she urged. "The lieutenants ordered the servants to start scrubbing the house and lay the dance floor outside by the portico for the ball. In a week's time they said. Run now. I can see that you are not pursued for a few hours."

"I cannot. I came to help the others."

"Then you are a fool, Duncan McCallum. After he arrives with more of his bullies you'll have no chance."

He kept walking. "Do you know the bay?" he asked when she caught up with him.

"Of course. When we were first married my husband and I sailed it for nearly a month in celebration."

"To the south is the wide ocean. To the north is the Susquehanna. Is it navigable all the way to the river? I need a map of the entire Chesapeake," he explained when she nodded. "Of the ports and towns. I want to understand where the lieutenants go."

She asked no questions. "There is one in the library. I could copy it by hand." A skein of geese flew overhead, low enough to hear their wings, and they paused until the birds glided onto the river.

"He bathes me," she suddenly said.

"I'm sorry?"

She looked away as she spoke. "When he stays here. The first visit, after Ramsey proclaimed that he was the new owner, my maid was washing my back as I sat in a tub in my chamber. Suddenly he was there, ordering her away." She paused, burying her face in her hands for a moment, then collected herself and continued, fixing her gaze on the geese now. "Every night he is here I must sit in a tub and he bathes me. Then he dresses me and makes me lie beside him in bed, in my nightgown. That's all. Nothing else. He is not capable of more."

They stood alone, in painful silence.

"He vowed to send me to die on his plantations in the Indies," Duncan said at last.

Her head slowly came up. "Why ever would he do such a thing?"

"Because I thwarted his plans to make his own fiefdom in the north. Because I have the affection of his daughter, which she will never give to him."

"Surely all children have occasional difficulties with their parents."

"She was captured as a child and was raised by the Iroquois, a child of the forests. When she finally returned she would not conform to his notions of the dutiful daughter. He tried and failed to beat the wildness out of her. He tracked down and killed her Iroquois father. He made plans to send her to surgeons in London who said they could tame her by removing part of her brain."

Once more tears welled in her eyes. "Surely you can't stay, Duncan. Please don't stay. You still have a chance . . ."

He gripped both her shoulders. "I will not tremble again before that monster."

"But you heard Dr. Lloyd. He's coming to the woods."

Duncan hesitated. "The woods?"

"It's what Ramsey calls this place sometimes, to mock it, because everything is so rustic here."

Duncan gazed at her in confusion, then pulled out the little flag again. "The castle and the woods!" he exclaimed.

"I don't understand."

"Something a friend said. A riddle from Shakespeare. The men at Galilee will die when the castle comes to the woods. It meant when Ramsey finally arrives at Galilee."

That night he huddled with Murdo and Webb over the letters Alice had provided.

"Hogsheads and firkins for September delivery," Webb said in a puzzled tone as he read the first. "Nothing but an order to a cooper from one of the plantation owners in the House of Burgesses."

"Mr. Dickinson sends congratulations on the betrothal of his niece," Murdo read. "He will make mention to the governor." Ross paused. "Dickinson is a member of the Philadelphia committee," he explained. "But there is nothing secret here."

They quickly examined the others, one of which was a letter from a judge to a nephew in the College of William and Mary, another a complaint from a merchant in Boston named John Hancock to a banker in New York. Duncan paused over the last of the papers, signed by William Johnson at Johnson Hall. It was a list sent to an Albany merchant for trunnel nails, pots of glue, six cones of sugar, a box of ginger, and four copper teapots, a favorite of the Iroquois.

"Why would the Krakens care about such trivialities?" Murdo asked. "Why pay coin for them?"

"They make no sense," Duncan agreed, but then recalled his exchange in the smokehouse. "Except that Kincaid said Sir William will die for trunnel nails and teapots."

CHAPTER SIXTEEN

The Judas slaves baked under the sweltering July sun, the hot wind churning dust that coated their sweating backs and parched throats. Insects worked at their eyes and ears. Impatient overseers worked at their backs. When whistles blew to call in the slave crews from the fields, Duncan and his friends were grateful for the unexpected midmorning break. But by the time they had lined up along the perimeter road behind the stable he could hear the drumbeat. A different group of overseers was coming.

The marines from the *Ardent* were being displayed in full scarlet plumage, marching in ranks of four to the beat of the drum, led by two mounted officers and followed by Gabriel and several of his dark riders. Duncan glanced in alarm toward the river. The cutter that had taken Kincaid and Hobart away had returned. Their soldiers paraded by the manor in front of the assembled servants and compound workers, then turned onto the northern perimeter track to pace along the assembled files of Africans.

Gabriel's pharaohs arrived to assist Trent and Winters, slapping the Judas slaves with batons to straighten their line. The company stood in silence, sweat dripping down their faces, flies buzzing around their heads, until finally the parade arrived. Kincaid and Hobart dismounted from their thoroughbreds for closer inspection.

As he paced along the line Kincaid randomly slapped men with his riding crop, snickering when they showed signs of pain. Hobart for some reason drew his sword, resting it on his shoulder as he languidly followed Kincaid, who halted to chastise one of the Pennsylvania men for his slovenly appearance, then Ononyot for his unwashed stink. Murdo, standing beside Duncan, tightened as Kincaid approached.

Kincaid wheeled to face Duncan. He brushed his crop against Duncan's cheeks, staring at him intensely. "How many brands will it take, McCallum? How many body parts can you spare?" he sneered, then stepped aside for Hobart, who slapped his drawn sword onto Duncan's shoulder. "You caused us a lot of trouble that day at Townsend's."

"You caused us a lot of trouble that day," Duncan shot back.

Hobart's eyes flared. He slid the blade across Duncan's shoulder until the cold steel rested against his neck. "Why is it always the neck for traitors, James?" He was addressing Kincaid now, who had stopped at the end of the row to use his snuffbox. "Stretch it or squeeze it or slice through it. Damned uninspired, when you think of all the other possibilities. The savages at least have this one thing right. They take a week or two to kill a captive then eat his heart." He twisted the blade and Duncan felt a trickle of blood on his neck.

"Delaware work," came a soft voice. Old Jaho was standing in line a few feet away.

Hobart, looked up, surprised, as he felt the Susquehannock's gaze. "You speak to me?" he asked in an oily tone.

"I was admiring the quillwork of your medallion," Jaho declared. "The Delaware always were the best at it." When Duncan had told him of the murders of Peter Rohrbach and his pregnant Delaware bride, a sorrowful, faraway look had settled over the old man's face and he had retreated to his altar.

Hobart glared at the old man. Duncan now saw that under his brass gorget he indeed wore a thin strip of painted doeskin holding a medallion, its finely worked quillwork woven into the image of a fish. The lieutenant lowered his sword. "I *am* rather fond of it," he replied, his voice dripping with contempt. "Trophy of war."

"The work of a Delaware maid," Jahoska said. The Susquehannock tilted his head for a moment, and Duncan realized he was listening to a rustling sound in the swamp reeds below the road.

Hobart and Kincaid exchanged an amused glance. "Is that what she was?" Hobart said. "A pity she was not fit for any sport. But then we had so little time."

Jaho's face tightened, and Duncan braced himself in case the old man tried to move toward the officer. Kincaid assumed a businesslike air. He stood in front of the company as an officer might on inspection, then drew his own sword and moved to the end of the line with a deliberate air. The first thrust of his sword came so fast Duncan would have missed it if Burns had not cried out. Duncan did not fully understand until Kincaid struck again, at Frazier this time. He was stabbing the tip of his sword into their feet. "Stand at attention, you sniveling worm!" the lieutenant growled when Hughes sank onto a knee as his foot was cut. The men beside him helped the ranger to his feet as Kincaid walked briskly along the line, drawing more groans as he quickly pierced the feet of Larkin and Joshua Townsend before wiping his blade on the britches of Morris, at the end of the line.

His business completed, Kincaid mounted. "All done, Robert. Let us go find refreshment."

As Hobart turned, Jaho spoke in a low voice, in his native tongue. A gasp escaped Winters, and the overseer took a hesitant step toward the old man.

Hobart halted in front of the Susquehannock. "What the hell did you say, you ancient bag of bones?"

Jaho spoke the words again, this time in precise English. "If you steal a god, the god will steal you back."

As Hobart slapped him, Chuga erupted from the reeds, snarling, spooking Kincaid's horse. The lieutenant reined in his mount and rode off laughing.

Jaho stared at Hobart without blinking. As Hobart hit him again the dog lunged at the lieutenant, baring its fangs. Hobart dodged the animal and drew his pistol.

"No!" Duncan cried as the lieutenant aimed at the dog, and was about to leap between Hobart and Chuga when Murdo's hand clamped his arm like a vise.

As Winters hastened toward them, Jaho shouted at the dog, who quieted and stepped backward toward the water, but Hobart still cocked the gun. Jaho leapt just as Hobart pulled the trigger, hitting the lieutenant's arm. The dog disappeared into the reeds and Jaho collapsed onto the bank, blood oozing from his skull.

"Good riddance!" Hobart spat. "Meddling old fool." He viciously kicked Jahoska's limp body, once in the ribs and once on the shoulder, before taking his horse's reins from a soldier and trotting toward the manor, the marines following in close order.

Instantly Duncan and Tanaqua were at Jaho's side, protected by Winters, who hovered over them, warning away the pharaohs, who laughed and rode away.

The bullet had gouged the flesh along the old man's left temple but had not entered his skull. Duncan pulled open his shirt, torn by Hobart's boot, touching his ribs, then asking Tanaqua to help remove the shirt so he could examine the shoulder.

A surprised gasp escaped Tanaqua's throat.

"He is just unconscious," Duncan assured the Mohawk. He paused, confused. Tanaqua was suddenly tracing the tattoos on the old man's body. Tanaqua excitedly pushed aside the tattered shirt and cried out for the other Iroquois, who dropped on their knees around the old man, wonder in their eyes.

Duncan stared at Tanaqua. Never had he seen such emotion on a tribesman's face. Never had he seen such an expression of both joy and anguish on any man's face. Finally he looked down and saw the tattoos clearly for the first time. An oak tree covered the old man's chest. Each shoulder was enveloped in an intricate tattoo of a bear skull.

There was moisture in Tanaqua's eyes as he looked up at Duncan. He had found the legendary warrior, his missing half king.

THE FIVE INJURED MEN WERE HELPED BACK INTO THE STABLE, their feet dripping blood behind them. Duncan called for a sleeping pallet, and they used it as a litter to carry the unconscious Jahoska inside. Trent led the remaining men back into the field, leaving Duncan, Tanaqua, and Webb behind with Winters and the crippled men.

"It wasn't just a fit of spleen," Webb said as he helped clean the ruin of Burns's foot, glancing at Winters, who sat in the doorway with his head in his hands. "They intended it all along. Kincaid selected five of the fittest. Hobble the fast horse so it can't wander far."

"They knew," Burns said, wincing as Duncan poured water on the wound. "They knew we were fixing to run."

"We can't have the bastard spy with us when we go," Frazier said. He sat a few feet away, watching the blood drip from his own foot. "He'll be the end of us. He'll have the pharaohs waiting with guns and dogs."

Webb and Duncan exchanged a worried glance. They had discussed the spy among them, more than once. They knew it was not any of the Pennsylvania men, who were all known and trusted by Ross. It was not any of the tribesmen, for the Kraken Club would never trust an Indian. It was one of the Virginians or one of the northern rangers, and it seemed unlikely it would be one of the frail or one of those just crippled by Kincaid, for the Krakens would keep their man healthy, probably giving him food when they pulled him into the smokehouse under pretense of interrogation. That narrowed the list to perhaps half a dozen men.

Duncan saw the angry way Webb studied Winters. "He doesn't know. They don't trust him."

Winters said nothing when Duncan produced his stolen medicines to treat the injured, nor when, after the overseer finally urged the fit men back to work, Webb obliged but Tanaqua and Duncan sat defiantly beside the still-comatose Susquehannock, lying on the platform near his makeshift tent.

They stayed with Jaho into the afternoon, at first just grimly staring at him. Duncan pieced together the tales he had told of his life, trying to calculate his age based on his tales of traveling with the Spanish and long-ago battles. The half king had lived at least eight decades, and his body offered testimony to a life lived hard, and wild, and joyfully. There were scars on every limb, including a deep, wide one on his abdomen that looked to have been made with a saber. He was missing two toes, and on his calf was a hollow in his muscle where flesh had been bitten off. On the inside of his thigh was a row of little tattooed flowers, done by an intimate hand, and above his knee was a tattoo of a man flanked by two children, holding their hands. In a better world, Duncan would have sat with the man for days, and recorded the remarkable journey of his life in a journal to preserve for all time.

Tanaqua was silent at first, despair often on his face as he wiped the old man's body with water, then after an hour he began speaking in his native tongue. "I am the shadowkeeper, the watcher of the sacred lodge," the Mohawk intoned in a near whisper. "The father of the father of the father depends on me. The grandmother of all rides on my strong back." He glanced uneasily at Duncan, and Duncan realized he was hearing a recitation of the secret society, one of the vows and verses of the guardians whose work could not be spoken of. Duncan gave an awkward nod and retreated outside. The men with the pierced feet had been allowed to stay in the yard and lay now under the big oak. Winters sat on one of the logs, staring at the manor, and did not react when Duncan stepped out of the yard and crossed the road.

He was gathering boughs of white cedar at the edge of the swamp when he heard a rustling in the reeds. He began his own low chant, the Gaelic words used by his father to comfort nervous animals on the croft, then slowly turned and lowered himself to the ground as the big dog with the curly russet hair emerged.

Duncan stood still as a statue, letting Chuga sniff him before stroking the broad back. "We are losing him," he confessed to the dog in a choked voice.

After a few minutes he collected the boughs he had dropped. The dog warily followed, staying at his side as he entered the stable. When Chuga spied Jaho he effortlessly leapt onto the platform, sniffed at his wound, then laid against the old man, licking his shoulder.

Tanaqua nodded his approval and went back to his own ministrations. Duncan arranged the boughs around Jaho then set a short candle in a bowl, stacked cedar twigs around it, and set it near the Susquehannock's head.

As the fragrant smoke rose, the half king's eyes opened. He silently studied Tanaqua, Duncan, and the dog. "When I was a boy," the old man said in a cracked, dry voice, "my mother used to say if you sat by the river long enough everything you need would eventually float by." He tried to smile but the effort turned into a grimace.

"The half king and the lost god have been reunited with their people," Tanaqua observed.

Jaho sighed. "I did not know about the killings the theft of the god caused. I am sorry. The path was too dangerous, these demons too greedy."

Tanaqua's face clouded. "But that was the British. You had nothing to do with it."

"Your friend Red Jacob," Jaho said. "The Scottish girl. The Philadelphia man. The Delaware and her husband. The Iroquois boy in Onondaga. My old friend Atticus, who deserved so much better."

"You had nothing to do with their deaths," Tanaqua insisted.

Jaho turned to Duncan, who was checking his weakening pulse. "He did," Duncan declared to the Mohawk. "Because he planted the idea of stealing Blooddancer with Kincaid and Hobart. It is why we are here."

Tanaqua shook his head in confusion.

"I was working with Titus in the great house when those British soldiers first settled here," Jaho explained in a near whisper, "when the prisoners started arriving. Those officers complained about the Iroquois being the impediment to their success, that the Iroquois messengers were too hard to stop. I had not heard men speak of the Iroquois as enemies for many years. I was not able to travel to Onondago to warn them so one night I suggested to them a way to distract the Iroquois, to scare them."

"Steal a god from Onondaga," Duncan suggested.

The half king gave a small nod.

"Because," Duncan continued, "you knew men would come from the north to find it."

"Because the right men would come."

Tanaqua and Duncan exchanged a forlorn glance.

"The right men?" Tanaqua asked.

Jaho motioned for another drink before he spoke. "When I was young I heard a sound from the forest like I had never known before, like a bellowing scream. It scared me but it also filled me with excitement. My uncle took me out in the night to a place deep in the woods where it seemed much louder. He told me it was the sound of the last wood buffalo in our river country, an old bull that could no longer find females. I said that was sad, and he said no, listen better. He said it was one of the real things I heard, one of the ways the world gave voice at important times, that the old buffalo was speaking to us, that it was a song of the spirits telling us that essential things could never be defeated. He said the ones who carried the song would change but never the song itself. I said how could he know that and he said because I had heard it."

It was Tanaqua who broke the silence. "Why would the half king need worry about taxes of the British king?" the Mohawk asked.

"I could never find a way by myself."

"A way for what?" Frustration built in Tanaqua's voice.

"To save the freedom men. They have to be saved. They must be saved. A new world is possible, but pathfinders must always lead the way. Freedom is what keeps our souls alive. Not everyone understands that, but the pathfinders do." The old man shuddered, and clenched his teeth against the pain. His eyes shut and he drifted off. It was several minutes before he stirred.

"Why grandfather?" Tanaqua asked him. "Why let yourself become a slave?"

The Susquehannock made a motion with his shoulders, an attempt at a shrug. "I am no slave, Tanaqua my son. It's just the way to be with these men here, and to be close to the earth. Young Winters always allowed me my walks out at night."

"Why the Blooddancer?"

"Because he always had the strongest magic. Once I had talked with the old Trickster, in his lodge in the north. It was the night I left for the last big war with the Carolina tribes. I visited with him often after that, in my dreams. I always knew he and I had unfinished business," he added. "One more battle." His attempt at a grin was interrupted by another seizure. Duncan mixed a sedative and propped him up for a long drink.

"We'll be missed," Duncan said as Jaho began sleeping. "If they come for us they may try to drag him out as well."

Tanaqua nodded and reluctantly followed Duncan back to the fields.

THE NEXT DAY TRENT, ESCORTED BY TWO SULLEN MARINES, OPENED the door before the morning bell to retrieve Duncan. Horses were waiting, including a mount for Duncan, who hesitated at the door, looking back at Jahoska. The old Susquehannock had not recovered consciousness all night, or at least not awareness. He had awakened in the small hours only to rave in his old tongue, not responding when they spoke to him. Duncan had seen the same symptoms in the Edinburgh wards of the aged. The brain might work but the tongue could not, or the brain would dwell only in places of the distant past. When Tanaqua had forlornly embraced Jaho, pleading with him to come back, the old man had patted him on the back and continued speaking in his lost tongue, as if comforting a frightened son.

Trent led the way at a trot, down the track that bisected the fields, past the African sheds toward the manor, and then up the slanting road that crossed the ridge to the mill. The other marines stood in a single rank near the dock, weary and frightened, their sergeant nervously watching the mill, where Kincaid stood on the porch with Alice Dawson and an African woman Duncan took to be Lila, the maid assigned to the mill. Only Alice moved, rushing to Duncan's side as he dismounted. "He was still warm," she said. "I thought there might be a chance . . ." Her words faded and she shrugged, then led him into the building.

Hobart's bedroom was at the end of the corridor, past a door with a crudely painted cross. Several crates had been pushed to the walls and were covered with the officer's clothing and belongings. A sword and pistol hung on a peg above the rope bed where the officer was sprawled.

Lieutenant Hobart was beyond Duncan's help. His face and hands were contorted, his eyes wide and terrified. He had died in excruciating pain.

"They say he played whist with the men until late in the evening, then no one saw him again."

On a chair near the bed, Hobart's spectacles lay on three folded papers. Duncan made no effort to conceal his motions as he collected the papers and pushed them inside his waistcoat. "The lieutenant came to his room alone last night?" he asked.

Alice pulled Lila from the shadows by the doorway. "Alone?"

The maid nodded but kept her eyes on the floor. "I thought he was going to call for me like he often does but he had had too much ale. I was on my pallet at the other end of the corridor and watched as he stopped at the spirit dungeon. He pulled his dagger out and stared at that door."

"Spirit dungeon?" Alice asked as Duncan began examining the body.

"You know, where they keep that Indian god. The lieutenant woke up from a nightmare last week, pushing me out of his bed onto the floor. He said they had to chain it and beat it, that it would learn not to mock him in his dreams."

"Speak sense, child," Alice chided. "Beat whom?"

Duncan answered for the frightened slave. "Blooddancer."

Lila gave a vigorous nod. "The god in that mask."

Alice put her hand on the woman's shoulder. "Surely you're not frightened of some old wooden curiosity."

"No ma'm. It's just that he wouldn't be concerned about you, now would he?" Lila declared with a shuddering breath. "He isn't your god and he has no feud with you. He's their god, our god, and the soldiers have been hurting them."

Alice took Lila's hand in her own to calm her. "I woke up when Lieutenant Hobart came out after one of his nightmares last night," the slave continued. "He stormed to the spirit dungeon, threw open the door, and fired his pistol at it, cursing the thing inside. Then he came back in here and didn't come out. No one came into the building, I swear it. No one flesh and blood."

Hobart had apparently passed out in his clothes. His gorget was still around his neck. Duncan lifted it and paused, seeing no sign of the stolen Delaware medallion, then fingered the lieutenant's right sleeve near the elbow, where two little circles stained the fabric red.

"What do you mean *our* god?" Alice asked the African girl.

"The Indians were born out of the land here, just like my people were born out of the land in Africa. It's why their skin is stained from the soil, like ours. The most powerful gods are the ones that bind a people to the earth." Lila's eyes widened as Duncan ripped open the sleeve. She pointed at the ruin of Hobart's exposed arm. "Like the god that sent the serpent that done kil't him."

Alice took a step backward and quickly surveyed the floor around them.

The snake must have been huge. The distance between the two fang marks was nearly as long as his thumb. The dead man's arm was grotesquely swollen and the skin around the punctures had turned a greenish blue.

"His door was ajar when they found him," Alice said.

"Snake come in, snake go out," Lila concluded. "Just like that red god done told it so."

Duncan quickly examined the rest of Hobart's body. "It could be an act of—" he caught himself.

"An act of God," Alice finished, with a hollow whisper, then seemed to collect herself. "We have huge vipers, water moccasins we call them, that live in watery places. A mill would always be home to mice, making it a good hunting place for them."

Duncan completed his examination, then looked back at the upended crate that had served as the officer's bedstand. "Hobart was drunk. It was dark. He had taken off his spectacles and may not have seen what it was. He may have swatted at the snake and angered it." He searched the pillows, and under the officer's blankets, finding nothing.

"It's gone," Alice said. He did not tell her he was not looking for the snake.

"Two nights ago," Lila confessed, "he dragged me into that room and told me to spit on the god. When I refused he slapped me, then he opened his britches and made water in front of the god, taunting it, saying 'how do you like my offering, you ugly old thing?' That's why he died. I went to the old grandmother in Ursa's shed for a charm—" Duncan now saw the bundle of feathers stuffed up her sleeve "or it might have kil't me too."

Duncan was not inclined to argue about the power of Iroquois gods. The snake may indeed have been sent by the twisted-face Trickster. But it had not been the snake who had taken the little quill-work medallion Hobart had stolen from Rachel Rohrbach.

When he finally followed Alice and Lila into the corridor, he saw the red back of a marine rushing outside. The door with the painted cross was now ajar. Inside, a candle had been lit below the red mask. In the wall beside the mask was a single round bullet hole. Underneath it, beside the rattle with four claws, was a freshly laid pile of British military hardtack and a cup of tea.

THAT NIGHT, AFTER CHECKING ON THE STILL-COMATOSE JAHO, Duncan gestured for Webb and Murdo, and brought out the papers he had taken from Hobart's room.

The first was simply a folded sheet bearing the simple word "evidence" and Hobart's signature on the outside, and as he lifted it, a single tax stamp fell out, one of those, Duncan suspected, that he had distributed to the company earlier in the summer. The next was a list of peculiar supplies, also in what appeared to be Hobart's hand. *Burnt bone dust, gum water, badger hair, prussian green, linen, lampblack, carmine.* They studied the strange list, futilely trying to connect its contents to some purpose of the Krakens, then moved to the third paper, which was in a different hand. *Larkin, oldster with black and grey beard,* it said at the top. Then, *Burns, red hair and scar above left eye, Frazier, powder scar on his cheek, Hughes, brown hair and bent nose, Townsend, youngster with blond hair tied at nape.* It was a list of the men whose feet had been maimed. Duncan handed the paper to Webb.

The major read it and went still, closing his eyes. When he recovered he pulled out a writing lead, took the first list, turning it over to its blank side, and rose. "Sergeant Morris," he called out, gesturing the sergeant forward. "I need a list of the men whose feet were pierced, ranked according to their ability to still walk."

Morris frowned, but took the paper and paced along the company before sitting on the platform and writing names. As he reported back to Webb he took no notice of Murdo and Tanaqua as they followed him. Webb studied the paper Morris handed him, then with a grave expression offered it to Duncan, who quickly scanned it before looking up at the sergeant.

"A well-trained spy would have concealed the handwriting," Duncan observed to Morris in a casual tone. "But then you never would have expected that I would be invited into Hobart's quarters to examine his body."

As Duncan extended the list of men from Hobart's chamber, Sergeant Morris took a step backward, only to have Murdo and Tanaqua each seize an arm. His face drained of color. Duncan read the names and descriptions he had taken from Hobart's room. "What was your price?" Duncan asked. "Six hundred forty acres? No," he decided. "More. You didn't just spy. Maybe two whole sections of Ohio bottomland? Was that your price for killing Devon and reporting on all that happens here? And no doubt setting the traps that snared all the Virginian rangers."

"You're going to hang, the lot of ye!" Morris spat. "Betraying the king!"

Duncan ignored him. "You didn't want to give up that cheroot made from the tax commission. You were going to take it as evidence. All you could do was give them a single stamp, the one I gave you." Duncan lifted the stamp. "You were most interested when Devon mentioned that Major Webb knew all the runner marks, but you cut him off when he wanted to speak about the water route." He dropped the stamp. Morris watched it flutter to the floor. When he looked up Hughes was holding his knife inches from Morris's neck. "Then you pounded a planting stick down his throat."

"I was lashed that day with the rest of you!"

"Of course. How else to keep your secret safe? And two days later Major Webb is brought in as a prisoner."

The sergeant frantically pushed back against Murdo and Tanaqua. Duncan put his hand on Hughes's arm.

"He must die!" Hughes growled.

"What is it about the water route we're not supposed to know?" Duncan pressed, still restraining Hughes's hand. "Where do the ships go when they leave here?" He let the blade inch closer to Morris.

"I don't know!" Morris groaned. "They call it the counting house, that's all I know. They take the boats to the counting house!" The blade touched his throat. "They would never trust me. I am just another commoner, one of their servants!"

Duncan knew he was right, and knew also that if they inflicted the punishment Morris so richly deserved, Gabriel's reaction would interfere with their escape.

THEY HEARD THE SOUND OF THE BAR BEING LIFTED IN THE EARLY dawn, then the gasp of surprise and the thud of the bar on the ground. Murdo kicked open the door but no one stepped outside. Trent began blowing his horn.

Framed in the open doorway they could see Morris, gagged and bound, suspended from the big oak by a rope looped under his arms. His body was badly bruised from the beating he had taken, and from the pebbles Sinclair had shot at him with his sling as he was suspended. Blood dripped down his face. His Virginia men had sewn the tax stamp into the skin of his forehead.

CHAPTER SEVENTEEN

Duncan did not understand the grin on Gabriel's face when he arrived to watch Morris be cut down. The pharaohs too had seemed amused as they laid the unconscious sergeant over a horse and led him away to the overseers' barn. An hour later, when the sun was burning their skin in the fields, they heard the groan of heavy axles and saw a crew of Africans hauling the cut timbers on oxcarts toward the knoll at the bottom of the fields. The Africans had been told they were cutting timbers for a new shed but Duncan knew better.

Workers in the manor compound stood on the lawn and watched as the slaves fitted the joints together, hammering in pins and positioning the joined pieces under the direction of some of the overseers. As the lunch cart began its slow journey into the fields, the ox teams began pulling, raising the frames as the men levered them into holes. The lunch had been served out by the time the company began to recognize the structure. Many stopped eating and just stared. By the end of the day the gallows would be ready, and beside it the gibbet for displaying their bodies.

"There is no time left. We must leave this place," Duncan said to Webb, who seemed unable to take his eyes off the knoll. "When Ramsey arrives with his tame magistrate he will be impatient to begin putting it to work."

The major spoke without turning. "Not with our best men crippled, and another eight or nine who couldn't run a quarter mile without collapsing. Barely half a dozen strong enough to resist if we are followed. Not to mention no one to guide us through the swamp. My God," he moaned, as the Africans levered up the first posts of the gibbet and dropped it into its holes. The major's hand went to his neck. "This is the end."

Duncan shook Webb's shoulder, pulling him around to face him. "Tomorrow night," Duncan pressed. "If Jahoska has not regained enough strength, I will carry him on my back so he can guide us. It has to be tomorrow night. Those who haven't enough strength will have to be helped by those who do."

They both looked back at their quarters. They had left Jahoska still unconscious, his pulse but a faint tremor. Trent had ordered all of them out, leaving no one to tend to the Susquehannock, whose aged body had no strength to recover from his injuries. Even Chuga was gone, for in that second night of his coma Jaho had awakened and, his arm draped over the mournful dog, had whispered for long minutes near his ear, then asked Duncan to take him back to the swamp before slipping back into unconsciousness. The big retriever had stayed dutifully on the bank, staring at the slave barracks.

Duncan had not seen Webb so despondent in all the long weeks of their imprisonment. The major cast a glance toward the young overseer. "Young Winters has a Christian heart. Maybe he will bring paper and ink if I ask. The men will want to write their families."

When Murdo straightened an hour later Duncan thought he had seen the water cart coming. "Sweet Mother Mary!" the big Scot gasped.

Duncan followed his eyes toward the far end of the field, where a horse stood, bareback, a stone's throw from the forest. "It's my Joanie, Duncan! It's little Joan of Arc!"

Duncan cupped his hand above his eyes to look at the chestnut horse. "Surely not, Murdo. It's too far away for us to know. She could never have—"

"But I know her!" Murdo insisted. "My Jess's favorite. *Fearsgar math!*" he shouted.

The horse's head snapped up at the Gaelic greeting and she trotted fifty feet closer. The Pennsylvania men were all watching now, confused grins lifting their despairing faces. Then something behind her caught the mare's attention. She snorted and wheeled about, kicking up her feet as she disappeared up the forested slope.

"Murdo!"

The call was from Sinclair, who was pointing to the end of their quarters. Sometime in the night the outlines of two buildings had been sketched there in charcoal. A school and a barn. They were the runner signs for the Conococheague and Edentown stations. The drawings were no more than five feet off the ground. He looked back in alarm to the slope where the horse had disappeared. It would be the height that Analie could reach.

Trent's split cane whip slashed the air over Murdo's head. "Sotweed!" the overseer barked.

The water cart, tended by Kuwali and his mother, was finally approaching when a cloud of dust appeared behind it. Several mounted figures were hurrying out of the compound, followed by a column of marines marching at double time. Duncan, and all the Iroquois, took several steps toward the stable as they saw Lieutenant Kincaid, Gabriel, and several overseers dismount by their quarters. Two of them ran inside and dragged out a limp figure.

"Jaho!" Tanaqua cried.

Duncan dropped his hoe and stepped deliberately toward the stable, ignoring the cane on his shoulder. He heard Trent curse and turned to see that half the company had done likewise. Winters had lowered his own staff to join the procession. Kincaid, spotting them, quickly dispatched marines, who ran to form a line, bayonets fixed, between the slaves and the stable yard. The Welsh sergeant in command of the squad cocked his musket and extended it from his waist. Duncan held out his arms and the men behind him stopped, twenty paces from the marines.

Kincaid ordered the overseers to release the old Susquehannock, who barely had the strength to stand. He raised a riding crop and slashed repeatedly at Jahoska's face, pummeling the old man so severely Gabriel stepped forward as if to intervene, only to have Kincaid turn on him, slapping the superintendent himself with the crop. In that instant of distraction Jahoska darted with unexpected energy past the marines who were facing down the Judas slaves, closing half the gap toward Duncan and his companions before collapsing. Winters dashed past Duncan to help, but Jahoska shook off his proffered hand then stared pointedly at Duncan as if to be certain he had his attention before dropping to his knees. To Duncan's bewilderment, he clasped his hands and lifted his head toward the sky in a Christian prayer. Then he staggered to his feet, walked a few more steps, ignoring the running boots behind him, and lifted his hands again, with a finger of each hand extended over his head, one pointing upright and the other at an angle along the side of his head.

As Kincaid and Gabriel reached the old man Winters stepped between them and Jahoska, earning a shrill epithet from Gabriel and a slash of Kincaid's crop on his cheek before a marine pulled Winters away. Gabriel pounded Jaho on the back with his fist, knocking him to the ground, but the old man managed to roll away. Duncan inched closer as the lieutenant approached Jaho, then halted, once more in confusion. Kincaid had stopped as well, staring at the Susquehannock. Jaho was back on his knees now, holding an uprooted tobacco plant out to the officer.

"Dottering old imbecile!" the marine officer spat, then leapt forward to knock away the tobacco and shove Jahoska to the ground. He angrily seized Gabriel's baton and had lifted it for a blow when a shape hurtled past Duncan, toppling two marines. Tanaqua was on Kincaid before the stunned officer could react. Tanaqua landed two vicious blows to Kincaid's jaw before the lieutenant began fighting back. The two rolled in a cloud of dust and fists, then marines swarmed over the Mohawk. One instantly reeled backward with blood gushing from a broken nose, another staggered back, crying out in pain, with two fingers hanging at a disjointed angle. Finally the Welsh sergeant's musket butt slammed down into the tangle of bodies and the soldiers pulled the stunned Mohawk away.

An overseer began blowing on his tin horn. His heart hammering, Duncan watched as Jahoska and Tanaqua were dragged to the stable yard and tied to the whipping posts. Gabriel's pharaoh riders galloped up and, with the marines, quickly herded the Judas slaves into a line around the logs that bordered the yard. They were to witness the punishment.

Kincaid retrieved Gabriel's baton and as he waited for the prisoners to be assembled he starting slamming its iron ball into one of the logs with furious, repetitive blows. His eyes were wild, his blows landing with such fury they were shredding the wood. Finally, the prisoners made ready, he twirled the club over Jahoska's head and swung down, stopping the treacherous ball inches above the old man's skull. "I will have satisfaction!" he shouted to the assembled slaves. "Give me the names of commissioners or these men die!"

Tanaqua, tied to the post beside Jahoska, looked up, exchanging a confused glance with Duncan. Kincaid's desperation was not about Hobart's death; it was about the name of the tax collectors whose commissions had been intercepted. Duncan looked back at the manor. Ramsey was coming, and Kincaid had not completed his mission. The lieutenant had to preserve the runners for hanging, but Jaho was not a runner.

"I will have the names! I will have them now!" Kincaid pulled away the leather covering of Gabriel's rivet-headed tails and cracked them against Jahoska's back. As he aimed the whip a second time a voice called out.

"Jonathan Bork, Esquire, Caroline County." It was Hughes.

Kincaid's lips curled in an icy smile and he pointed to his Welsh sergeant, who pulled out a paper and lead and started writing. He lifted the lash again.

"Josiah Randolph, Spotsylvania County," shouted another man, causing the lieutenant to pause again. The names were well known to those who had carried the messages. They had not given them up under torture but they would do so to save the gentle old Susquehannock.

Jahoska loudly interrupted, with a sharp speech in the tongue of his fathers that had the sound of rebuke. Suddenly he switched to English. "My name is Jahoska, born of the beaver clan of the Susquehannocks, masters of the mother river!" he shouted to the sky. "Men once quaked at the name of my tribe. I hunted wood buffalo when I had seen only nine winters, killed my first Catawba at fourteen, and the next year slayed the bear whose skull shielded my head in battle!" He spoke with an odd cadence, as if reciting a poem. "I saw the great Penn under the elm at Shackamixon and traveled the salt waters all the way to the great Spanish forts. In the year of the fire comet I rode on the back of a sturgeon as long as a canoe!"

Tanaqua stiffened. It was a death song. The soldiers, seeing how all the Iroquois had tensed as if to leap, leveled their muskets at them.

"Zebediah Sturgis of Accomac," shouted another Virginia ranger, as if trying to drown out Jahoska.

But the aged warrior continued, calling out the names of battles and brothers who fell in them, twisting in his bindings as he did so.

Suddenly an arm came free. Kincaid snarled and was about to strike down the old man's hand when he froze. Jahoska was extending the quillwork medallion that had adorned Hobart's neck.

The lieutenant trembled with rage. "By God! It was you who killed him!"

The lieutenant was deaf now to the names that were frantically shouted by the prisoners. He stepped back and viciously applied the whip. "You killed an officer of His Majesty's marines!" he shrieked. "You worthless old fool!"

It was no tribal shout that rose now from Jahoska as the steel tips began to shred his back. "*Sé mo laoch, mo ghile mear*," he called in a tight, cracking voice. Murdo turned to Duncan. The old Indian was speaking Gaelic, singing the defiant anthem that he had heard so often in the stable, the battle hymn of the Highlanders who had befriended and protected him. This was his war and he had to be allowed to fight it, the old warrior was saying to the young warriors. One Scot, then another, took up the song as the old man's skin was flayed. Jahoska sang ever louder as if to block out his pain, his words faltering as the lashes struck, then renewing, though always with fading strength. Tears filled Duncan's eyes, and he saw that half the men wept as they sang.

The Iroquois rangers who had run the woods with the Highlanders joined in, and the song took on the cadence of a tribal chant. "*Sé mo caesar mear!*" Raw flesh was exposed and ripped away. "*Suan na se an ni.*" Tanaqua sang even louder, twisting in his bindings to see the old man. Duncan shuddered with each stroke of the leathers. Jaho's voice died away. His eyes were locked on Tanaqua's now, and he was smiling even as the light steadily faded from them. Winters leapt forward to grab the whip and paid for it with a vicious lash to his face. Duncan took a step forward and found a bayonet point pressed against his belly. His heart withered in his chest. The old man was looking more like one of the anatomical specimens of Duncan's medical college than a living human.

Kincaid would not stop. Jahoska had known he would not stop when he had taunted the officer with the medallion. The Jacobite song faded away and in the terrible silence they could hear small animal-like moans coming from the old man each time the lash struck. Finally Jaho clenched his jaw and took up a war chant of his own people, the words rushing out between grunts of pain. Kincaid, tiring of his gruesome work, handed the whip back to Gabriel, who took up the task with renewed energy, working the lashes down the old man's spine until the bright ivory of bone could be seen. One of the marines turned away, retching. Gabriel's arm rose up and down as the blood pooled on the ground. The superintendent cooed like a satisfied bird.

At last there seemed no point in continuing. The mutilated body on the post looked like those left on battlefields after cannonballs turned men inside out. No one spoke.

"You will die. You will die hard for this."

It took Gabriel a moment to realize the vow had come from Tanaqua, still tethered in front of him. He raised his whip, then froze as an ungodly din rose from across the field.

The tribes from the far shore of the ocean had been watching. Just a stone's throw away over a hundred Africans were in a line, pounding their tools against buckets, sticks, and slop bowls, ignoring the overseers who shouted and slapped their backs with their short whips. Ursa was at the center, banging his hoe against the blade of a shovel. The sound was shockingly loud, with a treacherous, determined quality to it. The Africans' overseers backed away. When their tribe faced battle, Kuwali had explained to Duncan, pounding weapons on shields was a common way of terrifying an enemy, just as the Viking ancestors of the Scots had once done long ago.

Gabriel retreated several steps, calling for his pharaohs to surround him. Kincaid frantically ordered his men into a defensive formation and they too began retreating toward the road. No one stopped Winters as he stepped forward to cut Jaho's bindings. He dropped to his knees beside the old man's limp body.

Duncan took a step forward, then another. As Gabriel and his men reached the road, Duncan and the tribesmen rushed to the yard, releasing Tanaqua.

Duncan saw the bloodthirsty way Tanaqua eyed the superintendent but Murdo reached him first, gripping his shoulder. "This is not what he would want, my friend," the big Scot said. "Do not throw your life away."

"This is the hour of the half king's death," Tanaqua stated in an anguished voice.

Duncan's throat tightened. His voice cracked as he spoke. "Aye, it is the hour of Jahoska's death."

"He did not go to Hobart last night. It was not Jaho who took the viper into that room."

"But he was honored that you did, and that you placed the dead woman's medallion in his unconscious hand. This was the day he was going to die, Tanaqua. He just chose the hour. Kincaid's accusation of murder was his redemption, don't you see? Hobart's death was the beginning of the restoration of the lost god. The torture at the post was nothing compared to the torture of thinking the ancient Blooddancer would be gone forever, and all those deaths for naught. By being accused of the murder he knew what had happened, knew with certainty that the guardian of the god would not fail." He knelt by the old man and felt for a pulse before giving a mournful shake of his head. "You gave him a great gift, Tanaqua."

The Iroquois rangers formed a circle around Jahoska and began a mourning chant, one of the songs used to summon the spirits to greet a great soul. Tanaqua joined in for a moment but then his words choked away as Winters covered the dead Susquehannock with a blanket.

Duncan led him away to the water barrel.

The Mohawk dipped his face in the water, then gripped the sides of the barrel with his hands and stared at his reflection. "I would have taken him away had I known who he was earlier," he said.

"He would not have gone," Duncan replied.

"I do not understand," the Mohawk said. "Jaho knew he would just feed Kincaid's fury but he broke away to—" he searched for words, "perform that strange dance."

"He knew death was close. It was going to be the last thing he did," Duncan said, struggling himself to understand the last desperate movements of the half king.

"The blows to his head," Tanaqua suggested. "His wits were scrambled."

Duncan looked at the stable door and then at the patch where Jaho had halted, trying to reconstruct what he had seen. Jaho had stopped where he would be conspicuous to Duncan and his friends. The devout follower of the forest gods had offered a Christian prayer. He had made a pantomime with his hands to his head. He had offered a plant to the reviled English officer. Duncan nodded. "His wits were scrambled," he echoed in an empty voice, though he was not entirely certain that what they had seen was the result of a concussion.

CHAPTER EIGHTEEN

The moon was behind the clouds as Duncan slipped out of the stable to follow the tracks of the mule in the damp soil. By the time he reached Winters, the young overseer was already climbing the hill. A spade was on his shoulder and the body on the mule was wrapped with what appeared to be a linen tablecloth.

It was several minutes before either spoke. "The Judas slaves are required to remain in their quarters at night," Winters finally muttered.

"And you are supposed to be letting Gabriel stage a performance tomorrow," Duncan replied, "to demonstrate what happens to those who won't bend to his will." The Judas slaves had already been told to expect an assembly after breakfast at the base of the knoll.

"Gabriel gave orders to hang Jaho from the new gibbet in the morning," the overseer said in a brittle voice, then paused and looked at Duncan. "I could whistle right now and the dogs would come running. The pharaohs find great sport in turning a runaway into a meal for their hounds."

Duncan ignored the half-hearted threat. "He was my friend too, Jamie. May I call you that? That's how Alice calls you. Did she give you the linen?" Duncan rested a hand on the body. "If you hadn't taken him away I would have, whatever the cost." He reached out and Winters let him take the spade. The moon emerged from the clouds and Duncan saw that his face was streaked with tears.

"We're not going to the cemetery," Winters declared, then pulled on the lead rope and clucked for the mule to move faster.

They passed the flat clearing with the wooden grave markers and continued up the narrow path where old Jaho had disappeared the day they had buried Devon. After a quarter hour they reached a tall, steep bluff, the highest point for miles, that offered a broad view of not only the plantation but also the silvery ribbon of the river winding away to the east and the shadowy bulk of the Blue Ridge mountains in the opposite direction.

Duncan helped Winters untie the body and set it in a sitting position against a tree, then the overseer lifted the spade and stepped out onto the flat grassy clearing above the cliff. To Duncan's surprise he loosened a handful of soil then sprinkled it in each of the cardinal directions before dropping a few particles over his head and rubbing the remainder between his palms. It was a native purification gesture.

Winters gazed at the corpse. "I was only six when he first brought me here," he said. "My father was the pastor for the little settlement old Mr. Dawson started here. Mr. Dawson, he was a man of the Christian God, not a man of the forest, but he trusted Jahoska like a brother. Jaho had always been here, like the Chuga dog. Once I joked that maybe there had always been a man named Jaho here too, like Chuga. My father didn't laugh, just said because we worshipped the Old World God didn't mean we should make light of New World gods. My father sometimes called him Saint Francis of the tribes. I think now my father envied him, for his closeness to his gods and the effortless way he had with nature."

Winters turned to look out over the sweeping landscape. "In the autumn we would watch huge flights of ducks and geese flying along the edge of the bay. The passenger pigeons would fly overhead in flocks stretching from one horizon to the next. He would call out to them in his old tongue and they would fly lower as if they understood him, so low we could not hear ourselves speak for the sound of their wings. I was spellbound. I thought he was some kind of gentle wizard, for the way he understood nature and could coax wild animals to approach us. He always knew what nights to climb up here to show me meteor storms." Winters looked up at Duncan. "I will never forget those nights, and I will never fathom how he could know what nights the stars would fly like that. It was as if the pulse in his body came from the earth itself." As he spoke a huge owl swooped out of the darkness and landed on a limb above the dead Susquehannock. The bird cocked its head at Winters. Winters cocked his head at the bird. "He left special instructions for the burial hole," he explained, then started digging.

An hour later they had finished the peculiar grave that Jahoska had asked Winters to dig years earlier, a slanted hole that put his feet three feet deeper than his head, which itself was to be only a forearm's depth from the surface.

"He knew he would be here," Winters said.

"It's where he could see his land the best," Duncan ventured, then watched in surprise as Winters reverently unwrapped the cloth around the old man's head.

Tears streamed down the young overseer's cheeks. "I could have stopped it," he declared in a choked voice. "I let the gentlest, wisest man I have ever known be flayed alive by the cruelest man I have ever known."

"No," Duncan said. "You would have just gotten yourself killed. And that would have ruined the reverence of his death."

"Reverence? I saw only butchery. Gabriel will surely burn in hell."

Duncan turned back to the old man again, his body in ruin but his face so calm in death it seemed he was only sleeping, then after a moment gestured Winters toward a log near the grave. "Sit," he said, and lowered himself onto a flat boulder. "Tell me more, Jamie. Tell me more about your time with Jahoska as a boy."

Winters drew a long breath and nodded, as if welcoming the invitation. "He was always here, on the banks of the great river, here when there was nothing but forest and the ruins of some old lodges, here when my grandfather built the first cabin near the bank, long before the elder Mr. Dawson came and Miss Alice's family built their farm upriver. He never objected, never complained about Europeans taking his land. My grandfather said that, back then, old Jaho had a wife and two children but they were all carried off by smallpox decades ago, before I was born.

"My father remembered how in those early days Indians from the northern tribes would come visit, greeting him like he was some kind of royalty. They would speak with him of problems among the tribes of the confederation and he would offer advice. Sometimes he would disappear for weeks at a time, but he always came back. He was always alone but never lonely. There was often an animal of some kind at his side. Never did I know any creatures but other men to shy away from him. He knew all the herbs and medicines from plants, could cure any disease known to his people. But smallpox was a European disease." Winters's words cut off with a sharp intake of breath at a sudden movement on the trail. Chuga emerged from the shadows, glanced at them, then probed the body with his nose.

The overseer nodded, then explained how, when his grandfather had sold the struggling farm, the elder Mr. Dawson had promised to always give them gainful employment on his new debtors' work estate, and had even encouraged Winters's father to join the clergy and build a church for the workers. "Even as his precious forest had been leveled for sotweed fields old Jaho had stayed. My ma would say he was not so much a normal human as a land spirit in human form."

Chuga emitted a low, mournful cry, then sat beside the corpse, on guard.

"He wasn't just the wisest man in my life," Winters continued, "he was the strongest, and the best spoken. He always knew just what to say, and could say it with fewer words than any man I've ever known. Like a poet. Always so deliberate, so observant. It broke my heart to see him raving like some drunken fool out in the field."

The pantomime still haunted Duncan. He did not believe Jaho had lost his mind but his actions had indeed seemed deranged.

"Before he was the wise man of the river, he was a warrior," Duncan said, and spoke of Jaho's legendary prowess and the tales told of him at Iroquois fires. "If he had stayed in the north," Duncan concluded, "he would have become chieftain of all the tribes."

The last of the clouds blew away, leaving the world below glowing in the light of the moon.

"There were some little cedars down the trail," Duncan said. "We should burn fragrant wood. You can bring some while I spark a fire. Then we will lower him into the earth."

He cleared a circle of bare soil, grabbed some twigs, and extracted his flint, soon coaxing small flames to life. He looked back at Jahoska, keeper of the ancient secrets, then rose and extracted the fossil he had brought from Shamokin and dropped it into the old man's pocket.

Winters returned and they lit the cedar, waiting for the scent to fill the air before lifting the body.

"This was the day he was going to die," Duncan said after they had settled the body in the grave. "The day he intended to die."

Winters looked up from his grief as Chuga settled beside the grave. "He couldn't have known that Kincaid would drag him to that post."

"Of course he did. He taunted them, and knew they would take vengeance for Hobart's death once he taunted them with the medallion, knew he was not one of those who had to be preserved for the hangings. His body was failing him, so he chose his day. It is the way of the true warriors, the ones following the old ways, to make their deaths mean something, to fill their last acts with honor."

Winters gazed into Jahoska's face. The old man seemed to be listening. "I understand nothing." From somewhere below, a whippoorwill called, its lonely cry echoing down the slope. The overseer's voice cracked as he spoke. "How can you find honor in this?"

Duncan pushed down another tide of emotion. The words were painful. He had known others like Jahoska. Most were now dead, but Conawago was still among the living. "Remember how he would say he knew of no man left like him, a man of no mixed blood, a pure Susquehannock?"

The young overseer slowly nodded. "I found him up here once, at night. He had made a little fire of cedar, just like this one, and was talking with his ancestors about it, about what becomes of a tribe when there is only one left. I couldn't understand much, for he mostly spoke in his old tongue, but he explained that I was welcome as long as I stayed silent. Afterwards he said we had a duty to those who came before."

"That's what we saw today. The death of a noble tribe. He gave their lifeblood to us."

Winters gave a bitter snort. "Us? An overseer who hates himself and a bunch of slaves?"

"A man like that looks for a good death. The people of the woods are at the end of their time, knowing they were not bred to succeed in the new European world. They are not scared of death. They are scared of becoming beggars, of being cast off as rubbish in some settlement, their scalp taken in some alley to pay for a few pots of ale."

"He died because of Gabriel's temper. He died for nothing."

"Don't ever say that!" Duncan shot back. "He died for us."

"Died for us? I am the overseer. You are the slave."

"No. I am not a slave. I am a prisoner. And you are one of us, Jamie. I know that even if you don't. He gave his lifeblood to us."

"You mean for us."

"No. This was something different. Something happened today such like I have never witnessed. He was transferring something, passing something on to us."

The owl gave a soft call, answered by another on the adjacent hill. Duncan stared back over the landscape and his heart leapt as he made out the wide strip of silver to the east that had to be the mighty Chesapeake.

"I still don't understand."

"He was saving us."

"You're still a slave."

"Not like that. Remember how he reacted to that fossil? It gave him great comfort. He said it was proof that ages rise and ages fall, but that always there will be a next age, and the new age owes its existence to the one before. He knew he had arrived at an ending of the age of the tribes and of people who live close to nature, the age of the forest. But the wonderful thing about Jahoska was that he refused to mourn that age. Instead he rejoiced that he was present for the birthing of the new age. He saw something important in the Judas slaves. The freedom men, he called us. He had decided we had to survive, even at the cost of his life. He gave us hope. Today he gave us strength."

"I don't feel strong."

"Did you not see the fire in his eyes as he was being ripped apart? It spread through the company as they watched him die. The strength and the knowledge of the link between his world and ours. Freedom isn't something created in books or laws. Freedom was in his veins. If there is any word to describe the way of the wild, it is freedom. That's what he gave us. That is what we must stand for, he was telling us."

"Surely you are not saying that opposing the stamp tax is the same as keeping his Council fire alive?"

Duncan hesitated. "Maybe I am," he said, then rose and began covering the dead man's feet.

Winters stopped him. "He asked me to do two things," the Virginian whispered, then extracted a large acorn from his pocket. "He gave me this weeks ago. He said this was the perfect one." Winters held it out between two fingers for Duncan to see, then extended it toward the moon, as if Jahoska would have wanted it to approve. "I asked him why and he wouldn't say, just that I was to keep it safe. Then last week he told me what to do with it when the time came. I laughed then, and he just smiled and said he trusted me." Winters looked down at the corpse in the slanting grave. "It's why he wanted to be buried like this, with his head near the surface." As he held the acorn over Jaho's head his hand started shaking. "How could I do this? It's a nightmare . . ."

Somehow Duncan understood. He knelt and gently stroked the old man's hair, as he had seen Iroquois matrons do in mourning their dead. "I will sing a song in the forest tongue," he said to Winters, "and you will fulfill his wish."

Winters stared, transfixed, as Duncan began a low mourning chant of the Iroquois, calling first to the spirits to come and greet the dead, then for the forest animals that served the great gods. Finally, with trembling hands, Winters opened the last Susquehannock's jaw and placed the acorn in his mouth.

When he spoke, Winters's voice held a tone of wonder, as if he finally understood Jaho's intention. "He's going to become a tree," the overseer whispered, "with the roots following down his remains for nourishment."

"An oak," Duncan said. "The heart of the forest." He picked up the spade and began covering the body. They did not speak until the job was done, and afterwards Winters dropped onto the boulder as if utterly exhausted.

Chuga stood and made a circuit of the grave, touching the earth with his nose.

"Two things," Duncan said. "You said he asked you to do two things."

He was not sure Winters had heard. The young overseer sat staring at the mound Duncan was shaping over the grave.

"For you," Winters explained after a moment. "He wanted you to have this," Winters said, reaching into a pocket. "He said you were the one who would keep it now." The overseer dropped a stone into Duncan's hand.

"I don't understand what . . ." Duncan began, then his heart blocked his throat. It was the fossil from the ancient altar. Duncan had given him his own seed stone, and Jahoska had given him that of his people. He squeezed it tightly in his hand and turned to face the bay as moisture filled his eyes. The gift seemed to break something inside. A new wave of emotion surged through him. He felt a profound melancholy, but something new was burning now, deep inside.

Chuga opened his mouth and gave a mournful howl that seemed to go on forever, echoing down into the woods. When the dog was done he stepped to Duncan's side and looked up expectantly. Duncan knelt and put an arm around the dog, then rose and held the stone out in his palm, first for Chuga, then for the moon, to see.

Winters spoke again. "If . . . if you are trying to get the company away . . . I will help you."

Duncan turned back with a new glint in his eye. He knew with certainty what Jahoska had wanted for them. "We're not just escaping, Jamie," he declared. "We are stopping them."

It was well after midnight when they returned to the fields. They stopped as they reached the stable but Duncan showed no sign of going inside. "Is the manor house open?" he asked Winters.

"Titus sleeps lightly. He will let me in. But if you are caught, Duncan . . . why take such a risk?"

"Because Jaho was not demented. He was telling me something out on the field today. He was answering the question I did not know to ask."

Titus was instantly awake at Winters's tap on the door, handing Duncan a candle as they entered the kitchen. He left Titus and Winters behind and stepped into the hall, where bunting was being draped for the coming festivities. He paused by the reproduction of the Virginia charter, holding the candle close to read the artist's name. Jeremiah Bowen. He then entered the sitting room, forcing himself not to look up at the painting of Lord Ramsey as he studied the three smaller paintings in the room.

There was the Indian maid handing tobacco to the European, by the same artist. He stepped to the next, of the man praying, also by Bowen. The same graceful style and painstaking detail was so obvious in the third, that of the native in full tribal regalia, with tilted feathers on his head, that he did not need to look at the name in the corner. He stepped back so he could see all three paintings. Through the fog of his coma Jaho had heard Duncan speak with Murdo and Webb of the letters from the mill, puzzling over why such mundane writings could be considered so important.

"Is it true?" came a tight voice behind him. "That Gabriel killed Jahoska?"

Duncan slowly nodded at Alice Dawson, standing in the doorway in a dressing gown. She sobbed and sank into a chair by the door, tears flowing down her cheeks.

"He died on his terms," Duncan offered. "Before he died he was trying to tell me something about this man Bowen."

"He never showed resentment," Alice said, "all these years when we came and took his land Jaho just stayed and helped. He was so patient. It was like he was waiting for something."

"Who is this man Bowen?"

She looked up, scrubbing at her eyes. "Bowen could never earn a living from his painting. He became a miller."

"The mill over the ridge?"

"You astound me Duncan. Jaho is dead, the gallows are up, and you risk your life coming to talk about the miller?" She saw the fierce light in his eyes. "Yes. The same, the man who disappeared after Ramsey's men arrived."

Duncan gazed at the painting of the Indian and realized it was a much younger Jahoska, made up as a warrior. He still could not understand the dying man's message.

"A new edict came today. The Africans are no longer to be taught reading and writing. Gabriel complained about my classes to Lord Ramsey last month and now some official in the Colonial Office who never set foot in Virginia demands I stop. Edicts and commands come from London like the word of God."

Duncan found his gaze drifting up to the image of Ramsey, seeing now his ermine collar, his golden rings. The painter had included a soft glow around the lord's head like a halo. He suddenly understood. "That's it, Alice! The word of God! No edict could come from London in a month!"

She wiped away more tears and looked up in confusion.

"In his world Ramsey is god! He acknowledges no rules. Ramsey produces the edicts that serve him. Where is the miller?"

"You speak in riddles."

"There was a list of supplies in Hobart's room. Badger hair, prussian green, lampblack. Artist's supplies. They're using Bowen! That's what Jaho was trying to tell me. This artist made the perfect replica of the charter. So real it could be passed off as an official document. Where is he?"

"Gone away. They seized his mill and took him away on the cutter months ago."

"And then edicts started arriving?"

"Yes," Alice hesitantly replied. "A few weeks later."

"Ramsey is using Bowen to create a shadow government, to block the committees!" Duncan exclaimed. "He makes up his own edicts, creates letters in others' handwriting! William Johnson detected something false in the letter from Benjamin Franklin delivered by his son! We must find the miller!"

Ten minutes later they stood at the kitchen table, the map of the Chesapeake unrolled before them.

"He would be kept close, yet out of the way," Duncan said.

They stared at the map. "The cutter leaves," Alice said. "And if the wind blows fair she is back in three or four days."

"Annapolis," Winters suggested.

"Too big," Alice said. "Too many real officials. It would need to be somewhere very quiet."

Titus pointed to two other towns, Alice two more. Cambridge, Oxford, Chestertown, and Ononcock.

"There would have to be a printing press," Duncan put in.

"All but Oxford are county seats," Alice said. "County seats always have a printer."

"Not Oxford then."

"Surely the sailors must talk," Duncan pressed.

"Never," Alice replied. "They are too scared of Ramsey."

Titus's countenance suddenly lit with excitement. He slipped out the door and a moment later returned, dropping an oyster shell as big as his hand on the table. "The Commodore always wants his hogs," the butler declared, the gleam still in his eye. "A bushel comes back with the cutter every time."

"Hogs?" Duncan asked.

"Only one place these big ones can be found," Titus explained. "That's how they get their name. Chestertown hogs."

AN INJURED OFFICER HAS ARRIVED, READ THE MESSAGE FROM Alice Dawson that came as he worked the fields the next morning. *Please come at once.* Trent grinned as he handed the slip of paper to Duncan. "She says please, mind you."

As they walked alongside on the perimeter road Duncan realized that he too was studying the river.

"I wasn't aware a new ship had arrived," Duncan ventured.

"I ain't been near the river for two days. But there be no new mast showing. Probably just some powdered fool who scalded himself on his tea."

But the man lying on the upstairs bed bore the signs of battle. A cheek was badly burnt, with dark grains flecking his skin, and a long jagged splinter of wood was embedded in his shoulder. Blood oozed out of the wound. An empty vial of laudanum and a small tumbler lay on the nightstand, as did a suturing kit.

"Dr. Lloyd was denied permission to come onshore," Alice explained.

"But these are battle wounds . . ." Duncan began.

"Smugglers," the officer groaned through his pain. "They took half a dozen rounds from us. When we approached they let loose with two guns. Light ones, no more than six pounders, but one of the balls knocked a slow match onto a powder keg not ten feet from me. By then we were close enough for boarding. Our marines laid into them. The captain and half his crew are now food for Chesapeake gulls."

Duncan stepped to the window. The two new ships had been obscured from the fields by the manor house. A little brigantine lay anchored midstream, beside a heavy sloop that had clearly taken battle damage.

"The doctor from Philadelphia asked for you," Alice said to his back.

Duncan hesitated. Surely he had not heard correctly. "A physician who knows me is here?"

Before she could respond the door from the adjoining chamber was thrown open and a familiar figure hurried forward.

"Benjamin?" Duncan said. "You are supposed to be in Philadelphia."

"Duncan!" Rush proclaimed with outstretched arms. "Praise God you are safe!"

Duncan darted to the door and closed it. Alice closed the hallway door and leaned against it. "I am not safe, Benjamin, and neither are you. You must flee immediately, the same way you arrived."

Rush's smile flickered, fading and returning more than once as he struggled to understand. "That is problematic," he finally said. "You see, our ship is no longer our ship. There was a tragic misunderstanding with the Virginia navy."

"Surely you were not on the smuggler?"

The young Philadelphia doctor gestured Duncan to the window and spoke in a whisper. "Not a smuggler. We chartered the *Penelope* for an expedition of natural philosophy. Reports reached Philadelphia last year that the rivers feeding the Chesapeake contain sturgeon of unnatural proportions. Dr. Franklin and his scientific society suggested they may represent an as-yet-undiscovered species. We announced that we sought to capture some of the creatures for study." He lowered his voice. "A note came from the Conococheague Valley. It seemed a propitious time to launch an expedition." He extracted a slip of paper from his waistcoat and handed it to Duncan. It was in a child's scrawl. *Galalee on the Raphonock. Sayv thm.*

"Analie?" Duncan asked. "Is she safe then?"

"They came by horse, arriving in the hills two days ago."

"They?"

Rush seemed not to hear Duncan's question. "The captain had called at Galilee years ago and readily agreed to sail up the Rappahannock, to what he said was the best hospitality on the river. We were approaching the river mouth when the navy appeared and acted as if we were pirates."

His face clouded. "There were casualties. I fear our captain's luck ran out, may he rest in peace. When they questioned the crew and discovered the captain was the owner and had no heirs, they were ecstatic. With no one to object they would call the sloop a prize."

Duncan had a hundred questions, but the officer on the bed moaned, reminding him that there was more urgent work to do. He examined the splinter wound.

"I didn't dare take it out," Alice said, "for fear of a burst vessel."

"You did right," Duncan confirmed, then hurried to the basin to wash his hands. With Rush assisting, they had the treacherous piece of wood out within minutes. Rush began stitching the flesh together.

"And the crew?" he asked Rush.

"It was dusk when we anchored. Most slipped away in a boat to the far shore as soon as it was dark." Rush cast an uncertain glance toward Alice Dawson. "There are other injuries. The professor is doing his best, down the hall." He bent over the now-unconscious naval officer, taking his pulse.

"Professor?"

Rush cast a nervous glance at Alice. "I will finish here. Perhaps Mrs. Dawson can make introductions."

Alice did indeed take him into the corridor but stopped at the back window that overlooked the fields and outbuildings. "Gabriel was boasting about it at breakfast. The traitor's cradle he calls it." She was looking at the gallows. Four nooses now dangled from it.

She reached out and gripped Duncan's arm. "Gabriel brought in more of his thugs. They patrol the hills like soldiers. He says he hopes you all try to run, since a ball of lead costs a lot less than a good rope. I'm so scared, Duncan."

Duncan too found it difficult to look away. It was as if he were staring into his own grave. For years he had suffered nightmares of his father hanging on the gibbet outside Inverness, pointing at an empty noose.

Alice tugged at his sleeve, pulling him toward a room at the end of the hall. "The professor is a great scholar of the Old World. He spouts Latin and asks for Earl Grey tea."

Duncan glanced at the stiff back of the man in powdered wig and velvet waistcoat who bent over his patient, whose head was mostly obscured with a bloody bandage. Duncan took a tentative step forward, then his heart leapt as the professor extended his hand to adjust the bandage and he saw the tattoo of a turtle on his wrist.

It was all Duncan could do not to cry out when the man turned. For the first time in weeks he felt lightness in his heart. The professor nodded stiffly to Duncan, then bowed to his hostess. "My esteemed and beneficent Mrs. Dawson," came his rich, refined voice. "I beg your leave. We must perform a more complete examination of our patient's body, if you get my meaning."

"Of course, Professor Moon," he heard Alice say. "I leave you gentlemen to your . . . delicate affairs."

Conawago did not move until the door latched behind her, then he just grinned and slipped off the wig. "Scratchy damned thing," he said, tossing the curls on the bed. He seemed unable to speak for a moment as he examined Duncan. "You look thin, son," he observed, and extended his arms.

Duncan felt like a lost child who had found his home as he embraced the old Nipmuc.

"My God, Duncan, we feared the worse," Conawago said. "Thanks to Mr. Rush we had a fast boat from Philadelphia."

"We?"

His question was answered as the injured man sat up and began unwinding the bandage from his head.

"Patrick!"

"My Scottish doctor advised no travel for several weeks," Woolford said, "no strenuous efforts. But a boat cruise is no effort at all."

The questions came in rapid succession. Analie had sped north as soon as she had seen Duncan and his companions put in chains. "You were right, Patrick," Duncan declared. "They know the secrets. They mean to hang every one of us."

Rage gripped Woolford's face. "It's this damned black Admiral of Virginia! He may operate with leave of the Kraken lords in London but hanging men still requires a warrant. He has no warrant. He has no evidence of a crime!"

"The evidence will materialize as he needs it," came a worried voice from the connecting doorway. "And I've had a letter from a discreet friend in Williamsburg. The magistrate for our county has taken a huge loan from the Rappahannock Company."

"Meaning he's mortgaged his soul to Ramsey," Duncan spat, then saw the question on Woolford's face. "It's Lord Ramsey, Patrick Ramsey is the black Admiral."

The color drained from Woolford's face, then he looked with worry at his hostess.

"She knows," Conawago inserted.

Alice acknowledged the obvious question on Conawago's face. "I am a great admirer of the theater, Mr. Moon. You played your parts exceedingly well but you should have put more powder over the tribal tattoos on your wrists."

"I suggested bandages," Conawago explained with a peeved look at Woolford, "but Patrick thought powder would do. Not enough apparently." He bowed to Alice. "Forgive us. Conawago of the Nipmuc tribe, though I put on Socrates Moon when I don my waistcoat."

Alice smiled. "And an elegant one it is."

"A gift from my days in the French court," Conawago explained. Although the fashion of the velvet cut was dated by some decades, the overdone French jacket was, Duncan knew, one of his prized possessions. The old Nipmuc touched his fingers to his forehead and bowed again.

As Woolford offered a reluctant introduction, Duncan saw the suspicion lingering in his eyes. "She is a friend," he assured the ranger captain.

As Alice and her new acquaintances spoke, Duncan wandered to the window overlooking the river. A plank dance floor had been laid out by the portico. A launch was pushing off from the brig, rowing toward the mill around the point. A small party worked on the captured sloop. If the *Penelope* was to be claimed as a prize, they would want to rapidly repair her damage so she could be conveyed to a naval port for appraisal. Half a dozen dinghies and dugouts, used by river fishermen, were drawn up on the beach where the slaves were taken to bathe. A new boat had arrived, a little ketch with ornate paintwork and flying a long banner on its mast.

Below him a blonde girl ran across the dance boards, chased by one of the young housemaids into the lilacs. Titus watched, speaking with an auburn-haired woman.

Duncan did not realize he had made a sound but when he looked back his companions were staring at him. Conawago grinned as Duncan darted out of the room. Moments later, as his feet scattered the gravel of the garden path, the woman turned. Sarah's eyes welled with tears but she did not move toward him. Analie gave a little yelp of joy and darted forward, only to suddenly stop and back away, staring behind him in sudden fear.

Gabriel had appeared, with half a dozen of his bullies moving to encircle Duncan.

Another figure stepped from the shadows, resplendent in red silk waistcoat and white linen, his long periwig dangling around his shoulders. Lord Ramsey had gained weight and the sash of his invented rank, embroidered with crown and lion, stretched tight over his belly. An ox of a man followed, a step behind Ramsey. Teague's eyes were on fire. He touched the long, still-pink scar along his hairline as he approached, reminding Duncan that it was time for his vengeance.

In his hand Ramsey carried a pair of calfskin gloves. The black eyes above his heavy jowls gleamed with excitement. "Had I only known, I would have left you to rot in that Scottish prison!" he spat. He lifted his gloves and slapped them lightly across Duncan's jaw. Before Duncan could react Teague slammed his open right hand against the place where the gloves had touched. Duncan staggered but did not fall. He twisted at a cry from Sarah and saw her being seized by two of Gabriel's men. Ramsey slapped his other cheek with the gloves and Teague hit him there.

"Father!" Sarah sobbed. "No! I beg you!"

Ramsey seemed not to hear. He slapped Duncan's chest and Teague pounded it with a fist. There was no point in resisting. The men all around held clubs.

For a moment Sarah broke free, and shouldered her way into the circle, almost reaching Duncan before Ramsey touched her cheek too and Gabriel slapped her viciously, knocking her to the ground. Two men grabbed Duncan's arms, preventing him from reaching her. "You said you would not—" she cried.

"What I said," came Ramsey's oily voice, "was that I would not kill him when we met." Duncan had learned long ago to hate the thin cruel smile that formed on Ramsey's undersized mouth. He slapped Duncan again, in the belly, on his mouth, on his thigh, in his belly again. Teague landed a hammer-like strike at each spot his master indicated, until finally, as Duncan crumbled, he continued with his own unprompted flurry of kicks.

Chapter Nineteen

The freshly mounded graves had been arranged in neat rows, the simple markers nearest him spelling the names of his friends. Murdo Ross, Tanaqua, Patrick Woolford, Elijah Webb. The last was Duncan's own, still empty, waiting for him. From the dirt mound beside it a hand emerged, desperately reaching into the air, exposing the turtle tattoo on its wrist.

Duncan woke, his heart hammering. His first effort to move brought a paroxysm of pain. Teague's fists had bruised more than just a few muscles. His ribs ached, his kidneys hurt, and the flesh over his heart, where the Irishman had concentrated his final blows, was a swollen, tender mass.

He sat up, fighting a wave of nausea, and moved unsteadily toward a line of light, thinking at first he was back in one of the slave wagons, then he fell onto a packed earth floor. His dizziness subsided, and as his eyes focused he discovered three steps leading up to a slanted double door of rough timber. In the dim light, shelves were visible on the walls of the chamber, most lined with what appeared to be empty wicker baskets and demijohns. He was in the root cellar behind the manor house, the holding cell for those going to torture.

Duncan pushed on the doors. They were barred from the outside. As he pounded on them a spill of light broke through in a knot.

He dropped back to the floor, combing the darkness with his fingers until he found a stone, then began chipping away at the knot. In a few minutes he had knocked away the knot entirely, opening a hole as wide as his thumb.

Pressing his eye to the hole, he saw the manor lawn in repose, the only creatures in sight being the dozen sheep that kept the grass down, clustered near the big chestnut tree. Around the edge of the manor he glimpsed a stretch of the river that encompassed the *Ardent* at the dock and beyond it, anchored midstream, the captured sloop, the brigantine, and Ramsey's yacht. He studied the ships with a critical eye, considering the architecture of the vessels then trying to remember the timing of the tides that reached up the wide river.

His concentration was broken as Titus appeared on the rear portico, carrying a basket to a worktable below the kitchen window. He upended oysters onto it, the big Chestertown hogs, and two of the scullery maids settled down to open the shells. From somewhere to his right came the distant sound of an African work chant.

Benjamin Rush appeared on the kitchen porch, and soon was deep in conversation with Titus. After a few minutes the two men descended the steps and drifted along the lawn, distracted in conversation. Halfway across the lawn Titus abruptly threw an oyster shell at the nearest ewe, which gave a sudden cry and bolted, starting the others, who reacted in confused jumps and short spurting runs. The maids sprang after them. Titus started shouting, adding to the confusion as Rush darted to the cellar door. "Duncan!" he called. "Wake! I am here!"

"I am not asleep, Benjamin."

The sound of Duncan's voice so close gave the young doctor a start, then he saw the knothole. "Quite clever. Excellent. Did you see that stately African?"

"His name is Titus."

"From the noble Ashanti tribe! Have you noted the elongated jaw, and the huge ear lobes? He said I could measure his foot later."

"Benjamin."

"Oh. Sorry. I came to tell you that he is not going to . . ." Rush searched for words. "I mean I invoked the names of Dr. Franklin, Mr. Allen, the acting governor of Pennsylvania, and the Philosophical Society to get Lord Ramsey's assurance. Your life is to be preserved at Galilee."

Even in the darkness Duncan closed his eyes a moment, painfully aware of the truth that Rush's naiveté did not permit him to see. Ramsey meant for Duncan to have a long and painful death, far from Galilee. "There's over twenty others he means to hang, Benjamin."

"I've seen the gallows, Duncan. High on the hill on the open field, just where the weather is funneled between mountains and river. Ridiculous."

Duncan struggled to keep his frustration in check. "I need to see Woolford."

"Would that I had an almanac."

"Do not trust the men from the mill. Agents of the Kraken."

"An iron pot or tray perhaps."

"Sarah Ramsey. Is she safe?" Duncan had to ask the question twice to break through Rush's strange ramblings.

"In the charge of Mrs. Dawson, who provides her with all possible comforts, though an overseer stays close."

"Woolford? Conawago?"

"Arrangements are being made. I must go, Duncan. That man Titus said he could introduce me to warriors from the wild tribes of the Niger!"

"Do you have loose coin, Benjamin?" he asked, then continued when he saw Rush's nod. "There is an overseer named Trent. A bald man with thick shoulders, usually carrying what looks like a quarterstaff. I need you to find him. Say he needs to bring me water. Give him a shilling for the favor."

Less than half an hour later the sullen overseer was at the cellar door, carrying a demijohn. He did not realize Duncan could see him, and Duncan watched as he paused to study the marines who were approaching the manor house along the brick path. He spat in their direction and opened the door.

Duncan did not accept the demijohn when Trent extended it. "Come inside," he said, "and close the door behind you."

Trent scowled but complied, and as Duncan sat on a low shelf he settled onto the stairs.

"I could beat you into a lump of meat and say I caught you escaping." Trent said, as if for the record.

"Of course." Duncan nodded. "But what do you think of that sloop anchored in the river? And don't tell me you haven't studied her."

Trent hesitated, raising a brow at Duncan. "Cedar built, and spry as a thoroughbred. Sixty tons or thereabouts, and able to spread enough canvas for a vessel half again as big. Once her rigging is repaired she could cut through the water like a knife, though I don't know why her captain ain't added a third jib in the Bermuda style." He extracted a plug of tobacco from a pocket and bit off a chew.

"The *Penelope*'s captain is dead. He was the owner. He has no heirs. And now with a lie the Virginia navy makes claim to her."

"I ain't no sea lawyer if that's why you brought me."

"An old privateer knows about changing the identity of ships," Duncan suggested. "A clever master could alter the bowsprit, raise her rails, give her a new coat of paint. Maybe add that jib you mention. No one would recognize her. London's taxes are making wealthy men of those who are bold enough to evade them. The days of the pirate may be fading but America is going to become a smuggler's paradise. Of course you would need men to get her away. Say about twenty or so."

Trent stared at Duncan a long time, his tongue working the inside of his cheek. His contempt faded into curiosity. He looked at the earthen walls in the direction of the river. "The brigantine took damage but the *Ardent* would give chase and blow the sloop out of the water."

"She can sail much closer to the wind, and I hear the bay has much shoal water, too shallow for a ship as big as the *Ardent*. With a few hours lead the *Penelope* would be perfectly safe."

"Except that she won't have a few hours."

Duncan fought another spasm of pain before speaking again. "I will see that she does," he said. "The tide breaks about midnight. The sloop could ride the current out and by the time the *Ardent* can follow, the tide will be coming in, against her."

Trent listened, slowly chewing. "More like an hour after midnight," he observed, then spat juice and shook his head. "You're daft. And desperate. Desperate men have a way of ignoring hard facts. Like the patrols along the bay and the night riders with their dogs."

"You don't fit in here, Trent. You'll be leaving. The only question is whether you leave as a deserter or as master of a vessel that can give you a freedom, and a wealth, few men ever taste. And the night riders focus on the edge of the woods, not the water. I can see to it the dogs are not a problem."

Trent stood and stepped to the door, but then paused, staring at the circle of sunlight cast through the knothole. "My first cruise with a blue band on my sleeve was up the coast toward New England. Kincaid spied a swift little sloop moving south and had us come about to give chase, shouting for more sails. When the master complained that Kincaid would split his canvas, Kincaid hit him and sent him below, and declared there was a piece of silver for the man who could bring the sloop alongside. I told him I would do it, though mostly I just wanted to feel a ship's wheel in my hands again. It took nigh four hours but finally she lost a jib and we overtook her."

Trent still spoke towards the door. "Kincaid spoke to the sloop, asking who she was. She replied she was the *Nightingale*, out of Newport with rum for Philadelphia. Kincaid just turned to a gun crew and had them blast her out of the water. He tossed me a coin and said I was meant for glorious things, then he pulled a pistol and said he would shoot any man who lifted a hand to help those in the water. T'is a forlorn thing watching good men going down at sea, begging for mercy. All they ever were, gone in an instant into the deep."

He turned back to Duncan. "I would need papers to pass her off as mine."

"We're going to a man who makes papers as good as the king's own. Shall we say you bought her in Boston?"

A new gleam lit Trent's eyes. "Bermuda."

Duncan began explaining his plan.

An hour later he was on the floor, studying an image of the *Ardent* he had drawn in the dirt, when urgent whispers rose from near the door. He peered through the knothole to see a mass of bright dresses. Alice Dawson was scolding the cook. "Polly! Look what you have done, you clumsy creature! My basket of best buttons all over the grass!"

Polly and four kitchen maids were dropping to their knees, searching through the grass as Alice, standing so as to block the line of sight from the kitchen door to the cellar, made a show of pointing to the scattered buttons on the lawn.

"Duncan, I swear I never knew he was connected to Galilee." It was Sarah, kneeling by the knothole, obscured from the house by Polly.

"Of course not. But I would have come anyway."

"It's because of him and men like him that I said yes when Patrick asked if we would help the runners. I didn't want you to know. I thought I could shield you, in case there was trouble."

"Sarah, you must look to yourself. Leave now, while you still can. I beg you. You don't know the depths of your father's treachery."

She ignored him. "But I was a fool not to understand the dangers. Jessica warned me to be more wary of strangers. You warned me to send out patrols."

"What strangers?"

She turned away for a moment, and Duncan realized his question had distressed her. "That horrid Lieutenant Kincaid. He came to Edentown a few days before, as that circuit rider. I invited him to our evening meal. He even offered prayers, and said he would be traveling south soon if anyone had messages for loved ones in Pennsylvania. He led us in hymns before he left." Sarah scrubbed at her eyes as Polly urged her to hurry. "Jess gave him a note to carry to her mother and father, and explained to him how to find their house. The letter would have spoken about Edentown station and would have made it clear she and her father were helping the committee runners. It was her death sentence. I know that now."

"Surely, Sarah, you mustn't blame yourself for—"

"I have to go. That horrid pharaoh man follows us everywhere. You must hold on. Take no risks. I have made an offer to my father that he will never refuse. He can have it all. He can have Edentown and all its lands. I keep only one thing."

"No! Never in life!"

"Just one piece of paper. Your indenture. We can go into the wilderness, live with the Iroquois."

"Away from those doors, damn ye!" came an angry shout from the porch. The pharaoh had seen her through the confusion.

"Just two or three days, Duncan." Sarah pushed a finger through the hole. With a trembling hand Duncan touched it. Then she was gone.

THE SOUND IN THE LATE AFTERNOON STARTED AS A PATTERING OF light feet but soon rose to a louder trampling, accompanied by frantic shouts in English and African tongues. Duncan leapt to look out the door in time to see two large pigs trot by, snorting derisively as African field hands chased them.

Suddenly Titus was in front of the cellar, his waistcoated back to Duncan. As the melee of pigs and hooting slaves ran by again he backed into the door and, with hands hidden behind him, lifted the bar. In an instant the butler was inside, smearing something onto Duncan's face as someone else lifted his arms and pulled over his shoulders one of the long homespun slave tunics worn by many of the Africans. A tattered slouch hat was shoved over his ears, then Titus opened a pouch and poured a small pile of coal dust onto Duncan's palm. Duncan began rubbing the dust over his exposed forearms and hands.

Kuwali, Ursa's son, grinned and pushed Duncan up the steps and outside as Titus closed and barred the door, leaving the boy inside. "You staying alive in there, Mr. McCallum?" the butler asked through the knothole.

Kuwali's reply was a low moan, and a quickly muttered curse. Titus flashed a smile at Duncan. "Good enough for one who's been beaten and bruised. If the marines discover him he will say you tricked him when he brought you water." The Ashanti produced a piece of charcoal and made one of the African hex signs on the door. "And that will discourage the overseers from touching the door."

The slaves closed around him, and as the pigs were herded back into their pen, Duncan found himself being herded with them back to the tobacco fields, the impatient shouts of overseers behind them. Their ploy had been timed perfectly—as they joined Ursa and the other Africans the end-of-day bell sounded. With no more than the usual curses and impatient commands the overseers pushed the Africans back into their quarters. Ursa led Duncan inside as the others washed and prepared for their meager evening meal. The big African grinned as he gestured toward the burlap curtain at the end of the building.

Conawago was waiting for him. The Nipmuc elder sat on the floor before a bowl of smoldering sticks, beside the aged African woman Duncan had knelt before on his first visit. As Duncan sat down, the old African cupped her hands and pushed the smoke toward Duncan. It wasn't the usual cedar, he realized, but something sweeter, probably sassafras. Conawago grinned. The Africans too used fragrant smoke for summoning spirits.

"Conawago, you have to leave, up the trail back to Pennsylvania," Duncan pleaded as Ursa settled beside him. "Find Sarah and flee. There is too much death here."

"You will find death everywhere if that is what you look for." To Duncan's surprise, the gravelly voice was not that of Conawago but of the old woman at his side. He had not known she spoke English.

"Not like at Galilee, grandmother," Duncan said. "Here lives are bought and sold as cheap as grains of barley. Men die for speaking ill of those in London they have never met, who do not even know they exist."

"In our own land," she said, "our gods would impale such evildoers on thorn bushes and vultures would pick at their flesh for all time."

"Here," Duncan replied, "we are less patient for justice to be served. We will fight with sticks against their guns before we let them hang us. But I will not have you sacrificed in my fight."

Ursa, prince of the Ibo, smiled patiently, then gripped and turned Duncan's arm to expose the ugly brand. He pressed his own arm, with an identical scar, beside it. He spoke, and had the old woman translate. "There is not your fight or my fight," she relayed. "This is our fight. Afterwards, when the moon has set, Ursa says he will climb with nails and a hammer." Ursa stared at Duncan with cool determination, as if he had made a warrior's vow.

Ursa's wife appeared with bowls of food. "First you eat then wait for the dark," the old woman announced.

Duncan grasped enough about the Africans to know there was much about their ways he did not understand. "Nails?" he ventured, but Conawago pushed a bowl of stew into his hand, then began peppering Ursa with questions about his tribe. Duncan finished eating and kept watch out of one of the slit windows. An hour after sunset Sinclair climbed inside, extending Duncan's medicine bag before checking his sling and supply of pebbles.

Minutes later, Nancy, the maid from the house, appeared, holding another sack. "Bloodiest we could find," she said, then made a solemn bow to the old woman before departing. Ursa took the sack to the nearest platform and upended it, spilling out six cuts of raw beef, then looked up expectantly. Duncan reached into his medicine bag and handed him the last two vials of laudanum. Ursa made a clicking sound and three of the African men approached, wearing mischievious smiles.

"We go now, McCallum," Ursa stated. He embraced his wife, who waited at the loose plank, then led Duncan outside.

PATRICK WOOLFORD WAITED FOR THEM BY THE LITTLE CEMETERY above the manor house, silver buttons glistening in the moonlight. Duncan had seen him wear his captain's uniform perhaps five times in as many years but they had always been at formal, social occasions, not for a raid on the king's own soldiers. Woolford nodded to Tanaqua, Ursa, and Sinclair, best of the sling shooters, who stood at Duncan's side. Conawago gestured Woolford down the path over the hill as Duncan and his companions slipped into the shadows.

Hobart's surly sergeant was on guard duty by the brazier where the path split, branching toward the small mill dock and the mill itself. "Far enough, gents," he barked in his nasally Welsh accent as they approached. Duncan, listening at the side of the mill, gave a nod to Sinclair, who whirled his sling and released. The guard at the rear door to the mill, out of sight of the others, dropped to the ground. "These be restricted grounds," the sergeant warned.

Woolford stepped into the light. "Stand down, sergeant," he replied in his best tone of command. "I am here to speak with the officer in charge."

"The officer in charge right now be me."

"Sir. The officer in charge right now be me, sir." Woolford corrected. "You are addressing a captain of His Majesty's rangers."

The sergeant hesitated, studying Woolford's uniform suspiciously. "Thought all the rangers were disbanded after the hostilities."

Woolford glared at him.

"Sir," the Welshman stiffly added.

"Not all of us. There's still much to be done in the northern theater."

"This be Virginia, sir."

Woolford nodded toward the man's blue armband. "And you work for Virginia now. An officer in the standing army always has precedence over a militia officer."

"Normally that be right, sir," came the sergeant's airy reply. "But I just can't see how some northern forest walker has say over me." The arrogance on his face faded as Ursa and Conawago appeared at Woolford's side.

"You have an artifact stolen from the north. That makes it northern business."

"Art-i-fact," the sergeant repeated, motioning forward the third sentry, who paced along the riverbank. "Don't know what you mean, sir."

Duncan and Tanaqua stole around the building to the spillway by the millpond and knelt in the high grass to study it. The channel that powered the mill was blocked by four slats of wood, letting the force of the water spill into the river. Ursa nodded to Duncan, then threw a stone into the nearby brush. The sentry from the river turned and ventured toward the sound. As soon as he reached the darker shadows behind the building Sinclair dropped him with another stone. Duncan and Tanaqua darted to the mill and slipped through a window.

"A mask," Duncan heard Woolford say to the sergeant. "Painted red. Taken from our allies the Iroquois."

"Have to take that up with the chain of command, as they say."

Woolford impatiently shoved the man aside. The sergeant only laughed and watched the three men enter the mill. Duncan and Tanaqua waited for them at the end of the darkened corridor. As Conawago lifted the lantern that hung inside the door, a woman cried out and Lila rose up from a pallet. Giving up all pretense of subterfuge, Duncan hurried to meet Conawago at the door of the center storeroom. His heart sank as they looked inside. The plate of food offerings was crushed, the unlit candle broken. The mask was gone.

"The Commodore said it had to be secured," came the sergeant's gloating explanation behind them. "To keep the heathens down."

"Secured where?" Woolford demanded.

"Secured by Lieutenant Kincaid."

The sergeant gasped as a knife materialized from behind him, pressed against his throat. "Where?" Tanaqua demanded. "Where is the Blooddancer?"

"They—they didn't share the destination with me. I swear! The lieutenant just said it would make a pretty bonfire when all this was over."

"And she said over her dead body!" Lila inserted. The maid was standing at the doorway.

"Shut up, you bitch!" the sergeant growled.

"Who?" Duncan demanded. "Who said that?"

The sergeant recoiled as he recognized Duncan. "You be one of those Judas slaves, by God!" In one fluid motion Sinclair jerked away the man's musket and pivoted the stock up into the sergeant's jaw. He collapsed, unconscious.

"Who?" Duncan demanded again of Lila, who was grinning at the sergeant's crumpled body.

"That nice lady from up north, with the pretty chestnut hair. Mr. Kincaid had two of his soldiers bring her here, to keep her quiet. He told her his men would pack her bags 'cause Lord Ramsey ordered him to take her to London."

"London?" Conawago asked.

"The lord says he is to take her back to meet the man he has arranged for her to marry. A wool merchant from Yorkshire who is a cousin of the great lord's, the lieutenant said. They sailed away at last light."

Duncan sank onto a crate. It was not the first time Ramsey had kidnapped his own daughter. He had been determined to break her strong will for years but Edentown had always been her fortress. She had extorted his agreement to stay out of the New York colony but now, because of Duncan, she had abandoned her sanctuary and against all odds encountered her father.

Woolford saw his anguish. "Duncan, we tried to get her to go with Analie back into the woods."

"Back?"

"She insisted on riding with Analie from Conococheague, saying it would be faster than a boat from Philadelphia. I told her to go back to her horses and let us deal with her father. But she would have none of it, said she would not leave without you."

Duncan, numbed, slowly looked up. "You should have forced her."

"Force Sarah Ramsey? You know better."

"I can't help her, Patrick." The words stabbed at his heart.

"Not now, Duncan. Not tonight. Tonight we need you." When Duncan did not respond Woolford pulled him to his feet and shook him. "We need you now!"

Half an hour later, with the unconscious marines tied to a tree by the river, they stood on the ridge looking down at the mill. Woolford had had to lead the stunned Duncan away but he had revived when they reached the little pond behind the mill. Ursa had jumped into the raceway and lifted out the four boards that blocked the water from the wheel, then Duncan and Woolford piled four kegs of gunpowder on the flat grindstone in the mill. Duncan had emptied a cask of turpentine onto the stone and set a candle on it, where it would be upended when the grinding stone hit it. They waited until they heard the big wheel moving, turning the stones, then disengaged it with the long lever rising through the floor beside the grindstones. Sinclair would wait there, and when the candle had burned down two finger-widths he would pull the lever to engage the wheel before running back over the ridge.

Duncan nodded to Ursa, who disappeared into the shadows. Then Duncan led Woolford and Conawago down the path toward the manor, pausing as the harbor came into view. The cutter and the brigantine were both gone.

A shadow waited at the edge of the lilacs hedge. Trent tossed a coil of rope and an iron bar, shaped to an edge at one end by the African blacksmith, at Duncan's feet. "You're insane, McCallum."

"You were insane enough to join us," Duncan rejoined as he began unbuttoning his shirt. He slipped out of his shoes. "The rest is ready?" he asked Trent.

The overseer nodded. "At dusk two demijohns of rum appeared on board, below decks, while firewood was being delivered by slaves to the galley. But the marines on duty will never touch it."

"The off-duty seamen will," Duncan said. "The brawls will soon start below decks."

"And the marines will need to bring order below," Trent concluded, then helped loop the rope over Duncan's shoulder. Duncan lifted the bar in one hand and took a step into the water. Conawago held him back, placing one hand on Duncan's totem pouch, whispering a prayer to Duncan's protective spirit. He enclosed Duncan's own hand around the pouch, within his own, and repeated the words. Duncan felt the power of the sleek water creature rise within him as he slipped into the river.

BY THE TIME DUNCAN RETURNED TO THE JUDAS SLAVE STABLE, the air was what his grandfather would have called "weather heavy." A slow rhythmic drumming had risen from the African quarters. The old barn that housed the overseers and night riders showed many lamps through its windows. They were awake, as if expecting trouble. But there were no guards outside the stable door. Watching from behind the big oak in the yard, Duncan soon saw why. A squad of marines, bayonets fixed on their long Brown Bess muskets, was patrolling the edge of the field.

He slipped inside and paced down the row of waiting prisoners. Most had pouches slung from their shoulders, packed with their meager belongings. Those too weak or injured to move with haste lay on stretchers improvised from sleeping pallets.

"The men are scared," Webb confided. "Some say better the quick death of the noose than being torn apart by the dogs." Duncan eyed the men sitting on either side of the aisle in their assigned groups of five and six. At the end of one row Tanaqua stood, ever ready, one of the kitchen knives on a strap around his chest, holding his improvised war club. Every eye was on Duncan.

"This night is why old Jaho died," he declared to the worried faces. "He had lost his people but he found you, found us. He said it was men like us who would keep this land free. He believed in us and I will not betray his trust. Do this for your wives and children. I am doing this for an old Susquehannock who recognized something in us that we didn't see ourselves. Freedom is in the wild, he would say. Freedom is the wild, in this land we came to. You can't love this land without loving freedom—he made me see that."

He paused, pulling away Jaho's blanket to expose the escape hatch, and let the rhythmic drumming fill the silence. "The Africans beat their drums for us. They know they will not find freedom tonight. But they know we must. They say they will bring the weather we need. Three of their warriors are carrying meat into the woods, provided by the kitchen slaves, leaving a trail of blood. The meat is laced with laudanum. The dogs will find it and run no more tonight. But if those men are caught, if the kitchen slaves are caught helping, they will pay dearly for it. Do they believe in liberty more than we do?"

Hughes rose, pounding his fist into his chest, followed by Larkin and Frazier. One by one every man gave the old sign of the warrior.

As a gust of wind rattled the roof Duncan gestured the first squad outside, toward the bank along the swamp. As they moved out the door an explosion in the sky lit the fields. A lightning bolt threaded its way down and touched at the end of the field. Duncan, worried it would frighten the company, tried to ignore it, then saw the astonished looks on those beside him.

"Jesus, Mary, and Joseph!" Murdo gasped, and crossed himself.

The gallows had been struck. Its top beams had burst apart, and flames were spreading down the upright posts.

"Go!" Webb shouted.

Suddenly the bizarre words of Rush echoed in Duncan's head. Rush had spoken of the geography of the place, of the way the hills and river served as a weather funnel, had yearned for an almanac. Rush, the student of Dr. Franklin, had arranged for Ursa to affix nails and a metal tray to the top of the gallows, to lure the lightning. Ursa had said he would climb to attract the gods. And the gods had responded.

As Duncan watched, the marine patrol appeared in the light of the flames, frantically running about the burning structure, but powerless to stop the destruction. On the far side of the fields the Africans had started a chant, a weird ululation that seemed in syncopation with the gusts and rumbles of the clouds.

By the time the full company was outside, lying on the bank, the clouds overhead were roaring, the thunder echoing off the hill. More bolts of lightning were striking the hills. He looked one last time over the fields and in a violent flash saw Ursa standing in the field by the flaming gallows, hands raised toward the sky, laughing, as huge drops of rain began to fall.

Duncan led the men toward the washing cove, where Winters and Trent had beached the fishing skiffs. He nodded to Webb, who waited in the shadows with the other men, then with Tanaqua and the other Iroquois he ran to the closest boat. Duncan halted with a shudder as a figure rose up from its shadow.

"Surely you didn't think I would let you have all the fun," Woolford said.

"Patrick, you are an officer in the king's army. If they recognized you . . ."

Woolford stepped closer. His face was smeared with mud, his long black hair hung in braids, and two feathers dangled from a fur headband. "Tonight," he declared, "I am a Mohawk."

As he spoke the mill exploded.

CHAPTER TWENTY

The clouds bellowed as the shadows slipped over the railing of the *Penelope*. Only one marine was on deck, staring in the direction of the conflagration at the mill, whose flames now silhouetted the ridge beyond the manor house. He froze at the sight of the Iroquois warriors who materialized at his side, dropping his gun and not resisting as they gagged and bound him. Two of the marines below were playing cards as the third, their corporal, dozed in a hammock. One of the men sprang up, flinging his cards in Tanaqua's face and paid for it with a tap of the Mohawk's club that dropped him to the deck. The other soldier clamped his hands over his crown as if expecting to be scalped, and managed a strangled cry to his corporal, who tumbled out of his hammock and was pinned to the deck with Ononyot's moccasined foot.

They quickly searched the ship, distributing the weapons of the marines and others they found in a locker, then signaled for the other boats to approach. Tanaqua emerged from below with half a dozen weary sailors who were clearly terrified of the Iroquois.

"We be no enemy of yours," a wiry middle-aged man in a red cap ventured in a shaking voice, as he eyed his captors. "Whosoever ye be."

Duncan pushed Tanaqua's club down.

"You serve on the sloop?" he asked the man.

"Aye. First mate," the man said with a thumb to his own chest, and pointed to the man at the end of the line, then the others. "Bosun, the rest able-bodied seamen all."

"The *Penelope* is ours," Duncan declared. "If you're so inclined we could use your help. If not you can join the others," he said, motioning toward the marines, who were being gagged and tied like the sentry.

The mate looked back toward the dim shape of the brig. "The Virginia navy's claimed the boat, sir. And damned them to hell for killing the captain."

"Men pretending to be the Virginia navy took a pretend prize."

The mate pulled off his cap and scratched his head. "Everything on this river seems irregular."

"Completely irregular."

The man's expression softened. "The captain was a good man. They had no right." He shrugged. "But whatever the right of it there's no escaping those guns when she chases."

"She'll not be chasing. Not for hours yet. We'll be far out of sight by the time she reaches the bay."

"You mean because she'll not dare the river shoals in the night?" the mate suggested in a skeptical tone.

"Or with a broken rudder."

The mate frowned. "Rudder on a navy brig don't just break away."

"The *Ardent* spent too much time in the waters of the Indies without proper sheathing on her hull. Her wood is worm-eaten, which helped when I gouged out the planking around the rudder bolts. They are tied to two different pilings of the dock. The crew will be in a hurry to give chase when they discover the *Penelope* missing, and the current is strong. They will spring the bolts or at least bend them. If the pilings rip away they will foul the rudder. Either way, even with the best of luck they will be hours behind us. Most likely she will need a tow to a shipyard."

The mate contemplated Duncan in silence, then watched as more of the Judas company began climbing over the sides. "Ye be those white slaves they were fixing to hang," he said, more a statement of fact than a question. His men's eyes were all fixed on him.

"By the same men who killed your captain."

The mate gave a slow nod that sent a murmur of excitement through his men. "When do ye need the anchor hauled?"

Duncan surveyed the men who were climbing up from the boats. Trent and Woolford were rigging slings for the disabled. "In a quarter hour. We await a boat from the manor house. I need our injured safe in hammocks below. Is there a telescope on board?" He was troubled by the lights that had just appeared in the house.

A minute later, through the strong lenses provided by the mate, he could plainly see the figures of Rush, Conawago, and Alice Dawson in the open doorway. He confirmed that Winters and Sinclair waited for them in the cove with a scull, then saw a lamp lit in Ramsey's second floor bedroom. These were the most treacherous moments, when the guns of the brig at its moorings could easily reach them, when a single well-aimed shot could destroy their only chance for escape.

Five minutes later the skiff nudged the sloop and the mate barked out a command to weigh the anchor. Duncan ran to the rail as Winters, Sinclair, Rush, and Conawago climbed up.

He looked down into the empty boat. "Mrs. Dawson?" he asked.

Conawago shook his head. "She wanted so much to come, was talking about the new life she would be able to start with us. We were almost outside when he awoke, shouting for her, roaring with rage when he saw the burning gallows, screaming out the window for the marines. Then she brushed away a tear and said there was only one thing that would distract him, that something inside her had known she was not meant to leave her children. Then she went up to his bedroom."

Rain began sheeting across the river as the sloop edged away. Duncan watched the bedroom window until the driving rain obscured it, his heart a cold lump in his chest. He had failed Sarah, and now he had failed Alice.

Trent, at the wheel, let the sloop drift on the tidal current around the long point. As Trent and the mate directed the raising of the sails, Hughes called out and pointed to a dugout pulling alongside. Conawago straddled the rail and reached down, pulling up Kuwali, who surveyed the big sloop with round, frightened eyes. "Ursa said his son's freedom is his own freedom as well," Titus called out as the dugout drifted away.

"Edentown! He'll be in Edentown! We will send letters!" Conawago shouted to the old Ashanti as the dugout faded into the darkness.

The boy accepted Duncan's hand with a melancholy smile then darted to the stern, staring toward Galilee until it was obscured by the river bend. He had lost the misery of slavery but he had lost his family too.

Soon afterwards, Webb, Winters, and two of the Virginia rangers dropped over the side into one of the trailing skiffs. Webb and Winters hesitated at the rail. "You have hard riding to do," Duncan said.

"I know the roads," Winters replied, "and where to find horses." His face was lit with a new energy. "Duncan, you made me . . ." the young Virginian searched for words. "You made me understand," he said. "You showed me how to become the man Jaho always wanted me to be."

"You will make him proud, I am certain of it," Duncan said, as the young Virginian shook his hand. "And you are certain you can find that house on the Potomac?" he asked as Winters descended into the boat.

Webb put a reassuring hand on Duncan's shoulder. "He says we will make Mount Vernon by noon." The major put a leg over the rail before turning again to Duncan. "Praise God, McCallum. All would have been lost but—" Webb said, swallowing down his emotion.

"But an old Susquehannock showed us the way," Duncan finished.

Webb nodded. "Wilkes and liberty."

"Wilkes and Jahoska," Duncan replied.

The major nodded and slipped over the rail.

The *Penelope*'s surviving crew gave Trent a stiff reception at first but the overseer's churlish disposition seemed to have been left on land. He obviously knew what he was about, and though he was quick to chide the company men for their awkwardness in handling lines and stays, he was also quick to show them how the task was done.

It was three hours past midnight when they set the sullen marine guards on an island in the middle of the river. Duncan insisted on Woolford staying out of sight but let Murdo accompany them in a dinghy.

"I'll be busted for this," growled the corporal as they set foot on the little patch of brush and rock.

"Be grateful to be alive," Duncan reminded him. "My friends are short on compassion these days."

"Back to private, damn your eyes," the corporal groused.

"You're English I take it?" Murdo asked in a light tone.

"Of course I'm English, you Scottish hound. And when I—"

The corporal never finished his sentence. Murdo landed a fist on his jaw so heavily he stumbled backward and fell in the mud.

"Now ye can show the bruise to prove ye resisted us," Murdo hissed, then grinned at Duncan as he rubbed his fist. "That felt jolly good."

Back on board, Trent was wistfully aiming a musket toward the shadowy shapes on the island. "You're a soft-hearted fool, McCallum. They'll tell the brig our course for certain."

"They'll tell the brig what they heard," Duncan agreed. "But we said nothing about our true destination."

Trent lowered the musket. "You said the open sea, while means running past the patrols and through Hampton Roads."

"That will send the *Ardent* south if they reach the bay. We are jamming on every inch of sail she carries when we hit the open water and heading north. I have a craving for Chestertown oysters. Then we go up to the Susquehanna."

DUNCAN WATCHED THE SUN RISE FROM THE MAINTOP, WHERE THE mainmast joined the short topmast, one arm wrapped around the mast. He had told his companions he was climbing to the tallest point of the ship to keep watch, but Conawago had seen through him.

"There's nothing for it," the old man grinned, for he had seen the longing in Duncan's eyes. "You'll be good for nothing until you take a lark aloft."

For a few minutes after climbing the shrouds he felt as if he had shed years, the joyful memories of scampering in the rigging of Hebrides boats so overwhelming him that it was long minutes at the top before he remembered to look for a naval ship.

They were in the deep of the long bay now, and the wind and height gave him a sense of soaring above, as disconnected and free as the great osprey that flew close in the morning twilight. To the east lay the forested flatness of what was marked the Eastern Shore on their maps. To the west were the rolling hills of Virginia, cloaked in shadow. Between lay wind and sky, and a freedom he had not felt for months.

Freedom.

He glanced down at his companions, then with a more businesslike air studied the watery horizons. Several small fishing dories dotted the mouth of a river to the east. A sleek schooner, smaller than the *Penelope*, raced north ahead of them, probably headed for Annapolis or even Baltimore. His gut tightened as on the southern horizon he spied the square-rigged masts of what was in all likelihood a naval ship of the line, but then he realized that, bare-masted, she must be anchored.

He fixed his gaze on the now-distant point of land to the south that marked the mouth of the Rappahannock. If he had failed in his desperate attempt to disable the *Ardent*, if he saw her sails rising over the trees of the point, they would be doomed, for she would be close enough to spot the *Penelope* and her guns would soon reach them.

His gaze drifted back to the larger ship far down the bay. The murderous, lecherous Kincaid had taken Sarah. Her father had tried before to ship her back to England, to break her. She had even thrown herself into the Atlantic to escape Lord Ramsey, and she would do it again if given the chance. But this time Duncan would not be there to save her.

He watched the water until the mouth of the Rappahannock was long out of sight, no longer feeling the joy of the sailing but haunted by visions of Sarah as the prisoner of the man who had brutally murdered so many on the runners' trail.

The call of a thrush, incongruous on the bay, stirred him from his waking nightmares. Duncan looked down to see Woolford holding onto the shrouds a few feet below him. He motioned the ranger captain to join him.

"We're clear," Duncan reported. "The *Ardent* will not find us now."

Woolford nodded, and gazed out over the windswept bay. They did not speak for several minutes.

Duncan realized he had not had time to speak privately with his friend since Edentown, but he had seen the deep sadness behind Woolford's eyes. "I regretted not being able to stay for Jessica's funeral," he offered.

Woolford took so long to reply that Duncan thought he had not heard. "She took hold of my heart like no woman ever before." The ranger looked away, into the wind. "I carried my mother's wedding ring all these years. I was going to give it to Jess that very day, to wear on a chain until the Virginia business was over. Then I was going to take her back to Pennsylvania and ask the blessing of her parents so I could put the ring on her proper. Instead I buried her with it. My heart has been like a cold stone ever since."

There were no words Duncan could say. Woolford had lost Jess. He had lost Sarah.

"Lively!" came a sudden call from the deck. Trent was calling them down.

On a locker by the wheel, the mate had sketched a map of the Chester River on the back of a large chart. "Crabtown," he explained, indicating an odd square drawn in the center of the river mouth. "Fish weirs and floating pens to hold crabs and oysters for market, connected with walkways in a square, with shanties floating alongside for the watermen." He looked up at Duncan and his friends. "Take the *Penelope* any closer than Crabtown and the harbormaster will be out asking our business."

Trent, now at the wheel, took over. "So we lay in at the Choptank in another hour to call on the fishing dories."

"We have no time," Duncan protested.

"We must make the time. We cannot be suspected when we reach this Crabtown."

"He's right," Woolford agreed. "Any warning into the town and all we seek will be hidden away."

"So we need to foul the *Penelope's* beauty," Trent said. "We are going to cover our deck with bushels of fish and crabs."

"We need to make her stink," the mate agreed, seeming to warm to Trent's plan. "We need to make her ugly."

"We'll never pass for a fishing boat," Duncan objected.

"Not a fisherman, a market lugger. One of them that runs in to the villages along the bay to buy fish cheap then over to Annapolis to sell them dear."

There were always ways to rough up a well-run boat, but Duncan saw the chagrin on the crew's faces as they began slouching ropes and canvas over the rails and hauling up buckets of mud, dragged from the bottom, to drip over the hull. He watched for several minutes then turned over the chart the mate had drawn on, to find a map of the northern bay.

"Do London ships call on Chestertown or Annapolis?" he asked the mate.

The man scratched at the whiskers of his throat. "Not often, to be sure."

"Where then? If I were desperate to make passage, where would I go?"

"There's them that anchors in the Hampton Roads or even upriver toward Jamestown, though mostly when the tobacco harvest comes in. If you needed to be certain it would have to be Philadelphia. Three or four a week sail from there, I daresay."

Duncan pointed to the road on the map that ran northeast out of Chestertown. "And to get there from where we are going?"

"A fast horse east to the Delaware coast, I reckon, then catch one of the packets that run up the river."

"If I rode straight through to Philadelphia, without stopping?"

"Gawd, lad, you'd kill the horse and maybe yourself."

"How long?"

"Twenty-five, thirty hours."

"I can send messages, Duncan," Woolford said over his shoulder.

"To sit on some clerk's desk for days while half a dozen ships embark?" Duncan shot back. "And what do you say in a message? Stop a naval officer of good family who, no doubt, has a perfectly plausible letter from Lord Ramsey authorizing him to deliver his impaired daughter to England? No! The second we finish our business I will find two horses and run north, switching mounts as I go. I will swim out to every ship in the river to find her if I have to."

"I see. The runaway Scottish bondservant accosts the refined naval gentleman," Woolford snapped back, "who happens to be under the protection of a member of the House of Lords. I'll be sure to think of something witty from Shakespeare for your tombstone." He wheeled about and left Duncan staring forlornly at the map. Sarah was gone. He had destroyed that which he most wanted to save.

THE *PENELOPE* COASTED INTO CRABTOWN AT NOON THE NEXT DAY, reeking like a fish trader but with many of the company still grinning from the prior night's banquet of crabs, oysters, and rockfish procured on the Choptank. At the end of a maze of weirs spread across the river mouth, the odd collection of floating sheds and holding pens was connected by floating logs, planked over to make crude, uneven walkways. The ragged, boisterous watermen who were working the pens eyed them uncertainly but soon warmed when Trent brought up a cask of ale from the sloop's hold.

Duncan at first had such difficulty understanding some of the older men that he thought they must be speaking a foreign tongue, but then he caught the cadence and strange accents and realized they were using a very old English, the kind he might hear in a play of Marlow or Shakespeare. Their families, he realized, must have come over early in the prior century to this isolated region of the New World, and had never been diluted with immigrants from elsewhere.

The watermen seemed suspicious when he asked for a printer but soon, with the ale flowing, they explained there was but one print shop in Chestertown, though some of the watermen had the impression that the printer, Mr. Prindle, had been summoned elsewhere, for he had not been seen in town for weeks.

"A little golliwog of a man," a gruff figure with huge calloused hands explained. "But a good heart. I fear he's come to a woeful end. His big house's been rented out to the government."

"The government?" Duncan asked.

"Them water soldiers," the man muttered as he expertly lifted a crab in his fingers, examining it so closely it appeared he was trying to stare down the creature's stalky eyes. He glanced up. "Marines, they call 'em." He gestured with his free hand to a little cove tucked inside a curving point of land, where a familiar boat lay anchored. It was the cutter, one of the two boats that had sailed the day before from Galilee.

"Exactly the parties we want to see," Woolford ventured.

The waterman, lifting a second crab out of the basket, looked up suspiciously. "Thought ye wanted the printer."

The mate of the *Penelope* broke the awkward silence. "Only for a broadside to advertise our sailing schedule. Got to let those all in the little coves know when to expect us, eh?"

"Then wherefore see them marines?"

"Provisions for His Majesty's navy," Conawago put in. "They've got supply officers roaming all over the bay these days." He extended a mug of ale to the man. "Now exactly where we would find printer Prindle's manse?"

The waterman made a rough sketch on a scrap of wood then hesitated as he looked up to hand it to Woolford, noticing Tanaqua. "Folks don't go near the place these days. Fierce warriors be there, excuse me saying, sir," he added with an uncertain nod to Tanaqua. "Caused much ado in the town when they arrived in the spring."

"Warriors?" Conawago asked.

"Fighting savages brought from the north. Getting so womanfolk 'scared of going to church for fear of seeing them."

DUNCAN AND TANAQUA WATCHED THE BACK OF THE COMPOUND from the night-black river, only their heads above water. No one seemed to have taken notice of the dozen men who had appeared in the dusk, singly and in pairs, to wander the cobbled street. Murdo and two of his men sat on a bench in front of a tavern, Trent and two sailors on the stone step of the steepled church that shared the brick wall of the printer's compound. The guard at the gate onto the street appeared to be dozing. Duncan gestured Tanaqua forward and moments later they rose up out of the brackish water, using a stack of dories as cover.

Could it be possible the compound was so empty? They had not had the time to reconnoiter as Woolford had wanted. "Not the ranger way, to attack without knowing the enemy's strength," the captain had complained as they had studied the buildings through the telescope from one of the skiffs. But he had seen the cold determination in his companion's eyes. "Fine," he said to Duncan, and began checking the priming in his pistols. "We'll just do it the Scottish way. Charge forward without a care in the world."

"Not entirely," Duncan had chided. "If it was a true Highland charge we would be screaming like banshees. We will aim for a silent advance, in deference to the rangers."

The limb from the spreading chestnut of the church grounds hung over the wall, and as Duncan and Tanaqua advanced toward the back of the large house, a shadow dropped from the tree. The guard at the gate showed no reaction as Ononyot stole forward, knocked him unconscious, and dragged him into the shadows. Duncan and Tanaqua sprinted to the nearest window, which was cracked open, and climbed into the kitchen.

They inched through the darkened chamber, then into a dining room with a makeshift table made of planks on trestles. Duncan examined the room. The table could easily seat fifteen. Tanaqua hesitated over several white, curling objects on the sideboard, lifting one to show Duncan. They were collar stocks worn by British marines, slick with pipe clay.

"That cutter is anchored by Crabtown," Duncan whispered. "Maybe they went back on board."

But they had not gone back. In the front hall was a row of pegs on which hung eight uniform tunics and eight cartridge bags. Leaning along the opposite wall were muskets. The door on the opposite side of the corridor was closed but light leaked out along the bottom, and now they could hear quiet voices punctuated by exaggerated groans and exclamations. "Spades and diamonds!" someone called out. The marines were playing cards.

Duncan reached into a pouch and extracted Red Jacob's ranger disc, tossing it to Tanaqua, who nodded and set to work with the guns, using the disc to unscrew the flint from each musket. Duncan lifted away a bag and began stuffing it with the cartridges from the other bags.

Back in the kitchen, he carefully opened the latches of the two doors to reveal a pantry and a cellar stairway. "There is no printing press in this building. Too heavy for the second floor." He gestured to the squat brick building on the back corner of the compound that he had taken to be a boathouse.

The shutters were closed and the door of the building locked but its transom was open, and before Duncan could react, Tanaqua was in a tree, then on the roof and swinging through the narrow opening to release the latch. The air inside was laden with the scent of ink and wax. Tanaqua quickly lit a lantern and held it out to illuminate a printing press, a desk, and a large working table, below narrow shelves crammed with trays of type. Laid out on the table were three printed sheets with fresh seals affixed to them. The wax on the seals was still soft. "Tax commissions," Duncan declared, in a low, angry voice. "Made today."

Tanaqua picked up one of the papers. "I don't understand. How could a tax commission be issued in Chestertown?"

Duncan held the candle closer, reading the names, written in a hand that was remarkably close to the original commissions. Jonathan Bork, Josiah Randolph, Zebediah Sturgis. They were the names revealed the day Jaho had been killed. *You are directed to to deliver all proceeds to Lord Peter Ramsey, agent of the crown,* the last line said. The most predictable thing about Ramsey was his insatiable greed. If commissions were stolen the government would not expect revenue collected by the commissioners, and the commissioners would never expect a commission with an official seal to be fraudulent. In the backwater and remote towns of Maryland and Virginia, Ramsey was building his own phantom kingdom.

Duncan began searching the desks. The seal stamp used on the commissions was in the top drawer, along with several blank tax commissions ready to be completed. He set them on the desk, the seal on top of them, and opened more drawers. There was a ledger book with entries for Virginia and Maryland, evidencing tax collections that totaled several hundred pounds. The bottom drawer yielded several pots of ink and a locked wooden box. He extracted his knife and pried it open to find two packs of letters tied with red ribbons.

The red ribbons were used for filing in government offices but these letters were all to Lord Ramsey and Lieutenant Kincaid. On quick review the first stack were all receipts and lists of expenses for Ramsey's secret tax network. The second contained letters from New York, Philadelphia, Williamsburg, and Charleston. The first of these, an unsigned missive from Johnson Hall, read like a military report on the movement of certain Mohawks and Oneidas known to be closely allied with Sir William Johnson. With a chill Duncan recognized some of the names, all of them members of the ranger corps. A second letter described the movements of Woolford, Red Jacob, and other named runners. Still another letter, in a rough scrawl, reported schedules of trade convoys up and down the Susquehanna. It was signed simply "Bricklin."

There was a letter to Ramsey from the governor of Massachusetts raging over the disrespect shown by Samuel Adams, who, he haughtily pointed out, preferred the company of low farmers and sailors to that of proper gentlemen, and was rumored to be active in Boston's insidious committee of correspondence that was trying to foment dissent across colonial borders.

Tanaqua spun about, knife in his hand, facing the shadows at the rear of the building. Duncan too heard the noise now, a strange sawing sound from the darkness. He lifted the candle and inched forward, discovering more shelves and a ladder leaning in a corner. They paused, confused, until they heard the sound again, coming from under their feet. Tanaqua pointed to a large cast-iron ring in the floor, then to a bar with a handle and a hook that, when tried, fit into the ring. The Mohawk snagged the ring and heaved up, pulling away a square section of the floor. A fetid odor of unwashed human, fish, candle smoke, ink, and rum rose up from the darkness.

They slid the ladder into the hole and descended into a storeroom. On a narrow rope bed, beside an upturned crate holding an extinguished candle, a book, and a jar of rum, lay a snoring man. Long black hair was slicked over his bald crown. His hands were stained with ink. They had found the missing printer.

Duncan lifted Prindle into a sitting position, but when he released him he dropped back onto his pillow, senseless. The smell of rum was heavy on his breath.

"Prindle!" Duncan said, as loudly as he dared, then gestured for Tanaqua to help lift him to his feet. "Prindle, we are getting you out of here."

The drunken man's eyes fluttered open. "Ohhhh, aye. Well met," he slurred in a high-pitched voice, then his head sank toward his shoulder.

"Prindle!" Duncan pressed, then lifted the printer's chin. "Do you know a man named Bowen, Jeremiah Bowen?"

"Bowen, Bowen. Got to be a'going," Prindle chuckled.

"Where is he, man? Where is Bowen?"

"Buried like a mole," Prindle replied with a big smile. "But no more prisoners, prithee 'cause I'm fresh out of cellars."

They located the outside cellar door at the side of the house, shielded by rhododendron bushes, but to Duncan's dismay it was secured with a heavy padlock. "The door inside the kitchen!" he urged Tanaqua, well aware that they could be discovered by the soldiers at any moment. They had left the inebriated printer in his underground cell but did not know if their light in the print shop had been seen. "There was a stairway down to the—" He froze as he realized the tribesman beside him was not Tanaqua or any of their Iroquois companions.

There was anger in the man's eyes, but also curiosity. He ignored Duncan's greeting in the Haudensaunee tongue, and just stared over Duncan's shoulder. Tanaqua appeared beside him. "Seneca," Tanaqua declared with a tentative tone. Although part of the Iroquois League, many of the Senecas, the westernmost of the confederated tribes, had fought against the Mohawks in the war with the French and had often been the most bloodthirsty of those raiding settlers in the recent native uprising.

"Not another step," the Seneca stated, his voice raw with warning. "Go now and we will not draw blood." A war ax was in his hand.

Tanaqua inched closer but kept his open hands held out. "Brother, this is not your fight."

"Some in our village starved to death last winter," the Seneca said. "This is how we feed our families when the next snows come." The man was as big as Tanaqua. His grip on his ax tightened. "We do not care whose blood we take if it saves our families."

"And who," Tanaqua asked him, "will protect your families when the Great Council hears what you have done?"

"The Council is a circle of aging bears who have lost their teeth. Bricklin promised us flour and salted beef."

Duncan sensed the tension in Tanaqua. The Mohawk was struggling not to react to the insult. "It is not only the Great Council you need to fear," Tanaqua said. "There are others, in this world and the next, who will learn how you helped kill the Blooddancer."

The fight seemed to drain from the Seneca's face. His hand went to the totem pouch on his neck. "Do not say such things! The Blooddancer is safe in Onondaga."

"No," Duncan said. "He was stolen by the men you protect. Stolen to break the Mohawks who stand with us."

"You do not know of such things!" the Seneca spat. "You are not of the Haudensaunee!"

"We have tracked the captured god," Tanaqua stated. "He was in Virginia, just days ago. These men stole him. They would torture him and cut the chain that binds our people."

The Seneca glanced up at the window of the small third story of the house, then fingered his ax. "Not possible. I would know."

Tanaqua was done arguing. He abruptly raised his forearm, letting the moonlight catch its tattoo, evidence of his sacred trust. "I am the keeper of the secrets of Dekanawidah!" he recited in a furious whisper. He seemed to grow taller, more formidable, as he spoke, edging closer to the Seneca. "I am the shadowkeeper! I am the blade of the ancient spirits! Defy the spirits and the gate to the next world will be forever closed to you!"

The Seneca's jaw dropped open as he recognized the words of an Iroquois spirit warrior. His face clouded, his eyes widened. He backed away, all sign of resistance gone, then spun about and disappeared into the shadows.

In the corner of the kitchen Duncan opened the narrow door and climbed down. As they descended they saw light flickering on the stone flags and heard a quick metallic rattle. Tanaqua and Duncan exchanged a knowing glance. It was a sound they had heard often at Galilee.

A stooped, lugubrious-looking man sat on a stool in a corner of the cellar set apart from the barrels and crocks used for food storage by sheets suspended on ropes. From an iron ring in the stone wall a chain ran to the manacle around the man's ankle. A well-appointed bed, a nightstand stacked with books, and a commode with a pitcher, basin, and pot suggested he was not being altogether deprived.

Along one side of his linen-walled chamber was a long table bearing two bright whale oil lamps, with papers, paint pots, and brushes scattered across it. An easel had a muslin cloth tossed over it. The artist glanced nervously up at them, then back down at the floor.

"Mr. Bowen? Jeremiah Bowen?" Duncan winced at his fearful expression when he looked up again. "The miller of Galilee?"

"Miller no more," the man replied in a forlorn tone.

"Yes, well," Duncan said awkwardly. "I must confess we had to burn your mill."

Bowen cocked his head at them for a moment then shrugged. "Navy's loss, not mine. They requisitioned it. That was the word they used. Requisitioned in the name of the king. One lieutenant gave me a note saying they owed me seventy pounds sterling for it. The other gave me a note saying I owed them seventy pounds for not killing me. They had a great laugh over it, then fed both papers to the candle flame."

"Your work is most authentic," Duncan observed as he looked over the papers on the table. "I saw your replica of the Virginia charter."

"I describe it as the school of authentic painting," Bowen answered.

Several letters sat in a row as if awaiting inspection, each appearing to be in a very different hand. One was signed by Benjamin Franklin, one by Samuel Adams, one by William Johnson. Pinned to the sheet above the table were lists, notes, even ledger pages in different hands, but each with identifying names written in block letters at the bottom. They were the samples being collected by Kincaid's bounty hunters, the actual writings that provided the basis for the forgeries. Benjamin Franklin, said the first. As he pulled it down he saw the bloodstain along the top. *There is treachery in Virginia*, it said. *Hold all messages in Pennsylvania. Webb sent word. Let no one venture south.* It was signed simply *Franklin*.

A chill ran down Duncan's spine. It could only be the message taken from Ralston when he had been tortured and killed on the Susquehanna.

He examined more of the papers on the wall. Patrick Henry, he read, then James Otis, Samuel Adams, John Dickinson, Peyton Randolph, and half a dozen more. They were samples of actual handwriting. He paused as he studied the last letter in the row, then pulled it from the wall and stuffed it in his waistcoat before picking up the letter on the table bearing William Johnson's signature. It was an invitation to a French general to send troops up the Ohio Valley, and a description of the weaknesses of the British outposts, with an authentic-looking signature by Johnson. He remembered the list he had retrieved from the mill. *Johnson would die for trunnel nails and teapots.*

Beside the forged letter from the baronet were three more, each signed by one of the governors whose handwriting appeared on the wall. They were instructions to the chief officers of their legislatures, ordering that no members of the colonial legislature were permitted to travel outside the colony without their governor's permission. The Krakens were getting desperate in their efforts to block the feared congress.

When he finally looked back, Bowen gave him a bitter smile. "As you see, they keep me alive for my art. Using the stolen handwriting samples I have mastered fourteen different hands at last count. I could hang for even one. I have fourteen nooses waiting. After the first it didn't seem to matter."

"Not if you have been compelled against your will, sir."

Bowen hesitated, his brow creased with inquiry. "Why would you burn my mill?"

"To escape. We have a ship waiting. You no longer work for the Commodore."

Bowen's reaction was one of alarm, not relief. He shrank back as Tanaqua approached, but did not resist as the Mohawk bent over his manacle, taking out one of the pins they used to pop open such restraints. "No! No! He vowed to crush my hands if I tried to escape!"

"Do what we say, Mr. Bowen, and your hands will remain intact."

As Tanaqua worked, Duncan studied the room. The lamps had been positioned to illuminate the easel near Bowen's stool. A drop of chestnut-colored paint fell into a pool of a similar color at the foot of the easel. Bowen had not been working on another forgery when they disturbed him. As Tanaqua tapped at the pin with the hilt of his knife, Duncan pulled away the muslin cover.

His heart leapt into his throat. Although the portrait was not yet complete, the fiercely determined eyes, the high cheeks, the auburn hair, and soft yet firm chin were unmistakable.

"Where is she?" he demanded of Bowen. "Where is Sarah Ramsey? Where did you see her?"

"They didn't tell me her name. I—I didn't ask permission, sir, beg pardon. But she was so striking. Sometimes—" he gestured toward the table. "After all this sometimes I just want to paint a thing of beauty. I only saw her but a few minutes when she arrived, while I was in the kitchen, then again at noon today. I was showing the lieutenant some letters upstairs. She was asleep on a chaise by the window, with the sunlight playing on her hair. I didn't mean to . . ." his words faded into a stammer. He looked down nervously as Tanaqua pried open the manacle. "Please, sir. You misunderstand. I can't go up without his permission. Without my hands my life is for naught."

"Kincaid?"

"Not the lieutenant. The Irish giant. A gentleman named Teague."

A hungry, angry sound rose from Tanaqua's throat.

They had to practically drag Bowen up the stairs but he did not protest as they led him out the door to the print shop. They assured him he would be safe as they lowered him down with Prindle, who was snoring again.

From the house they finally heard movement. Shapes dropped from the lower windows into the boxwood and rhododendron around the house. The Seneca guards were positioning for battle.

Suddenly it was quiet. The boisterous men in the cobbled street had disappeared. An owl hooted from the stable across from the house. A whippoorwill answered from somewhere near the church, and urgent whispers rose from the Seneca hiding among the plantings. They recognized the Iroquois calls. An eerie drumming began from the loft of the stable. Hughes had found a drum in the church.

The owl called again, and the baffles of two lanterns fell away, one in the church steeple and one in the open door of the stable loft. Frightened gasps came from the shadows around the house.

A ghostly figure appeared in the light of the steeple. Bones dangled from the huge, angular, white body beneath a hideous, twisted face. It was an Iroquois spirit, or the closest effigy the rangers could manage in the short time they had to prepare. In the stable, the skull of a horse, found hanging on a peg at the back of the stable, had been adorned with horns of braided straw. Hung from a rope, it appeared to eerily hover over the lantern.

"Is this the night you pay the gods?" the figure by the steeple called out in the Iroquois tongue.

More whispers, some frantic, could be heard from the shadows, then quieted as Tanaqua spoke from behind a tree, only thirty feet from the house. "Brothers, come with us to the north. We will give you venison and warm robes for the winter. There is no honor in dying for these men."

The tall Seneca who had confronted them at the cellar door appeared in the moonlight. Five others joined him, including one with a musket who had been hiding only ten feet from Tanaqua.

Muskets roared from second-floor windows, aimed at the spirit figures. One ball hit the bell, raising a clear, solitary peal that lingered over the silent town. Angry voices rose from inside the house. A familiar figure leaned out as he saw the Senecas fleeing down the street.

"Damned cowards!" Teague boomed from the window. "I'll harvest every one of y'er scalps, damned ye to hell!" He fired a musket and one of the Senecas cried out in pain, holding his shoulder. His companions grabbed him and quickly pulled him into an alley.

The men in the house were prepared for a battle, but the rangers and Iroquois did not fight battles, they fought skirmishes with short, stealthy attacks. More second-story windows opened, and more muskets appeared, accompanied by angry curses as marines discovered their flints were missing. A rifle cracked from the stable, another from a tree, each wounding a man in the windows, who were angrily pushed aside as more of Teague's men returned the fire. Duncan was not worried, for his companions were trained to always move after firing a shot.

One of Teague's men darted out of the front door and was instantly rendered unconscious by Ononyot, who materialized out of the shadows by the door. Another man made the mistake of leaning out a first-floor window and was instantly pulled out, headfirst, by Hyanka.

Duncan, Murdo, and three rangers entered through the kitchen and warily approached the central hallway, where two of Teague's ruffians stood with muskets aimed at the front door. A shadow darted past Duncan, and Kuwali slammed a broom onto the back of the nearest man then disappeared into the darkened dining room.

"Goddamned little piece of manure!" the man spat and leapt after the boy. The broom handle shot out, tripping him, and Duncan heard the ring of an iron skillet on his skull. Analie appeared, victoriously waving her weapon from the kitchen. Kuwali and the girl had refused to stay on the sloop. The man remaining by the stairway backed into the pistol held by Trent. "Nice and gently now," the former overseer said in a whimsical voice as he reached for the musket. "The party's almost over and it'd be a pity to leave blood on the floor for folks to slip on."

The man yielded, and was led away to be bound with the other captives. Duncan and Tanaqua cautiously ascended the stairs. The chamber at the top, apparently used as a small ballroom, echoed with the retort of another musket aimed out the window.

Duncan spoke to the man who had just fired. "Sergeant, there are a dozen men out there who would rejoice at the chance of balancing their score with you. Surrender now and you will survive."

The sergeant spun about and reached into his cartridge box but his hand came out empty. "Fix bayonets!" he screeched.

CHAPTER TWENTY-ONE

Duncan's heart sank as the treacherous blades were dutifully clicked into place, then a hand was on his shoulder. Woolford, in his captain's uniform, pushed past. He casually set his cap on a chair. "Ensign?" he addressed the young officer who stepped past the sergeant. "It is ensign I believe?"

The officer gave a nervous nod.

"I am a captain in the king's infantry. You are a naval ensign seconded to the Virginia water militia." Woolford made a wide gesture toward the windows and the town beyond. "Perhaps you have noticed that you are on dry land. In the colony of Maryland."

The ensign glanced up the stairs that led to the third-floor bedrooms. He did not take his hand off his sword.

"These men," Woolford continued, "are irregulars under my command. What you do next is going to be one of the great decisions of your life. You can die. Or you take my order to stand down and walk away."

Murdo spoke sharply, in Gaelic, and two of the marines lowered their muskets.

"There's a barn across the street," Woolford stated. "Take your men there. Leave your firearms here for now. Get some sleep. Don't come out until I send word."

The ensign's hand slowly dropped from the hilt of his sword. He cast another uncertain glance up the stairs, then gave another command in a low, hoarse voice. The sergeant, his temper fueled hotter by the order, leapt forward, his bayonet aimed at Duncan's belly, and was promptly dropped to the floor by the butt of Woolford's pistol. His men removed their bayonets, picked up the sergeant, and followed the ensign down the stairs.

Teague was nowhere to be seen, but Duncan had lost interest in the Irishman. He and Woolford both moved toward the stairs to the third floor but Duncan held up a hand. "No. Only me."

He quickly climbed to the next level and pushed open the only door that showed light. Sarah Ramsey stood by a table in the center of the room. A huge weight seemed to lift from his heart. But then he paused, confused by the fear on her face.

The door was slammed shut behind him and Lieutenant Kincaid stepped out of the shadows, a heavy horse pistol aimed at Duncan.

"What opportunities America provides!" Kincaid exclaimed. He pushed the latch to lock the door then cocked the pistol. "The two things Lord Ramsey wants most in all the world! His insolent daughter off to be broken by some Yorkshire bulldog and the one man he is obsessed with destroying, both right in front of me. Not dead, he told us. McCallum may be broken but not dead, that was the order if we found you. He is a man of vast appetites, your father," Kincaid said with a glance at Sarah. The gun was fixed on Duncan's heart. "He reads books about the Crusaders. There was a torture used by the Saracens. The death of a hundred days. The lord has read the passage to us, at more than one of his dinners. So elaborate. It involves starving and hanging by the arms on a special apparatus that will carry the weight so the shoulders don't break right away." Kincaid gave a high-pitched, snorting laugh. "Ingenious really. Then slices of skin are removed from the lower body, day by day. There was something about hot wires pressed into the flesh and needles thrust into the privates, under the fingernails, then in the tongue and eyes. I think he has the passage memorized, like it was his personal Gospel."

"If you have touched her—" Duncan said in a voice savage with anger.

"Look at her!" Kincaid stepped closer, his gun still steady on Duncan as he lifted one of Sarah's curls. "Exquisite in every detail! How could she not be touched! She's made to be touched! Did I tell you I am to accompany her across the ocean? Adjoining cabins, though hers will be kept locked to all but me. I am authorized to administer doses to keep her quiet. Imagine that! I shall touch her, McCallum, I promise you. You'll be strung up in some Jamaican barn, begging to die, and I will be with Miss Ramsey, doing my duty. That impoverished woolmonger, her future husband, would never complain, given the size of the dowry he is getting."

Duncan inched forward. Sarah took a step around the table, out of Kincaid's reach. The lieutenant ignored her and raised the pistol toward Duncan's head. "You need to be alive," he declared in an amused tone, "but Lord Ramsey will understand if I have to put a ball in your knee or elbow. Or perhaps both?"

"The Iroquois kept saying it was a demon god who butchered those men in the north," Duncan said. "I never believed it was a spirit, just a man with a demon in his soul, a man like Ramsey but not Ramsey. You played the officer when convenient, even the circuit rider. But it's the role of the demon that best suits you. Now I wonder, with all the false papers here, do you even have a commission, Kincaid?"

The lieutenant gave an amused nod. "Bought and paid for by my father, the rich shoe merchant in Manchester. And the Kraken in the Admiralty will make me a captain by the time I'm through."

"You peeled the skin from living men. Cut off limbs."

Kincaid shrugged. "Teague said we should practice if we wanted to play the part of Blooddancer. So we tried our tools on the drunken

Iroquois who stole the mask for us. What a mess. He had already been
stabbed by that damned pest of a boy, who clung to his back all the
way to the river. We drowned that irritating boy then scattered that
drunkard's parts for the crows. Teague had worked in a butcher shop
so he had an unfair advantage in taking off limbs. But I tried. Don't
go straight for the joints, do the tendons first, he taught me."

"You sliced away the skin of a man just to spell a warning to us.
You killed him for no reason other than to frighten us."

"That African? Squealed like a pig."

Sarah's face drained of color. She backed away to the window and
cracked it open as if needing fresh air to revive.

Duncan inched forward. "Is that what Ramsey plans to do in
Lancaster, leave the mutilated bodies of the committeemen?"

"Of course not. A missing man on the frontier is one thing.
But some might consider killing members of the legislatures of
Pennsylvania and Massachusetts a bit reckless."

Kincaid failed not only to notice the opening of the window but
also the slow movement of Sarah's hand to the little pewter porringer
where red sealing wax had recently been melted. "Surely McCallum,
you should give us some credit. Ramsey will show them his forged letters. Mr. Bowen is a most remarkable man. It will be a shame to kill
him, but such a witness cannot be allowed to live. The handwriting
on the new letters is indistinguishable from their real handwriting
on the committee letters. Now that we have all the runners' marks
we can authenticate each one. Did you know those terrible gentlemen of the committees have been planning to build private arsenals
against the government, to organize smuggling against the tax, even
to conspire with our enemies in Paris? What entertainment we had,
deciding what crimes to create! Hobart wanted to construct some
intrigue between the governor's wife and Patrick Henry, but I said
mere acts of treason would suffice. With those letters Lord Ramsey

could throw them all in chains, ship them to London for trial and hanging." Kincaid paused and cocked his head at Sarah. She had made red lines on both her cheeks. He turned back to Duncan. "But of course Lord Ramsey will show his mercy. He will just keep the letters and have new puppets, new slaves in key positions in each colony. It will mean new charters for companies owned by Ramsey, new judges selected by Ramsey—"

Kincaid hesitated, looking again at Sarah, who now was whispering something toward the ceiling. Duncan took a step closer to the officer.

"*Jiyathondek! Jiyathondek!*" Sarah's words came more loudly now. It was an invocation, a request for the spirits to come to witness. "*Shatyykerarta!*" she declared. "*Enjeyeweyendane!*"

Duncan's spine went cold. *They are in their graves*, she had said. *They will be comforted.* It was a vow of retribution. He dared not rush Kincaid, for fear the pistol would discharge and hit Sarah.

"Dear God, woman, did I not tell you your father wanted you beaten if you played the savage again?"

"My claws are long," she continued in the Iroquois tongue. "Feel my strength."

Kincaid smiled as she stepped forward, extending her arms as if she wanted to embrace him. "What a wildcat! What a voyage we will have!"

"*Enjeyeweyendane!*" Sarah cried again and, stepping closer, flung her arms at him.

The thin smile on Kincaid's face froze for a moment, then he looked down in confusion at the bone-handled knife in his abdomen. Duncan recognized the blade as Tanaqua's. An instant later the Mohawk lifted the window and stepped in from the roof.

"You silly bitch!" Kincaid gasped, and swung the pistol toward Sarah. Duncan grabbed the barrel, resting his hand over the hammer, and pulled it from the lieutenant's weakening grip. Kincaid stepped backward, leaning against the wall, and with great effort reached for his sword. Tanaqua pulled the knife out of his belly then helped him pull his sword from the scabbard. He made sure Kincaid had a firm grip, then took a step back to give the officer room to swing the blade.

"Stupid heathen bastard!" With surprising swiftness Kincaid sliced his blade at the Mohawk.

Tanaqua brushed the sword aside with his war ax and plunged his knife into Kincaid's heart.

Sarah watched as the lieutenant's body slid down the wall to settle into a sitting position, his face locked in a puzzled expression, then stepped to the cabinet built into the corner and opened its door. The Blooddancer's crooked smile greeted them.

They worked quickly, collecting all the correspondence and records they could find and dispatching the men back to Crabtown in the wide flatbottomed ferry that plied between the town and the floating sheds. Duncan and Woolford found the frightened soldiers huddled in the barn, where they explained that Lieutenant Kincaid, whose body had been taken by the rangers to be weighted and dumped in the river, had fled and they should not expect him back. They introduced the remaining Virginia rangers and stated that the marines had to stay in Chestertown for ten days, under the guard of the rangers. After ten days they would all return to Virginia, where the rangers would attest that they had all been attacked by bay pirates and that Kincaid had valiantly died in the struggle.

Analie was in the kitchen with Prindle and Bowen, who had nodded off in a chair. In her hand she studied a little piece of jewelry, which she held out for Duncan to see. It was a watch fob, made of a little disc of polished oyster shell chased in silver. Something about it nudged at Duncan's memory.

"Mr. Prindle says they make them here in town, the only jeweler anywhere who does so." Analie looked up, searching Duncan's eyes. "I told you. Francis Johnson had one just like this when he visited Johnson Hall."

By midnight they had all reached the floating docks of Crabtown, from which skiffs were shuttling men out to the *Penelope*, still hidden in the little cove beyond the point where she lay anchored.

As Duncan, Sarah, and Woolford watched one of the last of the skiffs shove off, Ononyot, at the stern, cried out in warning. They turned to see a massive figure standing in a punt coasting toward them out of the darkness, holding a treacherous pointed fishing gaff in each hand. With a roar Teague launched one of the gaffs at Duncan.

Duncan had no time to avoid the spear. With an explosion of pain it ripped into his thigh, embedding in the muscle. He staggered then collapsed halfway off the dock, one arm and the wounded leg in the water, the weight of the heavy spear dragging him down. Sarah screamed and grabbed him, jerking out the spear and pulling him onto the dock. He clutched at his wound with one hand and tried to push her away with the other.

"Look at ye now," Teague laughed as he stepped onto the platform. "Christ knows I should have finished you both that day at Edentown. But Kincaid was in a hurry to get to the Susquehanna. Don't start a job unless y'er going to finish it, I always say." He balanced the remaining gaff in his outstretched arm as he approached them. Sarah threw herself over Duncan.

"Y'er such a wee thing," Teague said to her. "I wager I can skewer ye both with one thrust," he hissed. Through his fog of pain Duncan raised his hand, dripping with blood, to shove Sarah away, but she only rose enough to kneel beside him. As she reached for the bloody spear that had impaled Duncan a figure hurled past her with a furious

Gaelic cry. Murdo hit Teague like an angry bull, knocking the spear from his grip and flattening him on the planks. He pounded the Irishman three times on the jaw before Teague could react. With a furious bellow Teague arched his back and threw Ross off.

"Ye murdered my little girl!" Ross shouted as he recovered, facing Teague with clenched fists.

The words caused Teague to hesitate. He grinned. "And such a sweet morsel she was. I only wish I had had the time to linger over her. I told Kincaid we should take her to the river with us but he said we had no time for sport."

Sarah thrust the spear into Murdo's hands. The big Scot made a feint toward Teague then threw it. It lodged in Teague's side. With a howl of rage the Irishman tore the spear from his flesh and tossed it into the river.

"A darlin' bud of a girl," Teague continued as he inched forward. "When she tied on her petticoat that morn she never guessed she'd be gone by noon."

"Don't let him get close!" Duncan warned as he saw the cudgel in Teague's hand.

But Murdo's rage blinded him. He charged. The Irishman side-stepped and slammed the cudgel behind his ear. Murdo dropped with a groan then looked up, dazed, as Teague kicked him in the belly, knocking the wind out of him. The Irishman lifted Murdo's torso into a sitting position and, holding him up with one hand, began pummeling him with the other. Duncan struggled to his knees and began crawling toward his friend but Sarah pushed him down and began dragging him away.

Murdo began to recover, landing weak blows on Teague's shoulders, but the Irishman only gave a hideous laugh and hit him harder.

With a wild screech Analie burst out of a fish shed and launched herself at Teague's feet. The Irishman was so intent on battering Murdo that he seemed not to notice at first, then aimed a kick that glanced off her shoulder. As the girl retreated, crablike on the wet boards, the Irishman paused, then let Murdo fall to the dock.

The girl had tied a rope to Teague's knee. "Damned little banshee!" he hissed, then was about to turn back to Murdo when Tanaqua stepped out of the shadows. He was holding a heavy anchor stone. Teague hesitated, then cursed as he realized it was tied to the rope.

"You stole my god!" the Mohawk declared loud enough for the spirits to hear.

Teague frantically grabbed at the knot on his knee.

"You killed my brothers! Let the blackness take your soul," Tanaqua declared, then tossed the anchor in a long arc into the deep river.

The rope tightened and Teague was jerked through the air. There was no chance for him to struggle, no time for him to free the knot that bound him to the anchor. With a surprisingly small splash the big Irishman entered the water and was gone.

The *PENELOPE* slipped through the night, throwing white foam off her bow. Duncan, his jagged wound washed and bound, sat on a barrel watching the stars, the lantern at his side extinguished now that he had finished reading the letters taken from Chestertown. He sensed someone behind him but did not turn.

"It made no sense," he said, "that the name of Socrates Moon was on the forger's wall, with an example of the old gentleman's handwriting. Right up there with the leaders of the committees, with Samuel Adams and Benjamin Franklin. You knew all about the murders. You knew what was going on in Philadelphia and Boston and Williamsburg. You helped Patrick in his secret tasks and used Edentown, Conawago. I couldn't understand that day in Edentown when Jessica Ross kept looking at you when she spoke of the missing men from Pennsylvania. You invited her there to establish a station in the network."

"Not without Sarah's consent," the old Nipmuc replied as he leaned on the ship's rail. "She was going to tell you, in her own time." They watched a skein of ducks fly across the moon. "All my life I avoided choosing sides. I spent my years searching for my family. It was a fool's errand. I knew kings. I could have made a difference. But I chose to keep my world small, just as you did. Duncan, we have been obsessed with phantoms. My family is gone. Your clan is gone.

"When you and I were up on the St. Lawrence we could have changed the outcome of the war with the French but I chose to keep the Canadian tribes out of the final bloodshed and you chose to keep all those Scots from dying as traitors. What have we got for the trouble? The French would have peacefully coexisted with the tribes as they had for centuries. But the British king despises the tribes. He and his lords will annihilate the tribes if they have their way, just as they would shackle the colonists with taxes and laws. Helping that kind of king was wrong. I see that now. Such a king has no place in America. That is the side I have chosen now. Not the French side, which is long lost. And not King George's side. The side of this land. My land. Jahoska's land. Your land. Europe has no place here. We can make it different." A shadow emerged and stood beside the old Nipmuc. Woolford had been listening. He was not disagreeing.

"Words like that will get you killed," Duncan said.

Conawago smiled as if welcoming the remark. "The age is turning, Duncan. Jahoska the half king understood that before the rest of us. And at every turning there is a fulcrum, a small group of men who set the new age in motion. We are the agents of the turning. America is destined as the place of the turning. There is something new meant for America."

"It will get you killed," Duncan repeated. "Enough good men have died."

"I fear before it is over the good men who die will be like leaves on a tree," the old Nipmuc said. "Does that make it wrong?"

CHAPTER TWENTY-TWO

The angel on the sign swinging over the tavern door faced an old
man with a scythe on the opposite side of a setting sun. From the
stable across the road Duncan watched the sign sway in the breeze,
wondering if the austere Quaker innkeeper had chosen the image to
dissuade the revelers that frequented the other inns of Lancaster. The
World's End, though not the most prosperous, was certainly the most
respectable of the establishments in the community, well chosen by
the committeemen for its quiet location at the edge of town, with the
stable and Sabbath meetinghouse its only close neighbors.

The quick song of a lark came from the loft overhead and Duncan
edged closer to the partially open door. An ornate coach was arriving
from the direction of Philadelphia, the two guards riding on the top
beside the driver springing down before it rolled to a stop. Two more
men on escort horses dismounted, and hurried to assist the rotund
passenger out of the coach and into the tavern. Gabriel, attired in a
poorly fitting suit and tricorn hat, followed a step behind Lord Ramsey,
clutching a leather case and muttering in his usual surly tone.

As soon as the door of the tavern closed behind Ramsey's party,
Duncan and Woolford circled behind the building, entered the
kitchen, and slipped into the private dining chamber reserved by the
committeemen months earlier. They sat in the shadows behind the
half-drawn curtain used to divide the room.

The five men at one end of the long table by the row of front windows rose and politely greeted Lord Ramsey, then Gabriel, who was introduced as his secretary. As Ramsey sat at the end of the table nearest the door, the five introduced themselves and Gabriel opened a journal, produced a quill and ink pot, and made a show of recording their names, interrupting to ask spellings. Samuel Adams from Boston, Peter Hopkins from New York, Peyton Randolph of Williamsburg, John Dickinson of Philadelphia, and Mistress Deborah Franklin, speaking for her husband. Dickinson introduced Benjamin Rush as their own secretary. Ramsey's guards from the coach, each armed with a shortsword and a pistol in a shoulder holster in the style of Scottish troops, sat with stern expressions on either side of the door. Duncan recognized both as pharaoh riders from Galilee.

A maid appeared with a tray of cider and mugs, assisted by a girl with blonde braids carrying a platter of iced sweet rolls. The braids, and her bright white apron, gave Analie the look of an innocent serving girl. She had insisted on playing a role in their little drama.

"We were surprised at the announcement you sent from Philadelphia," the portly Samuel Adams lied, "but we are always honored to be joined by a member of the House of Lords."

"Join you?" Ramsey retorted, with a pompous gesture that seemed to dismiss Adam's words. "Only in the sense that we sit at the same table. Rather I ensnare you." As he spoke the remaining men of his escort, the two outriders, still wearing their cloaks, entered the room and sat, backs to Woolford and Duncan, as if to corner the committeemen.

Adams ignored Ramsey's opening. "We are here to discuss the particularities of a colonial congress," the Boston committeman continued, "but those of us habituated to public discourse can be so long-winded. Why if Dr. Franklin were here he would take thirty minutes just to warm his tongue and continue through at least three pitchers of ale. We know his better half will be so much more succinct."

Mrs. Franklin, a solid-looking woman with deeply penetrating eyes, offered a congenial nod in reply. She had played the gracious hostess to Duncan and his friends the prior week in Philadelphia, taking particular delight in demonstrating the household's electrical apparatus, and later insisting they all go to church to pray for Devon Gates when she had learned of his fate. "I am sure you would like to be spared the ordeal of our own discourse, Lord Ramsey," Adams declared in an attentive tone. "Prithee, if you have business with us let us hear you out first, sir."

An exaggerated sigh escaped Ramsey's throat. "I once found signs of rats in my country house in Wiltshire," the patrician began in a conversational tone. "My steward said it was to be expected, that they were doing no real harm. I told the fool that a rat feeling safe in the cellar will soon aspire to enter the kitchen, the dining room, and even the parlor itself. I ordered every barrel and rack moved out. We starved half a dozen terriers for a week then turned them loose. In the end we had nothing left but one very plump terrier." He cast a frigid smile down the table at the colonials. "We have rats in the cellar of the empire and it is time to loose the dogs."

With an air of ceremony Gabriel produced a thick bundle of papers from his leather portfolio and handed Ramsey the topmost sheet. "A secret letter from Mr. Hopkins of New York to Mr. Henry of Williamsburg." The patrician held it toward the window and made a show of scanning it before reading a passage. "The pompous Hanoverian is no longer my king," Ramsey recited. "He is a false idol which we must tear down." Ramsey wagged a finger at Hopkins, who silently glared at him. The lord continued with a letter from Adams to Franklin. "The gout in George's foot has spread to his brain," Ramsey read. "He who once strutted now only limps and babbles." He cast a censuring glance when a small laugh escaped Adams's throat. "We have no obligation to serve the infirm and incapacitated," Ramsey continued, then read from another, and another, all allegedly letters between known committeemen, all with similarly incendiary passages.

Ramsey glanced without acknowledgment at the two men who stepped from the kitchen and sat behind Rush and Franklin. "This is treason, gentlemen. Men have lost their heads in the Tower for less. In another century we would have had you drawn and quartered in the public square." He accepted another bundle of papers from Gabriel.

"More letters, these boasting of tax stamps stolen from the king. One shipment in New Jersey, another in Massachusetts. Contemptible!" Ramsey spat, heat building in his voice. "It makes you little better than a gang of cutpurses, damned your eyes!" He fixed Dickinson with a baleful stare. "Your agent Franklin in London is the worst devil of all!" he barked, pulling out a letter and waving it at Dickinson with a victorious air. "To the Committee of Philadelphia," Ramsey read, then paused as Dickinson held up a hand and pushed a quill and ink pot to Deborah Franklin, who began transcribing.

"To the Committee of Philadelphia," she repeated.

"I have led the king's men to believe that—"

"Prithee, sir," Mrs. Franklin interrupted with a matronly air, "more slowly."

With an impatient sigh Ramsey pressed on, "—to believe that the colonies will tolerate the dread tax to give us time to organize the congress. We will let the Parliament sleep until we awake it with a claw at its throat. What the king built in America shall be ours if we are but patient," Ramsey recited, ending with a flourish. "He should hang for this!"

When none of the colonials reacted he hesitated, then lifted the next five papers and read the names on each, the names of each of the committeemen at the table. "These are warrants for your arrest on charges of treason. With these I could have you clamped in irons today and shipped to London for trial."

Ramsey shot a peeved glance as another gentleman moved out of the shadows and settled in a chair along the wall. "But we are inclined to be merciful. We will hold the warrants and all of you, all the committeemen, will resign from whatever public offices you may hold and refrain from all public and political discourse. There will be no colonial congress."

One of the most recent arrivals, a spare, austere man in simple Quaker dress, stood and took a seat alongside that of Dickinson at the end of the long table opposite Ramsey.

"My name is William Allen," the newcomer solemnly announced as he placed a heavy brass seal on the table beside him. "I have the honor to serve on the Governor's Council, and in the absence of the honorable Governor John Penn, now at his English estates, I have full power to act for him. Last night," he said, producing a paper from his own leather portfolio, "I appointed Mr. Dickinson here as special magistrate. Of Pennsylvania. Surely even you, the most creative of accusers, would have to acknowledge that you are not in Virginia, but in Penn's Woods." The acting governor began arranging papers in front of him. "Where to begin?"

Adams cleared his throat.

"Very well." Allen pounded the heavy seal on the table. "This court is in session and Mr. Dickinson is presiding, assisted by Mr. Socrates Moon as clerk of this special court," he added, as Conawago, dressed in his European finery, rose from along the wall and sat just behind Dickinson.

Dickinson nodded to the acting governor and turned to the representative from Massachusetts. "Samuel Adams of Boston, did you write the letter Lord Ramsey ascribes to you?"

Mr. Adams suddenly lost his jovial air, shaking his head so hard it slightly dislodged his wig. "Never in life."

"Your name is on it," Ramsey snapped. "It is your handwriting."

"No."

"I assure you I can find witnesses to attest to it!" Ramsey scolded.

"No."

Ramsey simmered. "I tell you, sir, I have your name on a treasonous document."

"No," Adams insisted again, "but perhaps Mrs. Franklin can demonstrate the truth for the court."

Ramsey scornfully watched as Deborah Franklin, smiling earnestly at him, handed the transcription of the letter she had made to Conawago, who laid it in front of Ramsey.

An impatient rumbling rose from Ramsey's throat. "You don't seem to grasp the jeopardy in which you . . ." The lord's words died away as he studied the transcription. "I am quite sure I don't understand," he sputtered.

"The two versions are identical, are they not?" the magistrate asked. "Identical in every respect." He turned to Conawago. "Perhaps you can enlighten our guest?"

"Identical down to the curves on the *F*s and flourishes on the *G*s," Conawago elaborated. "Because your bounty men did not understand that Deborah Franklin acts as a surrogate for her husband while he is in London. You intercepted letters that you assumed were written by Benjamin, because they were signed Franklin, when in fact they were written by Mrs. Franklin. So your forgeries of letters from Benjamin are all made in her hand. The wrong hand. Your agent Francis Johnson did not know this when he delivered a letter purportedly from Benjamin to Johnson Hall. But his father, who has the pleasure of frequently corresponding with Deborah, immediately recognized her hand and saw that treachery was afoot."

"I have a commission from the governor of Virginia!" Ramsey snarled.

Allen nodded to Ramsey's outriders. "You have a vast imagination, sir, especially when it comes to your own abilities and authority," the governor declared. "It is you, sir, who presume too much. The traveling companions you hired in Philadelphia have had time to change to their official attire." The two men rose and removed their cloaks, revealing blue waistcoats trimmed with grey. "These stalwart lads you hired with the coach when you disembarked in Philadelphia are dragoons of the governor's guard, as is your carriage driver. Did I mention the owner of the livery is my brother-in-law? And perhaps you are acquainted with my two special bailiffs, appointed by my hand yesterday. It seemed the least we could do." As he spoke the door opened and Tanaqua and Ononyot, both wearing new waistcoats over buckskin leggings, moved inside so quickly that the two seated pharaohs from Galilee, stunned by their appearance, had no time to resist. The Mohawks pinned them to the wall with their war axes and relieved them of their pistols. A small strangled noise came from Ramsey's throat. He shrank back in his chair. He was, Duncan well knew, terrified of all Indians. Ramsey turned to Gabriel as if expecting him to come to his assistance, but the superintendent of Galilee sat frozen, the color draining from his face.

Murdo Ross came forward, leading the limping artist Jeremiah Bowen. Duncan had urged the Scot to stay away from the Pennsylvania officials because of the standoff in the Conococheague Valley, but two days before word had arrived of a truce in the valley. All prisoners had been released, and the governor had assured them the unfortunate episode in the valley was forgotten, and that all shipments to the western territory would henceforth be inspected by his personal representatives. Kuwali appeared behind Ross, helping Mr. Prindle the printer into a chair. Dickinson lifted a Bible, swore Prindle and Bowen to the truth, then began his new questioning. Ramsey said nothing, only crossed his arms and glared at Dickinson as the magistrate skillfully pieced together the story, carefully reviewed with

Duncan, Woolford, and the witnesses the preceding day. The full story of the forged stamps, forged commissions, and forged letters took hours to recount, with Rush recording every word.

"I have a commission from the governor of Virginia!" Ramsey finally protested, his voice thick with loathing. "I am a commander of the naval militia!"

Dickinson gave a lightless smile and waved another paper at Ramsey, then nodded to one of the dragoons. "Can you ask the colonel to join us?"

The tall, well-dressed man who strode through the door had the honest air of a farmer but his eyes were deep and his voice one of firm authority as he was sworn in. "Washington, sir," he declared to Dickinson in a polite tone. "Colonel of the Virginia militia."

"And commander of that militia?"

"That is my particular honor."

Dickinson handed him the paper and asked him to describe it.

"From the governor in Williamsburg, sir," Washington explained. "Signed in my presence and in my possession until I delivered it to you." He turned to Ramsey. "Your commission is terminated. The Virginia militia no longer requires a naval unit."

Ramsey's lips curled in a silent snarl.

"We apologize for troubling you in the harvesting season, Colonel," Dickinson offered to Washington. "You have a plantation on the Potomac I believe."

George Washington straightened. "When the integrity of the Virginia military is in question, sir, nothing is too much trouble."

"Your lenders in London will hear of this!" Ramsey screeched.

"Our Philadelphia friends have arranged for a colonial bank to pay off the debt the governor owes you, sir," Washington replied with a thin smile, "and perhaps Virginia planters need to learn to do without the lenders of London."

Dickinson excused the witness and Washington strode outside, where he could be seen lighting up a pipe with Woolford and Major Webb, who now waited with the Pennyslvania dragoons, a dozen of whom had arrived with the governor the prior evening.

The magistrate lifted one more paper. "From a judge in Maryland. A warrant for the arrest of Lord Peter Ramsey on charges of kidnapping and mayhem in Chestertown."

Ramsey's face turned crimson. The lace of his collar moved up and down. "Damn your impertinence! You have no proof I was involved!"

"Imagine the trials. British marines desperately trying to avoid court-martial and hanging by explaining they were taking orders from you to commit murder and false enslavement. Not to mention the use of a naval ship to sink private British vessels. Prominent citizens in Philadelphia, Boston, New York, and Williamsburg attesting to your attempt to deprive them of their liberty. Then there are the families of the men who died as a result of your scheme. Those are just the offenses of the Krakens. Imagine what the king would say if he heard of your attempt to defraud him of tax revenues." Dickinson extended the warrant toward the shadows and Duncan appeared to take the papers to Ramsey. "Do we also need to issue a warrant for embezzling the king's revenues?"

The pompous lord, who looked as if he might start throwing things at the governor, grabbed the papers, then glanced at Duncan and froze. His rage boiled over as Duncan coolly returned his stare. "McCallum!" Ramsey spat. "You can't be here. You are on a ship to . . ." he seemed unable to speak for a moment. "You mongrel! You did this! How dare you!" He pounded the table. "I will not have it! McCallum is my property! A runaway!"

"We understand his bond is to Miss Sarah Ramsey," Dickinson replied.

"She is incapacitated!" Ramsey furiously inserted. "Halfway across the Atlantic. She cannot . . ."

Sarah emerged from the shadows and stepped to Duncan's side. The cast of characters in their drama, which Woolford had insisted was as good as any of Shakespeare, was complete. "Actually, father, I am quite well, thank you," she declared in a chill tone. "And as you well know I am a landed free woman in the colony of New York. Mr. McCallum is bound to me alone."

Ramsey was beginning to look like a cornered beast. He spoke very slowly, vitriol dripping from every word. "I am a member of the House of the Lords!" Spittle flew from his lips. "I am cousin to the king!"

Deborah Franklin pushed back her chair and rose at last. With a ceremonial bearing she asked Kuwali and Analie to help her with a piece of folded cloth, and the two adolescents unfurled a flag, revealing the segmented serpent and its caption *Join or Die*, which they draped over the mantle, anchored by candlesticks. "I sewed the first of these with Benjamin all those years ago," she explained to Ramsey in a level voice. "It became one of his favorite treasures, so valued he took it to London with him. I was so honored to hear that dear Jessica Ross had sewn another that I had to make my own to fly on High Street."

She opened a worn leather satchel and produced a piece of newsprint, which Kuwali carried to Ramsey. "I helped compose this in my husband's print shop," she announced, "though Mr. Moon was of great assistance. It felt good to get ink on my hands again."

It was a prototype, a mocked-up page of Franklin's *Pennsylvania Gazette*. Half the page was taken up by a drawing of a giant eight-legged beast wrapping its tentacles around a map of the thirteen colonies. Beneath it was the caption *Kraken Feeds on America While the King Sleeps*.

"We typically send a hundred copies of each issue to London," Deborah Franklin explained, "though I daresay this edition would merit five or six hundred." She took off her spectacles and cleaned them on a linen napkin. "The article, of course, would include the names of members of your secret club, those we know so far. It will make our little paper famous all over Europe. Perhaps I will send duplicate plates to my husband in London so he can keep up with the demand there. A virtual goldmine for the news journals. The people do so love to read of how the high and mighty fall. With all the resignations from Parliament it will cause, I daresay, it will shift the balance of power in government. And they will all know you caused it."

Ramsey shrank before their eyes. Indictments from colonial officials meant little to the aristocrat. But the article Franklin threatened would destroy all that Ramsey held dear—his access to the king, his privileges in court, his private club memberships, the status that allowed him to strut and make people cower throughout London society. There would be no more balls, no more regal audiences, no more kowtowing at his presence.

Ramsey offered no protest when Conawago lifted away the stack of forged papers in front of him.

"We are prepared to refrain from such harsh actions," Dickinson announced. "We are willing to hold the writs in a private file and not prosecute them. Mrs. Franklin has reluctantly agreed to suspend publication of this most remarkable story. Provided—"

Ramsey leaned forward, reviving.

"Provided you leave Virginia and the northern colonies. You have plantations in the Carolinas and the Caribbean you can retreat to, not to mention your estates in England. You will discreetly give us the names of all members of the Kraken Club and we will make no official notice of them. You will give employment to Francis Johnson in England, far from the Iroquois and his father. You will abandon all efforts to block the committees of correspondence and the conduct of a colonial congress. And you will report that your informants confirm that such congress will not be held until next spring."

Ramsey's eyes were like daggers, stabbing at Duncan. He slowly turned to Dickinson then lowered his head and stiffly nodded.

Duncan leaned over Dickinson and whispered. "Ah, yes," Dickinson said with a slight blush. "You will abandon all efforts to marry off your daughter." The magistrate glanced out the window. Sarah had gone outside and was now laughing with Colonel Washington. "I have met Miss Ramsey and assure you she is quite capable of managing her own life. And you will sign a deed."

"Deed?" Ramsey growled.

Conawago placed another paper in front of the lord. "Sign this and the governor and magistrate will witness," Dickinson explained. "There was some confusion over ownership of a plantation on the Rappahannock. This deed transfers all ownership rights in Galilee to Mrs. Dawson, the widow and heir of the former owner."

"Colonel Washington," Dickinson added, "and Major Webb have graciously agreed to deliver the deed to Mrs. Dawson personally."

"Impossible!" Gabriel hissed, rising so fast he spilled papers across the table. "That is *my* plantation! No sotted Quaker prig is going to—" his words died away as Ononyot clamped a hand around his arm. Gabriel tried to twist out of his grip, to no avail. "Get off me you filthy heathen! If I had you back at—" Tanaqua appeared on his other side.

Dickinson raised a hand. "One final thing. Mr. Moon has reminded us that there is an old treaty with the tribes. Never abrogated after all these years. It promised comity, meaning each side would respect the enforcement of the laws of the other. There was an example, right in the text, that a murderer of a tribal member would answer for his crime under tribal law, and it is the policy of Pennsylvania that if any such fugitive from Iroquois justice sought refuge within our borders, we would turn him over. The murder of an aged Susquehannock would be a matter of tribal law, of course."

One by one Hyanka and the other Iroquois rangers who had been in Galilee filed into the chamber. Gabriel stood stricken, wide-eyed, and unable to speak, then suddenly reached into his waistcoat and extracted a small pepperbox pistol that he swung toward the Iroquois. Tanaqua pushed the barrel upward as it discharged, loosening its load into the ceiling.

No one spoke. Tanaqua pried the pistol out of his hand. As he set it on the table Gabriel gave a terrified squeal. Ononyot had slipped a prisoner's strap over his neck.

IT WAS LATE AFTERNOON WHEN THEY FINALLY LEFT THE TAVERN, having seen Ramsey off with his escort of Philadelphia dragoons. Governor Allen had to leave soon himself, but Adams, Mrs. Franklin, Washington, and Dickinson insisted on hosting a banquet that night for Duncan and his companions.

"In faith, McCallum," the governor exclaimed, "we are truly and deeply indebted to you. If there is ever anything I could do for you—"

Duncan smiled. He had prayed for the invitation. "We would not have succeeded without the Iroquois," he replied. "There is a merchant here named Hawley," he added, then explained what he had in mind.

"My God, McCallum. You presume much, sir."

Duncan silently returned his stare, until the governor looked away.

Half an hour later Duncan and the governor entered Hawley's establishment, followed by Dickinson, Conawago, and Tanaqua.

"Mr. Hawley," Conawago said to the man behind the counter. "Might I present his excellency Mr. Allen, the acting governor of the colony, and Magistrate Dickinson?"

The storemaster's jaw dropped open. He hastily removed his apron and offered a bow. "Honored I'm sure."

"I understand," Allen began, "that you hold a commission as paymaster of bounties on—" he cast an uneasy glance at Conawago and Tanaqua. "On hair," he concluded.

"Aye, sir. An active trade for our establishment, the most active commission in the colony by all accounts."

"Might I see it?"

Hawley frowned then excused himself as he hurried into a back office. When he returned, the governor unrolled the parchment on the counter. "Have you ink and a pen?" he inquired. As he waited again he read the words and his face clouded. "Not the proudest act of a Christian government," he whispered, as if to himself. When the ink arrived he lifted the pen and with a flourish wrote the word *Terminated* across the face of the commission and signed it. "You are done, Hawley. It's all done." He rolled up the commission and handed it to Tanaqua. "This colony is no longer in the hair business."

EPILOGUE

C hild!" Conawago growled to Analie. "The king will fall to
the deserved victor if you would but stop showering me with
Franklin's sparks! I swear I am going to write the great doctor in
London and let him know the French are perverting his science!"

Analie giggled, then drew another spark from Conawago's fingers with the glass rod sent by Deborah Franklin in Philadelphia and
skipped away, raising a deep laugh from their genteel host on the other
side of the chessboard.

"I've begun to suspect you have bribed the girl to distract me, Sir
William," the old Nipmuc said to his chess partner.

William Johnson, baronet and Superintendent of Indian Affairs,
looked up from his troubles on the board. "What an inspired sugges-
tion!" he exclaimed, and tossed a sweet biscuit to the girl before refill-
ing the china teacups on their folding campaign table. She broke it in
half to share with Kuwali, who sat on the carpet with Sarah looking
at a small slate where Sarah was teaching him the sounds of Iroquois
words. Duncan looked up over the gazette he was reading, relieved
to see the smile on Johnson's face. The pain of his son's betrayal had
been easing since joining his friends but the scar inflicted by Francis,
now gone across the Atlantic, would mark him forever. Analie grabbed
Duncan's hand and pulled him up from his reading. He handed his
paper to Woolford and let her lead him outside.

In his advanced years Sir William liked to carry his comforts with him when he traveled. Duncan and Analie stepped out of the pavilion tent's European world into a Haudensaunee town of bark-wrapped lodges. The castle of Onondaga, capital of the Iroquois nation, was a beehive of activity. Kettles of maize and venison stew hung over slow-burning fires. Dogs ran playfully with laughing children. Baskets of apples lined the front of one lodge, stacked pumpkins another. Duncan offered respectful greetings to matrons and chieftains as Analie pulled him toward the knoll behind the lodge of the Great Council.

The girl sobered as they reached the cairns of stones that flanked the path up the hill, and the warrior assigned as sentry gave them a stern inspection. She glanced down to make sure her bead necklace was not askew over her doeskin shift, then straightened like a nervous soldier. It was highly unusual for a child to be permitted up the knoll but, as the sentry well knew, she had been given special dispensation. The guard was Ononyot, and though a smile was in his eyes, their Mohawk friend gave the girl a strict examination, solemnly lifting and studying her beads before nodding his approval and gesturing them forward.

A slow, muffled drumbeat could be heard from the lodge at the crest of the hill. They passed the cedar-scented lodge where the sacred masks were kept and continued to the smaller, ivy-covered lodge behind it.

The grandmother of the Haudensaunee still lived. Adanahoe was weak but she was not the frail, fading creature to whom Duncan had given a vow months earlier. Her wrinkled face lifted with a smile as she saw her visitors and Tanaqua, so often now at her side, shifted to make room for Analie to sit beside the old woman. The celebration in the town was in honor of the tall Mohawk, for he was to be elevated to the Great Council that night, but he spent most of his time in solitude with Adanahoe. Duncan had seen despair on her face in the spring, and had known it was due not just to the stolen mask and death of her grandson, but also because she had been convinced she was dying and had not completed passing on the ancient ways to the next generation.

The Iroquois elder had insisted on hearing every detail of their experiences with Jahoska, and now had asked Duncan to come to relate what he had learned about the remarkable life of the half king of the south. She chatted amiably about the autumn harvest of pumpkins, the cherished gift of a teapot from Sarah, even the rumors of a white stag in the forest, until the cloth at the entry stirred and a young woman entered, carrying a small piece of skin stretched on a willow frame. As she settled in the shadows and extracted a charcoal stick from her cartouche, Duncan recognized her as one of the inscribers of the Iroquois records, an artist who produced the large pictorial chronicles on deer skins to memorialize people and events for the tribes. Adanahoe was making sure Jahoska was not forgotten.

For the rest of the afternoon they spoke of the half king and his long eventful life, with the Iroquois chronicler sketching notes as they spoke. By the time they finished, more drums were beating, and joyful chanting could be heard in anticipation of the approaching ceremony. Tanaqua seemed reluctant to leave the old woman, even when she struggled to her feet and pulled his hand to urge him to rise. Duncan did not understand the sadness on his face when he finally stood, nor the tear in Adanahoe's eye.

An hour later, the clans of the six great tribes—Mohawk, Oneida, Onondaga, Cayuga, Seneca, and Tuscarora—marched up the pathway to the circle of the Great Council, past trees whose gold and scarlet splendor was embellished with garlands of berries and gourds. The final clan to climb to the ceremony was led by Conawago, Sir William and his wife Molly, followed by Duncan, Sarah, Woolford, Analie, and Kuwali. The moon was rising. Torches were being lit along the path. Bowls of smoldering cedar lined the earthen amphitheater where the joyful investiture was to take place.

"*Jiyathondek! Jiyathondek!*" the eldest of the chieftains finally called, silencing the assembly with a call to the spirits of the forest. The other great chieftains of the League joined in the opening rituals, in which the gods were reminded of their faithful children the Haudensaunee, and the great things they had accomplished through the centuries.

The moon had arced through a quarter of the sky before the speeches were completed and Tanaqua had accepted his honor. Duncan cradled Analie against his shoulder as they finally made their way back to Johnson's comfortable encampment. He laid her down beside Kuwali on the blankets inside Johnson's tent, near Sir William's own cot, rubbing each of the children on the head. The two had quickly won the hearts of those in Edentown.

As he left the tent Ononyot was waiting for him. The Mohawk motioned Sarah and Woolford out of the shadows and silently guided the three of them back into town. Only Adanahoe's lodge remained lit with torches. Ononyot gestured them inside then turned to guard the door.

There was an unexpected heaviness in the air, a melancholy that seemed out of place in the festive night. Conawago and Tanaqua flanked Adanahoe at her fire ring. The ancient strand of wampum that had been awarded Tanaqua as a symbol of his new rank hung around his neck, but so too did a bundle of feathers and bear claws, wrapped in white ermine. The Mohawk was there not as a chieftain but as the head of the secret society that protected the ancient spirits, a shadowkeeper. With a chill Duncan saw that he had painted white and red stripes on his face, the sign of a warrior embarking on a dangerous mission.

"*Jiyathondek*," Adanahoe began, calling those on the other side to come witness. At first she used the familiar words of Iroquois ritual, but then after several minutes any sign of a ritual halted and she spoke in the tone of a eulogy.

"The spirits of the forest world grow weary," she said, "and are in danger of becoming distracted by fear and worry. It is time to find rest for the old ones, time to let them turn away from this world so they can grow strong in the next."

Sarah suddenly gasped and straightened. "Grandmother! No! You must not!" she interrupted. Duncan looked at her in alarm. It was unthinkable that she would show such disrespect for the venerated matriarch. He stared at her, confused, and with rising fear. She stood and leaned forward, as if she might physically stop Adanahoe. "You must not do this, grandmother! The people need—"

Conawago interrupted. "The people need to know their spirits are secure," the old Nipmuc said.

"Not like this," Sarah pleaded. "I beg you!" There were tears in her eyes as Conawago, rising, gently pushed her back to her seat on the packed earth floor.

"I had a dream," Adanahoe declared. "There was a cave on an island in a great lake. There were many white birches and an eagle lived in an oak atop the cave, a sentinel sent by the spirits. Conawago says he knows where that cave is, in the western lands beyond the inland sea."

"But the people . . ." Sarah said, her voice thick with emotion. "Our own world could become so hollow. Hope is already so difficult to . . ." Her voice trailed away as tears flooded down her cheeks.

Duncan's fear was turning to desperation. Something terrible was happening but he could not put a name to it.

"Not all go, child," the matriarch said. "The Blooddancer is restless and needs a new home, and four of the others. The Council met through the night last night to decide which ones."

Sarah's hand gripped Duncan's. Suddenly he understood why Tanaqua wore the badge of his secret office. The gods were leaving their centuries-old home with the Haudensaunee.

"It is only for a time," Adanahoe said, forcing a smile. "Surely there will come a day when our chiefs will decide it is safe for them to return."

Woolford's voice trembled as he spoke. "Grandmother, I beg you to speak no more with us of this thing. Do not let Europeans know of the destination. This should be a secret only for the tribes."

"The number of those we can truly trust grows smaller each year," the matriarch replied. "Only a few will know, but those that do must be those who know how to turn back evil when it seeks us. You stand with us. You have bled with us, and for us. We know now that your blood and our blood comes from the same ancient source, from the oak of the forest. And it will be those of that blood who will shape the coming age."

The honor being shown to Duncan, Sarah, and Woolford silenced all protest. They were three outsiders who would be trusted, three not from the tribes but still of the tribes. It did not include any of those from Johnson Hall, where betrayal had triggered so much death and suffering.

Only now did Duncan see that Conawago too wore a bundle of feathers, claws, and ermine fur on his arm, and his heart sank further as he realized what it signified. The old Nipmuc twisted two fingers around the bundle as he spoke now of their distant destination. There would be long rituals to perform once there, and a small, stealthy group of human shadowkeepers would be left behind to aid the eagle.

They left in the predawn greyness, a file of a dozen solemn men led by Conawago and Tanaqua, five of them carrying on their backs the special doeskin pouches in which the sacred masks were transported.

Duncan and Sarah watched from the shadows, their hearts laden with emotion. They were witnessing the retreat of a great people, for centuries the masters of the forests and guardians of the forests' secrets. The Haudensaunee would endure but part of their hearts would be empty. They watched in silence as the last of the sacred warriors disappeared into the morning mists. Not for the first time in watching his friend depart, Duncan wondered if this was the journey from which Conawago would never return.

Sarah led Duncan back to the little lodge where Adanahoe now slept, and they sat outside the doorway in silence until the sun had cleared the top of the trees.

Their encampment was full of laughter when they finally returned. Sir William had organized a lacrosse game among the adolescents, and Analie and Kuwali had accumulated so much grime from rolling on the soft earth that they were almost indistinguishable from their Iroquois playmates. A messenger had come from Edentown with letters, and Duncan sat with Woolford as they listened to Sarah read an account from Alice Dawson.

Smiles grew on their faces as they heard how surprised Alice had been when Colonel Washington and Webb had called on her, how shocked she had been to receive from the colonel the paper that returned the plantation to its rightful owner. Gabriel's overseers had been dismissed the following day. Ursa had taken up duties at the smithy and his first task had been to melt down all the leg irons. Alice was teaching Ursa to read and write so he could correspond with his son at Edentown. Winters had been put in charge of rebuilding the mill for Mr. Bowen. Chuga had miraculously appeared on the porch one morning, and now stayed at the manor house most days, though always leaving at dusk to sleep on the high bluff with Jahoska.

Sarah pulled a new *Pennsylvania Gazette* from the bundle and broke into a wide smile before handing it to Duncan. The Stamp

Tax Congress so dreaded by the Krakens had been officially announced, and would soon take place in New York, with at least nine colonies attending.

Reaching the final letter, she paused and pointed to the runner marks along the top. "It's for you, Duncan. Urgent committee business, the runner notes." Sarah looked up in surprise. "From that genteel Samuel Adams of Boston." She puzzled over the envelope. "But what's this? To *Duncan McCallum;* it says, *Son of Liberty.*"

AUTHOR'S NOTE

Our history books too often create the impression that American independence was abruptly born with the crack of a Lexington musket in April 1775. Their truncated perspective suggests that colonists woke up one morning and decided to cast off the yoke of oppression, launching a new nation. The truth is that the United States rose out of a long, deeply complex struggle featuring a stunningly diverse cast of characters who gradually recognized they had become something other than European. It may have been geographic quests that brought Europeans to America but it was thousands of journeys of self-discovery in the 17th and 18th centuries that gave rise to our country.

These are the journeys I seek to reflect in the chronicles of Duncan McCallum, the tragic, exhilarating, joyful, very human tales of Scottish rebels, woodland natives, wilderness missionaries, hardscrabble farmers, soldier adventurers, and the other outcasts, exiles, and original thinkers who inhabited the colonies. Such tales may escape the sterile pen of the historian, but they are often the most meaningful way for us to connect with our past. These people were living in an extraordinary time, when geographic, economic, and social boundaries were crumbling just as science and self-expression had begun to blossom, and many lived extraordinary lives.

America was coming of age in 1765, taking its first stuttering steps, not knowing where it was going but beginning to sense that its path was not aligned with its homeland. *Blood of the Oak* is framed around the profoundly important historic events of that year. The passage of the Stamp Tax, levied on not just all legal documents but also books, newspapers, diplomas, playing cards, and dice, was triggering the first widespread, coordinated protests ever seen in the colonies. Tax collectors were hanged in effigy, stamps were burned, and riots swept Boston, New York, Philadelphia, and many smaller towns. As colonies recognized their common cause, political discourse between them started in earnest, giving rise to the committees of correspondence that in the next decade would expand to play a vital role in creating common strategies for the colonies. Until this fateful year the government in London had adeptly kept the colonies isolated from one another, keeping colonial leaders always focused on England, not on their neighbors. Suddenly the colonies were speaking with each other and, to the outrage of officials in London, daring to suggest an inter-colony congress.

This was the year when many of those who later signed the Declaration of Independence and led the Revolution first stepped onto the public stage. In May Patrick Henry made himself heard in the Virginia legislature by passage of his Virginia Resolves, the first official rejection of the hated tax. Opposition to the tax brought together many unexpected allies, at all levels of society. Thus it was that William Johnson, Superintendent of Indian Affairs and adopted Iroquois chieftain, joined ranks with such charter members of the committees of correspondence as Samuel Adams and James Otis, America's foremost scientist Benjamin Franklin, and the hundreds of farmers, lawyers, merchants, craftsmen, and militia officers who began calling themselves Sons of Liberty. Another significant development, unheard of in the Old World, was that colonial women began actively expressing themselves in public demonstrations. While the Sons of Liberty receive more frequent mention, the Daughters of Liberty, who later provided vital aid to Revolutionary War soldiers, were also established as a movement during the protests.

Benjamin Rush, who became a leading figure in the revolutionary cause and the American Enlightenment, was a youthful nineteen in 1765. While his adventures here are fictitious, the peripatetic, inquisitive scholar-rebel who went on to become a signer of the Declaration of Independence and Surgeon General in the Continental Army had a lifelong interest, bordering on obsession, in the physiology and anatomy of native Americans and Africans. Soon after this tale is set, Rush was able to realize his ambition of receiving medical training at the University of Edinburgh. Later in life, established as a preeminent scientist, he was called upon by President Jefferson to train Lewis and Clark for their expedition to the Pacific and, in an intriguing twist of history, supplied their Corps of Discovery with hundreds of his laxative "Rush's Bilious Pills," the high mercury content of which has become an important marker for modern archaeologists tracking the campsites of the Corps.

There were, of course, those on the banks of the Thames who labored mightily to stifle all colonial dissent, and, most importantly, to stop the proposed congress. As early as the 1730s the British government had been intercepting the mail of political opponents, on such a scale that the postal service had its own "Secret Office" which not only clandestinely opened correspondence but was also known to forge letters to confound political enemies. Such practices escalated during the volatile 1760s. Ciphers and codes were used on both sides of the Atlantic, ranging from simple word substitution, such as that used by Thomas Jefferson the Williamsburg student to describe his amorous aspirations, to sophisticated "dictionary codes" that utilized book references and alphabet shifts to create nearly unbreakable ciphers, of which Woolford's Shakespeare code is a variation. The use of knotted strings and sinews to send messages was a system of the woodland tribes that undoubtedly predated the arrival of Europeans. Details of the many surprising ways codes, ciphers, and spycraft were utilized during this period—and the surprising people who used them—can be found in John Nagy's fascinating book *Invisible Ink*.

The Conococheague Valley in south central Pennsylvania, home of Murdo Ross, was indeed the site of the first armed uprising against the British army this same year, led by ranger James Smith and other Scots who could not abide the government's failure to enforce its own rules prohibiting shipments of weapons to the western lands. These rebels, risking life and limb in raising arms against their government, actually did capture a squad of Black Watch Highland troops sent against them from Fort Loudoun, as reflected in the novel. Although the chronicles do not reflect it, I have always assumed there would have been some awkward camaraderie between captors and captives once the whiskey and Highland tales starting flowing. While the complaints of the rebels were eventually addressed and the episode largely forgotten, it was an omen of things to come, and provides poignant evidence of the stubborn independence that had grown instinctive among frontier families.

Since the inception of the Virginia tobacco plantations in the prior century native American captives had been forced to work alongside African slaves—as well as many indentured Scots who essentially lived as slaves. The last survivors of Tidewater tribes and natives captured in the colony's Indian wars were disappearing into this harsh servitude well into the 18th century. While the Iroquois were not among those who were thus extinguished, the leaders of that once mighty confederation could no longer deny that their world was ending. Their numbers were dwindling and their traditional culture was rapidly disappearing, yet proud and determined chieftains, matriarchs, and warriors—some of them former rangers savvy in the ways of both the tribes and the Europeans—struggled to preserve their way of life. That remarkable native civilization, uniquely in balance with the natural world, had maintained the *Pax Iroquoia* for centuries in the Northeast woodlands but it was no match for the disease, rum, and timber axes brought by European settlers.

Ultimately British efforts to thwart the Americans failed and the Stamp Tax Congress proceeded in the autumn of 1765, with nine colonies attending. The resolutions it passed, though not as fiery as the Virginia Resolves, unequivocally rejected the authority of London to impose domestic taxes on the colonies. While the delegates tried to placate the king by asserting that England's monopoly on colonial trade should be deemed America's contribution to London, the Congress represented a vital turning point in relations between England and its American colonies. Its enactments were undeniably a joint action against Parliament, and while it infuriated many in London, including King George, it also strengthened the resolve of the colonists. The stamp tax was repealed a few months later.

Among those who stepped onto the public stage during this year of protest was John Adams, who until that time had been an obscure lawyer in Braintree. He recorded then that 1765 had been the most memorable year of his life, underscoring that the Stamp Act "has raised and spred thro the whole Continent, a Spirit that will be recorded to our Honour with all future Generations." It would be ten more years before muskets were fired on Lexington Green, and the intervening years were to be filled with more intrigues, triumphs, and tragedies, but the spirit of freedom that had been bred into the colonists had found a common voice. It would not be silenced.